HIDDEN IN
THE MIST

First Edition published 2022 by

Raven Witch Publishers

Copyright © Sue Penney 2022
The right of Sue Penney to be identified as the author
of this work has been asserted by her in accordance with the
Copyright, Designs and Patents Act 1988

Cover Design by Charlotte Mouncey with imagery from the author

Printed in Great Britain by Ingram Sparks

A CIP catalogue record for this book is available
from the British Library
ISBN 978-1-8384522-5-4

HIDDEN IN
THE MIST

SUE PENNEY

*To Jovi for all her help and continuing support
and
Vikki for her unwavering friendship*

PROLOGUE

She didn't remember what the time was. It couldn't have been too late, as she was sent to bed early at that age, but it was dark. Her mother had asked her to go down to the kitchen to get something. She didn't even remember what that was now, but it hardly mattered. What she did remember, though, was the fear. It gripped her heart like an invisible icy hand as it stifled her breathing and clutched at her throat.

She found it interesting, upon reflection, that as a small child who was very respectful to her parents, defiance certainly did not come easily, and for that same child to refuse to do a simple task should have been enormously telling. Looking back, she thought that her mother should have been aware that her very fear of going downstairs, even though it would induce her mum's wrath, spoke volumes. She didn't remember much of what the outcome was apart from the tears, but she remembered quite intensely that she did not go down those stairs.

She is still not sure whether her parents knew that she had watched them lift the body of her dead great-grandfather from its resting place on the hall floor, just beneath the ancient grandfather clock. His blackened eye seemingly stared up at her, but blankly, as it was starting to cloud with the milky film of death. She was sitting on the stairs looking through the banisters, a permanently curious child knowing, with a second sense, that something interesting was afoot.

Grandfather, or Gan as he was affectionately known, had been in a car accident a few days previously. His wife, Nan, a few years his senior in her early nineties, was in the cottage hospital just outside the village. He had been sent home to recover, but because he was in his late eighties and had been parted from his wife of several decades, it had proved too much for his heart.

She just watched with interest, not realising that he was dead then. She must have been around six or seven years old at the time and had never witnessed death as, due to her mother's allergies, they had never been allowed pets.

However, it wasn't this recent death that stopped her from wanting to visit those lower floors of the vast, sprawling house. It was the other things that lurked in the dark corners. The voices that whispered, and the glimpses of shadows just beyond her line of sight. Secrets dwelt in that house, and what annoyed her the most was that she knew that her mother knew, or was at least aware, of something strange going on.

Her mother knew more than anyone but, as an adult, had long since stopped being afraid – or so she presumed, in her childish naivety. She had inherited her mother's gift, and she wondered now if her mother knew back then.

She remembered the first time that she realised she was different. She must have been about five years old and was standing in the hall, looking out of the windows at the front of the house. She had been playing with her imaginary friend, who was a bit older than her, and was talking to him when her father asked her what she was doing.

She started to explain to him, but he was distracted by his work and didn't really listen to her. He just smiled and patted her head and walked back into his study, while the other child just looked on knowingly.

Chapter I

1973

Their schooldays in the village were happy times. They were a close band of children with lots of freedom, and they often walked down to the river when they were not at school or playing in the fields behind their homes. The river was of course a prohibited place, and the adults believed that their simple verbal instruction to stay away from it would render it off limits ... which obviously meant that it was where they spent most of their free time.

The gentle gravel slope down to the fast-moving shallow river had soft grassy banks, where they could watch its path as it tumbled restlessly over the stones and tree debris that lay twisting in the pockets created by larger rocks brought down on long-forgotten stormy days. People always said that they heard the river before they saw it – not quite a roar, as such, but definitely an urgent rush.

They were drawn to it, as probably their parents had known they would be, because they had fast-receding faint memories of a similar urge as children themselves. They remembered overhearing the adults talking about children having no fear and realised now how true those words were.

Not because children are less intelligent. They just lack experience. Their short lives are generally less marred by unpleasant experiences, so they live their lives with eyes full of wonder and expectation and want nothing more than to be free to run and explore and try out new things.

They were no different, and their parents should have realised that. Oh, how quick adults are to forget once they become bogged down in their busy lives full of the urgent but unimportant tasks that pull them to conform to the regimentation of adulthood. They had so much freedom then, and they wandered the lanes and the fields on foot and on bicycle, as their parents were keen to have them from out under their feet. Their memories of every day of their childhood were full of sun and laughter.

Until they weren't.

That day started like any other sun-filled day during the long summer holiday. There were five of them: Phillipa, Jennifer, Richard, Robert and Emma. Jennifer was the oldest, at twelve, so she was obviously in charge, and she was quite bossy but was always very kind to Emma. Phillipa was eleven, and as her and Jennifer's mothers were friends they naturally spent a lot of time together. Richard was the best friend of Emma's brother, Robert, and they were also both eleven. And Emma, at nine years old, was the youngest, and she was only really allowed to tag along because Jennifer was sweet on Robert.

Jennifer and Phillipa called round to Robert and Emma's house in the morning. The sun was shining, and it was already quite warm. Robert and Emma had had their breakfast and were in the garden. Robert was digging around in the vegetable patch looking for worms to throw at his sister, and she was swiftly climbing into one of the trees in the orchard to avoid this latest torment.

They both looked up when they heard the familiar squeak of the garden gate and saw the sun glint off the light brown bob of Jennifer's hair. Jennifer was dressed in a pair of dark blue cotton trousers with a white T-shirt and canvas shoes, and her ready air of self-assuredness preceded her as she confidently strode through the gate and walked towards the siblings. Phillipa, wearing dungarees and a pale top, followed her apologetically, her thick dark plaits tied with red ribbons and her head bowed as if she was avoiding eye contact. 'Rob?' Jennifer said, looking straight at Robert and pointedly ignoring Emma.

'Jenny,' he replied, with a lopsided grin on his face.

'You fancy going for a paddle? It's bloody boiling,' Jennifer said, looking pleased with her use of a forbidden word.

'I told her we're not allowed,' Phillipa said, looking nervously defiant, like one not used to standing up for herself for fear of losing her acceptance in the group.

'I'm coming,' Emma said, piping up from her vantage point halfway up one of the apple trees.

'No, you're bloody not,' Robert exclaimed. Emma scrambled down from the tree, eager not to be left out.

'Well,' Emma said, hands on hips in the haughtiest tone she could muster, 'if you don't let me come then I'll just tell Mum and then you'll all be in trouble.' She stuck out her tongue and pulled a face for good measure.

Jennifer looked at Emma then back to Robert. 'She's got you there, Rob. Come on, Squirt. We'll look after you.' They all turned and walked back towards the gate and let themselves out into the lane that led down towards the river.

Robert glared at his sister and muttered something under his breath that may have been, 'I'll get you later, you little brat.' Emma just ignored him and skipped along beside Jennifer as they walked towards Richard's house in silent unison. It would have been unheard of to go anywhere without him tagging along. Or Emma. They suffered her because Robert was usually left to look after her, so they didn't get much choice.

The sun was climbing ever more steadily in the sky as they

loped towards Richard's house, and on their journey there a casual teasing started between them. The gentle wind rustled the leaves and blew tall grasses along the side of the path. A grey and white cat watched them lazily from one sleepy eye as it reclined on a wall of one of the cottage gardens, basking deliciously in the shade of a tall lilac bush. Overhead jackdaws and magpies chattered, and a robin shouted out its territorial warning.

Richard's house came into view. It was one of the newer houses on the edge of a recently built estate – which was frowned upon by the older residents, who grumbled about any change that was cast upon their stable, never-changing lives. The front garden was a small, unremarkable patch of lawn with a concrete path that led up to a plain white front door. A couple of pots of bright red geraniums had been placed on either side of the door to try and brighten up this otherwise boring facade.

Richard must have been watching them approach from his bedroom window, as before they reached the front door it opened and he appeared with a cheeky grin on his face. With a backwards shout of his goodbyes to his mum he closed the front door and quickly came towards the group. 'Where are we going, then?' was his cheerful greeting.

'We're going to the river, of course,' Jennifer replied, slightly haughtily, as if daring him to challenge her self-styled leadership of the group. Richard just shrugged in a good-humoured fashion and followed them back up the path and onwards towards the river.

They came to the end of his road and turned right, which led to the lane that eventually ran behind Emma and Robert's house. It was a wide lane with impressively large houses placed at irregular intervals along either side of its length. The grass verges were substantial, and the pavements were set close to the houses. The road was covered in a fine sandy dust from weeks of dry sunny weather. The path to the river led off the lane and they walked steadily with the sun warm on their backs, relaxed and easy in one other's company, and talking about nothing in particular.

The path down to the river was bordered on each side by trees and other vegetation. There were fields beyond it, which lay full of crops of wheat or barley, or some other cereal crop ready for harvesting. The trees hung low over the path, making it shady and still. Birds flew between the branches, and they caught glimpses of sparrows, finches and a wren. Emma liked birds and loved listening to their ceaseless chatter and watching them flit about outside her bedroom window, always busy on a mission.

They could hear the steady, rushing rumble of the river as the path sloped gently downwards, and could see little stones being displaced by their feet as the boys kicked idly at them. A squirrel watched them warily from further along the path for a second before scurrying up the nearest tree and chattering its displeasure at their intrusion into its day.

The path came to an end, and they could see the five-barred metal gate that opened up onto a sandy, stony riverbank with tufted grass on both sides. There was no path leading along from where they were, just an area where you could sit or stand to admire the beauty of nature in all its glory.

Open fields spread out before them on the other side of the river, and the bank was much higher there. The fields were full of grass, and various types of livestock were kept in the fields from time to time. That must be why the end of the path they had walked along was gated: to stop any of the animals that got into the river to drink from finding their way to freedom up the lane. Even though the children had come to the river, which they knew was against the rules, they were still considerate enough to follow the code of the countryside, which had been instilled in them from birth, and they closed the gates behind them.

Emma saw him on the other side of the bank almost immediately. The sun was glinting off his blonde hair and his white shirt was blowing gently in the breeze as he stood there watching them. She called his name in delight and ran past the others towards the edge of the water, waving a greeting. She didn't see the uneven ground and the hole that must have been dug by a dog or some other animal in the soft earth and tripped, completely losing her balance, and fell heavily straight into the water.

The cold hit her like a physical slap. It knocked the air from her lungs, and as she gulped in fresh air it mingled with the water and she started to choke. The current there was strong. The river curved at this point and, although it looked calm enough on the surface, underneath it flowed strongly. Emma was swept along, pulled by unseen forces, and she felt the boulders cut into her legs and arms as she was knocked and thrashed against them. Panicking, she tried to breathe and grabbed at surfaces passing by, scratching her hands and ripping her nails. She could not get a purchase on anything that might save her from the inevitable.

Panic gripped her as she fought to save herself, and then there was a crack as her head hit a large rock and everything went black.

The other children looked on in horror, unable to do

anything as they watched Emma being pulled away from them by the sheer strength of the current. Fear clutched at their hearts, and they were too shocked to cry. There was no path along this side of the riverbank, so they couldn't even run after her and try to grab her out with a stick or anything.

They knew they would be in so much trouble. There was no way they could hide their transgression now. They'd be grounded for the rest of their lives and be given the worst jobs imaginable to make up for their disobedience.

But what if Emma died? They'd heard the warnings of children drowning, of course. Every parent regaled their children with warning horror stories in the hope that these alone would keep them safe through fear. For example, there were the books and stories they'd read at school about not walking on ice, of keeping away from swans in case they broke your arm, and not to stray onto building sites, to name but a few.

But the river? Well, that was different. Its lure was too strong, too powerful. It held a deep mystery that drew you towards it like misty tendrils. It got into your soul and called to something deep inside. Now that calling looked like it had taken one of their own.

Chapter 2

1973

John Peters had been fishing further down the bank on the opposite side. He'd noticed the children arriving with an inward smile as he remembered all the times he and his mates had spent in the very same spot, catching minnows to put in jam jars to scare his sister when he was a young lad. He was trying to catch some eels today. They made for good eating, even though they were not eaten by most people, especially not around there. He liked the firm flesh that very closely resembled salmon and, better still, they were free.

Life had not been unkind to John. He worked as a farm labourer and, although the hours were long and hard, he enjoyed his work, which followed the seasons in a gentle rhythm that had been played out over hundreds of years. He lived in one of the farm cottages which, although basic, was warm, dry and comfortable enough. His wife Sarah was a quiet and gentle soul who didn't ask for much and was content for the most part, although he could suffer the sharp side of her tongue if he came in late or too worse for wear after a few drinks at the Brown Cow with his workmates.

Theirs was a happy companionship born of many years together. He still remembered the shy young girl she had been who he'd first noticed all those years ago, working in the dairy, on his first day at work. He'd loved her on sight, but it took many months before he'd plucked up the courage to ask her to go to the village dance with him. Luckily for him she'd said yes, and the rest was history. They'd not been blessed with children, but with her sister's and his brother's and sister's children they had plenty of nieces and nephews to love and cherish.

He heard the splash and the shouts of distress as he was tending to his eel baskets. He thought that the kids were just messing about to start with, splashing and teasing each other like he and his siblings used to do, so he didn't really pay the noise much attention.

Then he saw Emma in the water. She was being thrown about by the current and disappearing under the water. Without thinking twice he jumped down into the river. His waders protected him from the worst of the cold. He grabbed the old boathook that he used to haul the eel baskets out of the river just in time and, as she came rapidly tumbling down the river, he managed to grab her clothes and pulled her towards him.

Her body was limp, her face was white, her lips were tinged with blue, and she was not breathing. He pushed her up onto the bank and scrambled up himself. He lay her face down over his lap and slapped her back hard. She started to cough, and water poured from her mouth. There was blood on the back of her head where it had struck the large rock in the middle of the river.

His hands shook as he started to think what would have happened if he had not come fishing today. He was supposed to be working, but one of the other farmhands had asked to swap days with him so he could go and visit his parents over the weekend and, as it was due to be a fine day, he'd readily agreed.

He turned her over gently. Her eyes were still closed but he could see that she was now breathing again and the colour was starting to return to her pale face. Her eyes fluttered open, their long dark lashes glistening with droplets of water. Her green eyes looked past his shoulder, fixing their gaze on something as she breathed out the word 'Tom,' and then she fell back into unconsciousness.

They heard him before they realised what was happening, as John Peters bellowed out a cry of distress. Emma had disappeared around the next bend in the river as they all stood there helplessly clutching at each other in emotional turmoil.

John ran along the other side of the bank towards them with Emma lying limply in his strong arms. 'Is she dead?' Robert cried, the terror and grief pouring out in those words.

'No, lad,' John replied, 'But she's mighty poorly. Run and get help as fast as you can. There's a phone box at the end of the lane. One of you call an ambulance … and go and fetch your mother, there's a good lad. Be quick about it.'

Robert was galvanised into action. 'I'll call the ambulance. Jen, you go and get my mother. Pippa, go with Jen, and Richard, come with me.'

John looked down at the little girl who lay unconscious in his arms. His heart was in his mouth as he remembered a time long ago when he had held another young child in his arms, watching his life ebb away, and had been unable to do anything to prevent the inevitable.

'Hurry,' was all he said.

Chapter 3

1973

Robert ran back up the lane, his arms pumping and his breath coming in short, panting gasps. The others ran with him. Nothing was said, as each of them was concentrating on their allotted task. At the top of the path they all turned left and Robert flew at the telephone box, his hand slipping and missing the handle to open the door in his earnest despair. He yanked back the door and picked up the receiver. The interior was littered with dog-ends and smelt of stale cigarette smoke and urine. He grimaced and dialled 999. Each turn of the dial felt like hours as he watched the dial turn with its whirring clicks as it spelt out the number to summon help.

The girls had peeled off and hurtled down the lane towards the back gate into Emma and Robert's garden. Richard stood against the open door of the phone box to allow fresh air to lessen the unpleasant smell inside. 'Emergency... Which service do you require?' came the calm female voice down the line.

'Ambulance. Please hurry. It's my sister,' Robert blurted out, the terror and panic quite obvious in his fast delivery of the short sentence.

'What's your location, please?' the call responder asked.

'The end of Vine Lane, Stoke D'Abernon, where the path to the river is.' He looked at Richard as if for confirmation. Richard nodded, his eyes wide and his features pinched in concern. 'Please hurry,' Robert added, a sob catching in his throat. 'I think she might be dying.' The last was a plea delivered with a sob released from impotent despair.

Jennifer and Phillipa sprinted down the lane, and they threw the metal gate into the garden open with such force that it smashed against the fence and let out a disgruntled metallic clang. They ran through the orchard and on through the wooden gate onto the lawns, which housed formal rose beds and other floral creations.

The gardener, who was edging one of the beds, looked up in alarm to see the two red-faced girls cannoning up the garden towards the house and jumped up to intercept them. 'Hey, ladies, where's the fire?' he asked in only mock jest, while looking beyond them to see what was causing their distress. After realising they were alone, he returned his concerned gaze back to them. Obviously, something was up. These girls would not normally act in such a frenzied manner.

Panting and trying to speak, they both stopped. Jennifer bent forward, her hands on her knees, as she tried to regain enough breath to deliver her news. 'It's Emma,' she managed to get out. 'She fell in the river. I think she's dead, and it's all my fault.' With this terrible message delivered, Jennifer burst into noisy sobs as Phillipa, her face solemn, looked on, not knowing what to do.

The gardener took charge immediately. He took off his gloves and put them on the ground in front of his muddy boots. 'Right, you two, you stay here and I'll go and fetch Mrs Morton. I'm sure everything will be just fine.'

He thought nothing of the sort. At the very least they were certainly going to be in a lot of trouble and at the worst... He didn't even want his mind to go there. He thought back to all those years ago, when he'd been a young lad working for another family in these same gardens. A life lost... He'd seen the light leave that little lad with his own eyes. He shook himself and returned to the task at hand.

He trotted down the side of the house and into the kitchen. He slipped out of his boots and walked through the dining room and into the large entrance hall. 'Mrs Morton?' he called, feeling uncomfortable about having entered the more formal rooms of the house. He only ever went in there to leave cut flowers on the side table for the lady of the house to create the attractive floral decorations that were liberally scattered throughout the many rooms when the cleaner was not there to take them for him.

'Jenkins, whatever is the matter?' she replied, a hint of irritation barely masked by her good manners. 'I saw those girls running through the garden. Has something happened?' Resigned to the fact that her busy schedule of lunch with her tennis club friends and church flowers was going to be interrupted by some nonsense or other, she sounded bored.

Jenkins shifted uncomfortably from foot to foot. He knew that Mrs Morton was always busy with some function or other. The children usually had an au pair to take care of them most of the time, but she'd gone home for the summer and so the children were free to play and wander the fields – which was what they'd all done as kids, and no harm had come to them. He thought back fondly at the memory. But no matter. This was important, and it was not his business to judge how other people lived.

'I'm sorry, Mrs Morton, but the children came with some distressing news. It seems that Miss Emma has had an accident down by the river.' He stopped speaking as he watched the younger woman take in what he'd just said.

'What do you mean, an accident? The river? How?' She was finding this all too much to comprehend. Her face started to pale, and she looked as though she was going to faint. Torn between impropriety and common sense, Jenkins moved closer and gently took her elbow in his large hand and led her to one of the chairs by the window. 'I don't know, madam. That's all the girls said. I thought you had better know straight away.'

Susan Morton felt the strength return to her limbs. She realised that something urgent had to be done so, mustering all the energy that she could, she stood up on slightly shaking legs, holding firmly to the carved wooden back of the hall chair. 'Girls,' she shouted at the top of her voice, sounding slightly reminiscent of a boarding school matron.

The girls – who had not stayed in the garden, obviously, but who had crept in through the kitchen and who were now cowering behind the door of the wood-panelled formal dining room – came forward uncertainly, both with eyes as wide and wary as a doe's. 'Tell me what has happened.' Her voice was pure steel.

At once both of them started to talk fast in high, urgent voices. They talked over each other and struggled to explain, apologise and absolve themselves all at the same time. 'Stop. One at a time, please,' Susan Morton said, putting the palm of her hand to her forehead to try to stave off the headache that was threatening to form. 'Jennifer, please tell me slowly and precisely what has happened and where, so I can act as quickly as possible.'

Jennifer paled and started to stammer out the events that had led them to this point so far that morning. 'Emma fell in the river, Mrs Morton.' Her eyes were wide with the self-in-criminating fear and guilt that washed over her young face. 'We only went to paddle. I am so sorry...' Her voice started to trail off as frightened sobs engulfed her and tears started their glistening track down her face, making dirty rivulets, where they mixed with the dust that had stuck to the sweat on her face as she had run to the house.

Sensing the urgency of the situation and realising that her friend was struggling to answer, Phillipa took over the story. 'Mrs Morton...' she began nervously. Susan Morton turned her eyes towards the smaller girl, taking in her calmer earnest expression and willing her to continue with a slight nod of her head.

Phillipa continued, feeling more comfortable now that she had been given silent permission to speak. 'We all walked down to the river, and as we walked through the gate Emma seemed to have seen something. She shouted a name. "Tom," I think she said.' She looked towards Jennifer for confirmation and Jennifer nodded, grateful to have been taken out of the spotlight for a moment.

'Well, before we knew what was happening, Emma just ran full pelt towards the edge of the river, then I think she tripped in a hole and fell. She just fell in and we were too far away from her to catch her or reach her or anything, and...' Her voice was getting faster and more frantic as she relived the episode in her mind. 'The river, it just took her away.'

Susan Morton gasped in shock, and a hand flew to her chest as she struggled to breathe. She fumbled in her pocket for her ever-present inhaler and took a couple of puffs to stem the constriction that tightened like an unrelenting band and threatened to choke her.

Phillipa glanced at Jenkins and Jennifer, aghast as the understanding of what the words she had just spoken portended. 'No, I mean... Mr Peters got her out. He said that she was breathing but she had blood on her head and she was asleep.

Robert ran to call the ambulance.'

Just at that moment the faint but unmistakable noise of an emergency vehicle's siren could be heard through the open window in the drawing room located directly off the large hall.

Pulled back to the moment with sudden clarity, Susan Morton jumped up and knocked over the chair that she had been sitting on as she did so. It clattered to the ground. 'Right,' she said, and ran towards the drawing room, whose metal-framed French windows opened out directly onto the garden. Without a backwards glance she ran down the garden towards the gate that led onto the lane and turned left towards the sound of the ambulance.

The girls and Jenkins followed suit, leaving the chair lying abandoned on the ornate Chinese rug that covered most of the polished parquet floor.

As Susan Morton ran towards the sound of the siren, which grew louder with every step, she felt the cold sweat of fear start to pool between her breasts and on her back. She was terrified of course for the life of her child, her only daughter.

But the fear went deeper than that. Had she heard correctly? Had Phillipa really said that Emma had shouted the name *Tom*? She had wondered several times before, of course, whether Emma was like her or not. Did she see what she saw and hear what she heard? There was that time, of course, when she had refused to go and get the sewing box that she had left in the kitchen on the table where she had been mending the tablecloth.

But she'd not really thought about it that much, and had brushed it off as her daughter simply being afraid of the dark. She remembered the conflict in Emma's eyes and the wary glance towards her father, but she had not pressed the matter.

She couldn't think about that now. Her child was in danger, and she needed to be there. She saw the boys standing at the entrance to the path leading down to the river. They had had the presence of mind to stay put to guide the ambulance men to where they were needed.

Everyone seemed to arrive together. The ambulance men jumped down from their vehicle and ran to the back, where they flung open the rear doors and grabbed a bag and a stretcher. 'OK, lads,' the younger man said, 'lead the way.'

The boys looked at each other, buoyed up by the responsibility vested in them, and pointed to the path leading down towards the river. Robert threw a guilty look at his mother, whose face bore a worried frown, and started to run down the path.

'She's down here,' Robert said as he ran, casting an anxious glance behind him to make sure that the men were following him. The two boys led the way, swiftly followed by the blue-clad ambulance men, with Susan Morton, Jenkins and the girls making up the rear.

As they neared the gate they could see John Peters through the light at the end of the tunnel made by the overhanging branches. Emma was still being held firmly by him, but was now conscious and half-sitting on his lap with her head resting on his shoulder. Everyone felt the relief wash over them – not least the children, who had of course witnessed the full horror of the drama only a short time before and had feared that they had lost their friend and sister to the unmerciful waters.

'Emma,' Robert and Susan shouted out almost in unison. The girl lifted a weary head and gave them a wan smile before resting her head back against John Peters's shoulder as he murmured comforting sounds to soothe the frightened child.

But almost immediately everyone realised that there was a logistical problem in reaching the child. John Peters and Emma were on the other side of the fast-flowing river, and although it was not as deep as John stood tall, its current was strong and powerful.

Jenkins and the ambulance men looked at each other, the unspoken thought resting between them. 'I'll go and get some rope,' Jenkins said, and turned on his heel. Then he re-entered the darkened tunnel of trees and walked back up the short path that they had all just emerged from.

Susan Morton turned to watch him go and looked questioningly at the ambulance men. 'I presume you are the child's mother,' the older man said gently. Susan Morton replied with an almost imperceivable nod of her head. Her large eyes were round with anxiety as she fought to divide the attention of her gaze between the would-be rescuers and her injured child.

'We need to get your daughter to this side of the river. The current is too strong for her to be carried across without help, so we will need to be sure that we have a strong hold on the gentleman there to help him come across without being pulled away downstream. Going round is simply not an option, as it will take too long, and as your daughter … is she called Emma?'

He looked Susan questioningly, and she nodded. 'As Emma has sustained a head injury and was knocked unconscious, we really need to get her to the hospital as quickly as possible.'

Susan's hand flew to her mouth as she took in the enormity of what she had just been told and the terrifying realisation of its implication. In order for her daughter to get to safety she was going to have to be carried across the river by the man who had fished her out, who could himself be dragged away to danger while carrying her precious daughter with him.

Chapter 4

1973

Emma came to, wrapped in a pair of strong arms. She could smell something faintly musty, like clothes that had been left to dry inside, mixed with the odour of farm and river. When she opened her eyes she realised that it was the smell of a man's old jacket. She felt exhausted, and it was all she could do to raise her head to look upon the stubbly chin of her rescuer.

Emma knew this man. This was John Peters. He was an uncle to a few of her friends, and his wife Sarah made the best shortbread she had ever tasted.

She was cold and shivering, her clothes were soaked through, and she felt as though she would never be warm again. She snuggled into the warmth of this man, feeling the soft brushed cotton material of his old checked shirt against her face. Her body was trembling, and she could hear his gentle voice soothingly speak calming words. 'Hush, lass, you're safe now. Your brother has gone for help. We'll soon have you warm and tucked up in bed with a hot-water bottle and some warm milk.'

She could hardly keep her eyes open, but she felt safe. Why had she fallen into the river? How on earth had she managed that? Then she remembered seeing Tom. 'Where's Tom?' she whispered. The effort of speaking was almost too much. John Peters's face was hidden, so she couldn't see the concerned frown cross his gentle features.

Emma heard the commotion and raised her eyes to look towards the bank and the gate on the other side of the river. Two ambulance men dressed in their smart navy-blue uniforms were following the red-faced puffing figure of Robert. Richard jogged to a spot beside them, and they were followed by Jenkins, her mother, Phillipa and Jennifer. Vaguely, in her befuddled state, she wondered why everyone was there.

Emma was glad but very wary to see the figure of her mother, but her face told her that she was concerned more than angry. However, she did not expect to be completely let off the hook for disobeying her. Mind you, Robert was much more likely to bear the brunt of her wrath, and her father… Well, they both knew what he was like.

She saw Jenkins turn and run back up the path with the sun glinting off the handles of the pair of secateurs he had thrust in the back pocket of his well-worn work trousers. John Peters hoisted her up slightly to make himself more comfortable. Even though she was small, she was a dead weight in his arms.

'Is it correct that she was unconscious for a while?' one of the ambulance men shouted across the river. It must have been frustrating for them to see her but not be able to reach her.

'Aye,' John Peters called across the water. 'She was that. She took in water and was not breathing when I pulled her out, but it was only for a moment. I slapped her hard on the back and out it came. She has taken a nasty bang on the back of her head, though.' The ambulance man nodded, and spoke with his colleague.

On hearing the news that she had come so close to death Susan's face noticeably paled, and Emma heard her sharp gasp and saw her hand fly to her throat as the realisation gripped her.

Robert moved closer to her and took her hand. 'I'm so sorry, Mummy,' he said in a voice so small that it belied his years. She took his words at face value and placed one hand on the top of his head, and drew him close to her with the other.

'OK, Robert, we will talk about it later. I suppose someone ought to tell your father.' The look of sheer panic that crossed Robert's face made her regret mentioning her husband. She knew that he was a hard man – more than most, for all his professional charisma and outward fine manners and bearing that came with his background.

She would have to try and cushion the children from his wrath at their plain disobedience, which had led to the situation that now faced them all. It was only a matter of time before he found out. And he would care more about what others may think about what had happened and how that reflected upon him than his daughter being injured. She shuddered and put the thought aside for now. One thing at a time. They still had to get Emma back across the river and to the hospital to see to that bang on her head.

Jenkins got to the end of the path. His breathing was hard and laboured and he was thinking quickly, and the sweat was starting to run down his face. He paused and rubbed a calloused hand across his face. There was plenty of rope in the garage, but that was quite a distance away, and was it thick enough?

He knew that there were a few houses along the road, where people kept boats. Maybe they would have some. Just as he stood there for a brief moment, contemplating the best course of action, one of the boat owners appeared out of his driveway and began to briskly stroll in his direction.

He looked at the gardener, who he knew by sight, as he'd seen him working in the Morton's gardens. 'Are you all right there?' he asked the older man, realising that something must be amiss for the gardener to be standing in the middle of the street, and he could see worry and confusion etched in the lines on his weathered face. He'd also heard the sirens earlier and caught a glimpse of an ambulance standing just a bit further down the road past the gardener's shoulder.

Jenkins looked at the man. He was about ten or fifteen years his junior and spoke with well-rounded vowels. He was dressed casually in light brown trousers and a pale checked shirt with a light blue sweater over his shoulders. 'Sir,' Jenkins said, with reference to the younger man's obvious higher standing in the community than his as a humble gardener, 'there's been an accident. The wee Morton girl, Emma, has fallen in the river and we need to get her across. I don't suppose you have any strong rope? John Peters has fished the poor lass out, but he is on the other bank and we need to take care in getting them both across without the river taking them both.'

The man put his thumb and forefinger to his chin and thought for a fraction of a second. 'Follow me. I am sure I have just the thing. It should be long enough.' With that he promptly turned on his heel and marched back up his driveway towards the garage to the left of his impressive brick house. Jenkins followed quickly, his feet crunching crisply on the thick layer of gravel that covered the driveway. He looked at the beautifully manicured low box hedges that edged impressive flower beds full of well-tended roses. There was not a weed to be seen, Jenkins noted approvingly.

He could hear the noise of heavy metal items being moved around in the garage as the man moved items aside to get to what he was searching for. The inside of the garage was cool, the concrete floor was smooth and clean under his feet and he could smell the odour of petrol and oil, as well as grass, which must be coming from the mower that he could see towards the back of the building. There were old oil patches staining parts of the floor and, as he looked up, he saw supporting beams housing ladders and other assorted paraphernalia.

'Ah, here we are,' the man cried triumphantly, holding up a coiled length of thick brown rope. It looked very heavy-duty. He also held a coil of thinner rope, which was slightly lighter in colour and looked much smoother to the touch. 'This one would be better to tie around Mr Peters, and we can loop it through the thicker rope so we have a good strong hold onto him and Emma,' he said as he gestured to the thinner rope. Jenkins nodded his agreement.

'We must hurry, sir,' came his urgent reply. 'The little miss took a nasty bang to the head, it looked like, so we need to get her across and to the hospital as soon as possible.'

'Indeed, indeed,' the younger man said, and he gave Jenkins the smaller rope to carry. Then he coiled the thicker rope, slung it over his head to balance the heavy weight of it across his body, and followed him back out into the sunshine and down to the river.

On hearing movement on the path again, Susan Morton turned her head to see Jenkins swiftly followed by Charles Munro, both of them carrying a rope. She was relieved to see the ropes, but as her eyes caught Charles's her heart started to race and she caught her breath. 'Charles, what are you doing here?' she asked.

Charles flushed slightly. He was still walking towards the ambulance men and holding out the rope, flexing it slightly between his hands as if testing the strength and weighing up its ability to manage the task in hand. 'Ah, hello, Susan. Nasty business, this. How is the little one bearing up?' This was addressed to everyone in general as he looked from Susan to the ambulance men and across the river to John Peters as he held the shivering child in his arms.

'Ah, right, I see,' he said. 'OK, chaps, where do you want me? What's the plan? Can I suggest the best course of action?' The ambulance men and Jenkins looked relieved to have someone in their midst who was willing and seemingly able to take charge.

CHAPTER 5

1973

It hadn't occurred to Emma that she would have to get back into the water to get across to safety. She didn't know what she had thought would happen, but as it began to dawn on her she started to panic. She became rigid in John Peters's arms and started to cry. Hot silent tears flowed down her face and soaked into the already sodden cotton shirt worn by her rescuer.

Sensing the change in her behaviour, John Peters looked down at her and started to speak again in his soothing voice. 'Come on, lass. We will soon have you safely across the water. I won't let anything happen to you now. I have you safe. Don't you worry.' His words did little to take away her fear, but she looked up at him and tried to give him a faint, watery smile.

There was an intense discussion going on across the river on the other bank. Charles Munro seemed to be taking charge and was fashioning a sort of double loop out of the smaller rope. He had attached it to the larger rope, which had a thick loop at either end. It looked like the sort of rope she had seen loop over mooring buoys on river wharfs and docksides on days out.

'John,' Charles called across the river in a loud bellow, to ensure it carried across the ever-present rumble of the fast-flowing water. 'We're going to throw this over to you. Please try and catch the smaller rope, which we have attached to the stronger one. When you get it, you will need to wrap it around yourself tightly so that we can keep a hold on you as you come across.'

John Peters seemed to understand what was required of him, as he nodded assent. He turned his kind blue eyes on Emma

31

and spoke again in his gentle voice. 'Now, lass, I'm going to have to put you down while I get the rope. Don't worry. I will then lift you down, and we will get you across the river so you can go and have that nasty bang on your head looked at.'

Her head was starting to throb with an ever-increasing intensity of pain and her vision was swimming alarmingly. Black spots danced in front of her eyes, and she was worried that she was going to keel over. She felt a wave of nausea wash over her and she clutched the front of John Peters's shirt tighter.

John Peters looked torn, but he knew that he had to put her down on the bank to be able to get the rope. Time was ticking on, and head injuries could be serious. But, as she clung to him tightly, he also wanted to ensure that she still felt safe. His protective instinct was very strong.

He gently started to peel her fingers away from his shirt, and weakly she relented and released her hold. Her strength was evaporating, and her fight was all but gone.

With a gentle splash John Peters stepped into the water and leant himself back against the high bank for support against the strong current that flowed against his thighs. His waders kept him dry and helped keep the worst of the cold at bay. 'Ready,' he shouted across at the group of men standing on the opposite bank.

Charles coiled up the larger rope and held it in his left hand as he passed the thinner rope into his right hand and stood side-on to the river. The sun was reflecting off the water, creating glinting sparkles that jumped from place to place as the water flowed over the larger rocks and crashed away in white frothy folds, to be replaced again in a fraction of a second. Its movement was hypnotically rhythmic.

Charles hurled the rope across the expanse of water, but

it missed its target and was drawn away towards the bend. Cursing under his breath, he hauled it back in again. 'Try throwing it upstream,' Jenkins said. 'That way, if you miss, the water will take it downstream towards John.'

Looking irritated that he had been outsmarted by a lesser man, Charles grunted and coiled the rope back in towards him. The rope was now sodden and heavy, and the water soaked into his thin summer clothing. 'Blast,' Charles exclaimed then added, 'Sorry, Susan,' on realising that there were women and children present. The girls sniggered into their hands and glanced at the boys, but they were too focused on what was happening to notice and were eagerly taking in the events unfolding around them.

Having gathered the sodden rope back up again and coiled it back into the right configuration to be able to throw it across towards John Peters, Charles turned even further to the left and threw the rope upstream, away from John. The rope skimmed the bank and fell into the water with a heavy splash about five feet from where John Peters stood. While holding onto the long grass on the bank with his left hand to steady himself, he reached out with his right and managed to grasp the smaller rope and hauled it towards him. He quickly wrapped the smaller rope around himself, crossed it over both his shoulders and back around his waist, and then fastened it securely back into the loop of the larger rope.

Now that he felt secure, he looked across at the others and saw that everyone seemed to have taken a hold on the other end of the rope. Satisfied that there would be enough ballast to ensure that he would not be swept away, he turned to face Emma, where he had left her sitting on the bank just about in line with his shoulders.

'Now, miss, I am going to have to carry you across the river. You will be quite safe, and I won't let anything happen to you. All you need to do is hold on tight, OK?'

Her head hurt and she felt weak, and the thought of going back into the river was frightening. She didn't move. John Peters looked at her kindly, as if he understood the turmoil going on inside her young head. He reached up and put his hands underneath her shoulders and lifted her gently. 'Put your arms around my neck, lass, and hold on tight, just like a koala bear, OK?' She nodded, which made her head hurt more and her vision swim.

She put her arms around his neck, as instructed, and held on tightly, wrapping her legs around him as he turned and grabbed a stronger hold of the thicker rope. She could feel the water starting to slap at her legs and feet, and she seemed to have lost one shoe. *Mother will go mad*, she seemed to recall thinking. Emma screwed her eyes tightly shut, as if not seeing what was happening would make everything all right and it would all just go away.

John Peters started to step out into the deeper part of the river towards the safety of the far bank and the rescue party. Almost immediately she could feel his body getting pulled to the left by the force of the current against his legs. The water was up to his waist already, and the bottom of her feet were dipping in and out of the water as he moved. He stopped and braced himself to prevent losing his footing.

Emma was very scared. She opened her eyes a fraction and saw the worried, intense expressions on the faces of everyone on the opposite bank. She quickly shut them again and tightened her grip with her legs and arms. One thing was certain. She was not letting go for anything.

Steadied, and once more in control of his balance, John Peters took a couple more steps. With each one the water was rising higher up his body, and Emma's too. The water was so cold, despite it being such a warm day. But she was probably in shock and was very frightened, which would have made it feel worse.

John Peters went to take another step and lurched forward, seemingly into nothing. He fell forward, and Emma's shoulder and the side of her head entered the water. She screamed with terror, but just as quickly he righted himself and pulled on the rope for support. The others were doing their best to keep the rope as taut as possible in order to give him more stability as he crossed the water.

They were past the middle of the river now, and the water was not as high up on their bodies. So John Peters started to move more quickly, and soon they were coming up out of the river onto the other bank. The ambulance men had a blanket and a stretcher ready for her.

Emma's mother ran towards her and enveloped her in a big hug. 'Thank you, thank you,' she gushed, turning her tear-stained face towards John Peters. 'You saved her life. I cannot thank you enough.' Her mother looked exhausted. Worry had caused the tiny lines at the side of her eyes to deepen, and her face had taken on a stricken, haunted appearance. Charles looked at her with obvious concern.

'Now, Susan, don't you worry about Robert. I will see him home, and then I am sure that Jenkins can watch over the lad until James gets home.'

Jenkins gently nodded his assent. 'Yes, madam, that will be no trouble.'

'James...' Susan said. Her voice started cracking with

apprehension. 'James must be told.'

'Don't concern yourself, my dear. I'll deal with James,' Charles said magnanimously. 'Just you worry about Emma. That is all that matters for now.' And with that he turned and started to issue instructions to the rest of the party.

Emma was placed on the stretcher and the ambulance men started to carry her up the lane towards the ambulance. 'We need to get her to the hospital as quickly as possible,' they said to her mother, who was trotting alongside them as they carried her up the lane, holding her daughter's hand. 'Head injuries can be tricky things.'

She could see the light playing through the canopy of the leaves as they made their way up the lane. It sparkled and glittered as it played its game of hide-and-seek with the thick green covering.

At the top of the lane they slid the stretcher into the back of the ambulance. One of the ambulance men came to sit beside Emma to check her over, and her mother climbed in.

Just before the other ambulance man shut the rear door Emma saw Tom standing at the end of the lane, leaning against one of the trees. She wondered how he had got there as he had been on the other side of the river, like her, and he didn't even look wet. Perhaps he had run all the way round.

I must have been unconscious for much longer than I thought, she said to herself.

Chapter 6

1 9 7 3

The rest of that day was a blur of doctors, nurses, big noisy machinery and a vicious headache. Apparently she had cracked the back of her head open on the rock and had a touch of concussion. She knew that she felt sick and woozy, and it really felt like she'd hit her head on a large rock.

They wanted to keep her in for observation, and she was tucked up in a huge bed with cool, heavy white sheets in a ward with other children. She was so sleepy that she just wanted to rest, but she was constantly jerked back awake by nurses wanting to prod and poke her and blow up her arm and stick things in her mouth.

She was starting to get irritable, and all she wanted to do was sleep. She was also confused about Tom. How could he have got to the other side of the river so quickly? She was just about to ask her mother if she knew when her father walked in.

Her father was a striking man. He was tall and slim with hair so dark as to almost be black, and he had piercing blue eyes. He was the type of man who brooked no argument. His word was law, and was to be followed without question. His orders were never questioned. However, this was engineered more from fear than out of any respect. His wrath was to be avoided at all costs. Robert and Emma had learnt this to their detriment a long time ago.

He strode into the room, nodding a mere acknowledgement at the nursing staff, who scuttled out of his way and came towards the bed. 'How on earth did you allow this to happen,

Susan?' he hissed between clenched teeth. His anger was only just held in check due to where he was, but its unwelcome presence could be felt simmering dangerously below the surface.

Susan flinched almost imperceptibly as Emma shrunk back into the bed, not realising at the time that her father would not be able to exact the usual punishment for any misdemeanour.

Her mother continued to hold her hand as she returned a cool gaze towards her husband's steely one. 'The children went out for a walk with their friends, as they usually do every day during the school holidays. You can hardly expect me to keep them cooped up in the house under lock and key,' she replied mildly, trying to keep the anxiety from her voice.

Emma watched their quietly conducted altercation with large, frightened eyes from the bed, her long dark hair fanned out now against the crisp white linen, as she waited with bated breath for the barely concealed wrath to explode its full fury in her direction. Her mother must have sensed Emma's anxiety, as her whole body tensed.

Emma was still holding Susan's hand, and she now gripped it with such an intensity that her knuckles gleamed white and almost matched the colour of the sheet they lay on. 'James,' Susan said quietly, and nodded towards Emma with the merest flick of her head.

Her father seemed to gather his senses and, remembering where he was and the eyes that were glancing in their direction from the nursing staff and junior doctors, moved towards Emma with a smile planted on his face, a smile that looked charming to all those not aware of his true character but which did not fool her for one moment.

'Well, Emma, whatever have you been up to now?' he said. 'What a fuss has been made over a simple tumble into the water. You can swim, I presume?' He cast a withering look of annoyance towards his wife.

'Of course she can swim, James. You know that. However, the current of the river is very strong, and I understand that she hit her head against one of the rocks and was knocked unconscious. She would have drowned if John Peters had not fished her out with one of his basket hooks.' Her voice caught on the last words as she choked back the emotion.

James just raised his eyebrows. 'Well, I think you've had enough attention for one day, Emma.' He grabbed his wife's arm and made to drag her away from the side of the bed.

'No, James. What are you doing?' Susan exclaimed, trying to shake his grip from her arm. 'I am staying here with Emma. The doctors have said that she has concussion and needs to be kept under observation for at least twenty-four hours.'

'Well, we will see about that,' James countered, and strode off to demand to see the doctor in charge of his daughter's care.

Her mother sank down into her chair and sighed deeply. The nursing staff looked over inquiringly but did not intervene. What went on between a man and his wife was none of their business, but they cast knowing looks at each other.

Her mother was embarrassed at having had others witness what usually only took place in private. Emma only discovered much later the extent of the suffering she had endured being married to her father. Back then, as children, they just knew that their father had a temper that was to be avoided at all costs. They knew that he was a very well-respected member of the local community and outwardly he was the handsome solicitor with the beautiful wife and the perfect home, complete with his two lovely children. If only they knew.

Her father, having found a doctor, and by using a

combination of charm and bullying tactics, which always seem to get him the results he craved, had somehow managed to secure Emma's immediate release from the hospital. 'Right, Emma, there's been enough of this nonsense. You are coming home now, and your mother is perfectly capable of looking after you at home.'

He cast a disgusted, condescending look down his nose at Susan, as if her very existence irritated him. Emma looked up at her mother with beseeching eyes. But she failed to meet them and, knowing that she was beaten, cast her gaze down at her lap.

Her father did, however, permit her to be placed in a wheel-chair to take her along the corridors and out to his car, which stood waiting in the car park. Emma was still very unsteady on her feet. Her head pounded and she was so tired. She just wanted to go to bed and sleep for a week.

She glanced at the peeling paint as she was wheeled in silence along the corridors by her mother walking a couple of paces behind her father, who strode down the long corridors with huge, purposeful strides, his head high and his body language exuding the essence of his own self-importance.

The peeling paint in the corridors increased her feeling of desolation. It seemed to embody the way she was feeling. Neglect oozed from its pores, the overhead lighting hurt her eyes, and every turn jarred her body and sent bolts of pain into the back of her eyes and down her neck.

As they reached the glass doors of the entrance the sun glared bright, and she winced and closed her eyes to shut out its intensity. Her mother stopped and took off her cardigan and placed it gently over her head to shield her from the worst of the light. 'Oh, stop fussing, woman,' her father muttered under his breath as he stalked off towards his waiting car.

Emma didn't remember much about the journey back home. She just remembered resting her head against her mother's shoulder as they both sat on the back seat. She must have fallen asleep, but she awoke as she heard the tyres crunch over the gravel of the large driveway. The car came to a halt, having turned around the large flower bed in the centre of the drive, and faced the entrance. Hopefully this meant that her father would not be staying, she thought.

Her mother got out of the car and came round to her side to help her clamber out. She gently supported her daughter as she leant against her as they walked towards the front door. They had hardly moved away from the back of the car when it moved off up the driveway so quickly that the back end swerved slightly in the deep gravel, which flew up and hit them both in the back of the legs. They stood dumbfounded by this latest act of arrogant aggression as the car reached the top of the driveway and spun a fast right turn, screeching slightly as the wheels protested against the tarmac. Her mother sighed resignedly as she gently put her hand against her daughter's back to guide her into the cool interior of the house. 'Come on, love, let's get you inside and into bed.'

Emma meekly followed her mother up the two flights of stairs to her attic bedroom, where she helped her undress and get into her nightdress. She closed the curtains, which were thin, so they still allowed the light to enter the room even though it was dimmed, but she was so tired that she could have slept in the full sun. The window was open, and the light breeze played with the thin material like a puppet dancing, guided by unseen hands. Her mother pulled back the sheet and the thin blanket and she got into the bed. The sheets felt cool and inviting. Her head still pounded but tiredness took her anyway, and she fell instantly asleep.

Susan Morton watched her sleeping daughter for a moment. She brushed her fine dark hair away from her flushed cheek and felt a combination of tenderness, fear and guilt wash over her all at the same time. She needed to do something about the situation she was in, but felt powerless to act.

Things were never going to improve – she knew that deep in her heart – but she had no idea where to start to make things any better. So she did nothing and allowed the intolerable situation that she found herself in to continue unabated, and lost a bit more of herself every day. But this – she looked at her sleeping daughter, who she knew should really have been in the hospital – this was the final straw. She needed to stand up for herself, for her children, before it was too late.

She left the room to go downstairs to find Robert and Jenkins. She really needed to apologise for the way she had treated them earlier. The pressure of living this constant lie for the sake of appearances was changing her very essence and she was acting out of character, filling her days with mindless actions to try and fit in to the role she was expected to play and to blot out the fear and loneliness that threatened to swamp her and pull her down into a dark, desolate place from which there would be no easy return.

As she walked distractedly from the room, she felt a brush of air and looked down to see Tom slipping in through the door. 'Watch over her for me, would you, Tom? There's a dear,' she murmured as she walked towards the stairs in search of the others.

She found them all seated in the kitchen. Jenkins had made a pot of tea and he, Charles, Robert and the two girls all sat around the table talking quietly. They stopped immediately as she entered the room and turned several pairs of expectant eyes in her direction.

'Mum,' 'Susan,' 'Mrs Morton,' they all said at once. She shushed them all with a wave of her hand, which reached up to her forehead as if to still the pain that throbbed behind her tired eyes.

'Where's Emma?' Robert asked anxiously. 'Is she OK? Is she still in the hospital? Why are you back here?' The questions tumbled out of him in a worried rush that brought a lump to her throat for the love that he obviously felt for his sister.

'She's OK, love,' Susan replied. 'She is upstairs in bed and sleeping.'

'Is that wise?' Charles asked, looking at her closely and realising that something was not quite right. 'Should she be back from the hospital so soon?' Susan sighed. Her breath was long, as though she had been holding onto it for a very long time. The fine lines around her eyes were accentuated, and she looked worn to the very core. She rested her hands upon the back of the chair that Robert sat in and looked directly at Charles.

'James came to the hospital. He made a scene, saying it was all a fuss about nothing, and bullied the doctors into allowing him to take her home. It didn't look good, he said, that his daughter had been in an accident because she wasn't being supervised properly.'

'That bloody man,' Charles said before a beseeching look from Susan reminded him of the others that were in the room, including the children. He opted instead to let out an irritated huff and folded his arms across his chest. Susan must have been at the end of her tether to let the mask of nothing more than a happy wife and homemaker slip, even for an instant, even though all those present, including the neighbours' children, had been witness to James's outbursts on more than one occasion.

Jenkins rested his kind, older eyes upon Susan's defeated face and spoke gently. 'Is Emma OK, though, Mrs Morton?'

Susan seemed to snap out of the trance she had temporarily fallen into and turned to face him. 'I think so, Jenkins. I hope so. I just…' Her voice cracked and she covered her face in her hands, overcome with the emotion of the fear she had felt on hearing about the accident, the relief that Emma was OK, and from having to hold everything together all the time to keep up the pretence that all was rosy in her world.

Charles stood to make a move to come towards her, but Robert leapt to his feet. He wordlessly put a gentle hand on his mother's arm and guided her to sit down in the chair that he had just vacated. He placed a cup of tea in front of her and then turned to the two girls and Richard, who were staring awkwardly at the unfolding situation in the kitchen. 'Come on,' he said brightly. 'Let's go and see what fruit is ripe in the garden, and maybe Mother can make us some pies or something later.' Relieved to be given an excuse to extract themselves from the oppressive adult company, they all jumped up quickly, hurriedly said their goodbyes and walked towards the back door.

Susan looked gratefully towards her caring son and shouted after him, 'Robert, please don't leave the garden. I need to know where you are, just in case… You know,' she finished awkwardly. Robert threw her a cheeky smile and a thumbs up and, following his friends, left the kitchen.

Jenkins looked towards the door 'He's an old soul, that one,' he said, as if it were a known fact. Charles muttered something unintelligible, which appeared to be an assent, but Susan said nothing.

Jenkins then stood up and made to move towards the door himself. 'If it's OK with you, Mrs Morton, I'll get back to work, and I can keep an eye on the nippers too while I'm out there.' Susan nodded and thanked him for his thoughtfulness.

'Well,' said Charles, after everyone had gone. 'What are you going to do?'

Susan just looked at him bleakly, with large eyes full of turmoil. 'I don't know,' she said honestly. 'I really just don't know any longer, but things cannot carry on like this.'

At that moment they both heard a call from upstairs that Susan recognised instantly. 'Mummy … Mummy.'

Charles looked at Susan. 'Is that Emma? You'd better go. It sounds urgent.' Susan sighed but didn't say anything. She just rose to climb the stairs to go and check on her daughter.

When she reached Emma's bedroom she gently pushed the door open and saw what she had expected to see. Emma was lying fast asleep where she had left her. Her breathing was even, and her cheeks were still almost as white as the sheets. There was a fine beading of sweat upon her forehead and she felt clammy to the touch. *She shouldn't be here*, Susan thought, hating herself for the weakness that prevented her from standing up to her husband.

Emma moved restlessly in her sleep and let out a soft moan. Susan sat down gently on the side of the bed and brushed Emma's fine dark hair, which was slightly damp from perspiration. 'Shush now,' she said quietly. 'I'm here.'

Emma opened her eyes sleepily and looked towards the window seat. She smiled in her half-sleep and said 'Hi,' then closed her eyes and dropped back into a deep sleep. A shadow moved between the window and the door, which Susan caught in the corner of her eye, but her gaze remained focused on her daughter. She needed to do something but had no idea what that something was.

Susan walked to the window and looked out onto the garden. She could see the edge of the terrace and the slope of the grass banks, which were interspersed with rose beds. The lawn was long and wide, flanked on either side with more large flower beds, and each boundary was marked by mature trees. There was a wych elm tree at the end of the lawn area that the children loved playing in during the summer as they were completely hidden by the canopy of leaves, which reached to the ground. Beyond that was the orchard, which housed a variety of fruit trees, and a small vegetable patch. This should have been an idyllic place and, had her husband been a different type of man, things would have been very different.

She had been happy at first, she remembered, when they had first met. James was clever and handsome and had been considered a great catch by her friends and family. He was all charm and manners and had swept her off her feet. Once they were married, however, and had moved into this house, the change in him was almost immediate. It was as though she had become his property, that after the chase was over and he had claimed his prize she no longer held any interest for him.

At first she didn't understand, so she tried so hard to be what he wanted her to be. She hosted lavish dinner parties to entertain his friends and business colleagues, but her quiet and gentle ways seemed to bore him. Because she was always left to her own devices she had tried to join in with the local set – lunching with the right people, playing tennis at his club – but whereas the other wives seemed to revel in this life that lacked purpose it just felt empty and meaningless to Susan.

She wondered silently if any of the other wives' husbands were cruel and cold. It was definitely not a subject that could be discussed in those kinds of circles. But who could she talk to? Was this just the normal way of things? She thought of her own father, who had been so gentle and kind. He never raised his voice in anger, let alone his hand.

She couldn't discuss this with her parents. Her father would be heartbroken for his only daughter, and her mother would just tell her to get on with it. She could not cause them the social embarrassment of a failed marriage. But what could she do? She looked down the garden and could just catch glimpses of the children playing some sort of made-up game of pirates or something that involved sword fighting with sticks, and smiled. She looked back towards Emma and resolved to find a way to fix this awful situation.

When Emma woke up it was getting dark. Her head still hurt but it was bearable. She saw that someone had left her a drink and a plate of biscuits on a stool that had been placed by the side of her bed, and she realised that she was actually starving. She leant across the bed to grab a biscuit, which caused a shooting pain in her head.

Her vision swam and she felt sick. She clutched at the bedsheet, her knuckles whitening with the force of her hold. She caught a movement out of the corner of her eye and looked across to the window and saw Tom sitting there, watching her with a quizzical look on his face. The last rays of the day's sun washed over his pale face, leaving the rest of him in shadow. 'Hello, Emma,' he said quietly. 'How are you feeling?'

He walked over to the bed and stood by her side. Then they heard the faint sound of footsteps coming up the stairs. 'I'll see you later,' he said, and with that he left her. Her mother's voice carried along the corridor.

'Emma,' she called out. 'Is that you speaking? Are you OK? Do you need anything?' She hurried into the room looking concerned, but brightened when her eyes alighted on her daughter's face, which had started to show a bit of colour returning to its fine features. Always a pale child, this mishap had stolen away what little colour Emma did have, giving her an ethereal appearance.

'You look a bit better,' she said, resting a cool hand on her forehead and frowning slightly. 'Mm… You are still a little too warm for my liking, though,' she said. 'I think perhaps we could ask the doctor to pop out and see you just to check that everything is OK. Have you had a drink?'

Emma lifted the glass of juice to her dry lips and took a small sip. It tasted like nectar on her parched tongue, and she drank deeply. 'Slowly,' her mother said chidingly. 'We don't want you being sick or coughing and jarring your head, now, do we?'

She took the glass in her hand. 'How is your head feeling?' she continued.

'It still hurts, especially when I move,' Emma admitted. 'Well, try not to move, then, darling,' her mother suggested, plumping up the pillows. 'Are you hungry? Could you manage a sandwich or some soup?'

'Maybe a cheese sandwich,' she replied in a small voice. 'Thank you, Mum.' Susan smiled at her daughter, so small and slight in the bed.

'OK, one cheese sandwich coming up.' She turned to leave the room to attend to her daughter's needs.

'Is Father home yet?' Emma asked hesitantly. Her mother didn't fail to catch the trace of fear in those few words.

'Not yet, sweetheart,' she replied. 'Now you rest there, and I'll get you that sandwich.'

As she made her way back down the two flights of stairs to the kitchen on the ground floor, Susan had plenty of time to reflect on the fear she had seen in her daughter's eyes and the tremor in her voice when she spoke of her father.

This just could not carry on. She hoped that tonight would be one of those nights when James Morton did not return at all.

The man in question was sitting at his desk contemplating what to do. He really should be seen to be at home with his family after one of his offspring had been involved in a near drowning incident, but he had already arranged to take that pretty little blonde out for a discreet dinner.

He just could not face an evening in that stifling house pretending that everything was fine. His wife bored him. It was as simple as that. Oh, she was pretty enough, he supposed, and it had done him no harm to be seen with her on his arm, but she was… Well, she just wasn't eighteen, blonde and hanging on his every word, was she?

So he decided that he would take his chances and go out for dinner with Clare. They could be discreet, go out of the way, where no one would know either of them. She could just be a client he was meeting to discuss a case if anyone did notice them. Yes, it was fine, he persuaded himself.

He picked Clare up as arranged, at a bus stop down a quieter street. It was starting to rain, which brought a welcome relief to the stifling heat earlier on in the day. Clare was waiting for him as arranged. She wore a short flared red skirt, teamed with heels and a thin sweater, which clung in all the right places. Her long blonde hair fell loosely down her back, and she held a plain black umbrella in her hand. She started to close the umbrella and gave it a little shake as James pulled the car into the bus stop and leant over to open the door for her.

She smiled shyly at this polite gesture. Most of the men she had been out with before would have driven through the puddle that was rapidly forming in the dip at the side of the kerb and thought it highly amusing to soak her through, perhaps thinking she may be tempted to remove an item of clothing or three. Clare shuddered at the thought.

Not James, though. James was different. He was sophisticated and had perfect manners. He was always so attentive, and complimented her. Oh, she knew that he was married, but he had been pushed into the marriage at far too young an age and his wife was cold, aloof and unfeeling, so who could blame him for looking elsewhere for some fun and relaxation? Hadn't he told her himself?

'Good evening, Clare. I hope I have not kept you waiting for too long.' His words cut through her reverie and pulled her back to the moment at hand. 'You do look pretty tonight,' James continued.

'Thank you,' Clare replied, lowering her eyelids and fluttering her lashes slightly. 'No, you have not kept me waiting. You're right on time, as always.' James knew this to be a fact. He always prided himself on his timekeeping – was fastidious about it – but it never hurt to be reminded of the fact.

'Well, let's get going then, my dear, so do your belt up. I thought we could try a new restaurant a bit out of the way. It has some very good reviews.'

As Susan sat in the drawing room looking out over the garden, a fox crossed the grass and disappeared behind the wych elm. *Where is James?* she wondered. She didn't actually want him to be at home because it was so much more peaceful and relaxed without him. No one had to tread on eggshells all the time or be scared about when the next outburst was going to erupt when he wasn't there. *He is like a walking volcano,* she thought. Nothing she ever did or said seemed to be right.

She was tired, weary to the very core with it all. She had seen Robert off to bed around thirty minutes ago and popped up again to see Emma. She seemed to be looking a little better, but she would get Dr Walker out to see her tomorrow just to be on the safe side.

She sat in her favourite wingback chair overlooking the garden, holding her cup of tea and watching the sun make its gentle descent behind the trees and casting long shadows across the lawn. It was such a beautiful garden. For all James's temper and forceful nature, she did love this house.

The grandfather clock in the hall struck nine. Momentarily distracted from the garden, she looked back and thought she caught a glimpse of red between the branches of the trees. Intrigued, she rose from her chair and walked through the French doors, across the terrace and down the slope onto the lawn. The grass was still damp from the earlier rain, and she left a trail of wet footprints as she walked across the grass towards the trees. She heard a child's soft laughter and saw the flash of clothing again. She followed the sound round behind the trees and came to the hedge which bordered the garden, but there was no one there.

The giggling noise came again, this time from the orchard. She walked quickly up to the gate and through the orchard and there it was again, that same giggling sound. She heard the back gate open and shut, so she half-ran towards it and flung it open. But again there was no one there. The path was clear on both sides and the large expanse of grass verge right in front of her was empty. Shaking her head, she walked back down through the orchard and followed her footprints back to the house.

She took her cup into the kitchen and rinsed it and put it in the sink, deciding she would wash it up properly in the morning. She locked the back door and walked through the dining room and started to climb the stairs to the first floor. She got herself ready for bed and went to check on Emma one last time before going to bed. Happy that all was well, she looked in on Robert, who was snuffling gently, and walked down to her own bedroom at the end of the corridor.

It was only as she was starting to drift off to sleep that she realised what had been troubling her about the noises in the garden. She had definitely seen and heard someone, but what she hadn't seen were any other footprints. Where were the footprints?

CHAPTER 7

1973

It was another sunny day but not as hot as the preceding few days, for which everyone was exceedingly grateful. James must have come back at some point and left again before Susan was awake, because one of the spare bedrooms had been slept in and his dirty clothes lay discarded on the floor where he had taken them off the night before. She sighed and picked them up, then straightened the bedclothes absent-mindedly as she walked around the bed.

She wondered whether he had even looked in on Emma, whether he actually cared at all. She knew that he had not really wanted children but that it was expected of him to have them to carry on the family line. His precious family... You'd have thought they were descended from royalty, the way his parents went on.

She had been desperate for children and had fought James tooth and nail to prevent him from sending Robert away to school. He did seem more interested in his son than his daughter, but even that was fleeting, with only the occasional enquiry about how he was doing at school. He never played with them, never kicked a ball around in the huge garden. He was a distant, remote and oppressive figure in their lives and for that she was doubly sad, especially when remembering her own childhood with her kind and loving father. James could not have been more different.

She had already checked on Emma first thing that morning and now prepared a breakfast tray for her. A boiled egg and some nice toasted bread that she knew she liked and a glass of milk. She carried it up the two flights of stairs to her daughter's bedroom in the eaves of the house.

She supposed that these four rooms would have been servants' rooms once upon a time. They really did not need to live in such a vast house, but that was James: prestige and outward appearances were everything. She would have been happy with a little cottage with a rambling garden, but that would not do for James. That would not suit him at all. He didn't have to keep this vast house clean, though, did he?

She pushed the door to Emma's room open with her hip and saw that her daughter was sitting up in bed and, although still very pale, was looking much better. Susan sighed inwardly with relief. 'I've made you your favourite for breakfast, darling,' Susan said gently, with a kind smile on her face. 'Do you think you can manage a little?' Emma shifted herself into a more comfortable position to be able to take the tray from her mother and grinned at her.

'Thanks, Mum. I am hungry.'

Susan gave her the tray and sat down at the end of the bed. There was a light cold draught coming from the window and she got up to close it, but it wasn't open. She shivered slightly and went and sat back down on the bed. 'How is your head feeling today? Is it still sore?'

'It is a bit,' Emma admitted. 'But it is much better than yesterday. I don't feel as tired, either. I think I just have slept for hours.'

Susan smiled. 'You certainly have,' she said. She wondered whether she should ask if her father had been in to see her too but thought better of it. 'I think I will ask Dr Walker to come and check on you this morning to see if he is happy with how you are healing. Is that OK?' Susan asked her. Emma merely nodded and continued to tuck into her eggy bread, which was trailing spots of yellow over the tray and down the front of her nightdress.

Not the best choice for a breakfast in bed, Susan said to herself. She went to wet a flannel in the sink by the window and dabbed at the stain. 'Sorry, Mum,' Emma said, but she knew that her mum was not really cross with her.

They both turned at a clatter of feet running up the stairs, and a second later Robert thrust his grinning face round the door and bounced into the room. He threw himself onto the bed, nearly upturning the tray and spilling some of the half-empty glass of milk onto the tray, which mixed with the drying egg. 'Careful, Robert,' mother and daughter cried in unison. Then they all looked at each other and broke into a collective giggle.

It sounded good. Laughter had been sorely missing from their lives lately, and Susan vowed that she would do something to rectify this as soon as possible. She would speak to someone, someone who wasn't likely to report back to James. She thought about it for a moment, then decided to call Charles later that day.

Robert tried to resist bouncing up and down on the bed, but he was so pleased to see his little sister looking so much better that his pent-up relief oozed out of every pore. 'Well, what are you going to do today as an encore?' he asked his sister teasingly.

'Oh, be quiet, Robert,' she retorted. 'You're just jealous that I got breakfast in bed.' Glad to see that normality had returned by witnessing their gentle teasing and bickering, Susan collected the tray of dirty dishes and walked towards the door.

'If Dr Walker pronounces you fit and well later, you can go and sit in the garden if you keep yourself quiet,' she said as she exited the room and walked down the stairs back towards the kitchen at the other end of the house.

Dr Walker was an older man, probably somewhere in his late fifties, with a bristling moustache and a ruddy complexion. He had a cheery manner, which was coupled with a booming voice that should have caused fear in the nervous and in small children, but everything combined to make him appear like a friendly Father Christmas sort of character.

He always wore clothes that would not have been out of place on an old-fashioned country squire, and today was no different. He appeared at the front door wearing a tweed suit and a brown checked shirt and a waistcoat, complete with a pocket watch. On his head he wore a hat with a couple of feathers in the band, which reminded Susan of a fishing fly. 'Morning, Susan,' he bellowed. 'How's our young patient today, then?'

Susan ushered him into the impressive hallway as the grandfather clock at the bottom of the stairs struck 11.15 a.m. 'She seems a bit better this morning, Doctor. But I would like you to check her over just to be on the safe side, since James bullied her out of the hospital yesterday.'

'Hmm,' Dr Walker mumbled, but said no more. He knew that things were not all as they should be in this house and had treated Susan Morton on more than one occasion for a 'slip' or 'fall', which he had always suspected had happened by other, less innocent means. *She must be getting to the end of her tether, though, to have even alluded to her husband being any less than perfect just now*, he thought with concern. *What has the bloody man been up to this time?*

The doctor had always thought him a nice enough chap – a bit uptight and full of himself, but nice enough. He would have a word with his wife and see if she could have a discreet word with Susan. He would do what he could to help, but only if help was sought.

They walked up the two flights of stairs, the doctor wheezing slightly from the excess weight he carried from too frequently partaking of a glass of port after a fine dinner. *If only my wife was not such a remarkable cook*, he thought with slight amusement.

They rounded the corner at the top of the second flight of stairs and entered Emma's bedroom. The girl was lying back against the pillows. Her face was still pale but her eyes were bright, and she turned her head towards the door as she heard them enter the room. 'Well, now, young Emma,' Dr Walker said loudly. 'What scrape have you been in this time?' His eyes twinkled and his moustache quivered, and Emma let out a little giggle from behind the hand that had covered her mouth.

'I fell in the river, Dr Walker. I didn't mean to. I know we are not allowed to go to the river, but the others were going and I didn't want to be left on my own.' The words tumbled out of her like a torrent, as if getting everything off her chest would make it all better and the pain would go away of its own accord.

Dr Walker nodded gravely. 'Well, young lady, I am sure that we have all done things that we realise we shouldn't have, and lucky for you old John Peters was there to fish you out.' Emma nodded, making her head hurt again. The wincing pain registered on her face, which did not escape notice by either the doctor or her mother.

'Then I saw Tom, and I wondered why he was there, so I called out to him and ran to talk to him, and then I must have tripped and fallen into the river…' She trailed off then, screwing up her eyes to block out the memory of swirling in the dangerous cold water and swallowing gulps of the smelly river water.

At the mention of Tom both Dr Walker and Susan Morton exchanged a glance. Dr Walker's was questioning, and Susan Morton just shrugged her shoulders but did not comment. 'Anyway, young lady, let's take a look at that bump on your head then, shall we?' And he moved towards the bed, where Emma shuffled up to a sitting position and awaited further inspection of her wounds.

After looking at the back of Emma's head and feeling the swelling, Dr Walker checked her eyes with a light, listened to her chest with his stethoscope and took her temperature. He felt her throat and neck to see if her glands were raised and then changed the dressing on her leg. 'I think you'll live,' he said with a smile on his face. 'Rest this morning, then you can get up this afternoon. But no running about, please.'

'I said that she could come and sit in the garden if you pronounced her well enough,' her mother said to the doctor.

'Yes, a bit of fresh air will do her good,' the doctor replied as he packed his equipment back into his bag.

The adults both left the room and walked down the stairs. As they got to the hall Dr Walker paused and turned back towards Susan. The expression on his face was of kind concern. 'Susan, you know that I am here to help. If you ever need to talk, or… Well, you know,' he trailed off.

Susan shook her head. 'I know,' she said quietly. 'Maybe. We'll see.' The doctor nodded. He realised that she was a proud woman, but he wanted her to know that she should not suffer in silence.

Things had changed, and were continuing to change. You did

not have to stay in an unhappy marriage any longer. The shame of divorce was not as strong as it had been in their parents' day. 'Well, you know where I am if you need me,' he said.

And with that he walked through the front door and Susan closed it quietly behind him.

CHAPTER 8

1973

Jenkins was in the garden deadheading the roses and some of the other plants while whistling to himself. The sun was warm on his back, and he was enjoying his work. There was always something to do in a garden this size, and he spent a couple of hours a day keeping on top of everything.

Then there were all the other jobs to be done around the place: gate hinges to oil, cars to wash, things that always needed mending. The lawn took three hours just to mow in the summer, and that needed doing at least twice a week. Then there was raking up the grass... The list went on. He liked to be busy, though. He had worked in this garden for forty years now, and had sort of been inherited by the current family when they bought the property from the previous owners.

He shuddered involuntarily when he thought back to the sad memories of that time. He looked up as a shadow crossed his path to see John Peters walking down the lawn towards him. He raised a hand in welcome. 'Hello, John,' he said. 'What brings you down to these parts?' but he already thought he had a good idea.

This was confirmed as soon as John Peters started to speak. 'Thought I'd come to see how the young lass was doing. She is all right, isn't she?' he added quickly, suddenly worried that something bad may have happened and worried that perhaps he shouldn't have come.

'Aye, she's right enough,' Jenkins replied, and witnessed his friend's anxiety slip away with the lowering of his shoulders and the release of a long breath that he had been holding.

'Well, thank the gods for that,' he said as he breathed out in relief. 'The missus said she'd be as right as rain, and you know Sarah and her premonitions.' Both men nodded at each other sagely.

'Anyhow,' John Peters continued, 'Sarah sent me down with some of her shortbread for the lass. Gave me strict instructions not to touch any on the way down, neither.' He smiled with recollection of her stern words and the warning look on her face as she stood framed in the kitchen door with hands on her hips as she issued her warning. 'My wife knows me too well,' he said to himself, with a smile creasing the features on his face.

'Happen she's still at the hospital?' he asked Jenkins, who shook his head gravely.

'Nope. The boss stormed down there and pulled her out. There was quite a to-do, from what I heard through the grapevine. What he was thinking I don't know. But I think that Dr Walker has just been to see her and, as he left with a smile on his face and she is still here, I am presuming that she will be just fine.'

'Poor mite,' John Peters said, shaking his head gravely. 'And the boss's wife? Is she OK?' It was an open secret that James Morton was none too kind to his wife, which was sad, because she was such a lovely lady.

'Who knows what goes on in there really?' Jenkins put in, and returned to deadheading his roses while John Peters carried on up the garden towards the back door which led into the kitchen.

He knocked on the open back door and walked into the kitchen. Then he walked across the large room to the door that opened into the beautiful wood-panelled drawing room and stuck his head around the corner and called out, 'Mrs Morton, are you there? It's John, John Peters,' he added for good measure, just in case she was wondering.

Susan was in the drawing room and called out, 'I'm in the drawing room, John. Hang on. I'll come through.' It would save him from having to take off his work boots, which he would no doubt be wearing, she thought. She knew that Sarah would have drilled that into him before he left her, and she smiled to herself at the image of the large man being directed in etiquette by his tiny wife.

As Susan walked towards the dining room she noticed that the flowers on the hall table were starting to wilt. She would have to ask Jenkins to pick some more for her today. James liked the house to look presentable at all times, and for her to have overlooked something so obvious to him as he walked through the door would just cause another row.

She sighed at the thought and continued through the dining room into the kitchen, where John Peters stood with a tin in front of him, looking slightly uncomfortable being inside the large house, even if it was only in the kitchen. On noticing his uncomfortable manner Susan nodded at the tin and asked, 'What have you got there, John? Please tell me it is something delicious, made by your lovely wife.'

Smiling broadly with pride now, John Peters nodded his agreement. 'Aye, that it is, Mrs Morton. Some special short-bread that Sarah knows the kiddies love.'

'I don't know why you insist on calling me Mrs Morton, John. You've known me long enough now, and you did save my daughter's life yesterday,' Susan said, flapping her hand at him and taking the tin that he offered to her in his outstretched hand.

'Aye, I know, but it doesn't seem right – you married to Mr Morton, and all that.' John Peters rubbed his chin as he spoke. 'How is Emma? Jenkins told me she was back from the hospital. Is she OK?' The look of concern was back on his face and his eyes looked troubled as he recalled the events of the previous day.

'She will be fine, John, thanks to you. I don't know what would have happened if you had not been there.' Her voice started to break with those last few words and her hand flew up to her heart. 'What can we ever do to thank you?' she continued, quickly gaining control over her emotions before the floodgates opened. If she allowed that to happen, with everything else going on she did not know when they were likely to close.

'I don't want or need anything,' John Peters continued, 'just as long as Miss Emma is OK. That is enough reward for me. Please tell her that Sarah sends her love too.' And with that he turned and walked back through the kitchen door and headed down the garden and towards home.

Emma and Tom watched him go, then Emma turned to Tom and said, 'I am going down to the garden now, Tom. Can you come with me?' With a slight, wordless shake of his head Tom declined her offer and sat back down on the window seat to watch her from there.

Emma was sitting in the garden at a small wooden table doing a jigsaw with her mother when her father came home. Finding no one in the house to greet him, he moodily crossed the hall and walked through the drawing room to the French doors. In the garden the happy picture of his wife's head bent over a puzzle with their daughter was clearly visible. But just seeing the cosy family life – that he paid for – made his blood boil.

When had he started to feel like this? Had he always been this resentful?

He searched his memories and feelings, and realised that it was soon after they had moved to this house. Because he had always wanted to be seen to have a certain position, he had been determined to buy an enormous house, one far larger than his family could possibly ever need, and had brushed aside his wife's concerns.

What did she know? Stupid woman. All she ever did was spend his money on her clubs and flowers and God only knows what else. He conveniently forgot that it was he who urged her to join the country club to butter up the wives of his prospects and the wealthy businessmen that he wanted to forge relationships with. Also, it was he who insisted that there were always fresh flowers in the hallway and in the other main rooms of the house.

He stormed across the terrace and flung himself down in the remaining chair at the table. 'Well, this all looks cosy,' he said sneeringly. 'Susan, make me a gin and tonic, will you? I'm tired. It's been a long day.' Susan eyed him warily, wanting to make some comment about his late-night return – no wonder he was tired – but knew that it was not worth incurring any further wrath from this man, who was becoming more distant by the day.

She rose silently and then turned to her daughter. 'Emma, will you be OK, love? Do you want a drink too?'

'Of course she will be OK, woman,' James snapped at her. 'I'm her father. Can I not spend some time with my own daughter without you questioning it?' Emma viewed her father warily but shook her head quickly at her mother and looked back down at her puzzle, trying to avoid looking directly at her father. She did not know what would make him angrier: staring at him or ignoring him. Her hands started to tremble.

Seeing the reaction of his daughter only incensed James more. 'What's wrong with you now? Cat got your tongue, has it? Look at me when I'm talking to you.' Emma raised fearful round eyes that were starting to fill with tears.

Just then the telephone could be heard ringing. After a short pause Susan called out into the garden, 'James, it's for you,' and Emma breathed out a long breath as her father got up from the table and walked back into the shadows of the dining room.

She looked up to her room and saw Tom's pale face looking down into the garden at her with a look of anger crossing his small features, which gave Emma pause, and she felt a shiver run the whole length of her body.

After slamming down the receiver, James Morton ran a nervous hand through his hair. He needed to get out of this oppressive house, even though he had only just arrived home. Everything about it annoyed him. Everywhere he looked he just saw money oozing out of his pockets. He wished he could just walk away from this life.

He paced the drawing room, trying to think. His behaviour emulated the caged animal that he felt like inside. Someone must have seen Clare and him together, he thought.

He picked up his briefcase, and without a word to his family he stalked across the hallway and slammed the front door behind him. His tyres crunched noisily against the gravel, and he sped away from the house to try and fix the mess that his life was becoming before it all tumbled down around him.

Susan watched him go through the kitchen window and wondered what on earth was wrong this time. She wasn't sad to see him leave. His presence in the house always made everyone nervous. His moods of late had been getting worse, and the children were starting to suffer now too. If only she was strong enough to speak to him about it, but fear of his temper always made her hold back. But now it was starting to affect the children…

She bit her lip while frowning and rubbing her temples to try to ward off the tension headache that was starting to brew. Then she poured out four glasses of fresh lemonade, set them on the plain white tray she had placed on the table along with the tin of shortbread Sarah Peters had baked, and walked through the utility room and out of the door and around the side of the house to the terrace, where she placed it all on the table.

'Robert, Jenkins, a glass of lemonade for you both, and I also have some shortbread from Sarah Peters,' she called, handing Emma a glass and taking a slow sip from her own before sitting back down in the chair and closing her tired eyes.

Emma watched her mother with sad eyes. She looked tired. *Why is Daddy always so horrible?* she wondered. She was so relieved to hear his car speeding away. Hopefully he wouldn't come back until she was in bed asleep.

Robert and Jenkins approached the table to claim their refreshing glasses of lemonade, excited at the prospect of tasting Sarah Peters's wonderful baked offerings. 'Thanks, Mum,' and, 'Thank you, Mrs Morton,' they said in unison. Robert had been climbing one of the trees in the orchard and his hands and knees were covered in green and brown stains. Susan could smell the earthy scent and smiled.

'You'll need to have a bath before dinner, Robert,' she said, smiling at her kind, funny son, who was so unlike his father.

'Where's Dad gone this time?' Robert asked his mother.

'I don't know, dear,' she replied, sounding worn down by it all.

'Well, I'm glad he's gone,' Robert continued. 'He's nothing but a cross bully, always shouting at everyone and being unkind,' he burst out.

'Robert,' his mother said warningly in a shocked voice. 'He's your father, and you must never speak about him like that. It isn't right.'

'It's not right how he treats us all, especially you and Emma, Mum. Why don't you stop him?' he cried out in frustration. 'I hate him.' And with that he stormed off into the house, slamming the door behind him so that they would not see the tears already starting to spill down his face at the unjustness of it all.

His poor mother. He had heard the shouting and had listened to her muffled sobs night after night. Did she not realise that he knew what was going on? If only he was older, stronger, bolder. He felt so impotent and useless… He could not do anything about it.

He heard his mother calling his name as he marched along the corridor to his bedroom, and after slamming the door behind him he threw himself on his bed face down and sobbed his anger into his pillows until they were wet through with his tears.

If only they had not gone to the river that morning. It was his fault. He could have said no. And if only Emma had not fallen in. He knew that this had made his father even angrier than normal. Why couldn't he be like his friends' fathers, always ready to play a game of cricket or rounders? His father had never so much as picked up a bat or played catch with him.

Jenkins sat down at the table in the chair that had been rapidly vacated by Susan. 'Well, now, miss,' he said, looking at her with kind brown eyes. 'Happen that your brother is feeling a bit helpless right now.'

Emma eyed him with a curious look. 'Helpless? Robert? Why do you say that?' she replied, eager to understand.

'Well, young Robert is a kind, honest and upstanding young man, and he obviously doesn't like what he sees in your father's behaviour.' Emma continued to look at him, hanging on his every word. Jenkins rubbed a dirty hand across his face. 'Perhaps I should not be saying anything. It's not my place, now.' With that he selected a piece of shortbread from the tin and walked back down the slope from the terrace and went back to his gardening.

Susan returned to the table looking more stressed and worried than she had been before. 'Mummy,' Emma said, 'Jenkins said that Robert was feeling helpless. What did he mean?'

Susan patted Emma on the hand. 'Ah,' she said softly. 'Our Jenkins is a very perceptive man.' But she did not answer the question. 'Let's see how much of this puzzle we can finish before I need to start cooking your tea, shall we?'

Emma, realising that she would get no more out of her mother right then, agreed, and started to sort the puzzle pieces once again into different colours. She filed the question away to ask at another time.

CHAPTER 9

1 9 7 3

Robert lay on his bed, looking at the ceiling. The sunlight was making patterns in the shadows where the curtains blew gently in the light breeze. He was fed up and frustrated by his father's behaviour, although he didn't understand fully why his mother allowed him to carry on like he did. She was an adult, after all. He knew himself the fear that the thought of his father's sharp tongue and hard hands induced in him. He knew that he made his mother cry, so maybe she was scared of him too.

He pushed himself up on his hands and got off the bed. He didn't know who he could talk to. Not his mother. She had enough to worry about without him adding to her woes. *And Emma is just a baby*, he said to himself, a frown wrinkling his brow slightly.

But Jenkins seemed to know the lie of the land. He was ancient too. Perhaps he could help him know what to do. He was still deep in thought, with his hands shoved deeply in his pockets, when he felt a sudden cold draught pass over him. He looked at his door, but it was still tightly closed from where he had slammed it in his frustration. The window was open slightly, but there was only a slight breeze.

He shrugged his shoulders and grasped hold of the door handle to exit the room. As he closed the door behind him he just missed a book being pushed from the shelf above his bed. It fell onto the covers with a soft thud and lay open at a page with a picture showing an image of a small boy looking out of a window onto a garden much like his own.

Robert ran down the stairs, pausing at the huge arched window that overlooked the front of the house and the driveway, and checked that his father had not returned home during the time he had been in his room. The driveway was clear, and he let out the breath that he did not realise he had been holding and slid his hand along the banister as he trotted down the rest of the stairs.

In order to avoid seeing his mother, as he was slightly embarrassed about how rude he had been earlier and knew that he must apologise to her, he went through the front door and through the garages to reach the garden that way. He skirted along the long privet hedge that bordered the neighbouring property and along a thin strip of grass, which had a large B-shaped flower bed on the other side. This housed tall plants that hid him for most of the way until he could flit behind the wych elm and reach the orchard and vegetable patch at the end of the garden.

Jenkins was there, forking material onto the compost heap and raking dry gardening debris into the bonfire area. Jenkins looked up as Robert approached him, an expectant look on his face. He was not surprised at his arrival, and had in fact been expecting to receive his young visitor at some point in the next few hours.

'Hello, young Robert,' he said, stopping what he was doing and pushing the fork deeply into the soil so that it had a firm enough hold on the earth for him to lean against. 'I thought you might come along to see me today.'

Robert looked up at the old man, surprise etched on his young face. 'You were? How? I mean, why…?' The words fell from his mouth in a rambling torrent. Jenkins leant on his fork, his arms and hands deep brown from all the hours spent in the sun. A kind, knowing smile was spreading on his weathered face.

'When you've lived as long as me and seen the things I've seen, you get to know and recognise a thing or two, lad.' He paused before continuing, 'Patterns, lad. Life is full of patterns. Take the flowers, and leaves, the feathers on the birds and behaviour in people and animals. The song of a bird and the cry of a fox. They are all patterns, and behaviour is just another pattern. You were upset, and now you need to make sense of what is going on. You need to talk to someone who may understand but will not be upset or judgemental or treat you like a child, and you thought of me. Am I right?'

Robert looked at the older man with wonderment. Was Jenkins some sort of wizard or magician? How on earth did he know these things? Is this just what happened when you became old? When did this knowledge start, or was it just suddenly there?

All these questions must have shown on his face as Jenkins watched him and laughed out loud at the confusion and astonishment as it played out for all to see. 'Oh, lad,' he said wiping his eyes with the back of a dirty hand, 'if only you could see your face right now.'

Robert looked at the ground, unsure of what to do or say. Jenkins sat down on the grass and beckoned the young boy to join him. 'Come on, lad, take a seat. And let's see if we can help you get some of those woes off your chest, shall we?'

Robert, not knowing what else to do, folded up his body and joined the gardener on the grass. He started to pull at the tufts of long dry grass that were allowed to grow in the orchard to create an ambient environment for the wildlife, and rolled them idly between his fingers as he wondered where on earth he could begin.

As if reading his thoughts, Jenkins spoke softly. 'Where do you want to start, lad? Anywhere will do and it will probably lead to where you want things to go, so just start anywhere.'

Feeling encouraged, he began to speak, slowly at first, and then everything sort of just tumbled out in a rush. 'I just don't understand. Why is my father so beastly to everyone, especially Mother, and why doesn't she do anything? Why does she let him treat us all this way? It's not fair. Why did he even have any children, when he obviously doesn't want us, or even like us…?' Hot tears sprang to Robert's eyes, which he dashed away, but as fast as he tried to stop them more welled up to take their place.

Jenkins's heart went out to the child. He was not blind, and often heard James berating one or another member of the family. James was a rude, arrogant man and his family bore no resemblance to him at all, which was a blessing in some ways, but a little resilience would have helped them all to cope better. 'Well, lad, sometimes people are just inclined that way. They are unhappy and do not know what to do about it, so instead they lash out at those closest to them. It doesn't mean that it is right, or that the people being treated badly have done anything wrong. Your mother is probably doing her best to protect you and your sister from the worst of it, so she absorbs more of his bad temper herself.'

'Why does he not just leave us alone, then, if we make him so unhappy?' Robert said.

'Oh, lad,' Jenkins continued, placing a large hand on the boy's shaking shoulder. 'It's not you that makes him unhappy. It is him … himself. He doesn't know what to do or what he wants to do, which makes him frustrated. Maybe he feels trapped or under pressure to provide for you. I don't know the exact reasons behind your father's behaviour, but I have seen enough in my time to recognise the signs. As to what to do... Well, that is a more difficult one to figure out.'

Robert looked at him, his eyes still wet from the tears he had shed. 'Is there anything I can do?' he asked in a small voice. 'I know he bullies my mother, and I just want her to be safe.'

'I know, lad. I understand,' Jenkins said sadly. 'But it is not your problem, even though it does affect you. You just try to keep yourself and your sister out of the way and leave it to your mother and father to sort it out themselves. I'll have a quiet word with your mother. Now you can help me pick some of those crab apples, as I know your mother said that Sarah Peters could have some to make some jelly.' With that he stood up and held out a hand to Robert, wondering what he could do to help with the situation, which was now getting completely out of hand.

Susan had watched her son as he flitted between the flower beds. She knew that he would have been heading to speak to Jenkins and, knowing that Jenkins would give him an ear to air his problems, her mood lifted slightly. Jenkins was a complete godsend. They really had sort of inherited him with the house when they had bought it as a young couple. He had worked these grounds since he was a teenager, or so she was led to believe. She knew the stories of the families who had lived there before but had never really taken that much notice of them.

She wondered whether James would return that evening, and shuddered at the thought. If he did it would be best if everything was ordered just as he liked, which might help to curb the worst of his temper.

She shook her head sadly and rose from the chair, then

walked towards the kitchen to start on tea for the children. She would eat with them but would make sure that there was something prepared and ready for James just in case he did return and demand a hot meal.

A shadow passed across the hall as she walked towards the dining room en route to the kitchen. She watched it progress across the floor towards the stairs while feeling the hairs on her arms start to rise. Then a loud knock at the door made her jump sharply, and she brushed aside her nervousness and turned towards the front door. The shadow stopped in its wake, as if waiting for its next move, then it was gone as if it had never been.

Susan reached the large oak door and pulled it open, revealing a middle-aged blonde woman with a slightly harried expression on her intelligent face. She was well dressed in a smart navy suit and carried a cream handbag in the crook of her arm. 'Ah, Susan,' the lady said, 'I'm glad you are in. Could I come in for a brief chat?' Susan was a bit surprised to see the doctor's wife on her front doorstep, but good manners prevailed and she opened the door wider and ushered her inside.

'Mrs Walker?' Susan asked as she followed the older woman into the hall. 'What a – er – lovely surprise. I – um – was just about to start preparing tea for the children.'

'We can chat in the kitchen, then. I will help you, and please do call me Barbara. *Mrs Walker* makes me sound like my mother-in-law,' she said with an exaggerated shudder, which had the desired effect of bringing a smile to Susan's face. 'Through here?' the doctor's wife asked, nodding her head towards the dining room.

Knowing what defeat looked like when she saw it, Susan murmured her acknowledgement and headed through the dining room towards the kitchen beyond. 'Hmm,' Barbara said. 'I always did like this room. We used to have huge birthday parties in here when I was a girl,' she said as she remembered those days fondly, 'until… Well, that was all a long time ago.'

Barbara broke off and returned her thoughts to the present. Susan was such a kind, pretty woman. How could she help her? She recognised that cowed, worn-down expression, the droop of the shoulders and the gaze not quite meeting her eyes. If she was not very much mistaken, her husband's suspicions had not been far off at all.

They entered the kitchen, which was flooded with light from three sides. One was the door of the utility room, which had been left open, and the door to the garden, further on, was open wide so that Susan could hear if the children needed her.

They could hear the distant voices of Robert and Emma bickering gently over who was better at jigsaw puzzles as Susan walked towards the large ancient fridge to see what she would make them for their tea. Cheese on toast would probably go down very well for them, but she would need to make something more substantial for James in case he did care to join them later that evening.

'Well, what can I do to help?' Barbara said briskly, rubbing her hands together in a no-nonsense fashion, which reminded Susan of her mother. She took some cheese out of the fridge and laid it down on the large table and went to get the bread out of the bread bin. 'It's OK,' she said, 'I'll only make cheese on toast for myself and the children. That won't take any time at all.'

'And James?' Barbara countered, sensing her opportunity to steer the conversation in the direction she wanted it to go. 'What will he have, or is he out this evening?' Susan held onto the table to steady herself. Her eyes were downcast, and the worries of the past few days were starting to catch up with her as she swayed slightly. Pain was shooting into her temples, making her wince involuntarily.

Concerned for the younger woman, Barbara moved quickly to her side. 'Now why don't you sit down and take the weight off your feet for five minutes and let me help you with this? You look done in, and I expect nobody ever does much to help you really, now, do they?' It was more of a statement than a question. A look of defeat passed over Susan's face as she relented, all fight gone out of her as she sank wearily into the chair and stared blankly at the wall.

Used to her role of supporting her husband with the local needy families and helping out weary mothers, Barbara grabbed a breadboard and the loaf of bread and started slicing thick wedges of soft white bread. After she had sliced what she had deemed a sufficient amount she laid down the knife, dusted the flour off her hands, and looked at the younger woman in front of her as she assessed in her mind the best way to tackle the issue without Susan clamming up.

'Susan,' she began in a soft, coaxing voice, 'you know that you are well liked and respected in the village and are known to be kind and supportive of others.' Susan continued to stare blankly ahead. 'You don't have to suffer in silence. You do know that, don't you?' Barbara continued, trying to convey a level of concern in her voice.

'It's been reported that James marched little Emma out of the hospital yesterday.' She raised her hand to stop Susan, who had started to protest, and made to rise from the chair. 'It wasn't right – you know that as well as I do – but neither was it your fault. Now I know that it is wrong to meddle in a marriage, and no one really knows what goes on behind closed doors, but we are not daft either, love. We can see just by looking at you that things aren't right.'

Her voice became even gentler and quieter, and she came and stood beside Susan and rested a hand on her arm in a confidential manner. 'If he hurts you and the children, we can help you before it goes too far.'

Susan looked up through weary tear-stained eyes. 'I just don't know what to do,' she said in a voice full of emotion. 'Nothing I do is right. He is angry all the time and goes out at all hours, and sometimes does not even come home at all. It's better when he's not here, but then we are all forever listening for the sound of the car and...' She trailed off, dropping her head into her hands.

'I don't know what's wrong with him. He seems to be getting worse, and can see that his behaviour is starting to be noticed outside our family. Yet he blames us for everything.' Susan fished a handkerchief out from her sleeve and dabbed at her eyes and blew her nose. 'Anyway,' she said, standing up and straightening her clothes, 'This won't get tea made, now, will it?'

Feeling confident that she had planted the seed of friendship and support, Barbara decided that she would leave the conversation there and went to fill the kettle with water to make a pot of tea. Susan lit the grill and put the bread under to toast on one side. 'Will you stay for a bit of cheese on toast with us, Barbara?' she asked.

'No, you're all right, love,' she replied. 'I must be away to make George's supper. That man works so hard that I like to have a bite to eat ready for him when he gets home. Now you think on what I said, and do not suffer in silence. You know where to find me if you need to talk.'

Susan nodded her acceptance with a weak smile. 'OK, thank you,' she replied, and with that Barbara let herself out of the back door and walked around the front of the house and out onto the main road to walk back home.

After the children and she had had their tea and the children were bathed and in bed, Susan went and sat back downstairs in the drawing room to read her book. She thought back to the visit from Barbara Walker and wondered what had prompted it. Was it Dr Walker's visit or someone from the hospital? She needed to talk to James, but she was afraid of his temper. She didn't even know if he would be coming home that evening and silently hoped that he wouldn't. But again, apart from allowing her some peace and quiet, it wouldn't solve anything.

A breeze blew lightly across her face, and she could hear the gentle noise of children's laughter coming from somewhere. She placed her book down on the small wooden table by her chair and stood up to look out of the French doors. *Funny*, she thought, *the doors are closed, so where is the breeze coming from?*

A door slammed shut and she heard the sound of hurried, purposeful footsteps. She moved quickly towards the hall. James must have come home and she had not heard his car pull up.

'James?' she called, quickening her pace and looking up the staircase but hearing nothing else.

Then she heard the unmistaken sound of a child calling, 'Mummy, Mummy.' She ran up the stairs two at a time towards the children's rooms. She looked into Robert's room. He was fast asleep, and his book had fallen on the floor beside him. She picked it up and placed it on the table beside his bed quickly and turned towards the staircase leading up to Emma's room.

She heard the call again… 'Mummy.' She ran up the stairs

and flew into Emma's room, her heart pounding hard in her chest. Emma was also fast asleep, snuggled up with her favourite toy cat and snoring gently. Apart from Emma sleeping soundly, the room was empty.

The front door banged hard, making Susan jump out of her skin, and even from up on the top floor she was able to hear James calling her name. 'Susan, Susan, where are you? Is my dinner ready? Susan…'

Sighing to herself, Susan let herself out of her daughter's room. She turned back to look at her and noticed that the little doll's crib was rocking. Another insistent shout from her husband took her attention away swiftly and she walked back down the stairs to attend to him. Her stomach lurched painfully as she hurried through the large house.

CHAPTER 10

1973

James had had a trying day. Nothing seemed to be going his way and people in his office were starting to look at him strangely, as if they couldn't quite understand what he was saying at times.

What is wrong with people? he wondered, not for the first time. Questions, always questions. Why could they not just do the job they were paid to do and leave him alone to do his work? Then, when he got home, instead of being greeted by his wife with a hot meal she was nowhere to be seen. What was the point in having her there at home at all if she didn't do her job properly either?

He raked a hand through his hair in an exasperated manner and was just about to shout again at the top of his voice when she appeared at the top of the stairs. He rounded on her crossly and handed her his coat and briefcase to put away for him. 'Where have you been? I expect you to be down here ready for me when I get home.'

Susan bristled at his tone but replied as meekly as she could for fear of further antagonising him. 'I thought I heard one of the children calling for me so I went to see, but they were both asleep.' He turned a scornful face towards her.

'Hearing things now, are you?' he said, his voice scathing and full of menace. 'Well, perhaps we need to get the doctor to come and see you, do we?'

She sighed. 'No, James. Emma may well have called out in her sleep. She could have been having a nightmare after her narrow escape.'

'Huh,' he continued. 'I'll tell you what a nightmare is: coming back here to this house day in, day out after a long day working my backside off to support you and those children, and what for? To have my wife squandering her time and pandering to the whim of those mollycoddled brats. You spoil those children, Susan.'

Susan took in a deep breath, willing herself to stay calm. 'I do not spoil our children, James.' She emphasised the *our* as if he needed reminding that they were his responsibility as well as hers. 'If you mean going to see what is wrong when one of our children is crying out, then that is what a mother should be doing.'

Bored now, he just huffed and stormed into the dining room. 'I'll have my dinner now, if you please, and make sure that it is something hot. I give you enough money for housekeeping. I expect to get a proper meal and have it waiting for me when I get home.'

Susan did not point out to him that if he would deign to let her know when he might be coming home, she may be better able to acquiesce to his demands. It was not worth inciting more arguments from him about his status, his busy workload and things she could not possibly understand, because she was only a lowly woman.

Neither did she mention that the meagre amount she was given to run the household was barely enough to cover the cheapest food, let alone clothes and other necessities for the children. If it were not for the generosity of her parents the children would be running around in rags, and without Jenkins's skill in the garden to grow their vegetables and her skill in the kitchen James would be having bread and water for his supper.

James watched his wife walk towards the kitchen and wondered just what it was about her that drove him to such anger. Why did she not fight back? Was she just as spineless as she appeared? She never used to be so weak. What on earth was wrong with the woman? She looked like a faded version of the vivacious young girl he had pursued and married.

No wonder he was looking elsewhere. What was left of her to interest a man like him? He didn't want to behave like this, but she made him. Did she antagonise him on purpose? Didn't she understand that it was her duty to look after him?

A shadow flitted across the dining room from the hall and merged into the dark corner behind James. Its existence was felt faintly by his subconscious as a brooding presence. He shuddered as a chill passed down his spine. 'Close the door, woman,' he shouted. 'There's a bloody draught in here.' *Damn old house*, he said to himself. *It's always bloody cold, even in the heat of summer.*

Susan merely looked up as she stirred the stew that she had made earlier, which she was now warming on the hob. There were no doors or windows open. What he had felt had nothing to do with a draught and everything to do with whatever caused a malignant presence to be in the house whenever he was home.

She moved to the table and set out a tray, then she cut a huge hunk of bread from a loaf and placed some butter in a dish and set it on the tray beside the bowl, which she poured a generous helping of stew into. Then she added cutlery and condiments and took the tray through to the dining room. She set the tray down in front of James and he picked up the spoon and started eating without even looking up at her.

Not even a word of thanks, Susan said to herself as she walked to the sideboard and poured her husband a glass of wine and set it down on the table beside him.

She made to leave, but he grabbed her wrist. She turned and looked at him and he stared up at her, searching her face for any hint of what had first attracted him to her. It was still there, but buried deep.

The shame he felt for his behaviour towards her just made him even angrier. What was wrong with him? Her questioning gaze fell to his hand on her wrist and he tightened his grip. His fingers bit into her arm. 'James,' she cried, 'you're hurting me.' A loud crash came from the kitchen, breaking the moment, and as if recalled to his senses James let go of his wife's wrist.

Susan fled to the kitchen to see what had caused the noise. On the floor she saw the tin containing the shortbread from Sarah Peters lying in the middle of the floor. *How on earth could that have got there?* she thought. It had been on the top of the dresser behind the lip that held things in place.

As she bent to pick it up she caught sight of a raggedy old bear lying under the kitchen table. *Now how on earth did that get there?* she said to herself as she stooped to pick it up. She placed it on the top of the dresser along with the tin of short-bread and wondered what on earth was happening.

James wiped his mouth on the cloth napkin Susan had placed on the table for him and screwed it up into a ball. He pushed himself away from the table and stood up, brushing his hands down his trousers and then rubbing his face with his hands. What had come over him? It was like a rush of anger that had taken him over. He had to get out of the house. It felt as though the walls were closing in around him.

He held onto the back of the chair for a moment to steady himself and then walked out of the oppressive panelled dining room into the brighter hall. A large chandelier hung in the centre of the room, casting its crystal light, but failing to reach the far corners where the shadows held on, lurking there, watching him.

He had intended to sit down and speak to his wife that evening, try to sort out the growing distance between them. He had even planned the words he was going to say on the journey home, but the minute he set foot in the house everything vanished, and he was swamped by feelings of resentment and anger. Emotions invaded him like a poison, and tendrils entwined themselves around every part of him until it was as if he was becoming someone else entirely.

Fear gripped his heart and he struggled to breathe for a moment. It was as if this rage – his torment – belonged to someone else.

Then, as suddenly as it had come upon him, it was gone. He sank down into one of the chairs by the windows in the hall. The steady ticking of the grandfather clock beat at half the speed of his heart, which he willed to slow to match the rhythm of the ancient timepiece.

He could hear Susan in the kitchen clearing away as an owl hooted outside, and he felt his fraught nerves returning to normal. What on earth was going on? The fear was being replaced with frustration. He was tired. The dark episode had taken more out of him than he realised. He would go to bed and try and get some rest. He was probably just tired, or more like exhausted with work and the stress of leading a double life. He would put a stop to this nonsense with Clare.

He headed towards the stairs, and as he started his weary ascent he didn't notice the shifting of the shadows in the hallway below.

When Susan had finished in the kitchen, she locked the

doors downstairs and made her way up to her bedroom. When she opened the door she was surprised to find the bedside light on and James curled in the foetal position, snoring gently. She went down the corridor to the nearest bathroom and flushed her face with some cold water and brushed her teeth and got changed into her nightie. She walked back to the bedroom and got into bed carefully to avoid waking James and turned off the light.

She lay there for a long while, watching the shadows dancing across the ceiling where the tree branches moved gently in the breeze and were illuminated by the soft moonlight. James turned towards her in his sleep and threw an arm across his wife's body. He pulled her towards him and nuzzled into her hair. 'Clare,' he murmured gently.

Susan sighed. *So it is Clare this time, is it?* she said to herself, feeling nothing but resignation. Any love she had once felt for her handsome husband had long since been destroyed. She closed her eyes and tried to fall into the oblivion that only sleep could bring.

CHAPTER 11

1973

When Susan awoke James had gone, so she busied herself with her morning ablutions and went downstairs to make herself a fortifying cup of tea. It was still early, and she took her cup and went to stand in the drawing room.

She set down the cup on her small table by her favourite chair and opened the French windows to let the morning into the room. The dew was still sparkling on the grass in the early morning light and a female blackbird was running across the lawn. The sun was rising steadily and a slight mist was still snaking its cold tendrils at the far reaches of the garden, but it was being chased away by the growing warmth of the day.

Susan picked up her tea and stood in the doorway. She leant against the frame and sipped slowly. She really loved this view. She knew that the house held its secrets and that it had not always been a happy place, but she felt safe here. Even James's behaviour was forgotten in the moment as she looked out onto the serene view. Sparrows and finches danced around the bird table and she watched them in delight in her quiet, private moment.

She heard the back gate open and close and supposed that Jenkins would be making an early start. Then she heard that laughter again, faint as if carried on the breeze, and saw that same flash of red between the trees. She set down her tea and made her way across the terrace and across the lawn. She approached the orchard and there it was again, still faint but unmistakable, a child laughing, as if they were playing a game of hide-and-seek. It was a delightful sound, full of freedom and fun. A male voice beside her made her start in shock.

She looked to her right and saw Jenkins in the vegetable patch watching her. 'Sorry, Jenkins. You made me jump,' she said in a breathy voice, waiting for her breathing and heart rate to return to normal.

'I'm sorry, Mrs Morton. You looked like you were in a daze. Were you looking for me?' he replied.

'No, I thought I heard…' She faltered, not really knowing what to say.

'What did you hear?' Jenkins said to prompt her.

'Oh, nothing. Never mind,' she said, then continued. 'It looks like it is shaping up to be another glorious day.'

'Indeed it does,' Jenkins replied thoughtfully.

Susan turned and started to make her way back towards the house, wondering if she was really going a bit mad, like James kept hinting. *At this rate he is going to have me locked up, then he will be free to see who he likes and do whatever he likes*, she thought bitterly. Then she thought of the children and her heart was gripped by an intense fear. *Never*, she thought. *Never will I allow him to separate me from my children.*

Jenkins watched her go and wondered. Had she heard the children playing too? He'd watched and heard them for the best part of forty years now or thereabouts, he thought. Always the same game, always the same laughter. Like children everywhere, he supposed, although his own were long grown now and had fled the nest years ago. He enjoyed playing with the grandkids, though, when he was not working, and always made time for Robert and Emma when he was there.

He stuck the fork in the earth and started digging over the vegetable patch. The heavy clay soil was hard, which made the going difficult. He would mix in a good load of manure, he thought, to mix it up a bit, and then he could get planting. A robin eyed him hopefully from its perch on a low branch, waiting for the worms to be unearthed, and swooped down close to his feet as a juicy specimen was unveiled.

The sun was rising higher in the sky and the day was already warm. *It is going to be another scorcher*, he said to himself as he rhythmically turned the earth.

His thoughts strayed back in time to when he had first started working at this house. There had been many more staff then, of course: two gardeners, a housekeeper who doubled as a cook, and her husband, whose role covered many different aspects from chauffeur, secretary, butler and goodness knows what else. There was also the nanny-cum-governess, who looked after the family's two children.

His boss then had been Dr Edward Winter. He was a very good doctor, well respected and liked by all. His wife, Sophie, had been a lovely woman, kind-hearted and always pleasant to the staff. She was a devoted mother, and the children were polite and well behaved. It had been an awful wrench for the family when she had died in childbirth with her third child.

The doctor, a busy man and still young and handsome, had taken a second wife – the governess, as it happened. Louisa … she was pleasant enough, but was not like her former mistress. There had always been something about her that he couldn't put his finger on. She was ambitious, but he suspected that beneath all the outward pleasantries a darker side lurked.

He couldn't remember what made him think that now. It had just been a feeling, as though she watched everyone, storing up anything she found to use against them. He had tried to keep out of her way as much as possible. The children would often be in the garden asking him questions, getting him to fetch their balls from trees. He smiled as he recalled their antics.

The smile faded on his lips as he recalled the traumatic events that had happened on that fateful day, so long ago now, but the memories resurfaced as if they had happened yesterday. The screams, the thud, the blood on the ground, the unseeing eyes looking up to a sky that they would never see again.

Such a waste – so young – and the devastation that followed. The grief and the pain. How it destroyed the young family. They moved away afterwards, he recalled, shaking his head as if to dispel the unwanted memories that were drawing a cloud over the otherwise beautiful day.

Why had he remembered it all today? he wondered. It was nearly forty years ago. What had brought all those long-buried memories flooding to the surface?

Chapter 12

1936

The rain was hitting the pane of his bedroom window in a steady patter. It was still quite early, and the sound had awoken him. Tom lay in his bed watching the trail of the raindrops as they traversed a path down the glass. The light behind them was a light grey, and the ivy that covered the back of the house was tapping against the window in the wind.

Tom sighed and turned over in his small bed and pulled the covers tightly around him. The windowpane shook as a fierce gust of wind took it by surprise, and he shivered. He had been looking forward to climbing the trees in the orchard again today so that he could hide in the branches and spy on his sister Cassy. He liked hiding, because he found out lots of interesting snippets of information when people didn't know he was there. Especially when the servants gossiped. Even at his young age he found people fascinating. He liked to watch them, and it was funny how they often spoke about other people in quiet voices with sharp comments but to their face they would be all smiles.

Well, the weather was turning bad, and he would be cooped up in the house that day, which was never an enjoyable experience. Louisa would find something to complain about. Some small misdemeanour that he had unwittingly or even unknowingly committed would be taken out and dissected in its minutiae.

Louisa… *Why is she so difficult all the time?* he wondered. She didn't seem to persecute Cassy like she did him, or perhaps she did and he didn't notice. Or, even more likely, she did it in secret, as befitted the spiteful way in which she seemed to conduct herself most of the time. Not for the first time he wished that his father had never married his old nanny, or governess as she had preferred to be known.

Once he realised that sleep was not going to bless him with her presence until nightfall, Tom swung his legs over the side of the bed and stood on the sheepskin rug that was placed on the floorboards of his room. That was another thing. Why had he been relegated to the servants' quarters up in the top of the house while his father and Louisa and Cassy had rooms in the main part of the house? Not that it really bothered him. It kept him out of the way, and he had such a lovely view of the garden from the huge window seat set into the eaves.

The rain was still making its steady stream down his window as he shrugged himself into his slippers and dressing gown and went in search of any potential treats that Maggie Graves, the housekeeper-cum-cook, may wish to give him. *I am, after all, her favourite*, he said smugly to himself.

He trotted quietly down the stairs and along the corridor that housed the other bedrooms on the first floor, in order to avoid waking his father and the dreaded Louisa. Cassy would not be awake for ages yet, so he didn't need to worry about her.

He rounded the top of the landing and started to walk down the second flight of stairs, but stopped as he heard the front door open. A moment later his father appeared, walking backwards into the large hall and shaking an umbrella in from of him before laying it down on the quarry tiles of the porch, still open, to dry. He brushed the worst of the raindrops off his heavy overcoat before hanging it on one of the pegs just inside the cloakroom, then turned to walk into the hall after closing the outer door behind him, as if that would separate him from the brewing storm outside.

He made to walk purposefully across the hall but he stopped short when he caught sight of his small son standing on the stairs. 'Tom,' he exclaimed in surprised delight. 'What are you doing up so early?'

'The rain woke me, Father, and I was hungry, so I thought I would go and see if Maggie was up and ask if I could have some bread and jam.' He was pleased to see his father, since he saw so little of him.

Edward Winter ruffled his son's hair and smiled at him. 'You are always hungry, Tom. I don't know where you put all that food you eat. Come on. Maggie will probably be making some breakfast. She knew that I had been called away in the night because Cedric answered the telephone in the early hours. Mrs Lacey is having another baby and it decided to make an early appearance into the world, which took us all by surprise.'

Tom looked at his father and nodded solemnly, as if he understood. He knew that babies that came unexpectedly or otherwise could often cause sorrow as well as joy, and he thought back to when his own lovely, sweet and kind mother had been taken from him before he had even really got to know her.

As he looked at his son's grave face his father seemed to realise what his train of thought was and patted him on the shoulder. 'Come on,' he said. 'Let's go and feed that hungry tummy of yours,' and they walked in unison towards the kitchen.

Maggie looked up from the table where she was kneading dough when she heard the father and son approaching. Her hands and arms were dusted with flour. 'Why, Master Tom,' she exclaimed good-naturedly, 'whatever are you doing out of your bed at this hour?' She glanced at the kitchen clock that hung on the wall above the doorway to the dining room, where it ticked its steady passage of time, and whose hands currently marked the hour at not quite 6.30 a.m.

'The rain woke me up,' he replied, then followed with, 'I'm hungry. Can I please have some breakfast?'

Maggie chuckled. 'Now when are you not hungry, young Tom?' She nodded towards the dough. 'Let me just finish this, and I'll make you some eggy bread and bacon. How does that sound?'

Both father and son responded in unison with a resounding, 'Yes, please,' which made her laugh.

They sat at the other end of the table, where Edward took out a newspaper that he had folded under his arm. He gave it a shake. 'I think I will stay in here with Tom and share breakfast with him, if you don't mind,' he said conversationally to his housekeeper. This behaviour would be frowned upon by Louisa, but as she would not be up for a couple of hours yet. So she wouldn't know that he had lowered himself in her eyes and fraternised with the staff.

He didn't really understand her logic. Sophie, his beloved first wife, had never had airs and graces, and had been kind and loving to a fault. But Louisa? Well, she was different. It may be that she felt she needed to prove something, having been a governess and rising in the household ranks upon becoming his wife. He had never understood such things, really. As far as he was concerned, people were people and that was that.

Maggie finished kneading the dough and moved it to a large cream and blue ceramic bowl to rise. Then she placed a piece of cloth over the top and sat it on top of the oven in the warm. She moved towards the sink to wash her hands before starting to prepare the breakfast for the two early morning visitors to her domain. 'Mrs Lacey had a little girl in the end,' the doctor said conversationally, after lowering the paper so he could see his housekeeper.

'Aw, that's lovely,' Maggie replied. 'Was everything – well, you know – OK?' she asked in a quieter tone, knowing that the baby had been early and that the good doctor had lost his wife in childbirth himself a few years earlier.

'They will both be fine,' he reassured her. 'It was a difficult birth. The baby was breech. But, being early, she was small, which helped. Mavis Jones was the attending midwife and she had things in hand. She didn't really need my help, but called me just to be on the safe side.'

Maggie nodded her head. She knew Mavis, and her reputation as an excellent midwife was well known. 'Well, I'm glad everything is OK,' she said, and busied herself with making breakfast.

Edward looked at his son over the top of his newspaper. He was a cheerful lad, never one to complain, but he had been much quieter of late. His daughter, Cassy, was always sunny-natured and confident. He thought of her fondly. She would be fast asleep upstairs right now, oblivious to the fact that this hour of the morning even existed apart from perhaps on her birthday or Christmas mornings.

Tom was reading a book that had been left on the kitchen table, probably from the last time he had been in there. Tom took after him, he supposed – always with a nose in a book and with an unquenchable thirst for knowledge. His had been all about nature and science, and he had found medicine fascinating as an older child. All he had ever wanted to do was study to become a doctor. He wondered whether Tom's interest in literature had more to do with escapism than education, though.

Tom, feeling his father's gaze upon him, looked up and smiled questioningly at him. 'I was just thinking, Tom,' his father said, 'how I always had my nose in a book from about your age. What are you reading?'

'*Black Beauty*,' he replied. 'It's quite sad in lots of places, but it is still very good. He reminds me of the horses on the farms.'

His father nodded enthusiastically. 'When I was a boy we didn't have cars. We all used horses or ponies and traps,' he said. 'That's why we still have the stables and the paddock. We don't need them now, really. I was thinking about selling the land, but have not really had time to think about it.'

Tom thought about the fun he had playing in and around the stables and was a bit sad at the thought of it not being theirs any longer, but he supposed his father was right. Now that they had a car, they didn't need the space. All the same, he wished he could have had a pony, and said as much to his father. 'Your mother loved horses,' Edward replied sadly. 'You must get that from her.'

At this point Maggie bustled over with their breakfast and thrust plates of bacon, eggy bread and mushrooms in front of them. Father and son exchanged glances of pure pleasure and started to tuck into their welcome guilty feast.

When they had finished Edward stood up and brushed down his shirt to knock the crumbs away and wiped his mouth with a napkin. He let out an appreciative sigh and, turning towards Maggie, who was stationed at the sink, elbows deep in suds, said, 'Well, that was amazing, as always. Thank you, Maggie. You are very kind.'

Maggie flapped a suds-covered hand at him, which threw a

cascade of soapy bubbles across the floor. 'Oh, away with you both,' she said, and returned to her washing-up, but a warm smile was deeply etched on her face and it matched the glow in her heart of a job well done.

As Tom and his father made their way back through the dining room towards the hall, Edward put a finger to his lips and said to Tom, 'Now, not a word to Louisa,' and winked down at him.

As they walked through the door they heard a shrill, haughty voice call out, 'Not a word to Louisa about what?' They entered the hall to see the very person standing on the bend of the stairs, her hands on her hips and a pout on her lips. Edward and his son looked at each other with guilty expressions and then both burst into laughter. Louisa was not happy. Her eyes turned hard and steely.

Her voice was steeped in scorn as she spoke. 'Well, what little secret are you keeping from me this time? No wonder I feel like an outcast in my own home if you are both speaking about me in secret.' Wanting to avoid a full-blown outburst of his second wife's fury, which would do no good to anyone, least of all herself, Edward put on his most coaxing voice.

'Louisa, my dear, we were just having breakfast in the kitchen, which Maggie kindly cooked for us as Tom here was up early. I had just come back in from attending to Mrs Lacey who, by the way, gave birth to a healthy little girl this morning.'

Louisa sniffed huffily. 'Well, if you ever gave me a tenth of the attention that everyone else seems to get from you, perhaps I would not feel so left out all the time.' And with that she turned abruptly and marched back up the stairs.

'Oh dear,' Edward muttered, realising that he would have to work hard to mollify his wife. Why was everything such hard work with Louisa? Everything seemed such an effort. It had never been that way with Sophie. She understood and accepted without ever complaining when he was called away to his patients. But Louisa seemed to regard the time that he had to spend away from her as a personal affront.

Not for the first time he wondered whether he had been too hasty in marrying for a second time, but it had seemed the right thing to do at the time. He shook his head and ruffled his son's hair. 'Come on, Tom. You had better get dressed and I need to get changed myself.' And with that he bounded up the stairs two at a time in search of his wife to see if he could make peace with her.

Tom wandered back upstairs more slowly than his father. It was still raining steadily outside, and he wondered what he would do that day. He could hear Louisa's sharp tongue berating his father. He didn't understand why she couldn't be happy, as she was the only one in his life who marred his happiness. It was just unfortunate that she was such a big part of it. He knew that she wanted to send him and his sister Cassy off to boarding school, but his father refused, having promised his mother that he would keep them at home and send them to the local school.

His mother had wanted them to make friends with the local children and grow up without feeling lonely and abandoned, as his father had done when he was a boy. She had loved her two children deeply and the thought of her brought a sudden tear to his eye when he remembered the kind and caring person she had been. He had felt truly loved and safe when she had been alive.

Now... Well, he knew that his father loved him in his own way, but Louisa? She had always been faultless in her care of her charges as nanny and governess, but she had never been loving. Now she seemed to positively resent their presence and any demands on their father's time that they made. She hid this well when their father was about, however, not wanting to show this distasteful side of her nature to her husband. However, he was sure that she would get her way one way or another. His father was such a kind and trusting person. He would not consider for one moment that he was being manipulated by his new wife.

He went back up to his bedroom and sat down on the window seat. He leant against the wall and looked out of the rain-streaked window at the garden below. No birds flew and danced around in the garden today. They were probably all tucked up safely in their nests, sheltering from the rain as well, he thought.

He opened the book that he had carried up from the kitchen and carried on reading about the adventures of the black steed.

Louisa was incensed. How could her husband have been so careless of his position of master of the house to have eaten breakfast in the kitchen with a servant? She blamed the boy. He was allowed to run amok and was thoroughly spoilt by his father. Well, she knew just how to tame that wild streak. She would find some mindless task to occupy him.

And as for Maggie... Well, if she continued to act above her station she would find herself looking for another position. Just see if she wouldn't. She crossed her arms in front of her chest and let out a forceful breath. Why did no one in this house treat her with the respect that she deserved?

She picked up one of the ornaments, which had belonged to Sophie, that sat on the dressing table in front of her. She looked at its exquisite design – it must have cost a fortune – and ran her fingers over its beautiful lines. Then she opened her hand and let the precious object fall to the floor. She mouthed the single word 'Whoops,' as the beautiful figure broke into tiny, splintered fragments.

On hearing the crash her husband popped his head around the dressing room door, a look of concern on his face. 'Is everything OK?' he asked, looking at his wife with an anxious expression.

'Yes, darling,' she crooned sweetly. 'I am sorry. I appear to have had a slight accident and have knocked one of these trinkets on the floor.' She pointed to where the ornament now lay shattered. Splinters of it reached across the floor towards the bedroom door.

Edward looked crestfallen. Sophie had loved those ornaments, as they had been given to her by the children as gifts, although obviously Edward had paid for them. He would get Maggie to pack the remaining ones away for safekeeping. 'Stay there,' he said to his wife. 'You have nothing on your feet, and the pieces may be sharp. I will go and get a dustpan and brush and sweep it up.'

He made to leave the bedroom and Louisa said sharply, 'Darling, really, just send Maggie up. It's not really your place to clear up when you have staff to do it for you, now, is it?'

Knowing that it was pointless to argue, he turned and walked out into the corridor and across to one of the cupboards that were recessed into the walls along its length. He was sure that one of them must hold cleaning materials of some kind. He opened the first, to find assorted bed linen and towels, all neatly ironed and folded with sachets of lavender. He breathed in the scent. It reminded him so much of his beloved first wife.

He thrust the thought from his mind and opened the second

cupboard, and found what he was looking for. Along with mops, brooms, buckets and a collection of bottles and powders, there, hanging from a hook on the wall, was a dustpan and brush. Feeling pleased with himself, he walked back towards the bedroom brandishing the dustpan and brush, only to be confronted with a barely concealed look of scorn on Louisa's pretty face.

She huffed her displeasure at her husband's reluctance to call the housekeeper. 'Really Edward, why are you doing this yourself when you pay people good money to look after the house?'

Edward bent down and started to brush the broken fragments carefully into a pile, lifting and shaking the sheepskin rug gently to ensure that any small pieces caught in its soft fleece were removed. 'Louisa,' he said in a calm but stern voice, 'Maggie has enough to do with a house this size. I am not beyond sweeping up a few fragments of a broken ornament when leaving it could result in one of the children, or you, needing my medical assistance if you stepped on it.' She opened her mouth to argue but he stilled her with a look as he raised his hand to gesticulate to further emphasise his point.

'I don't understand why you seem to have such an issue with propriety all of a sudden. Maggie has been with us for years. She is one of the family, and I seem to recall that you were employed at one stage, so why do you keep carrying on as if there is some huge divide? It really is beyond me.'

He rubbed a hand across his face in exasperation. He really was tired and could have done with going back to bed, but he had his morning surgery to attend to and then a full list of house calls to make. 'I'm sorry, Louisa,' he continued more gently. 'I need to go. I will see you and the children later. Perhaps you can try and organise a trip to the theatre or something for us all. That would be nice.'

He leant forward to kiss her on the head, and with that he headed down the stairs, taking the dustpan and brush with him.

Louisa just sat on the stool in front of her dressing table mirror and stared miserably at her reflection as the rain continued to fall in a steady stream outside.

CHAPTER 13

1973

Emma heard a crash from her parents' bedroom and headed downstairs to see what had happened. She thought that everyone was downstairs or in the garden. She had heard some laughing earlier and thought that perhaps Jennifer had come round to see Robert. She swung herself around the bottom of the stairs, turned and walked down the corridor to her parents' bedroom, then opened the door to see that an ornament had fallen onto the floor and had broken into lots of pieces. She started to pick them up, but they were tiny and one of them pierced her finger. She winced and sucked the blood that had started to pool. She thought she had better go and tell her mother.

She walked down the stairs and found her mother in the drawing room reading her book by the window. 'Hello, darling,' her mother said warmly. 'You look better. How are you feeling?'

She stood up and enveloped her daughter into a loving embrace. 'My head still hurts a little,' Emma replied. 'But I do feel much, much better, thank you.'

Her mother noticed the drop of blood on her finger, which had started to form again. 'What have you done there? Let me see.'

'Oh, I tried to pick up the pieces of an ornament or something that had fallen on the floor in your bedroom, but the pieces were very small and one of them got me.'

'Come on, let's go and see,' her mother replied, wondering what on earth could have fallen on the floor, as she didn't have any ornaments on her dressing table. Perhaps it was a perfume bottle or something, but she thought they were all in the drawer.

They went back upstairs together and entered the bedroom. Susan scanned the floor to see where the pieces might be. Emma looked confused. 'But they were right here, by the door. It looked like pieces of china or something. I ... I don't understand...' She broke off, looking at her finger, which was a little sore from where it had been pierced.

Susan looked at her daughter's bewildered face and shook her head. She had definitely cut herself on something. 'Oh, well, there's nothing here now. Let's go and see if Robert has left any of the jam tarts I made this morning.'

They walked back towards the stairs as the cupboard door in the corridor banged shut and a breeze blew past them and down the stairs. Mother and daughter exchanged a nervous glance and walked back down towards the kitchen in search of sugary sustenance.

Robert was already in the kitchen clutching at least three jam tarts in his hands, which he started to try to hide behind his back before he realised that it was useless, as he had been caught red-handed. Instead, he plastered a cheeky grin on his face and shrugged his shoulders by way of explanation. His mother eyed his cheeky face and put her hands on her hips and turned to her daughter. 'It seems as though we were just in time, Emma. What was I just saying...?' Then they both laughed and Susan ruffled her son's hair, and as soon as Emma had taken a couple of jam tarts herself she ushered them both into the garden.

'Go and see if Jenkins would like a couple of jam tarts and a cup of tea,' she called after them, and busied herself with sweeping up the crumbs that Robert had left scattered all over the floor. She heard a door bang loudly upstairs, which made her jump, but she didn't have the energy to go and investigate. What with all the goings-on in this house of late she was thought she was just as likely to find a couple of rogue chickens wandering the upper corridors, and she could do without dealing with any other bizarre discoveries at the moment.

She would sort out something to make for dinner and hope that James would be in a better mood when he got home. She needed to discuss the problems in their marriage and see if it was salvageable, if only for the children's sake. He wouldn't like it, but they couldn't continue like they were.

She opened the elderly fridge and looked inside. *What can I make for James that he won't turn his nose up at?* she thought as she scanned the contents of the fridge. There were a couple of pork chops. They would do, with some potatoes and vegetables. The children could have cheesy potatoes and a small salad.

The problem was never knowing when James would be home. He seemed to expect a hot meal to appear in front of him, as if by magic and with no effort, the minute he stepped through the door. *Well*, she said to herself wryly, *there is no effort on his part, is there?*

James was tidying up his desk at the end of the day. He was looking forward to the end of the week, when he could enjoy a relaxing weekend at home. He reminded himself that it was only the beginning of the week and he was already looking forward to the weekend. Perhaps he should try and make a bit more of an effort, as he was expected to socialise with his wife at various company events. And, although she had never actually refused to attend them or had let him down, he acknowledged grudgingly, Susan was looking more and more jaded every time he saw her.

She was always so jumpy, which made him nervous. *Perhaps she is seeing someone else*, he said to himself. The thought made him angry. Perhaps that was it. Well, she had another think coming if she thought she could push him aside.

His desk phone rang as he was putting the last of his papers into his briefcase. He picked it up absent-mindedly. 'James Morton,' he said, in an assertive, clipped manner. His voice cooled noticeably when he heard Clare's whining voice on the other end. 'James,' she said in her wheedling voice, which he used to find sexy, 'I thought you were taking me out this evening.'

James looked at his watch and realised it was going on seven. He was tired and not in the mood for entertaining. 'Sorry, Clare, something came up. Another time, maybe?'

She heard the curt dismissive manner of his voice, and her tone became sharper. 'Oh, it's like that, is it? Have your fun with me then dump me to run back to wifey?' Her shrill tone grated on his nerve endings, and he fought against the urge to slam the phone down. 'Well,' she continued, 'I wonder what the wife would say if she found out that her beloved husband had been playing away from home?' And with that the line went dead, leaving James seething in anger and frustration. He looked at the receiver before slamming it down with such force that the telephone nearly fell off the desk.

James strode from his office, anger coming off him in waves. Who did she think she was? The jumped-up little nobody. How dare she threaten him?

He wrenched open the door of his car and threw his briefcase onto the passenger seat. He turned the key and the car stuttered into life. He screeched away from the kerb and hurtled down the road, making a small boy jump back from the kerbside in alarm.

The drive home did little to stem James's anger, and as his car sped into the driveway and slammed to a halt Susan looked out of the kitchen window with her heart sinking in dismay. She opened the fridge to retrieve the two pork chops and lit the grill. *Here we go again*, she said to herself as she busied herself in preparing her husband's dinner.

James slammed into the house, threw his briefcase down on his desk in his study next door to the drawing room and sank into his desk chair. He put his head in his hands. He took a few deep breaths as he tried to still the rage that was brewing inside him before he went to find his wife, who he supposed would be in the kitchen.

By the time James had calmed himself down and arranged his work papers into order to deal with after dinner, he caught the delicious aroma of meat coming from the kitchen. He stood up and walked towards the dining room with his back to the corner of the room, where darkening shadows were gathering, barely visible, like dark tendrils of mist seeping into the corners with a whispering hiss.

Susan was just finishing off James's meal when he put his head around the kitchen door. Seeing him appear made her start so forcibly that she almost dropped the plate she was holding. 'James,' she said cautiously, as if testing the air to see which way the wind of his mood was blowing. 'Your dinner is ready. Would you like to sit at the dining table and I will bring it in for you?'

James didn't reply. He just went and sat in the dining room as Susan busied herself with cutlery, condiments and his meal. She poured him a glass of wine and placed his plate of steaming hot food in front of him. She hovered in the doorway, uncertain whether to make a start on the washing-up or to see if there was anything else he wanted.

James took a couple of mouthfuls of food and chewed rhythmically. He motioned with his fork for her to sit in the chair closest to him and she reluctantly walked across the room to join him. He sighed after noticing her hesitation, which made her tense even more. He wished that she did not have to irritate him so much. Couldn't she see what she was doing to their relationship with her behaviour? He looked at her for a moment. She didn't look too bad for her age, he supposed, and there was no denying that she was a good cook and an excellent mother to his children. But where had that spark gone? Where was the easy laughter, and where was the fun they had once enjoyed?

The shadows curled unseen beneath the door and melted into the woodwork. The room chilled suddenly, and Susan shuddered involuntarily.

'What's the matter with you?' James shouted, spitting the words.

Susan flinched, but kept her gaze neutral. 'I don't know what you mean, James. I felt a draught, that is all. Is your dinner to your liking?'

As if forgetting that he had been eating happily and savouring the food a moment ago, James threw down his knife and fork into his plate of half-eaten food, causing splashes of gravy to soil the white tablecloth. He pushed himself to his feet, and with one hand he pushed his half-eaten meal onto the floor where the plate promptly smashed and the shards of china mixed with the remnants of food and splashed up the wall onto the oak panelling.

James sneered at the look of horror on his wife's face and

stalked from the room, slamming the door behind him, and went in search of a glass or two of whisky in his study.

Resignedly Susan went to the kitchen to find a bucket and mop and some newspaper to wrap the broken china in before putting it in the bin. She didn't see Tom standing by the wall in the kitchen, watching her with a look of pure desolation on his small face. The shadows slipped beneath the door in search of their quarry in the study.

Robert heard the crash from downstairs and the slam of his father's study door. He was sitting on his bed and had been reading a book, one of his old annuals, which he had received in his Christmas stocking last year, and he had jumped so much that the book had fallen out of his hand. He wondered what to do. He didn't want to risk bumping into his father, but he wanted to make sure that his mother was OK. He couldn't get to the kitchen, where he presumed she would be, without walking past his father's study.

How he hated this feeling of uselessness. His hands plucked at his crocheted blanket, which his mother had sat making for hours from odd scraps of wool, while he considered what to do.

His door creaked open slightly and a small head appeared around the door frame. Emma appeared, her wide eyes full of fearful tears. She looked so small in her long nightdress, clutching her threadbare toy cat. 'Did you hear the crash, Robert?' Robert nodded glumly. 'What do you think we should do?' Emma continued in a whisper.

'I don't know,' Robert said, rather shamefully. He wanted to take care of his little sister and make sure his mother was OK, and he was furious with his father for behaving how he did. 'Come and sit with me, Em,' he said instead. 'We can look at my annual together, or you can get one of yours and read that if you prefer.'

Not wanting to leave the relative safety of her brother's room, Emma opted to share Robert's book and together they read about the dastardly deeds of Dennis the Menace.

Susan found the pair of them curled up asleep together when she went up to bed later that evening after having cleaned up the mess in the dining room and putting the kitchen straight. She wondered suddenly if they had heard the commotion downstairs. She would have thought that it was too far away from them, but the children seemed to hear everything, even though she tried to hide the worst of their father's behaviour from them.

She hadn't seen James again. He had not emerged from his study. She wished she knew what was going on and why he was so angry all the time. His behaviour was definitely escalating. She would have to think up some excuse to get herself and the children away from him as soon as possible.

James sat in the study, having worked through his stack of papers. He was sitting in his chair with his second whisky in his hand. He twirled the amber liquid around in the cut crystal glass and watched the way the light from his desk lamp lit up the different facets of the glass. The movement soothed him, and the tension started to ease from his shoulders.

He had no idea why he had turned on Susan like he did. The meal was good, and he had been enjoying it. In fact, he was damn hungry now. What had she done to anger him so much? He took a sip of the whisky, savouring the feeling of heat as it moved down his throat and into his stomach. Just thinking about Susan made him angry. Well, he just wouldn't think about her.

He stuffed his papers into his briefcase. As he put his brief-case back on the floor he spotted his overnight bag in the corner of the room, which he had packed to go to a residential conference in Aberdeen a few weeks before. But at the last minute he had not been able to attend it, due to an urgent case needing his attention closer to home.

He picked up the bag and his briefcase and walked towards the study door. He was about to open the door, thinking he would go to see Clare, when he remembered their earlier argument. He wasn't so sure that she would be that happy to see him right then, and it was too late to buy any flowers for her because the shops had closed hours ago. He sighed and, setting the bag back down again, he poured himself another glass of whisky and headed upstairs to one of the empty bedrooms.

Susan heard James coming up the stairs and her body involuntarily tensed. However, when she realised that he was not going to continue his terror in the bedroom and had chosen to sleep elsewhere, she let out the breath she had been holding and put the book she had been attempting to read down on the bedside table and turned off the lamp.

Her body felt sore from constantly holding onto all this stress and tension. She would work on a plan to escape this hell in the morning, but in the meantime she needed to try and get some sleep. She heard James's snores coming from further down the corridor and finally allowed herself the oblivion of sleep.

CHAPTER 14

1936

Louisa looked at the cards she and Edward had received inviting them to various soirees, dinners and other various events and occasions. They varied in design and thickness of card, depending upon who they had received them from. The good doctor, her husband, was in constant demand, being of impeccable character and great company. Also, she supposed, his marriage to his former nanny would have piqued the interest of the gossips. She resented this feeling of being an object of curiosity. She could just imagine the demeaning comments whispered behind their hands, which were barely disguised by the manners expected in polite society.

Well, she would hold up her head and stand proud. Who cared what the other wives thought of her? Edward had married her, not them, and he did not seem to have a problem with it. Her fingers caressed the edge of an ornately decorated cream card that was inlaid with a beautiful silver-edged swirling design. It was from Lord and Lady Sinclair, inviting them to a formal dinner to celebrate the betrothal of one of their daughters. Edward had probably saved the simpering child from some disease or other during her miserable life.

Well, this one would do, she supposed. She sat down at her writing desk to craft a suitable response. Edward would of course have to buy her something appropriate to wear, she thought, as a cunning smile briefly pulled at her lips. In fact, she thought gleefully, if she accepted all these invitations, not only would it give her something to do, but she could get a completely new wardrobe in the process.

Thinking along these same lines, she considered the possibility of persuading Edward to allow her to organise something at their home. That would mean that she could get the little decorating jobs done that she had wanted to tackle for a while now. She needed to put her own stamp on this house and eradicate once and for all the lingering personality of her predecessor. Feeling buoyed up by this plan, she started to rapidly reply to all the invitations so she could spend the rest of her day making notes of everything she would get changed in the house.

Tom was in the garden, talking to the undergardener. Louisa eyed him warily through the window of the upper room, where she sat at her writing desk. She didn't know what it was about Tom that unsettled her. Maybe it was the way she saw his mother reflected in his eyes. And she was sure that the little boy watched her. She shuddered, and turned her gaze back to the letters of acceptance she was composing.

Tom had felt Louisa's eyes on him and glanced up. When she saw him watching her she had turned her focus back to whatever she was doing and pointedly ignored him. He shrugged. Jimmy Jenkins, the new apprentice gardener, was much more interesting anyway. Jimmy had been with them for a few months now and always had time for him, unlike his family.

Cassy was not interested in anything he wanted to do, feeling that to play with her brother was childish and she was now beyond such trivial things. All she seemed to be interested in was clothes and ribbons and stupid stuff like that. Jimmy had made him a catapult and shown him how to knock cans off the wall. Jimmy's brother used his to hit birds, but Tom, who loved all creatures big and small, would never have been able to bring himself to injure another living being.

Jimmy – or Jenkins, as he was supposed to call him – was currently in the process of building a bonfire from all the prunings from the trees, which had been laid out to dry in a pile. He was explaining to Tom the importance of checking for hedgehogs before lighting the fire because they liked to crawl in and make cosy nests for themselves in the stacks of wood. Tom was excited. What little boy didn't love a good bonfire?

He was helping Jenkins move piles of sticks from the separate drying piles to the area where the bonfire was to be lit. Louisa looked out of her window and sighed, torn between not wanting to have to entertain the small boy and not wanting to allow him to demean his status as the son of the household by carrying out menial gardening tasks with the lower echelons of the hired help. She decided to ignore it for now and decided to take it up with the head gardener that afternoon when she took her daily stroll in the garden to obtain cut flowers for the entrance hall display.

Tom was in his element. He really enjoyed being outside and Jenkins was so interesting, talking about his friend's fishing trip and the huge pike that had got away, and how his friend John Peters had nearly fallen in the river trying to keep a hold of it. He was doubly embarrassed as his sweetheart, young Sarah from the farm where John Peters worked as an apprentice, was walking by with her friend Sally at the time, and the pair of them had been sniggering at the two boys and walked away pointedly ignoring them, with their chins high and their noses in the air.

Tom relished listening to the tale, wishing that he could go fishing and that he was able to have the freedom to get involved in all sorts of antics that other boys his age seemed to be involved in. He had never even been allowed to go to the river, even though it was only a short walk from his house, he believed, from what Jenkins was saying. Mind you, who would he go with? His friends all lived a long way away from him, and Cassy wouldn't want to get herself dirty.

He thought for a minute and then said to Jenkins, 'I have never been to the river. Would you take me? Could I go fishing with you and John Peters?'

Jimmy Jenkins looked a bit sheepish as he replied. 'Well, I don't actually know, Tom. I am not sure that your father would allow it.'

'If he says I can, will you take me?' Tom asked, his young face eager with excitement.

'Well, if you had permission then of course I could take you on my day off,' he replied. Jimmy liked this young boy. He was kind and quiet. He obviously loved the outdoors as much as he did himself, and he needed space to let off steam.

Tom grinned with glee. He would speak to his father the very next time he saw him, but he would make sure that Louisa didn't overhear as she was sure to put a stop to any fun he might have planned.

As it turned out, Edward Winter thought that it was a marvellous idea that his young son learn to fish, and was only sad that he never had the time to indulge him in such boyhood activities himself. He spoke to Jenkins, thanking the young man for being considerate enough to take care of his boy on his day off. Jenkins was thrilled to have been praised so highly by his boss for doing what he considered something that anyone would do. He spoke to his best friend John Peters, and they arranged to go fishing and to take young Tom with them the following Saturday when they both had a day off work.

Maggie got to hear of the planned escapade and promised to

make a picnic for the three of them. She was pleased that Tom was getting some attention, as he often seemed to be left to his own devices and drifted around the house like a lost kitten looking for mischief.

Louisa was predictably unimpressed by the news, but Edward was adamant, and no argument was to be permitted on the subject. Anyway, Edward had been reasonably happy about her having accepted the invitations that she deemed the most suitable and had not forbidden her from organising a social event of her own, so she was putting most of her energy into planning that and the rest into trips to buy the new outfits she would require.

Edward was very lenient with his purse strings, and she could usually spend what she liked within reason. She would have a chat with Maggie about menu plans, she thought, a smile for once lighting up her pretty face. She left her room to walk down to the kitchen in search of Maggie.

Upon entering the kitchen Louisa eyed Tom's book, which lay on the edge of the table. She frowned. *Why does that boy seem insistent on spending so much of his time with the servants?* she asked herself.

Maggie walked through the utility room door with her arms full of produce, which she must have just collected from one of the gardeners. Her eyes narrowed as she saw who was in *her* kitchen, as she thought of it. She schooled her face into an open expression, and after laying down the vegetables on the large, scrubbed kitchen table she faced Louisa. 'Louisa,' she said curtly, 'what brings you down to the lower depths of the house, then?'

Momentarily caught off guard by the older woman's obvious hostility, she was determined not to be put off her task.

'Maggie, Edward has agreed that we can host a small dinner party in response to the many invitations we have recently accepted. I was wondering whether you could devise a menu for the evening.'

Louisa was out of her depth with this, and she knew that she needed to have the other woman on her side. Apart from rustling up sandwiches and small snacks for children, she had never had the need to learn how to cook. Her parents had always employed a cook themselves, and when they had died within months of each other she had taken up the position with the Winter family as nanny and governess, and as such had had all her own meals provided for her.

Maggie looked at Louisa suspiciously and folded her arms. Her position of authority over all things culinary gave her an air of superiority. 'How many people are you thinking of inviting?' She knew that the table in the dining room would seat at least twenty adults comfortably. If Louisa was thinking of having that many guests, then she would need help with both the preparation and serving.

After relaxing a little and easing into her stride, Louisa continued. 'Well, I was thinking of Lord and Lady Sinclair,' she flushed slightly, feeling a sense of self-importance wash over her by even considering having these highly regarded patrons of society gracing her dinner table. She continued by saying, 'Dr Metcalf and his wife, Mr and Mrs Mortimer, Giles Green and his daughter Clara, and a few of Edward's most highly regarded patients.' She finished speaking, and Maggie was still regarding her quizzically as if waiting for her to slip up.

After a few seconds Maggie spoke into the chasm of silence, which had started to feel slightly uncomfortable. 'Have you forgotten about Gerald and Caroline Watson?' Maggie was referring to the retired doctor and his wife. The doctor had worked closely with Edward until Edward had taken over his practice several years previously, and they also coincidentally happened to be Sophie Winter's parents.

Louisa blanched. 'Well, really,' she started, an unbecoming blush creeping up her neck. 'I hardly think that they would be appropriate guests…' She trailed off, her words dying on her lips under Maggie's unwavering stare. 'Fine,' she said huffily, like the spoilt child she had never seemed to have grown out of being. 'I will speak to Edward about adding them to the list.'

'I think you will find that he would have taken it for granted that they would be on the list already, Louisa,' Maggie said pointedly.

However, apparently placated, Maggie slowly unfolded her arms and retrieved a couple of large books from an upper shelf. She wiped the thin film of dust that coated them, which gave testament to their recent lack of use, accusingly. 'We can start with these,' she said, and thrust them across the table to the obviously deflated Louisa. 'What sort of meal were you thinking of? Plain and simple country fare, or something more lavish?'

Maggie knew that Louisa would want to show off, but she also needed to rein in this young upstart and make her realise that the guests who she spoke of would not be impressed by an 'exciting menu', and it would do her no favours at all if the reason behind this sudden interest in hosting a party was to further herself in society.

Louisa, although pushy and ambitious, realised when she had met her match and decided that she needed Maggie at this moment much more than Maggie needed her, so was sensible enough to allow herself to be guided by her obvious wealth of knowledge in the eating habits of the middle and upper classes.

She presumed, correctly, that Maggie had lots of friends who were also in service, and they often discussed what went on in their own establishments, gossip being a favourite pastime. Hence, Maggie was in a very good position to know what the majority of the guests liked to eat.

The two women, their differences momentarily set aside, started to plan a menu that was agreeable to them both. Louisa had set the date for a couple of weeks away on a Saturday, and the invitations had been sent and the acceptances received.

Louisa was in a rare good mood. It appeared as if she was being accepted at last. Edward and she had enjoyed a few evenings at various parties, and she believed that she had held her own. Edward had been attentive and had complimented her on her appearance. Louisa had even been slightly less acerbic with Tom. He was going fishing the same day as her party, so he would not be in the way during the preparations and distracting Maggie and the girls she had enlisted to assist her for the occasion. Edward was just happy that his wife seemed to have cheered herself up. Her constant moodiness baffled him, and he just wanted to stay out of her way when she was in one of her tempers, which just exacerbated the situation.

There had not been time to do much more than polish the floors and give the house a thorough clean, although Maggie and the daily cleaning lady made sure that the housework was always kept on top of anyway, so there was not much extra work required. Louisa herself had seen to the floral arrangements. Apparently, Sophie had always had fresh flowers in the house and, as her parents had been invited, Louisa didn't want them comparing her more unfavourably to their precious late daughter than was necessary.

In her more upbeat mood Louisa did mentally reprimand

herself for her unkind thoughts, as Sophie had been a lovely person, she admitted slightly reluctantly to herself, and her parents were both open and kind people who would probably not think anything of the sort.

But it never hurt to be too careful.

CHAPTER 15

1936

The day of the party dawned clear and bright. Tom jumped out of bed very early, keen and excited to go on his very first fishing trip. He had been so excited the night before that he had found it difficult to sleep, but he must have drifted off at some time, he thought with a grin, or he would not have just woken up.

He dressed quickly in his oldest clothes and ran down the two flights of stairs to find Maggie, who was in the kitchen, stirring a pan of porridge on the hob. Three parcels wrapped in tinfoil sat on the kitchen table, and beside them stood a flask and three apples. There was an old canvas rucksack and several bottles of home-made ginger beer. There was also a round red and green tin, which would have once housed some fancy biscuits, but which now Tom sincerely hoped contained some of Maggie's famous baked offerings.

'Morning, Tom,' Maggie said, with a smile on her face as she continued to stir the porridge in a concentrated fashion. 'I thought you might be up with the lark today, so I made some porridge. It's nearly ready, so pour yourself a glass of milk and I will put some in a bowl for you.'

Tom did as he was bid and sat down at the table. He was ravenous, as always. He cut himself a large hunk of the bread that was sitting on the table and buttered it and then spread some jam on it and took a huge bite. Maggie shook her head and with a chuckle. 'I don't know where you put it all, young Tom, I really don't.' Tom just grinned at her and continued munching his bread and jam while he waited for his porridge to cool enough for him to eat.

As Tom was finishing his porridge his father came into the kitchen reading his newspaper, which he held in one hand, and carried his bag in the other. He nearly walked straight into Maggie, who was sweeping by the door. Maggie tutted at him good-naturedly as he apologised and sheepishly tucked his newspaper under his arm and shrugged his shoulders as he winked at Tom.

After noticing the parcels on the table, Edward looked at his son's beaming face and realised that today must be the day Jenkins was taking him fishing. He walked over to his son and patted him on the shoulder. 'Ah, Tom,' he said wistfully. 'It's such a perfect day for a fishing trip. I really wish I had the time to come with you but, alas, duty calls.' He grabbed the piece of bread that Tom had not finished, and waved it in the air while grinning at Tom's protestations.

'Remember to be home in time for Louisa's party tonight, Edward,' Maggie called after him as he took the back way out of the house. She could hear him calling a cheerful greeting to Jenkins as he walked down the side of the house and round to the front of the property, where he had left his car outside rather than parking it in one of the garages.

Jenkins came into the kitchen moments later, rubbing his large hands together, and looked to be nearly as excited at the day's proposed escapades as his young charge. Maggie smiled fondly at the pair of them. She thought how kind it was of Jenkins to be taking his boss's son out on his day off. 'Do you want some porridge, Jimmy?' she asked him.

Jenkins, who had already eaten bacon and eggs at home before setting off this morning thought for a minute before answering. 'Yes, please, Maggie, but just a small bowl, mind.' Maggie smiled. She knew his mother and knew that he would have already been fed, but she also knew how much young men and boys could eat.

She put a steaming bowl down in front of him and nodded towards the parcels on the table. 'I've made you three packed lunches and there is also some of my ginger beer there, and I'll make a flask of tea for you now.'

Jenkins beamed at Maggie. 'Thanks, Maggie. You're the best.' With a flap of her hand Maggie turned away, but she was smiling at the young man's kind words. She put the large flat-bottomed kettle on the stove to boil and turned to the washing-up. Once done, she wiped her hands on her apron and busied herself making a flask of tea for the three of them to take.

Maggie placed the flask on the table and pointed to the canvas rucksack. 'Put the lunch in there, Jimmy, and mind that you put the heavy items at the bottom. You don't want to squash the food and spoil it.' Thinking that nothing much could spoil Maggie's food, Jenkins allowed himself to be guided about the correct way to pack a picnic bag. Once everything was stowed away to Maggie's approval the two of them jumped up and, after hauling the rucksack onto Jenkins's back, they walked out into the sunshine.

Tom was so excited that he was talking nineteen to the dozen. Jenkins smiled to himself. He could remember the first time he went fishing with his father. He had been much younger than Tom, but he had still been very excited.

The novelty had never worn off, either. The hours spent sitting on the bank watching the float bob about on the water and occasionally dip below it … the excitement of reeling in the line to see what may, or may not, be on the end of the line. It was therapeutic, and he loved the calmness of just sitting and watching nature. He loved to see the bright blue flash of a kingfisher and the grace of the swans, who always expected him to share his lunch with them.

They got to the gate at the bottom of the garden, which opened out into the lane beyond, and saw John Peters walking towards them pulling a small handcart behind him laden with fishing paraphernalia. There were two large boxes, at least three folded chairs and two long canvas-type bags – which must house the rods, Tom thought.

John grinned at the pair of them. 'Ready?' he asked, taking off his cap and wiping the sweat from his forehead. He spied the large rucksack that Jenkins was carrying. 'Aw, please tell me that Maggie has had a hand in what is in that bag.'

Jenkins and Tom grinned back at him. 'Oh, yes,' they both replied in unison.

'Well, praise all that is holy,' John said and sighed theatrically, and the three of them dissolved into peals of laughter.

They walked down the lane, which was dry in the early morning sun. The rain from a few weeks ago was now a distant memory, and the dust kicked up around their feet as they walked. There were not many people about yet and it was very quiet.

They passed a couple of people on horseback and the baker's van, which was taking the lane as a back road to deliver to one of the local shops around the corner. There were only a few shops: a butcher, a greengrocer and a sweet shop and general store, which also sold a few loaves of bread. That was probably where the baker's van was going. Usually, the two lads would have called in there to grab a couple of cakes, as it was so close to the track that led down to the river. But today they had been spoilt by Maggie's famous offerings, which they were looking forward to as much as the day's fishing.

They ambled along in companionable silence until Jimmy spoke. 'So, Tom, what is this big party that you are having tonight all about, then? Your stepmother was all hot and bothered about her flowers yesterday. Had to have the biggest and best of the blooms, etc. I heard her complaining to Mr Graves. He was not very happy, I know that much.'

Tom shrugged his shoulders in response. 'I don't know. I never get told anything. Cassy would know, but she doesn't tell me either.' He sniffed, completely uninterested in the goings-on at home. The less he was involved the better as far as he was concerned.

Changing the subject, he turned to the day at hand. 'What do you think we will catch, then? Maggie said she would cook it for my tea if I caught a trout,' Tom said excitedly.

Jimmy and John both exchanged a glance and smiled at each other. 'If we catch a trout, young Tom, I'll cook it myself, wearing Maggie's pinny,' Jenkins said, and they all fell about laughing at the thought of Jimmy dressed in Maggie's apron.

They came upon the track to the river. The branches hung low across the entrance in the summer, almost obscuring it completely from view. The smell of grass hung in the air, and this mixed with the intoxicating smell of wild flowers that grew in abundance in the hedgerows. Birds flew across the track and the dappled light fell softly on the path leading them down towards the gentle rush of the river.

The gate that ended the path was new. The previous one had been replaced after it had finally fallen apart from years of neglect and being clambered over by people too lazy to open it. It creaked gently as it opened to reveal the sandy bank and the fast-moving river that flowed around the bend. The tall reeds that lined the banks swaying gently in the movement. The opposite bank was much higher, and Tom could see cows far away across the fields.

Tom felt ecstatic. He was so excited to just be by the water. He could never have imagined that such a wondrous place existed so very close to his home. He breathed deeply, inhaling the scents of the vista before him, and drank in the images as if to burn them permanently into his memory.

Jimmy and John manoeuvered the cart through the gate, and as its wheels instantly became buried in the sand they decided to unload the cargo so that it would be easier to move it out of the way. They had a bit of a discussion about the best place to set up and decided to start to the right of the gate.

This side of the river had no path, so there was not much of an area to choose from. But Jimmy decided that to try casting from the position he had chosen would allow the river to take the line downstream into the shadow of the bend, where he hoped the larger fish might be hiding.

CHAPTER 16

1973

When Susan awoke it was very early. It was not quite light but the birds were singing gaily, so she assumed that it must be around 5 a.m. She got out of bed and stretched away the sleep, and then went to the basin and splashed cold water on her face and cleaned her teeth. She pulled on some clothes and walked towards her bedroom door, and after opening it slowly she stopped to listen. She couldn't hear any movement, so she padded quietly towards the stairs.

The doors to the other bedrooms were all closed, and she couldn't see the front of the house from there so she was not sure whether James was still in the house. She shuddered. What had things come to, where she was tiptoeing around her own home in fear? She shook her head sadly.

She had been so determined to speak to James about their future – or lack of it, she thought – but his behaviour had prohibited any such move on that front. She just wanted to be free from this poisonous man. His behaviour was wearing her down and she was starting to fear for her safety, she had realised.

As she rounded the end of the landing and started to make her way downstairs she was sure she could hear the sound of someone singing. *Who on earth would be singing?* she wondered, intrigued.

At the bottom of the stairs she stepped into the hall and slid her feet into the slippers that she kept hidden discreetly next to the grandfather clock tucked under the return of the stairs.

Yes, she could definitely hear someone singing or humming. It sounded like an old song. Perhaps someone had left the radio on, but it was a bit early, and even Jenkins was unlikely to have been in the kitchen at this hour.

Susan glanced out the windows in the hall, but it was still too dark to see outside properly so she couldn't see if James's car was there or not. She continued to walk through the hall, past the doors to James's study and the drawing room and into the dining room. As she crossed the threshold into the dining room the air felt tense.

The singing was coming from the kitchen. It was the gentle, melodious sound of someone enjoying a task and accompanying it with a happy tune. Was it the radio? Susan walked past the dining table, the scene of the previous night's row, and grimaced.

As she placed her hand on the handle of the kitchen door the sound stopped abruptly. Susan pushed the door open, expecting to see Jenkins sitting at the table with the radio at his side, but the room was empty. After pressing the light switch and frowning, Susan moved to the door into the utility room and tried the handle of the back door. It was locked, and the key was protruding from the lock. Totally confused now, Susan spun round and entered the kitchen again. It smelt of sweet peas and freshly baked bread, but there was still no sign of anyone.

Susan flicked on the kettle and sank into one of the chairs. What on earth was going on? Was she actually losing the plot now? Her foot nudged something under the table so she bent down to see what it was, and as she lifted her foot she saw a wooden object that was painted red and green. It had a bulbous middle and tapered out to a very thin rounded point at either end. It looked like a fishing float. Why on earth would a fishing float be lying in the middle of the kitchen floor?

Deep in thought, she almost jumped out of her skin when a loud knock rapped at the back door. She jumped up cautiously and walked to the door, and was relieved when Jenkins's familiar face appeared. 'Morning, Mrs Morton,' he said cheerfully. 'I saw the light and wondered if there may be the chance of a cuppa.'

Smiling, Susan opened the door and stepped back to allow the older man to enter. 'Yes, of course, Jenkins. I have just put the kettle on.'

They walked into the kitchen together, and Jenkins gasped when he saw what was lying on the middle of the table. 'Now where on earth did you find that?' he exclaimed, a smile of wonder lighting up his features and a lopsided grin nearly splitting his weathered face in two. 'It was on the floor under the table this morning, I nearly trod on it. Why, do you recognise it?' She looked questioningly at Jenkins, whose former excited expression had morphed into confusion tinged with potential apprehension.

She watched his face as the conflicting emotions rode over it, each vying for supremacy while she waited for his response. 'What is it, Jim?' she asked. Her use of his Christian name seemed to pull him back to the present.

'I, er, that is to say…' He faltered, rubbing his hand over his face as if unsure as to how to go on. 'It's mine,' he finally managed, 'but I've not seen it for nigh on thirty-odd years. The last time was on that day when John and I took young Tom fishing.' He sat down heavily at the table and looked up at Susan's open and enquiring face. There was still confusion on his face, etched with something else. Was it pain or sadness?

Not knowing how to respond, Susan remained quiet and

busied herself with making tea for the pair of them.

'That was some day,' Jenkins said eventually. He let out a huge breath and shook his head sadly.

CHAPTER 17

1936

Having chosen the spot to fish from, the two older lads started to unload the cart. They placed the two large tackle boxes on the ground. Tom took the chairs, and they told him where to place them. Then they started to prepare the rods. Tom watched in fascination as with practised hands they threaded the line and added metal weights and brightly painted floats.

They selected hooks and placed the rods on the ground. 'Now for the bait,' John said, with a note of glee in his voice. He pulled a metal bait tin out of his canvas bag and removed the lid. Tom looked on with fascinated revulsion at the wriggling, squirming mass of fat creamy white maggots that filled the tin. The older lads grinned at each other.

'The girls hate these,' Jimmy said, and laughed.

Tom could just imagine Cassy and her friends screaming at the sight of the tin full of horrors and joined in with the amusement. 'Oh, I wish I had a tin of these at home when Cassy has her annoying friends for tea,' he said, imagining how much havoc he could wreak.

'Right,' John said. 'Let's get the bait on the rods, and then we can show you how to cast out.' John selected a maggot and pierced it onto the hook. He walked down to the water's edge. 'OK, watch what I do, young Tom.'

He released the bail arm on the reel, took the line gently in his left hand and swung back the rod with his right. He flicked the rod expertly and aimed for the centre of the river.

The float could be seen bobbing gently in the water and the current moved it towards the reeds. John pushed the bail arm back on the reel and motioned Tom to sit in one of the seats they had positioned earlier.

He handed the rod to him and said, 'Keep your eyes fixed on the float. If it starts to move, let me know. If it bobs below the water that means that a fish has taken the bait and you need to start winding in the line. Just let me know and I will come and help you, OK?'

Tom, not taking his eyes off the float, nodded. The other two exchanged an amused glance and busied themselves with their rods. They had a couple of V-shaped rod rests and placed their rods in them so they didn't have to hold them all the time, and then went to look for a suitable stick for Tom to use to rest his rod.

Once they were all set up, Jimmy Jenkins took the flask out of the canvas bag and poured them all a cup of tea. Under instruction from the others, Tom had placed the bottles of ginger beer in another bag and put this in the river near the bank and tethered it to a stick through the handles, as this would keep the contents nice and cold. They placed their packages of food in one of the tackle boxes to keep the bugs from getting to them and handed round some shortbread that Maggie had given them to dunk in their tea.

All three sat back in their chairs, mugs of tea and biscuits in hand. 'Ah, this is the life,' said Jimmy.

'Aye,' replied John, 'it is indeed.' Tom looked from one to the other, feeling privileged to be included in their outing. He couldn't remember having ever been happier in his entire life. The sun was warm but not scorching, and a gentle breeze was blowing. The sun shimmered off the river like dancing lights illuminating the silver water, and the sound it created as it hurried along on its way was like subtle music to his ears.

Tom had turned his attention back to his float when suddenly it bobbed and dipped below the surface. In his haste to jump up out of his chair he spilt his tea down his front. 'The float,' he exclaimed excitedly, pointing and jumping up and down.

'Grab your rod, Tom, and start to wind in the reel like we showed you,' John said, a big smile on his face. It was typical that the youngster got the first bite.

Tom, whose gaze fixed on the line as he carefully reeled it in, was full of nervous concentration. He caught a flash of silver as a twitching fish came into view. 'Slowly now,' John said, as he moved to help the boy land his fish into the large green net in the water. It was very small, but Tom was elated.

John expertly removed the hook from the fish's mouth and showed the fish to Tom. 'Shall we throw this one back, Tom?' he asked. 'It's only a little 'un. But very well done for catching the first fish.' Tom, torn between wanting to keep his first ever fish and wanting to do what was right, nodded solemnly. Jimmy patted him on the back and added his own words of congratulations, remembering how he himself had felt when he had caught his first fish.

Jimmy caught the next two fish and then John had a run of luck catching three in a row. Tom was just as excited to watch the other two as he had been catching his own.

They decided to have a break for lunch, and busied themselves handing out the parcels of food that Maggie had put together for them. There was a large sandwich each with cheese and pickle and a big slice of pork pie. There were slices of fruit cake and an apple each too, all washed down with the ginger beer that Tom had retrieved from its cooling place in the river.

'My, but Maggie is a fine cook,' John said, wiping the back of his hand across his across his mouth.

'Aye, she is that,' Jimmy said. 'You're one lucky lad, having her as cook in your house, young Tom. There's no denying it.'

Tom would not have dreamt of denying it. He knew only too well how amazing Maggie's food was. She seemed to have a soft spot for him too, and was always keeping special titbits to spoil him with. He smiled at his acknowledgement of the undisputed fact.

Just then the sun went behind a cloud and they all looked up at the sky. In the distance the sky was a threatening black. There was an ominous low rumbling and the black clouds flickered with yellow light. 'It looks like our trip is coming to an abrupt end, boys,' Jimmy said jumping up and folding his chair. 'Come on, let's see if we can get packed up before the worst of the rain hits.'

Another huge crack of thunder let rip above them and the first fat drops of rain started to fall around them and almost sizzled on the ground. Tom, who had never been a fan of thunderstorms, shivered in apprehension. Sensing his disquiet with the change of events, John busied him with jobs to take his mind off the looming storm. However, another huge crack of thunder that followed almost immediately, with a blinding flash of lighting, made Tom cry out in alarm as he covered his head in fear.

'Come on, Tom, it's only a storm,' Jimmy said coaxingly as he hurried to pack the remaining items into boxes and load them onto the cart. 'Quick, run under the trees by the gate there and get out of the worst of the rain.'

The rain seemed to have been released by the last crack of thunder, almost as though it had ripped a hole in the fabric of the sky itself to allow the flood to drop in a single torrent. In seconds the three of them were drenched to the skin. The rain was running through their hair and down their faces into their eyes, making it impossible to see what they were doing.

Before either of them could issue a warning to Tom to be careful, he had raised up his rod to put it on the cart. At that very second a flash of light so bright that it blinded them all momentarily hit the ground in front of them, scorching a black line in the soil and throwing all three of them to the ground.

Terrified, John and Jimmy jumped up to see Tom still lying on the ground, not moving. The rod he had been holding was on the ground beside him and the scorch mark was right by his feet.

Chapter 18

1973

Jenkins hadn't seemed to want to elaborate on the meaning behind the old fishing float and so Susan, sensing his discomfort, decided to leave it. She handed him his steaming mug of tea and, after thanking her graciously, he went back through the door and out into the garden.

Susan busied herself making some porridge for everyone and then sat at the table with her own mug of tea and a small bowl of porridge. She had little appetite at the moment and her nerves were in shreds, but she knew that she must eat. She needed to keep her strength up and her wits about her to be able to think straight. She clearly needed to get away from James's increasingly erratic and aggressive behaviour, but how could she do that and where might she go?

She heard a noise in the hallway and her heart rate increased. She took a deep breath and tried to calm herself. The sun was fully up now and beams fell sharply through the windowpanes, illuminating items as brightly as if they had been put under a spotlight.

One of the beams highlighted the old float, mocking her with its bright red and green paint. As she watched it rolled off the top of the oven, where she had placed it, and skittered across the floor to place itself at her feet. Wearily she bent to pick it up and rolled it between her fingers. She wondered how on earth it had come to be lying in the middle of the kitchen floor. It's not as if they had a cat or anything that could have hooked it out from under one of the cupboards with its paw.

The noise in the hall came again, and reluctantly Susan got up to see what it was. As she entered the hallway it was to see her husband flinging items into his briefcase and closing it with a self-satisfied click. He placed it on the floor beside his overnight bag and, sensing her presence, turned to face his wife. 'I have a conference in York,' he said by way of explanation.

'Oh,' she replied, 'you never mentioned it. When will you be back?'

James sighed exasperatedly at her. 'Oh, for goodness' sake, Susan, I told you ages ago.' He gesticulated his irritation by flapping his hands at her in a shooing motion. 'I'll be gone for two nights, if it's all right with you.' He sneered at her, as if challenging her to complain.

Susan tried not to let the relief in her face show. With two whole days and nights without having to tread on eggshells she could plan their escape without fear of being caught in the act.

Taking the look on her face to be dismay, James felt a frisson of excitement tingling in his belly. His sadistic nature was rewarded by causing what he mistook as pain on his wife's face. With a smug smile he picked up his travel bag and his briefcase and without a backwards glance walked across the hall and out the front door, closing it behind him with a controlled click.

Susan let out the breath that she did not realise she had been holding and felt relief flood through her body. She knew that James had not mentioned anything about a conference. She was meticulous about recording his appointments in the kitchen calendar, if for nothing else than to help her with meal planning because she knew how much James abhorred any sort of waste.

Feeling suddenly energised by the relief of two whole anxiety-free days, she ran up the stairs to wake the children. They could do some baking or go for a walk or do some painting in the garden, whatever they felt like doing, without the shadow of James breathing down their necks.

As she reached the first landing the grandfather clock chimed seven o'clock. Its melodious tone filled the house. Susan opened her son's door. Robert was still fast asleep but his dark lashes moved slightly as his eyelids twitched out the dream playing behind them. 'Robert,' she said softly. His eyes flickered open and she smiled at his sleep infused face. 'Come on, darling, wake up. I've made some porridge and thought we could go for a picnic or something today if you would like that?'

As he rubbed the sleep from his eyes Robert sat up and stretched. Yawning, he grinned at his mother. 'That would be great, thanks, Mum,' he said enthusiastically. 'Shall I wake Em up?'

Knowing that Robert's idea of how to wake his sister up would be very different to hers, she shook her head, smiling down at him. 'No, you get dressed and I'll go up to her now.'

After closing his bedroom door behind her, Susan mounted the stairs to the second floor and hesitated before she opened her daughter's door. She could hear her speaking. Was she reading aloud or playing with her toys? Grinning, she opened the door and stopped.

Emma was indeed reading from one of her books, a very old copy of *Black Beauty*, which she had found in the kitchen and left on the side. But she was not reading to her toys. Instead she was sitting in the window seat. 'Morning, darling,' Susan said, 'How lovely to see you reading. I love that story.'

'Yes, me too, Mummy. Tom says it was his favourite book too, and that's why he left it for me.'

Feeling slightly uneasy but not wanting to show it in front of her daughter, Susan smiled. 'Ah, yes, Tom,' she said. 'And how is Tom today?'

Looking pleased that her mother was showing an interest in her friend Emma replied, 'He was sitting here listening to the story until you came in. He's gone now.' Emma nodded to the pile of cushions on the opposite side of the window seat to where she was sitting. Susan caught a glimpse of something red and green jutting out from underneath one of the cushions and stepped closer to take a better look. Her hand flew to her mouth as she gasped in shock. She reached down and pulled out the small wooden float that she had last placed on the kitchen table before she came upstairs to get the children for their breakfasts.

Her heart racing Susan held the offending article in front of her. 'What's wrong, Mummy?' Emma asked in alarm.

'Where did this come from, Emma?' Susan asked, trying to keep her voice neutral.

'Oh, that. I don't know, Mummy. I think Tom was playing with it.' After getting down from her perch on the window seat Emma turned to her mother. 'Can I have honey on my porridge, please, Mummy?'

Susan took her daughter's small hand in her own and dragged her gaze away from the window seat with difficulty. She looked down at her daughter, determinedly planted a smile on her face and said, 'Of course, darling, and then we will prepare a picnic to take on a walk.'

'Yippee,' Emma cried and ran in front of her mother.

I really need to get away from this house, Susan said to herself as she followed more slowly in her daughter's wake.

Still holding the red and green float in her hand, Susan made her way into the kitchen. She opened the right drawer in the large pine dresser and placed the float in it. Then with a shudder she closed the drawer and lit the gas under the pan with the porridge inside and stirred it absent-mindedly.

The house had always seemed to have its fair share of strange goings-on – shadows moving in the corner of her eye and unexplained sounds – but over the last couple of months they seemed to have increased and she seemed to be the only one aware of them. While trying to put it out of her mind for the moment, she focused on getting breakfast ready for the children and wondered where she should take them for their picnic.

Emma and Robert both sat at the table with bowls of porridge in front of them. Susan asked them what they would like in their picnic. They both started reeling off a huge list of items, some of which were more practical than others. As their suggestions got more outrageous, they all burst into laughter when Emma suggested rainbow pie in response to Robert's dinosaur leg with octopus sauce.

It was visibly noticeable that the children had caught on to her much more relaxed way of behaving now that their father had left for a couple of days. They never seemed to ask after him. In fact, she often wondered whether they actually felt anything for him at all.

It saddened her. Her own father, although strict, was a kind and gentle man and had always made time for her when she was a child. James had no idea what he was missing out on, and he brought it all upon himself.

Having made a pile of sandwiches and added fruit, slices of cake and a large Scotch egg, which she intended sharing between them, she placed some plastic containers on the table and packed the food in carefully. She put the containers in a rucksack and found another rucksack, which was purposefully kept packed for picnics, and which housed plates, cutlery and a chopping board, among other useful items.

She filled some bottles with some squash, made sure that the picnic rucksack also had some beakers in it, and put everything together on the table. After looking in several cupboards she found the old picnic blanket folded up in one of the wall cupboards in the utility room. She placed this in a smaller rucksack and went into the garden to look at the sky.

It was already warm and the sky looked blue and clear. They wouldn't be going too far away, as she couldn't drive. And even if she had been able to, James had the car.

They would walk down to the church, where the children could play in the park for a while, and then they could feed the ducks in the pond. After that they could walk back past the house and towards the village and cross the bridge over the river to get to the fields on the other side. They could leave the picnic here and grab it on the way back past the house. No need to carry it until they had to.

Pleased at having devised a nice route for the day, Susan called the children, who were in the garden chasing butterflies without much success and much to Jenkins's amusement.

She could pack her sketchbook and do some drawing while the children played after lunch, if they allowed her the time. Perhaps she could put in a ball and some racquets. That should keep them amused for a while. Smiling to herself, she went to change her shoes for something practical before gathering up her small charges, and they all walked down the garden towards the gate at the back of the orchard and out into the lane.

They turned left and followed the path down to the small row of shops. The sweet shop on the corner must have been there for years, Susan thought. It was very old-fashioned, but that lent it a certain degree of charm. There was a wool shop, which also sold shoes, for some reason, a greengrocer's, a butcher and a general store, which sold practically everything that you could ever need and lots of things that you never would, or so Susan thought.

The children chattered happily, pointing out different things of interest to each other as they walked. It lifted Susan's spirits to see them like this and not bickering for once. 'Can we have some sweets, please, Mum?' Robert asked. 'Yes, please, Mum,' Emma added pleadingly. Susan smiled, as she had been anticipating this and had brought some small change with her for this very reason.

'You can have ten pence each,' she said, handing each child a shining silver coin, and with eyes lighting up with pure glee the children pushed the door open with a cheerful jingle.

The shopkeeper, wearing old but clean overalls, appeared behind the counter. He had a gentle twinkle in his eye, and he nodded at Susan before giving his full attention to his two young customers. 'Well, Master Robert and Miss Emma,' he said, 'what can I get for you today?' Behind him there were shelves full of glass jars full of brightly coloured goodies. The counter he stood behind housed even more treats, from licorice whirls to gobstoppers and Black Jacks and Fruit Salads.

Realising that this could take some time, Susan excused herself and went to look in the windows of the other shops. She didn't need to buy anything today. As James was not going to be at home she could make a simple soup with some bread for their tea, and she had everything she needed at home for that.

After about ten minutes the children left the shop and came to find their mother, carrying white paper bags full of goodies in their hands. They obediently handed these into their mother's care, knowing without having to be told that they would not be permitted to eat any of their carefully selected purchases before their lunch. 'We bought you something too, Mummy,' Emma said, beaming at her mother with such loving kindness radiating from her small face that Susan's heart almost skipped a beat.

'Well, thank you, my darlings,' she said. 'Shall we go to the park now?'

The children spent a happy half an hour or so playing in the park. There were a few other children in there too, who they all knew, and Susan chatted with the other mothers for a while to pass the time. As a rule she didn't get to spend much time with the local children's mothers, as James preferred her to spend time with his associates' wives to build relationships that would favour him and his needs and aspirations. Susan didn't have much time for those types of people but knew that James would be unhappy if she didn't do as he asked so, as usual, she swept her own feelings under the carpet.

After a few minutes chatting with these local mothers, Susan realised that she would much rather spend her time in their easy company rather than the competitive falseness of James's associates' wives, who were all about trivial fripperies and being seen in the latest fashions – all things that Susan couldn't give a fig about. These women, however, seemed to have an easy camaraderie between them. Their friendships were forged in honesty and fierce loyalty to one another.

Susan suddenly felt very lonely and isolated. She also felt angry with herself for allowing herself to have been so easily manipulated into this situation by her husband. The realisation hit her with such unexpected clarity that she felt suddenly faint. She paled noticeably and felt her legs tremble.

The other women, seeing her change in colour and spotting

that she had become unsteady on her feet, rushed to her side and guided her to the bench to sit down. Overwhelmed by their concern and kindness to her when they did not know her at all made tears prick at her eyes, and she brushed them away before they threatened to spill unchecked down her cheeks.

'You all right, love?' one of the women asked her gently. 'You looked like you came over all faint, like.'

Susan forced a wan smile onto her face and looked up into the kind, concerned face of the other woman. 'Thank you. I'm fine. I don't know what came over me. I'll be OK in a minute.' After glancing over at her children, who thankfully seemed oblivious of her embarrassing situation, she looked back at the group of three women, who were all looking at her with interest.

'I'm Stacey,' said the woman who had helped her to the bench. She had blonde hair pulled back into a ponytail and wore jeans and a pink T-shirt. 'This here is Jane,' she said, pointing at a slight mousy-looking woman who was rocking a pushchair in which sat a sleeping child, 'and this is Julie.' The last woman was slightly taller than Jane, with darker hair, which was cut into a bob, and she wore a pair of denim shorts and a white blouse. Stacey herself also wore jeans and had a black T-shirt, with a pink cardigan knotted round her waist.

All three women continued to stare at Susan. Realising that she was supposed to respond in some way, Susan said, 'Oh yes, sorry. I'm Susan. I thought I'd bring the children to the park to have a bit of a run about. They have the garden, of course, but it's nice for them to see the outside world too.'

The other women turned and followed her gaze to the children. 'Ah, yes,' Julie said. 'Emma and Robert. Emma is in the same class as my son and Robert is in Debbie's class.'

Feeling embarrassed that she didn't recognise the mothers of her children's playmates, Susan reddened. As she could not drive, the children got the bus to school or Jennifer's mother took them all.

Understanding her embarrassment, Stacey nudged her gently with her elbow. 'I didn't realise that you and the kids lived near here. Mine always mention your two, saying that they are both nice kids.' She smiled kindly at Susan. 'Perhaps you could all come by for tea one afternoon if you're not busy.'

Susan was stunned. These women had only just met her, and yet they were showing more kindness than she had experienced in over twelve years of her experience with the wives of James's cronies. And they were offering her the hand of unconditional friendship. She had obviously been looking for friendship in completely the wrong area.

While smiling her thanks up at Stacey she reached into her back for a notepad and a pen and scribbled down her telephone number and handed it to Stacey. Stacey ripped a piece off the bottom of the piece of paper and, after holding her hand out for the pen that Susan still held in her hand, she wrote her own number on the scrap of paper and handed it back to her.

'How about tomorrow afternoon?' she asked Susan. 'Would you and the kids be free then? The others here are coming round and we've put a paddling pool up in the garden. The kids can have a splash about, and we can sit down and put our feet up and have a natter.' Thinking that nothing had ever sounded nicer in her life, Susan nodded her thanks. 'That would be really lovely. Thank you so much.' She noted that Stacey had written her address on the piece of paper too and smiled to herself.

If James knew his wife and children were frequenting an address in Stratton Road he would explode. 'About three o'clock suit you?' Stacey asked, her head cocked on one side.

'That would suit us perfectly,' Susan replied. After standing up and calling the children to her she smiled at the trio of women and waved their goodbyes.

Feeling further buoyed up by the interaction with the three women, Susan felt elated. How long had it been since she felt even a glimmer of such joy in her heart? This is how she used to be, she remembered, frowning slightly. What had she allowed to happen to her? All the more reason to make sure she had a plan to get out of the cloying suffocation that her life had become.

She felt the strength and determination return to her limbs. She watched Emma and Robert skipping along the lane and her heart filled with joy for being blessed with two such beautiful children.

They retraced their steps along the lane towards the house to collect the rucksacks. The morning had warmed up even more during the time they had been at the park, and it looked perfect for having a picnic. The spot that she had chosen was by the river and had some beautiful willow trees along the bank that they could sit under if it got too warm. The bank was too high and steep for the children to paddle that side, though, but after Emma's accident previously she doubted whether not being able to get in the water would bother her.

They reached their back gate and walked through the garden to the house. Jenkins, as usual, was pottering around in the garden. The children ran up to him and he smiled affectionately at them. Susan walked to the back door and picked up the three rucksacks from where she had left them earlier on the table. The house had a strange, brooding atmosphere that she thought was weird. It was as if it were waiting for something.

Normally when James was about, she felt the oppressiveness, but with him not being there this felt wrong.

She shrugged her shoulders. She wasn't going to mar today with worrying about what may or may not be going on. She had two whole days without James, and she was going to make the most of them.

As she went out of the back door she didn't notice the swirling black mist curl itself around the legs of the table as if searching for something. It moved slowly, snaking its tendrils as if feeling its way and testing the air. As if realising what it was searching for was not there it moved towards the door to the dining room and disappeared into the wooden panelling.

As she entered the garden Susan called the children to her to help her carry the rucksacks. She gave the smallest one with the blanket in it to Emma, the medium one she gave to Robert, and she hefted the largest one onto her own back. After mentally checking that they had everything, Susan led them back down the garden and, after calling over to Jenkins, bade him farewell and said that they would all see him later.

'Watch out for the storm, Mrs Morton,' Jenkins called after them. Susan looked up at the sky. It was still blue, without a cloud to be seen, but perhaps that was the feeling she had picked up on when she was in the kitchen. Perhaps a storm was brewing.

'Thanks, Jenkins,' she replied. 'Hopefully we will be back before any storm breaks.' And with that the trio exited the gate and turned right to access the path that led towards the farmland.

It took them about ten minutes of walking along the lane before they turned left to walk along a rutted track that gave access to the farms. They crossed an old stone bridge and carried on for a short while before they came to a stile, which would take them into one of the fields.

'This is where John Peters works, I think,' Susan said to the children.

Robert nodded. 'Yes, John and Sarah Peters live in one of the cottages down there,' he added, pointing further along the track they had been walking along. 'Some of his nephews and nieces are in our class. They are always very popular when Sarah has been baking,' he added with a wink.

His mother laughed. 'Yes, I'm not surprised. Sarah's short-bread never does last very long, does it?'

'Not when greedy Robert is about, anyway,' his sister added.

'Oi,' Robert said in protest and started to chase his sister across the field. Shrieking with delight, Emma dodged and darted about until Robert finally caught her and tumbled her to the ground and started tickling her. 'Greedy, am I?' he said to her in mock horror.

Susan laughed. 'Come on, you two, you'll spoil the lunch. Last one to the trees is a—' She didn't get to finish her sentence before the children both shot off in the direction of the group of willow trees. *Goodness knows we all needed this*, Susan said to herself as she walked swiftly in the wake of her children.

Feeling pleased that she had not given the children anything breakable or squashable to carry in their rucksacks, she started to unpack the discarded bags. She placed the blanket on the ground and put the other bags on top to hold it in place. Robert and Emma were playing some sort of tag game with each other, swinging around the large trunks of the graceful trees whose boughs dipped towards the water, and the long fronds of their leaves gently swayed in the light breeze.

Susan drew in a deep breath and savoured the sweet summer

air, rich with the scent of grass and the hedgerow flowers. It was so peaceful there that she could almost forget how stressful and burdened her life had become while sitting in this secluded spot, watching her children play with carefree abandon.

She took her sketch pad out of one of the bags and began to draw. Each stroke of the pencil acted to soothe the tension that had accumulated in her shoulders and neck. She leant against the trunk of the tree under which she had positioned their picnic site and sighed.

She looked down at her sketch and smiled. How long had it been since she had done anything like this? Her life had become filled with nonsense and falseness, and everything had been engineered to fuel James's career.

Her own life had become empty, a sham of the promise that it could have been. She had given up her own identity and instead accepted the mantle of an identity thrust upon her that bore no relation to her true self. What had she been thinking? She had become so brainwashed that she had had no space to think clearly. No wonder James had become impatient with her. She had become insipid.

No, she said clearly to herself. There was no excuse for James's behaviour towards her. Yes, she had allowed it to become this bad. But when he was so angry it was difficult to stand up for herself, as that would make things worse. She needed to make a plan to leave. She needed to confide in someone and get advice. But who? Oh, why was it all so difficult? She would do it later. No point spoiling the picnic and this precious time with her children.

Susan turned her attention back to the children. They were walking along the bank, stopping every now and again to pick something up. They were probably collecting pebbles, she thought. She looked at her watch. It was 11.45, and by the time she had set out the picnic and called the children over it would be more or less time to have their lunch. She was glad she had wrapped up a damp cloth in a tea towel as they would probably have very mucky hands and would need, at the very least, to wipe them clean before they started eating.

Satisfied that everything was to her liking, she called the children and they came bounding over to her with their pockets full of their finds, which they proceeded to show their mother, who looked at every item with interest before passing them the damp towel to wipe their hands on and handing them both a plate. 'Tuck in, then,' she said to them, and they did not need to be told twice.

Once they had eaten their fill Susan told them to go and play for a bit while she cleared up the debris that remained from their enthusiastic plundering of the picnic.

As she was just putting the last items back into the rucksacks a cloud passed over the sun, swallowing up the dappled brightness that speckled the ground underneath the tree. When she glanced up Susan noticed that the sky was bruised with dark grey clouds that seemed to have risen out of nowhere. *Jenkins was right*, she said to herself as she jumped to her feet and hastily shook out the blanket before folding it and stowing it deftly in the last rucksack.

Thinking that they would be lucky to get back home without a complete soaking, Susan called the children to come quickly – just as an ominous rumble rippled the sky above, followed moments later by a bright flash of lightning. Robert grinned and Emma cowered. Susan loved storms, but not particularly when she was out in them with no cover and with two children in her care.

The rain started to fall in slow heavy drops. 'Quick,' Robert called, grabbing his rucksack and heaving it onto his shoulders before helping his sister on with hers, 'Let's run to Sarah and John Peters's house. Sarah is bound to be in, and we can shelter there. She might even give us some shortbread.'

Before Susan could respond Robert had darted off across the field, dragging his sister behind him. Susan followed at a slower jog, wondering to herself how Robert could think he had space for any more food after all he had eaten already.

As they reached the stile the heavens opened, and the rain came down so heavily that they could hardly see where they were going. It was hitting the ground so hard that it was bouncing back up, and the potholes in the track were already filling with water. They were absolutely soaked to the skin and the thunder was cracking so loudly above them that it felt as though the sky itself was about to fall upon them. Bright flashes of lightning lit the sky and forked down into the field beside them. Shrieking in terror, Emma grabbed her mother's hand and the three of them ran up the lane towards the group of three cottages huddled at the side of the road next to the huge barn that belonged to the farm.

As they reached the gate of the first cottage Robert threw it open and ran to the door, pounded on it with his small fists and shouted for Sarah to let them in. Almost immediately the door was wrenched open and John Peters stood there, filling the door frame with his huge frame. He ushered them inside and shut the door quickly behind them. The three of them stood in the middle of the quarry-tiled kitchen floor with the rain running off them in rivulets. They looked like a trio of half-drowned kittens.

Emma and Robert shook their heads, and droplets of water

flew across the room and all over John Peters. Sarah appeared in the doorway to one of the other rooms that led off the small kitchen and, hands on hips, looked at the group and said, 'Well, what do we have here? John, why are you just standing there like a big lump? Go and get some towels. I will put the kettle on and make you all a hot drink. Poor things, you'll catch your death.'

Galvanised into action, but still not having uttered a word, John Peters went off in search of towels while Sarah bustled about and filled the large kettle with water and placed it on the stove to boil. Pools of water had already started to collect around the soaked Morton family by the time John Peters had hurried back into the room with an assortment of towels.

He handed one to each of the dripping visitors. Sarah took Emma's towel and helped her to dry her hair, while Susan and Robert dried themselves the best they could. 'Thank you so much for this,' Susan said apologetically. 'It is really kind of you.'

'Nonsense,' Sarah replied. 'You couldn't have walked all the way home in this, now, could you?' She handed the towel back to Emma and the young girl started to rub at her wet clothes to try and soak up some of the water.

The rain continued to lash down against the windows. The wind had also got up, and the sound of it howling around the cottage and down the chimney made the group stare at each other. Another flash of lightning lit up the room and a crash of thunder made Emma squeal. 'Come and sit yourselves down by the fire,' Sarah said. 'The kettle is boiled so I'll soon have some tea made, and I'll find some shortbread for you all.'

Grinning at his mother and sister in an 'I told you so' kind of way, Robert moved closer to the fire. John Peters was still quiet. Sarah glanced over at him, concern etched on her face, and said, 'Our John is not keen on storms, are you, love?'

John just shrugged his shoulders and busied himself by taking back the now soaking wet towels and placing them on the table. His wife tutted at him and took the towels, and after taking a wooden clothes horse out from behind the overstuffed sofa she erected it in front of the fire and started to place the towels on it to dry. 'He was caught in a storm just like this years and years ago when he was out fishing. Just a lad he was, but a young boy was hurt. Storms have made him nervous ever since.'

'Aye,' was the only comment John made as he took the mug of tea proffered to him by his wife and settled himself in one of the pair of armchairs that graced the room. As his thoughts drifted back to the day in question he rubbed a weathered hand across his face and eyes and took a long sip of tea, as if to bring himself back to the present.

CHAPTER 19

1936

John and Jimmy Jenkins raced over to Tom, who was lying perfectly still. The rain was bouncing off his prone body, such was its force, and creating rivulets in the sandy ground. 'What do we do?' wailed John, his face stricken. 'Is he even breathing? Is he dead?' The last came out as almost a whisper.

Jenkins looked closely at Tom's young body. His chest was rising and falling, but with very shallow movements. 'Help me lift him up,' Jenkins shouted above the noise of the storm. The wind was whipping through the trees and the rain was lashing down so hard that it almost obliterated the sound of the thunder that still rumbled overhead. The angry sky was splitting every now and then with more flashes of lightning.

The pair of them lifted Tom and, between them, laid him on the handcart. 'I'm not sure whether it will be faster to run with him over my shoulders or to pull him on this,' Jenkins called out to John. After considering this for a moment, John Peters seemed to come to the conclusion that once the cart was out of the sandy soil they could get up a faster speed with their injured young charge on the cart than if one or other of them carried him, and that he would also get jostled around a lot less.

'Maybe one of us should run ahead and make sure that Dr Winter knows what has happened and is available,' Jenkins said. 'Do you think I should do that or you?'

'You run ahead, and I'll get him there as quickly as I can. Let's wrap the picnic blanket over him to keep off the worst of the rain.' Jenkins grabbed the blanket, and after tucking it carefully round Tom he ran to the gate and wedged it open with a stone before coming back to help John drag the cart through the wet sand.

Once they were through the gate the ground was much firmer, so it was much easier for one of them to pull the cart on their own. After closing the gate, Jenkins edged past John and the cart and set off up the track as if the very hounds of hell were after him.

Jenkins ran down the lane as fast as his legs would go. His breathing was hard and his muscles were screaming, but he bade them no attention. The rain was sheeting down, the sky was dark under the leaden clouds and the noise from the combination of the rain and the thunder was immense.

He reached the garden gate and swung himself into the grounds. He ran straight through the orchard and splashed up the lawn. He could see that there was a light on in the drawing room and made straight for the room, all thoughts of propriety forgotten. He grabbed the metal handle and threw the door open wide. Dr Winter was in the drawing room looking in his bag for some item or other. He looked up with a start as the door was flung open, bringing with it a sodden gardener and the full force of the storm, which was blowing an absolute gale by now.

'Jenkins,' he exclaimed. 'Whatever is the matter—?' He broke off on seeing the look of sheer panic and misery on the young man's face. Dr Winter spoke in a calm but urgent tone now. 'Jenkins, tell me slowly what has happened.'

Jenkins, his hands on his thighs, was bent over, trying desperately to catch his breath. Rain was pooling on the fine Axminster carpet, and he knew that there would be absolute hell to pay when Miss Louisa spotted it. He shook his head to clear the hair from his eyes, sending droplets of water all over the room. 'It's Tom', he managed finally. 'The storm... We were just packing up and he held up one of the rods – high, like – before we could stop him. He didn't know. He didn't realise the danger, see?'

Dr Winter studied the young man's face before replying. 'Jenkins, what happened? Where is Tom?'

'The lightning. I think he got struck by lightning.' Jenkins's face was ashen now. 'John Peters is bringing him on the cart. I said I'd run ahead to make sure you were here'.

Dr Winter ran from the room, through the hall and out into the cloakroom. He grabbed his mackintosh and re-entered the drawing room. Hearing all the commotion, Louisa left the dining room where she had been putting finishing touches to the table decorations for her dinner party. She was determined that the evening was going to be perfect and that it would elevate her status as a hostess to be reckoned with. She had been enjoying herself enormously, despite the vile weather outside, and was glad that she had made Jenkins pick the flowers for her before he went out on his day off.

Louisa entered the drawing room to see a soaking wet carpet and her husband and Jenkins about to exit through the French windows.

Louisa stood hands on hips and called after the men. 'What one earth is happening? Edward, the carpet... Our guests will be arriving soon... Where are you going?'

But her words fell on deaf ears as the door was flung shut behind them to stop any more of the storm forcing its way into the house. Immediately a fresh sheet of rain was flung against the double doors with a strong gust of wind. A long bright flash of lightning illuminated the garden just long enough for

Louisa to make out three figures at the very end of the lawn and some sort of trolley or cart.

Tutting to herself, Louisa flounced out of the room. Well, Edward was just going to have to pass whatever emergency had happened onto his locum. She had insisted that he engage the services of a locum for the evening as she was determined that the party would be perfect, and her husband being called away for some emergency or another did not factor into her success.

Louisa flounced back through the dining room to the kitchen to check on the final preparations that Maggie and her specially recruited assistants were putting together. It was a hive of activity in there, and warm from the heat of the ovens despite the chilly air outside.

The rain could be heard above the chatter of the team of women and the low volume of the radio as it hurled itself relentlessly against the windows. The flashing lightning was occasionally accompanied by loud cracks of thunder. 'My, will you just listen to that?' Maggie said, her hands on her hips and her head on one side. 'That is some storm. I've not heard the like for many a year. I'm glad I'm not venturing out into that any time soon.' Her small team all nodded and muttered their agreement.

Louisa's thoughts suddenly turned to her husband and to Jenkins, who had run out into the garden and were at this very moment out in this tempest.

Before she could utter a word of response Jenkins came crashing into the kitchen and skidded to a halt in front of the group of women. 'Now, Jimmy,' said Maggie, 'Where's the fire?' Panting and gasping for breath, Jenkins couldn't speak for a moment and just stood there, water dripping from him and creating pools at his feet on the tiled floor.

After regaining his senses he spoke, the fear and worry evident on his face and in the words which tumbled from his mouth. 'It's Tom,' he managed. 'Dr Winter says we need hot-water bottles, blankets, boiling water—' He broke off, trying to remember the list of items the doctor had instructed him to seek. Maggie started to fill the large kettle as she threw her own questions back at him.

'What has happened to Tom?' she asked gently, but with urgency in her voice.

'It were the lightning,' Jenkins croaked. 'Master Tom was hit by lightning.' And with that Jenkins sank down into one of the hard wooden kitchen chairs and sat there staring into space, his face drained of all colour, his clothes and hair still continuing to drip water onto the floor around him.

Maggie turned to Louisa and her team. 'Right. The blankets are upstairs in the cupboard on the first floor. Louisa, would you mind getting some? We can see to the rest down here.' She turned to one of the women in her team. 'Mary, young Jimmy Jenkins here is in shock. Make him a cup of strong sweet tea.'

Louisa bristled slightly at being given instructions from Maggie, but did not want to lose face in front of the other women by making a point. Besides, it was hardly the time to pull rank. She decided to speak to Maggie about it later, after the dinner party perhaps.

The dinner party… *For goodness' sake*, she said angrily to herself, *what on earth is going to happen with that?*

All her efforts and planning… She couldn't expect Edward to get a locum to tend his only son. That really would be going a bit too far.

She angrily stomped up the stairs. Wondering what all the noise and commotion was about, Cassy put her head out of her bedroom door. Louisa called to the girl. 'Cassy, come and make yourself useful. That pest of a brother of yours seems to have somehow managed to get struck by lightning and the whole of downstairs is in a hubbub.' Cassy looked at Louisa with a mixture of shock and horror on her young face.

Not particularly caring what Cassy thought, Louisa stormed past her and flung open the door of one of the cupboards situated in the corridor, and after grabbing an armful of blankets she turned and walked back down the stairs to the drawing room.

After plastering what she hoped would pass for a concerned look on her face, Louisa walked into the drawing room to find Tom lying on one of the sofas. He was soaking wet and as white as a sheet. John Peters stood at the side of the room looking completely forlorn.

Edward was gently removing Tom's sodden clothes and, as he saw Louisa approach, he held his hand out for the blankets. 'Louisa,' he said quietly, 'please can you ask the girls in the kitchen to find some towels and make a hot drink for Peters here?.' He nodded towards the young man. 'Why don't you go into the kitchen? Maggie will sort out some clothes for you both and get those wet things dried for you.'

Then Edward immediately turned his attention back to his son. Tom's breathing was shallow, and he was still unconscious. Once Edward had finished removing his wet clothes he wrapped him gently in the blankets. Mary entered the room with a couple of hot-water bottles and Edward asked her to light the fire, which was set ready in the grate. 'We need to get him warm,' Edward said to no one in particular.

Tom stirred and groaned. Edward was immediately at his side. He took his small hand in his and rubbed it gently. 'Tom,' he whispered, 'can you hear me? Everything is going to be all right.'

There was a muffled sob. Edward looked up to see that his daughter had entered the room. She looked stricken. Edward beckoned her over to his side. 'Cassy, can you sit here with Tom while I go and get my bag from my study?' Cassy just nodded, great sobs escaping from her. She pushed her long blonde hair out of her eyes and took her father's place at Tom's side and held his hand. She had never really had that much time for her younger, annoying sibling, but she vowed to be kinder to him and make more time for him if he came round safely.

Edward walked out of the drawing room and into his study to get his bag so that he could better aid his son. As he did so he caught sight of Louisa standing in the corner of the hall looking out into the darkness. 'He'll be OK, Louisa,' he said, mistaking her look of misery for concern over Tom. She turned to face her husband. Her expression was bleak. 'I suppose we will have to cancel the party now,' she muttered.

Not trusting himself to speak, Edward just turned away from his wife and, shaking his head, walked into his study, grabbed his bag and returned to the drawing room to tend to his injured child.

Louisa bit her lip. She realised that she should not have spoken those words out loud. It was obvious that they could not have guests come now, not with Tom hurt, but she felt as if he had stolen her moment from her.

Resentment bubbled up from deep inside her. She clenched her hands, and it took all her strength not to bang her fists against the window and throw her head back and howl at the injustice of it all. Instead, she turned and walked sedately upstairs to start to make the calls informing her guests that there would be no party being held at her home this evening.

At that moment there were two bright flashes and a crash as lightning struck the roof of the house and one of the trees and the gate at the bottom of the garden, and then the house was plunged into instant darkness.

CHAPTER 20

1973

As she sat by the fire that Sarah had stoked up to a roaring blaze while waiting for the kettle to boil on the stove, Susan started to feel the warmth permeating through her body. She was still very wet, but out of the wind it was not actually that cold. The rain still fell in lashing sheets, which hit the windows with an angry fierceness that made Susan all the more grateful for the hospitality offered freely to them by this kind old couple. Sarah had found her ready tin of baked sustenance and the children were greedily tucking into shortbread, their obvious delight verbally acclaimed in the loud oohs and aahs coming from their direction. Susan and Sarah exchanged a glance and smiled.

'Whatever were you doing, having a picnic with the storm coming?' Sarah asked, while adopting her customary stance of her hands on her hips with her head slightly cocked to one side. 'Didn't Jimmy warn you before you left?'

Susan stopped, her mug of tea halfway to her mouth, and looked at the older woman in astonishment. She laughed as she replied, 'How did you know, Sarah?' She added, 'Jenkins did warn me that a storm was coming. I just couldn't see it. The sky was so blue. Not a cloud in sight.'

'Ah,' Sarah replied, 'we country folk have our ways and means. Isn't that right, John?' John Peters, who was sitting in his chair and busily reading something that looked like some sort of farming journal, obviously had half an ear on the conversation, for he nodded his head and muttered 'Aye,' as his response.

Sarah waved a tea towel at her husband. 'Oh, John Peters, ever the great conversationalist.' John merely grinned and resumed his intense scrutiny of his paper.

Sarah offered the tin of shortbread to Susan, who took a piece with thanks and started to nibble on it absent-mindedly. These local people were so much kinder and friendlier than the crowd that James had her encouraged to mix with. Why on earth had she not seen this before?

She thought ruefully that she had been brought up in the same sort of circles that James now insisted that she mixed with, so had never realised. Nor had she witnessed the lives of those less fortunate than herself.

But, she suddenly thought, who was more fortunate? Her, for having the trappings of apparent luxury, but all the time being bereft of kindness and friendship? Or these much simpler folk, whose lives were not measured by material trappings? Their lives were shared, and were based on true, deep-rooted kindness and love.

She shook herself mentally. This was no time to give into feelings of self-pity. She had chosen her life and she would have to get herself out of it.

Sarah, watching the younger woman's face, saw the play of emotions carry out over her delicate features. She knew that her life was troubled. Jimmy and John had been and still were best friends, and stories were carried back to her from the goings-on at the Morton residence.

There was no judgement on Sarah's part. She understood only too well the confines that marriage could bring to women's lives. Not her own, though. She had been so very lucky with her wonderful, kind husband. But her father had been a tyrant, unkind and spiteful, and she, her siblings and her poor dear mother had suffered terribly under his wicked hand.

She saw the same look of fear mixed with guilt and desperation etched in the fine lines of Susan's face and in the way she carried herself and the careful way in which she spoke, always guarded and on edge, as if to reveal too much could bring instant retribution tumbling down upon her.

She wanted to be able to help the troubled woman, but also understood that she would have to find her own way to escape. She would make it understood, however, that should she ever need it, Susan had a solid and dependable friend in her.

Unaware of Sarah's scrutiny of her, Susan continued to nibble on the shortbread. So engrossed in her own thoughts was she that she scarcely registered the play of sugary, buttered ecstasy that unfolded on her tongue.

She was suddenly jolted back into the present by Emma exclaiming loudly to her, 'Mummy, I told you that Sarah makes the very best biscuits ever, didn't I?'

Laughing, and suddenly awakening to the delight of the tastes in her own mouth, she acknowledged that her daughter was absolutely correct and thanked Sarah profusely for her kind hospitality and amazing baking skills. After waving away the high praise with a flap of her hands Sarah smiled gratefully and wondered how best to offer this lovely young woman and her children her and her husband's unconditional support without making her feel uncomfortable.

Sarah thought for a moment while she busied herself at the kitchen sink. She turned to face Susan. Then, while wiping her wet hands on her ever-present apron and looking squarely at the younger woman, she said, 'Have you ever thought about taking the children away for a holiday?'

Taken aback by the sudden question, Susan offered a faltering response. 'I, er, that is to say, um…' She bit her lip, not knowing really how to respond to the question. She desperately yearned to go on a family holiday, but James was always too busy and only ever wanted to stay in swanky hotels, which would not really be much fun for the children. Nor did he like to spend much time with the children and showed no interest in them when he was forced to, because it always put him in a bad mood.

'Er, James doesn't really have time for holidays.' She decided that this was the best response that she could make without going into the nitty-gritty of all the underlying reasons.

Sarah smiled. 'Well,' she said, hands on hips in that customary stance she seemed to always adopt before imparting some snippet of wisdom or other. 'James doesn't have to go with you, does he? My sister and her husband have a lovely farm in West Sussex, and they would be more than happy to have you stay with them. The children would love the space and the animals, and you could help my sister if it made you feel better. There is always work to be done on a busy farm, and she could show you what to do, so you wouldn't need to worry about that.'

Susan felt excitement well up inside her. It wouldn't answer all her problems regarding where to go to escape the awful situation she was in, but it would give her respite and time to think. Sarah watched the battle of emotions once again and stepped in before Susan could decline the offer.

'The children still have at least four weeks or so before they go back to school, is that right?' Susan nodded meekly. 'Well, then,' Sarah continued, 'I will write to Joyce today and we can make arrangements.'

Susan thought for a moment about what James would have

to say about this latest development, but realised that she didn't actually care. If the worst came to the worst, she would go straight to her parents' home after the holiday and they would just have to accept that she could not stay with James a moment longer. Buoyed up by the thought of being able to escape her awful life, Susan nodded her acceptance and thanked Sarah profusely.

Just at that moment the sun broke through the clouds and shone directly into the cottage, brightening everything it touched. It must be a sign, both women thought, independently of each other.

After a while, as the rain had also stopped, Susan gathered the children and their bags together and they had a soggy walk home. It was only about twenty minutes or so and they were very nearly dry by then, but Susan had decided that they were all going to have a nice warm bath before she started to cook the soup for their tea.

The children jumped in and out of puddles, their faces wreathed in beaming smiles, and the sight and sound of their obvious happiness lifted Susan's spirits even more. She felt lighter than she had in months. Today was turning into one of the best days she had had for a very long time.

The children had chattered and played nicely the whole way home and the sun was dazzling against the rain-soaked leaves, bouncing off the path and glinting on stones and windows as they made their way towards home. Susan felt calm and peaceful as they reached the garden gate.

She reached out her hand to push the gate open but then jumped back suddenly, as if she had received some sort of electrical shock. She rubbed her hand against the damp leg of her trousers and looked at her palm. There was a slight red mark, but that could have been caused by her rubbing her hands, she supposed.

The children looked at her quizzically. 'What's the matter, Mum?' Robert asked, a slight look of concern crossing his face. He looked from his mother to the gate and back again.

'Er, I'm not sure, darling,' Susan replied. She moved her hand towards the gate slowly and then retracted it again, deciding to err on the side of caution, and pushed the gate open with the toe of her shoe instead. The gate opened innocently enough, and they passed through it.

Susan kicked it gently shut with her foot again and thought she should go and speak to Jenkins, to see if he could explain what might have caused the sudden shock she had just received – that is, if she hadn't imagined it. So many strange things were happening at the moment, and the electrical storm that they had been caught in could have something to do with it, she supposed.

The children ran down towards the house, obviously intent on beating each other in some swiftly concocted game of chase. As Susan neared the house she looked up at the windows. The sun was glinting off the uppermost panes of glass and reflecting its golden, burnished tones down towards her. She thought she caught a slight movement from Emma's room, but with the glare she could not really determine anything definitively.

She heard Jenkins before she saw him. He was whistling some undefined melody as he pushed a wheelbarrow round the side of the house. He stopped when he saw her and rested the wheelbarrow on the ground. 'I see you got caught in the storm,' he said, by way of a greeting. He took off his cap and rubbed his forehead before replacing it firmly on his head. 'That was one hell of a storm. I expected to see you much soggier than you appear. Did you manage to find some shelter somewhere? Not under a tree, I hope?'

Susan laughed. They had all had that warning drummed into them as children about not sheltering under trees in a storm. 'No, Jenkins,' she said and smiled. 'Robert ran up to Sarah and John Peters's cottage and they kindly allowed us to take refuge with them for the remainder of the storm. It was not too much of a hardship, as Sarah had some of her wonderful shortbread on hand.'

Now it was Jenkins's turn to smile back at his boss's wife. 'Ah, yes, the famous shortbread. My, John is a lucky man.'

He made to pick up the handles of the wheelbarrow again to carry on with his work, but Susan stopped him with her next question. 'Er, Jenkins,' she started hesitantly. Jenkins waited patiently for her to continue. 'When we came back just now, when I went to open the gate, as soon as I touched it, I got what felt like some sort of shock. What on earth do you think could have caused that? Do you think it could have anything to do with the storm?'

Jenkins looked at Susan, confusion and concern etched on his face. He rubbed at his chin with his thumb and forefinger and looked off into the middle distance, remembering a night a long, long time ago. 'I'm not rightly sure, Mrs Morton. I will take a look, though, to see if it's anything dangerous.'

And with that he took up his wheelbarrow and made his way towards the end of the garden. All the while the events of long ago were playing through his mind like a horror film.

Upstairs in Emma's room, the curtains moved slightly as Tom got up from the window seat, where he had been watching and listening to the conversation being played out below him in the garden, and left the room.

CHAPTER 21

1936

Louisa screamed as everything around her went dark. She had not yet started to climb the stairs, so was still in the hall. She had never liked the dark. Even now, as an adult, it unnerved her. She inched her way from the staircase and started to feel her way across the room. The drawing room door was ajar and there was a small amount of light coming through from the fire. She heard Maggie's comforting voice telling everyone not to worry, that she had plenty of candles and she was bringing them now.

Louisa wondered for a moment whether the phone lines would be down as well. How on earth was she going to be able to let her guests know about the party being cancelled? Everything was turning into one disaster on top of the next.

She made it to the door of the drawing room just as Maggie bustled through from the dining room holding what seemed like armfuls of candles. They must have been left over from the war, Louisa thought mirthlessly.

The sight of Maggie's completely unflappable stout figure carrying armfuls of candles made the rest of the company relax. She set a couple in the candlesticks on the sideboard in the drawing room, where everyone seemed to have congregated, and struck a match from the box she had retrieved from one of the drawers. The flame hissed into life and flared against the wick.

Maggie lit the second candle from the same match and then handed some more candles around to the others. She ushered the girls out of the drawing room to give Dr Winter and Tom some space and called the lads after her to come and get something warm to eat and drink in the kitchen

Louisa lifted the telephone off the cradle and listened but there was no dialling tone. 'The line's dead,' she said dully to her husband, who remained crouched down by Tom's head.

Edward raised his head towards his wife. 'Sorry… What was that, Louisa?' he asked distractedly.

'I was just saying that the telephone line is dead,' she repeated. 'I was going to telephone our guests to cancel this evening.'

'Oh, yes,' he responded quietly. 'The party… Well, I shouldn't worry, Louisa. No one with much sense will be going out tonight in this monsoon. The roads will be flooded, and no one will be getting from the village up here tonight anyway. You know how the river always bursts its banks on the road into town.'

Louisa bit her lip. She was trying hard to hold back the tears. She had put so much effort into this evening and it was now all ruined. She was so furious with Tom that she didn't really consider that the storm would have most likely put paid to this evening anyway.

Tearfully she turned away from her husband and left the room in search of Maggie to see what could be done with all the wonderful food that had been cooked. It would be such a waste, but she hardly wanted the likes of the gardener and the hired help to profit from her loss. She would rather see it go in the bin.

However, when she entered the kitchen, she saw to her abject horror and disgust that Jenkins and John Peters as well as the kitchen helpers were tucking into parts of the lavish meal that was supposed to have been being served to her guests.

She stood in the doorway, her hands on her hips and exclaimed in a loud voice, 'Well.' The five young people sat around the kitchen table stopped and looked at her in shock, forks suspended in mid-air. 'What on earth is going on here?' Louisa demanded, anger making her voice shrill.

Maggie wiped her hands on the tea towel she held in her hands and placed it down on the side with deliberate care. 'Now, Louisa,' she started, but Louisa was having none of it.

'Don't you "Louisa" me,' she spat. 'It's Mrs Winter to you, Maggie Graves, and don't you forget it.'

Maggie eyed her calmly, but her eyes were like flint. 'OK, Mrs Winter,' she continued, ice dripping from every word. 'These young men are soaked to the skin. They have very likely saved young Tom's life and Dr Winter asked me to feed them and the girls, who will have to most likely wade part way home tonight. The food will otherwise be going to waste, what with the party being cancelled, so would you rather have me put it in the bin or feed it to these kind people?'

Louisa's face reddened as she held back the retort that she would very much rather see it put in the bin or fed to the pigs on John Peters's employer's farm than be eaten by these people, who she deemed unworthy to grace even her kitchen table.

Instead she turned on her heel and stormed out of the kitchen and back through the dining room to go up to her room. In her haste to leave she had forgotten to ask for some candles to light her room, but pride forbade her from returning. She would just sit in the dark and feel sorry for herself.

Maggie shook her head. She had never really warmed to Louisa when she was the nanny, and now she had just become a rude upstart who was much too big for her boots. The others were still sitting there in suspended animation, forks still poised midway to their lips.

Maggie waved her hand at them. 'Come on, eat up. I don't want my fine food to be wasted now.' They didn't need telling twice, and soon the kitchen was again filled with the noise of companionable conversation and the gentle clatter of cutlery on plates. Maggie smiled and thought about Louisa. Something needed to be done about that one, and no mistake.

Back in the drawing room Tom was coming round. His father was perched on the edge of the sofa by his side and was gently patting his hand. Tom looked at his father with unfocused eyes as he fought to make sense of where he was and what had happened. 'Ah, Tom,' his father said in a cheery voice. 'Decided to join us again, have you?' His voice was light as he did his utmost to mask the concern that he naturally felt at the sight of his only son having been injured in such an unpredictable way.

Tom blinked a couple of times to try to clear his vision, but his head swam and a thumping pain seared through him and down his left side. He tried to move but it felt like he was being held in place. He looked inquiringly at his father again.

'Father,' he whispered through parched lips, 'what happened? Why am I here? Why can't I sit up?' Although relieved that his son was speaking coherently, the fact that he seemed unable to move added to the worry. When Edward got up from his sitting position on the side of the sofa, he realised that this apparent paralysis might actually be due to the heavy blankets that were covering Tom, which he had pinned him down with by sitting on them. He folded the blankets back and tried to help his son into a seated position.

Relief flooded through Tom as he realised that it was only

the heavy, weighted blankets that had prevented him from moving, and nothing more sinister. He shuffled back up the sofa into a more comfortable half-sitting position and took a couple of sips from the glass of water that his father had offered to him. Exhausted by this effort, he sank back down and closed his eyes again.

His father squeezed his hand, relieved that it appeared as if Tom would make a full recovery. 'What happened?' Tom asked again sleepily, his eyes still closed, as if opening them was just too much effort.

'It seems like you were too close to a lightning strike,' his father replied. 'It seems to have missed you, or not hit you directly, as I cannot find any actual burns on your body. But it may have struck the fishing rod you were carrying and used your body as a way of earthing itself. You have had a very lucky escape, Tom.'

Being only a young child, Tom did not fully understand the severity of what had happened and what the potential outcome could have been. Besides, he was just too tired and all he wanted to do was to sleep.

As soon as he realised that the best thing for his son would be to sleep, Dr Winter lifted his young boy into his arms and proceeded to carry him up to his bedroom. Maggie had, in her usual efficient manner, lit candles in the hall, the corridor at the top of the stairs and in all the bedrooms that were in use.

Using this gentle light to find his way, Dr Winter walked through the house with his sleeping charge and up to the top rooms, where Tom had badgered him to be allowed to have his bedroom, even though it really was supposed to be for the servants. He nudged the door open with his foot and, while bending down, moved the covers back to reveal a stone hot-water bottle that Maggie must have placed in there to warm the bed.

Smiling in gratitude, he pushed it aside while with the other arm he lowered Tom into the bed. He then pushed the hot-water bottle to the bottom of the bed, where it could continue to do its job. He tucked the covers up around Tom's chin, kissed the top of his head and left the room. He would pop back and check on him regularly through the night. Thank goodness Louisa had insisted on having a locum for this evening, he thought wryly.

Edward went in search of his wife and found her sitting in her room in the dark. He entered the room and he saw her turn to look at him, the side of her face illuminated by the moon, which cast its soft light gently into the room. 'Louisa,' he said gently. 'Whatever are you doing sitting here in the dark?'

He walked towards his wife and extended a hand to her, pulling her to her feet and into an embrace. Louisa allowed herself to be held and rested her head on his shoulder. 'Everything is ruined,' she wailed in a childish, whining tone.

Edward pushed her away so that he could look at her face. 'What do you mean, Louisa? Is this about your dinner party?' he said incredulously. 'There will be other parties,' he continued, trying to sound placatory instead of annoyed, as this was the emotion that was bubbling to the surface. Did she not understand how serious Tom's accident could have been? And the storm… Even if Tom hadn't been injured, how many people would have been able or indeed willing to venture out in that?

Louisa looked at the ground, her face sulky, her arms by her side. 'I know,' she said in a quiet voice. 'I'm sorry, but I just wanted it to all go well … to be accepted by your friends as your wife … to actually be able to do something right for once in their eyes. It feels as though I am cursed.'

Edward looked at her in shock, a hardness stealing into his eyes now, which was matched by the tone of his voice. 'Now, you listen to me, Louisa,' he said, his tone brooking no argument. 'I will not have any such talk in this house, do you understand me?' She nodded, but still did not look him in the eye.

He sighed and, putting his finger under her chin, he gently raised it until she was looking at him. 'Louisa, listen to me,' he said, in a much milder tone. 'You are blowing this all out of proportion. No one thinks badly of you or is judging you in any way. Do you understand me?' She nodded and dropped her eyes to the floor again. He drew her back into a close embrace and lightly brushed the top of her hair with his lips.

Louisa allowed herself to be held by her husband, but as she leant into the embrace and once again rested her head on his shoulder she thought silently to herself that he really did not have a clue about society and how it worked, or even about his own family and the condescending looks that were cast in her direction.

She allowed silent tears to flow down her cheeks and soak into her hair and felt the despair wash over her and thought that she would now have to start all over again.

Chapter 22

1973

Susan walked round the side of the house and into the utility room. She thought she could hear the sound of someone humming quietly. *Perhaps the radio is on*, she said to herself.

Eager to get out of her still damp clothes and into a bath, she hurried into the kitchen, whereupon the noise stopped. Susan faltered, listening hard, her head cocked to one side as she tried to stretch her hearing abilities as far as they could go. Nothing. What on earth was going on? Tired, and getting cold now, she removed her damp shoes and stuffed them with old newspaper, then did the same with the children's discarded footwear and sat all the shoes on the radiator.

After slipping on a well-worn old pair of slippers she walked through the kitchen, into the dining room and out into the hall. The light was starting to fade gently now, and she had not realised quite how late it was. *We could all just have beans on toast for supper*, she thought. She did not have the energy to make soup, with all that chopping involved, and the kids wouldn't care. They would probably rather have beans on toast anyway.

She started to walk up the stairs and froze. It sounded like someone was in the drawing room. She cast her gaze quickly towards the windows in the hall and looked out towards the drive, but she couldn't see James's car.

She walked back down the stairs and padded silently towards the drawing room door, which was slightly ajar. There was a faint glow of light coming from the room. She had not remembered leaving a light on, but what with everything else going on she could hardly remember her own name sometimes.

There it was again, a faint murmuring as if someone was speaking quietly in a very low voice. The hairs on the back of her neck started to rise, but she continued to walk towards the room. As she put her hand on the door and slowly pushed it open the noise stopped. The room was empty, but she shook her head slowly in disbelief as she surveyed the room because there were several lit candles dotted around the room, and they were what was creating the glow of light she had seen from the hall.

Her hand flew to her mouth. How could there be candles? No one else had been in the house. Jenkins would have told her if there had been, and there is no way he would have done this. She saw him walking back down the garden towards the house in the twilight, the dark clouds making it seem darker than it would normally be at this time. She almost ran to the French doors and opened them.

Seeing the distress on Susan's face, Jenkins jogged towards her down the garden. 'Jenkins,' Susan started, the concern etched on her face, 'do you know why there are all these candles in here?' She gestured backwards with the sweep of her arm to indicate the entire room behind her.

Jenkins looked confused. 'Candles?' he said. 'No, Mrs Morton… I mean … I have no idea.' He moved towards her, up the steps onto the terrace, and looked through the doors into the drawing room beyond.

It was dark. There were no candles to be seen anywhere, but he could smell the telltale scent of the candles that had just been extinguished. Susan had joined him by then, and on seeing that the candles, which only moments before had burnt brightly, were no longer in evidence, she looked up at Jenkins with fear blazing in her eyes.

'Jenkins, they were there, I swear.' Jenkins did not know what to say. There were no candles there now, but he could definitely smell that there had been. He knew that strange things were going on, what with his old fishing float appearing from nowhere, the shock that Susan had had from the gate earlier, and now this. It made him shudder, and it took his thoughts back all those years ago to Tom's accident.

Seeing how white Susan Morton had gone he decided to throw caution to the wind, and he took her arm and steered her back along the terrace and into the kitchen. He pulled out a chair and gently lowered her into it, and then after filling the kettle he placed it on to boil and grabbed a couple of mugs and the teapot. Once he had finished he turned to face her. Susan still had a shocked look on her pale face, but she lifted her eyes to meet him and said, 'What on earth is happening here, Jenkins? Do you have any clue?'

Jenkins leant back against the cooker with his feet crossed at the ankles and blew out a long, slow breath. 'No, I don't know what is going on, but certain things seem to be mirroring events that happened a long time ago. I was here then too. And it were a right bad time, I don't mind admitting it.'

Susan continued to stare at him, giving him silent permission to continue. 'I still don't fully understand what happened, but it weren't good,' he continued, in his calm and gentle manner. 'But as to why strange things are happening now, I couldn't say.' Susan nodded and sipped her tea. The house had always seemed kind, somehow, to her.

James had never really liked the house, although he had been the one who decided that they should buy it. But that was more to do with the prestige of owning a large house than anything else. She however, had always felt safe and sort of protected by the house, which she realised was rather fanciful. But, nevertheless, that is how she felt.

Drinking the tea provided by Jenkins had started to fortify her and she decided that whatever was happening, strange though it may be, did not seem to be threatening. It was rather disconcerting, and candles being lit on their own could prove a potential fire hazard, but apart from that she realised that she didn't feel at risk. Actually, James frightened her more than anything the house could throw at her.

She smiled at Jenkins. 'Thanks, Jenkins. You have been very kind. I am sure that I will be all right now.'

Jenkins nodded at her. 'Well, you know where I am if you need me,' he said, and with that he ambled out into the dark and off towards his flat over the garage.

Starting to feel chilled now, Susan went upstairs and started running a bath for the children before running one for herself. Once the children were dry and dressed she went into her bathroom and ran herself a bath. She wished that she could lie in it forever, letting the silky bubbles soak away the stresses of her life with them as the warmth of the water soothed her aching muscles. She was so tense all the time that it couldn't be good for her.

After stepping out of the bath she grabbed a towel and quickly dried herself and got dressed. Feeling better for being warm and dry, Susan called the children as she descended the stairs and retraced her steps back towards the kitchen. No strange sounds greeted her this time, and she switched the radio on and was pleased to hear that a play was just starting.

She cut some slices of bread, slotted them into the toaster, and set a pan of beans on the stove to bubble gently as she grated some cheese. The children came into the room just as Susan finished setting the table. She was humming gently to herself and realised once again how much happier she felt, just knowing that James was not going to be coming home. The children too seemed to be more relaxed. She spooned the beans onto the hot buttered toast and pushed it in front of the children, poured them both a glass of milk and settled down beside them with her own steaming plate and cup of tea.

'Tomorrow we are going to visit those nice children you played with at the park,' Susan said to them. Both children looked at her in stunned silence with their mouths open. They looked at each other, still not speaking. Both of them were thinking that they never met up with the village children apart from Jennifer, Phillipa and Richard, and they had not seen them for over a week after Emma's accident, as they were probably grounded for the rest of their lives.

Robert spoke first. 'OK,' he said hesitantly. 'We don't really know them very well, though, Mum.' Susan smiled. She could sense what they were both thinking, and she realised that due to her constant fear of her husband's snobbish censorship the children had missed out on making many local friends. Well, she would see what she could do about that in future.

'It's time you made some more friends,' Susan said. 'Jenny, Pippa and Richard are lovely, but the village is full of children and I know none of the mothers, and don't really have that many friends of my own, so I think now is as good a time as any to start making some, don't you?'

Wondering what on earth had come over their mother, they both stared at her as if she were about to sprout a tail or donkey ears or something equally as strange, and just nodded mutely with wide-eyed astonishment. Once they had finished their tea Susan shooed them off to play for half an hour or so before they went to bed and started to clear away the dishes.

As she placed the last dish on the draining board, she wiped her hands on her apron and turned away from the sink. She gasped and her hand flew up to her mouth in shock. Behind her three lit candles were lined up on the dresser, their flames dancing gently in a gentle, unfelt breeze as if mocking her with their gaiety.

As Susan moved towards the candles to blow them out she heard the ominous rumble of thunder in the distance, and with a bright flash of lightning a sheet of rain hit the windowpane so hard it sounded like someone had picked up a handful of gravel and flung it at the glass.

Eager to be out of the kitchen, she moved through the dark dining room and into the hall, but as she reached the hall the lights flickered ominously. Susan looked up at the lights fearfully. She would have to go and get some candles in case the electricity cut out because of the storm – which, of course, were in the kitchen.

Cursing under her breath, she retraced her steps back towards the kitchen. As she walked towards the kitchen door she thought she caught sight of someone walking into the kitchen. She rubbed her eyes. She really was starting to go mad, she thought.

Cautiously she pushed open the kitchen door and entered the kitchen. It was in darkness, as she had left it. She switched the light on and started to rummage through the dresser drawers for some candles and matches, scooping up the candles from the dresser. She was just closing the door when the lights flickered twice and then went out.

Blast, Susan said to herself, but was glad that she had found the candles while there was still some electric light to guide her. She placed the candles on the table and, holding one, she lit a match and was pleased when the wick caught and flared into life. The flickering light cast dancing shadows on the walls. The light served to soothe her inflamed nerves slightly.

She inhaled deeply. She needed to go upstairs to the children because they would probably be fretting about the power going off too. She put the matches in her pocket and grabbed the unlit candles with one hand so that she could hold the lit candle in the other to guide her way through the house.

A large crack of thunder was accompanied almost immediately by a bright flash of lightning, which illuminated the garden and made it almost as bright as day. As Susan glanced up she saw a figure lit up outside the kitchen window, and she let out a loud, terrified shriek and promptly dropped the candles on the floor.

Jolted out of her fear by the more immediate danger of potentially setting the house ablaze, Susan grabbed the lit candle, which had amazingly stayed alight, and started to retrieve the other candles just as there came a loud knocking on the back door.

Susan jumped again. She put the lit candle on the table and, patting at her chest, she wondered how many more shocks her heart could take. The banging came again, accompanied by Jenkins's concerned voice. Relief washing through her, Susan half-ran to the door. After releasing the bolts and turning the key, she swung the door open to allow Jenkins in. 'Jenkins,' she said in an admonishing tone. 'You nearly gave me a heart attack.'

Jenkins smiled sheepishly. 'I'm sorry,' he replied ruefully.

'Just with the power going out and all I just wanted to check that you were OK, and also to see if I could borrow some candles.'

'I need to go and check on the children,' Susan said. 'There are plenty of candles in the dresser drawer, so help yourself. Would you like a cup of tea once I have settled the children?'

Realising that she really hoped he would say yes, and that she would rather not be on her own at the moment during the storm, which continued to rage unabated outside, and with all the strange things going on in the house, it hit her that she actually felt quite lonely and overwhelmed. Luckily, Jenkins seemed to have realised that she craved some company and agreed, and even started to make the tea as she headed upstairs to check that the children were OK.

When Susan reached the corridor on the first landing, she heard the children calling her. She walked down the corridor towards the large arched window at the foot of the second flight of stairs and opened the door to Robert's bedroom.

She found both her children huddled together under a blanket on Robert's bed. Emma was wide-eyed and a bit tearful, and Robert was doing his best to pretend that he was not afraid of the storm one little bit, but he seemed to look rather relieved to see his mother appear at his bedroom door. 'I've brought you some candles,' Susan said. 'The storm appears to have caused a power cut, that's all. The power will probably be back on soon.'

'Can I stay here with Robert, please, Mum? I promise we won't argue or fight or annoy each other or anything. I'll be really good, and I won't touch his things.'

Susan smiled. 'If Robert doesn't mind,' she started to say, but Robert agreed almost immediately, making Susan realise that he also was afraid of the storm. 'OK. Let me light some of these candles for you. Please don't touch or move them, though, or even go near them.'

It didn't look as if either of them was likely to move from where they were both huddled under the blanket, so she need not really have worried too much. 'Jenkins is downstairs too, so we are quite safe,' Susan said as she lit the candles and made sure they were safe too.

'I will leave the door open, so just call if you need me. I will just be downstairs having a cup of tea with Jenkins and then I will come up to bed, so I will just be down the corridor.'

'OK, Mum,' they both said in unison.

CHAPTER 23

1936

The morning dawned bright and clear. Dr Winter had checked on his son several times during the night and was happy that he was going to make a full recovery. He was now extremely tired, and decided to go and have a quick nap before afternoon surgery. He had telephoned the locum the previous evening and requested that he cover the morning surgery to enable him to get some rest, as he had been up most of the previous night.

He was more troubled, however, by Louisa's behaviour. She seemed to be moodier than ever, and he just did not understand what the matter was. He vaguely realised that society and appearances were important to women, but his mother, sisters and indeed Sophie had all made it look so easy and natural. His father and he had never had to do more than be directed to where to turn up and in what attire.

He sighed. For all her prettiness and nice manners Louisa was becoming hard work, and he had noticed that the staff did not seem to warm to her either. He would have a discreet word with Maggie later and see if she could throw any light on the situation and give him any advice about what he could do. But first he needed a rest before he fell asleep where he stood.

As he rounded the top of the stairs and started to walk along the corridor to the bedroom he shared with Louisa he saw her coming out of the room. He tried to not let the feeling of dismay he felt show on his face. He really did not have the energy for her right now.

Louisa looked at her husband, carefully scanning his face, and saw that it was schooled into the patient expression he reserved for his most tiresome of patients.

She scowled. Really, this was beyond annoying. Her party ruined last night, Tom taking up all his time and most of the night, and now it looked as if he didn't even want to speak to her.

'Edward, we really need to talk about reorganising the party.' Louisa's voice was earnest and slightly whiny. Edward sighed. This was exactly what he had wanted to avoid.

He turned and faced his wife and spoke to her in a voice that really allowed no room for argument. 'Louisa, I am very tired. I have been up all night with Tom, and I must get some rest before afternoon surgery starts. We will have to talk about this another time, or just organise something yourself. I really do not have the energy.'

Louisa nodded but there was a half-smile on her face. It sounded like she had been given free rein to host another party. 'Perhaps you could go and sit with Tom for me while I get some rest.'

Louisa's smile faltered. She had just been about to skip down the stairs and speak to Maggie about getting her new plans in place, but she stopped and turned slowly and walked back past their bedroom and down the corridor to the stairs leading up to Tom's bedroom. Her head was down, but it didn't completely hide the sulky, sullen look on her face. Edward rubbed his hand over his face. He was weary to the bone. He just ignored his wife and went to try and get some sleep.

Louisa walked up the stairs towards Tom's bedroom, trying to contain her anger. She blamed Tom, even though she also realised that the ferocity of the storm would have ensured that the party was cancelled anyway. Her resentment of the time his father had spent with him the previous night also irked her. Edward never seemed to have enough time for her these days.

She heaved a great sigh and pushed open the door to Tom's room. A fire was burning brightly in the grate and the room felt warm and cosy. There was a tray on the small table beside the bed with a half-drunk glass of milk and the crusts from a piece of toast.

Tom was sitting up in bed. His face pale but his eyes were bright. They scanned her face as she entered his room as if gauging her mood. This sent ripples of irritation through her body. She put her hands on her hips and frowned at him. 'Your father wants me to sit with you,' she said with absolutely no warmth and compassion in her voice, which gave Tom the message loud and clear that this was the very last thing Louisa wanted to be doing.

Tom shrank back slightly against his pillows and replied in a small shaky voice. 'It's OK. I am fine. You don't need to sit with me, Louisa. I am sure that you must have lots of other things to do.'

Pleased that she had elicited the response she wanted, Louisa smiled a tight smile, which got nowhere near touching her eyes. 'Right,' she said, and nodded sharply at him. 'I'll send Cassy to look in on you. Maybe you could play a game or something.'

Tom pulled a face but remained quiet. 'It's OK,' he replied. 'I am happy to read my book,' and as if to show Louisa just how fine he was with this, he picked up his battered copy of *Black Beauty* again and started to read.

Louisa turned and walked towards the door. 'I'll send Cassy up anyway. It's time she actually started doing something useful.' And with that she left.

Tom laid his book down on his lap and let out a long breath. *What was my father thinking?* he said to himself. Why one earth would he think that either he or Louisa would want to spend time together? Was he mad? Anyway, he was fine, if not a little tired.

He heard light steps coming up the stairs and turned to face the door just as his sister's cheeky face peered around it. 'You all right, squirt?' she said. 'You had us all scared earlier. You looked like a soggy wet rat. In fact, not much different to normal, then.' They both grinned at each other as she pushed the door open and came and plonked herself on the bed. 'Princess Lah-de-dah asked me to come and sit with you, but I was going to come up anyway. How do you feel?'

Tom's eyes were wide. Had his sister just called Louisa Princess Lah-de-dah? He thought that they were bosom buddies. He looked at her with such astonishment that Cassy burst out laughing. 'What?' she said. 'You didn't think that I actually liked Louisa trying to muscle in on our mother's position, did you? She is not even a slight patch on our mother, Tom. I know that you were tiny when she died but believe me, she was the sweetest, kindest person. Everyone loved her. Louisa, by comparison, is not even slightly close. To be honest, I think Father must have gone slightly mad when our mother died, I really do.'

Tom did not know what to say in response so just said nothing. Cassy, sensing that he was slightly shocked by her words, just leant over and ruffled his hair. 'Come on, then, Tommy, shall we play a game? Let's see what we have, shall we?' And with that she jumped off the bed and started to rummage underneath it and dragged out an old box full of equally ancient board games.

Relieved of her babysitting duties, Louisa went back downstairs in search of Maggie so that she could work out a new plan for a party.

As Louisa entered the kitchen, all smiles and conciliatory manner, Maggie sighed and only just managed to stop herself from eliciting an audible groan. What did she want now? Louisa only ever came to the kitchen if she wanted something, and it usually meant extra work for her, Maggie thought tiredly. Well, she didn't have time for her this morning. She had enough of her regular work to be getting on with, thank you very much.

'Maggie,' Louisa began cheerfully, totally unaware of how unwelcome her presence was, 'we need to discuss plans to arrange another party after yesterday's washout. I will telephone everyone today and arrange another date, but I would like it to be soon. I am not sure how everyone will be fixed, though, as there are so many other events in the diary and we only just managed to squeeze this date in as it was.' She started wringing her hands as Maggie looked on, stoically saying nothing.

Realising that Maggie was not making any comments, Louisa stopped and put her hands on her hips. 'Maggie, are you even listening to me?' she barked in her haughty tone, all smiles and false brightness replaced by her usual condescending manner.

'Yes, Louisa, I am listening to you,' Maggie replied wearily. 'However, I am waiting to hear what it is that you actually want me to do. So far I have not heard any instructions come forth.'

Annoyed by her tone, but realising that what Maggie had said was actually correct, Louisa huffed out an annoyed, 'Well, really,' and flounced from the room. Both women's thoughts about the other were closely matched irritation.

Maggie let out a breath and started to scrub at the kitchen table with more force than was strictly necessary, mumbling her words of irritation under her breath. Jimmy Jenkins walked into the kitchen from the back door and found her thus occupied. 'What on earth has that table done to offend you, Maggie?' he said with a grin, and was rewarded with a wet cloth being thrown in his direction that narrowly missed his face.

Maggie straightened up and smiled back at the young lad. 'I'll give you three guesses,' Maggie replied.

'Nah,' Jimmy replied. 'I'll only need one, and I guess it is Madam Louisa, Queen of the Residence,' he said, grabbing a slice of toast from the plate on the dresser that Maggie had placed there moments before Louisa had entered the kitchen.

'The very same,' Maggie replied, and, picking up a piece of toast herself, she began to chew a piece slowly. 'I still have no idea what Edward was thinking in marrying that one,' she said as she settled herself in the chair at the head of the kitchen table.

Jimmy Jenkins did not reply, but he knew well enough. Louisa was a very attractive woman, but her beauty masked a darkness inside, which he personally would have wanted to stay as far away from as possible. But then he had not lost the love of his life and been left with two young children to care for.

Louisa was filled with a fury that she did not quite understand herself. She wanted to go back upstairs and rant at her husband, but she knew that this would not serve any purpose other than to alienate one more person against her. So she crossed the hall, walked through the drawing room and strode out into the garden. *Why does no one take me seriously and give me the respect I deserve as lady of the house?* she said crossly to herself as she marched down the garden, past the wych elm and into the orchard.

She grabbed the swing that had been crudely fashioned from some rope and a plank of wood and hurled it hard into the tree, which startled a flock of birds into taking flight. She cursed loudly and started to kick at the trunk of the tree until her anger abated. She was panting and a slight sweat was pooling under her breasts and starting to trickle down her back. She did not fully understand these rages, but they seemed to be getting worse.

She needed to get herself back under control before Edward decided to prescribe her some of his medicine for crazy people. She took some huge, gulping breaths and, looking down at her feet, realised that she had completely ruined her shoes. She would need to hide them, she thought, in case anyone wondered what she had been doing.

After smoothing her hands down her legs she retraced her steps back through the garden and sedately re-entered the drawing room. She removed her ruined shoes and, holding them in one hand, walked in stockinged feet up the stairs to her dressing room. She would hide the shoes in her wardrobe until she could wrap them in some newspaper and put them out with the rubbish, she thought. She then decided that she should start to make the necessary telephone calls to apologise for yesterday's cancelled party and try and arrange a new date.

She did not realise that Tom had been watching his stepmother's unbalanced behaviour from his bedroom window and was now more concerned than ever, but he had no idea what to do or who he could even speak to about it. Would they even believe him, being but a child?

He decided to confide in Jimmy Jenkins. Jimmy was nearly an adult, and he was bound to have more of an idea about what to do than he himself would. Even if Jimmy couldn't help him personally, he was sure to know who could.

Feeling a bit better, now that this was decided, Tom pushed

himself off his window seat and went to walk downstairs. However, as he reached halfway down the stairs, Louisa exited her room and shooed him back up into his bedroom, hissing at him under her breath and forbidding him to come downstairs until he had been given express permission from his father, who was currently sleeping.

Tom hung his head and turned slowly to walk back up to his room. Louisa's smug smile of triumph, however, was not missed by him, and he was even more determined to do something about her.

CHAPTER 24

1973

Susan walked back downstairs. She was bone-tired but knew that she wouldn't sleep if she went to bed then. She was jumpy after the power cut and the strange goings-on, and the flickering candle flame was casting huge shadows as she walked back towards the kitchen. It was very quiet and, apart from the flickering light of the candle, the darkness was complete. She was relieved to see Jenkins still in the kitchen when she walked through the door, and even more relieved when she noticed that he had put a huge pan of water on the stove to boil.

She seated herself at the kitchen table as Jenkins put some teabags in the pot and poured in some boiling water. 'I thought you could do with this, lass,' he said and, after adding some milk and the tea to a couple of mugs, he pushed one of the steaming drinks towards her and joined her at the table.

Susan thanked him and nursed the mug in her hands, allowing the comforting warmth to soothe her. 'I just don't know what is happening here, Jenkins. It is one thing after the other. The float, the candles, the gate. What on earth is going on? It's like I'm missing something or the house is trying to get my attention, or...'

She trailed off, thinking that she sounded crazy. Jenkins just watched her with his kind dark eyes. 'Aye,' he said and sipped his tea. 'It's just like being back here all those years ago, what with the storm an' all.'

Susan looked at his face, memories dancing behind sad eyes and furrowed brow. 'What happened, Jenkins?' she said in a voice so quiet that it was almost a whisper. But Jenkins didn't reply and continued to sip his tea as he stared into the middle distance as though lost in thought, drawn back to a time long ago but as though it only happened yesterday, its images burnt so deep into his mind as to forge the very essence of all that had come after.

He shook his head and sighed. 'It was a very long time ago, lass, and it is all best forgotten. Nothing good will come from raking up the past. Not now, with everyone gone now.'

Susan reached over and laid a gentle hand on his arm. 'But you're not gone, Jenkins, are you?' she said quietly.

He raised his face and looked at her, sadness seeping from every pore. 'No,' he said, relenting. 'There's still me, John Peters, Sarah and a few others who remember. Young Cassy is probably still alive too, I expect, though where she might be now I have no idea. The family all left, see.'

Susan had no idea of the history of the local area, really, so didn't know what had happened. And, as Jenkins had said, it was all such a long time ago, before the country and the whole world had gone to war for the second time, the horrors of which eclipsed any local tragedy.

The two of them sat in companionable silence in the candle-light with the flames casting dancing patterns on the ceiling. Each one was lost in their own thoughts as they continued to sip their tea.

Tom stood in the doorway, watching as the swirling dark mist coiled itself around the bottom of the kitchen door and felt its way across the dark floor towards the couple sitting at the table, its smoky tendrils advancing slowly like a snake's tongue tasting the air.

The couple shivered as a cold draught settled around their

feet. Alarmed, they looked at each other and pushed their chairs back in unison just as the lights came back on and the mist evaporated.

Even though the lights had come back on, flooding the room with light and banishing the shadows to the deepest corners, the two of them still looked at each other in shock. Finally, Susan spoke. 'Tell me you felt that, Jenkins. It wasn't just my imagination, was it?'

Jenkins rubbed his chin slowly and nodded. 'Aye, I felt it sure enough.'

Susan gripped the edge of the table hard, and her knuckles stood out sharply against the skin. 'What is going on in this house, Jenkins? I never felt scared of the house, but this feels wrong.'

Jenkins shrugged, lost for words, but concern was etched on his face. 'It feels OK now, though, doesn't it?'

Susan took a deep breath to still her nerves and mentally scanned how she was feeling. Jenkins was right, she thought. The malevolent feeling that they had both felt just moments ago was gone. She shook her head slowly. 'I think that I'll just go to bed. I am meeting some of the local women and their children tomorrow, so I need to try and look less haggard than I probably do right now.' She tried to force a smile onto her lips, but it looked more like a grimace.

Jenkins moved towards the back door and bade her goodnight. But all the while his thoughts were dragged back through time to the horrors of long ago.

Chapter 25

1936

Edward Winter awoke feeling disorientated. He glanced at the clock on the mantelpiece of his bedroom fireplace and saw that it was 11 a.m., and realised that this must be eleven in the morning due to the light coming through the curtains. He threw back the blankets and jumped to his feet.

The memories of the night before came flooding back. He dressed quickly and almost ran up the stairs to his son's bedroom. As he neared the door he heard quiet voices, and hesitated for a moment. It sounded like Cassy, but why was she there when he had asked Louisa to sit with Tom?

He pushed the door open, but not before fixing a determined smile on his face. He was pleased to see that his son was awake and looking much more like himself. He smiled at his daughter and walked over to his son and ruffled his hair gently. 'How are you feeling today, Tom?' he asked.

'Much better, thank you, Father,' Tom replied. Turning to his daughter, Edward looked at her quizzically before asking, 'How come you're up here, love? I thought Louisa was sitting with Tom while I got some rest.'

Cassy just snorted and shrugged her shoulders before turning away. Edward looked at her back for a second before turning to Tom. 'Tom?' he asked gently.

Tom hung his head and looked uncomfortable before replying quietly, 'Louisa did come upstairs, Father, but I think she thought that I would prefer Cassy to be with me than her. I didn't ask her to stay with me, so she went and sent Cassy up instead. We've been playing nicely, Father. We haven't been arguing or anything.'

Seeing that Tom was obviously distressed about something and wanting to reassure him that he had not done anything wrong he said brightly, 'Well, that's all fine, then. Thanks, Cassy, for being such a good nurse to your little brother. It was very kind of you. Your mother would have been very proud of you.'

At the mention of her mother Cassy's cheeks flushed slightly, and she felt puffed up with pride at her father's kind words.' 'Thank you,' she replied shyly. 'It was not any bother at all. We had a nice time, really. I didn't sit with him the whole time, though,' she added quickly, being an inherently honest child. 'I did go downstairs for a bit when Tom looked tired but came back up again after about an hour.'

Realising from her statement that Louisa must have told Cassy to go and look after her brother instead of herself as Edward had requested made him irritated. What was the matter with Louisa at the moment? Surely a simple request to sit with his son while he got some rest was not too much to ask. She had been the children's nanny, for goodness' sake. It wasn't an arduous task.

Sensing his daughter's unease, he realised that the emotions he was feeling must have been playing out on his face so he put a reassuring hand on her shoulder and said, 'It's fine, Cassy. You didn't do anything wrong.'

He turned to leave the room, but Tom spoke up quickly. 'Father, please may I go out into the garden for a little while? I promise I won't overtire myself or anything.'

Confused at his son's request, he turned back to see the earnest expression on his little face. 'Why, of course you can,

Tom. Whoever suggested that you had to stay up here?' As Tom's gaze fell from his own to the floor Edward realised just who had told his son not to leave his room and, after smiling briefly at both his children, he promptly left the room to go in search of his wife before he had to leave to go to take afternoon surgery in the village.

Edward found Louisa sitting in the drawing room with a cup of tea. She looked elegant, seated in one of the wingback chairs facing out into the garden. She heard him approach and slowly placed her cup back onto its saucer and turned to face him.

The smile on her face faltered as she saw the grim expression on his face. She went to rise from her chair but his hand on her shoulder prevented her from doing so. He rubbed his face with his other hand before he spoke, his voice sounding weary and irritated. 'I've just been up to see Tom and I see that Cassy is up there with him instead of you. Was it really too much to ask of you to sit with Tom while I got some rest?'

Louisa schooled her expression into calm innocence before she replied silkily, 'Edward, my darling, why would Tom want to have me sit with him reading a boring old book when he could play a game with his sister? Anyway, he said that he didn't need me to be up there with him. So, instead of leaving him on his own – his choice, by the way – I asked Cassy to look in on him. Was that so wrong?'

Edward could understand her logic, but the whole thing just felt off somehow. He continued, 'And I also understand that you forbade Tom from leaving his bedroom until I said so.'

His eyes blazed their challenge, but Louisa was ready for him. *God, those children will pay for this later*, she thought venomously. 'I thought it best that you double-checked that he was OK before he was allowed to go romping around the garden.

I would never have forgiven myself if anything had happened to the poor little mite. Now please excuse me. I need to and check something with Maggie in the kitchen.' She got up with exaggerated grace and walked slowly from the room, leaving Edward staring at her in her wake and wondering what exactly had just happened.

Louisa was seething, and her anger was barely under control. It took all her effort to walk calmly from the room and across the hall to the dining room. Knowing that Edward had little time left before he had to leave to be at the surgery, she knew that she only had to keep things together for a very short time.

She marched through the dining room and into the kitchen. Maggie was kneading dough on the table as Louisa entered, her head high, her eyes darting all around the room as if determined to find something amiss.

Maggie continued kneading the dough, and, not looking at her, said, 'Something the matter, Louisa?' Louisa just glared at her and marched straight out through the utility room and into the garden. She tried to take deep breaths to still her anger, but found that they just came in great gulps.

What on earth was going on? *What is the matter with me?* she thought. The intensity of her anger was starting to scare her. Unless she managed to get a grip on herself she would ruin everything, and that must not happen.

She turned back. But instead of walking towards the garden she walked back past the back door and turned to walk the other way, towards the front. There were a couple of large old trees there, and it was very shaded.

She leant against the side of the house and let the coolness of the brick seep into her bones, which diffused some of the angry heat held in her body. She needed to calm down. She forced herself to breathe slowly, and gradually felt the anger lessen and leave her body. After a few minutes she heard Edward's car start and crunch up the drive through the gravel and knew that it was safe for her to re-enter the building.

She hadn't seen Tom who, on being given permission by his father to leave his bedroom, had jumped out of bed and run downstairs, through the kitchen, and grabbed a jam tart from the counter, which had elicited a quick shout of admonishment from Maggie as he made for the utility room.

On reaching the back door something made him stop and look both ways before running through the door. When he looked to his right he saw Louisa leaning against the wall, her eyes closed and her fists clenched, muttering to herself. The expression on her face was furious. He didn't stop to find out who had caused this latest bout of her wrath but turned left and sprinted up the garden in search of Jenkins and the answers to his predicament. *So much for my promise to father not to wear myself out*, he thought dryly to himself, but some things just couldn't be helped.

He found Jenkins sitting on one of the old logs down by the vegetable plot enjoying a sneaky cigarette and a mug of tea. 'Hey, Tom,' he called to him as he saw him running towards him, 'where's the fire?'

Tom stopped and took a seat on one of the other old logs. And, panting, said with half a smile on his face, 'Not a fire, Jimmy. More like a fire-breathing dragon,' and started laughing. The strain of the past few hours left him as he relaxed in the company of Jimmy Jenkins, who he now felt to be a true friend, even though he was so much older than himself.

'A fire-breathing dragon, eh?' Jenkins said with a grin, 'And does this dragon have a name?' Tom looked up at him and grinned, 'That she does. Mind you, Cassy calls her Princess La-de-dah,' and, snorting at his own joke, he broke into giggles again.

Jenkins rubbed his chin. He was in a difficult position here. On the one hand it was nice that the young lad felt comfortable with him, but on the other… Well, if the boss's wife ever got wind of him encouraging the young lad to speak out against her he'd be for the high jump.

'Now, Tom,' he said, a serious expression fixed on his face. 'You mustn't be unkind. That is your stepmother I presume you are referring to.'

Tom looked at Jenkins, the amusement dying on his lips. 'Yes, Jimmy, I know. But, well, she is a bit crazy, and she is getting worse. It's really scary, and I don't know what to do, and so I thought I'd speak to you to see if you could help me…'

This was all said in a quiet voice. Tom's head was hung low, and he was starting to bite his bottom lip. Sensing that the young lad was close to tears, and also realising that he probably didn't have anyone else to confide in, Jenkins patted his leg and said, 'OK, so you can tell me. Get it off your chest, OK? Then I can have a think and see what we can do. How does that sound?'

Tom looked up, his eyes wide and bright with unshed tears. 'Thank you, Jimmy. I knew I could count on you.' And then he proceeded to tell Jenkins about everything he had seen and witnessed at first hand that had been bothering him about Louisa.

When he was finished Jenkins ran his hand through his hair and considered his next move.

CHAPTER 26

1973

When Susan awoke the next day it was bright and sunny. There was a very gentle breeze but nothing to testify to the previous day's events, either in the house or in the weather outside.

She stretched and got out of bed. She looked out of the window onto the drive and was pleased to see that James had not returned early from whichever conference or other he was supposedly attending. She had a bath and got dressed and went to wake the children. She was looking forward to meeting Stacey and the other women today. Perhaps, if she felt brave enough and the conversation went that way, she may even discuss her possible options with them.

They had a leisurely breakfast, with extra for Jenkins by way of thanking him for his unconditional support the previous evening. She spent the morning pottering around the garden and making some soup that they could have for supper, before getting them all ready to walk to Stacey's house.

Soon enough it was time to leave. Although it was another bright and sunny day, the forecast was for rain later. Susan decided to take the children's coats with them just in case. She certainly didn't want a repeat of being caught in the storm from the previous day. The children skipped along quite happily, and Susan was feeling relaxed. There had been no more strange occurrences in the house, and for that she was somewhat relieved.

She glanced at the piece of paper in her hand with Stacey's

address on it. She vaguely knew where the road was, but that part of town was a bit of a rabbit warren. Following her instincts, she was relieved when they rounded a corner and saw the road name just a bit further up ahead on the right. The houses were all relatively small and either terraced or semi-detached and were a far cry from her own prestigious address. But she thought that there was a lot to be said for community housing, from looking at the well-tended gardens to the way that groups of children were playing together.

While glancing along the street Susan said to the children, 'We are looking for number 16 Sunmerhay Gardens. Can you see it?' The children raced along the street and shuddered to a halt outside a house with a white gate, whose front garden was bordered with privet hedging that looked as though it could do with a bit of a trim. There was a child's bicycle lying discarded on the front lawn and a pile of shoes outside the front door bearing testament to the number of people who were likely to be found inside. From closer inspection it looked as though they all belonged to children. Susan smiled to herself. James would have a fit if he came home to something like that.

She knocked on the door and it was flung open almost immediately by a child of about six, judging by the gaps in her huge smile where she had lost her milk teeth. 'Mum, they're 'ere,' she shouted back over her shoulder, without taking her gaze from the three visitors. When they made no move to enter, she followed up with 'Well, come in, then. Don't just stand there gawping.'

On hearing this last comment, her mother, who had by now come to the front door, cuffed the child gently around the head and said, 'Now, Lizzie, don't you be so rude. Run along and show ... Emma and Robert, isn't it?' She looked at Susan for confirmation, who just nodded. '… Emma and Robert into the garden, and show them where the juice and snacks are.'

Not needing to be asked twice, the two children, grinning up at their mother, followed Lizzie through the house and into the back garden, where a cacophony of children's delighted sounds of playing awaited them. Stacey rubbed her hands down her apron and, smiling, turned back to Susan. 'Aw, God love 'em, they've been that excited today to have some new blood to play with. I've had me hands full keeping 'em down. Come in, come in.'

This last request was enhanced by rapid beckoning movements from one hand, while she pulled the door wider to allow Susan to gain entry to the house. The noise from the children playing was even louder, and Susan thought that a school playground was probably quieter. Sensing her bemusement Stacey said, 'I always allows 'em to run riot during the day. I hope beyond hope that they might tire 'emselves out and go to bed early, but who am I trying to kid, eh?' She looked at the children playing with such fondness that it almost brought a tear to Susan's eye.

This woman did not have the airs and graces and fortunate upbringing that Susan herself had been afforded, but she also seemed to have a much simpler, more honest and rewarding lifestyle. Susan was determined to change her life for the better with immediate effect and would learn all she could from this kind woman.

They entered the kitchen, and sitting at the table were the other two women from the park plus another slightly younger woman with a baby on her hip. They were all smoking, and the glass ashtray was overflowing with cigarette butts and ash. Seeing her glancing at this, Stacey gestured for the ashtray to be passed to her and she promptly emptied it into the bin and handed it back to the group of women and lit up a cigarette of her own, offering the pack to Susan, who politely refused. 'Cup of tea?' Stacey asked her, and when she accepted Stacey made the introductions.

Somewhat overwhelmed and feeling like a fish out of water, Susan nodded her acceptance of a cup of tea and wished that she was more like the children who, with carefree abandon, had joined in with the games outside.

Stacey switched on the kettle and eyed Susan quizzically. She thought that she looked tense and overwrought, as if a puff of wind could blow her over. She looked smartly dressed in her casual fawn trousers and light blue shirt, but there was a fragility to her.

Stacey sighed to herself. If she was not mistaken, Mr Morton did not treat his wife as he should, which outward appearances belied. She had seen enough in her life to spot the signs a mile off, and perhaps unconsciously this is what had prompted her to invite this relative stranger into her home.

'Sit down, love,' Stacey said, motioning to the vacant chair at the table with one hand while handing Susan a cup of tea in the other. 'We don't bite.' Susan smiled weakly, and after taking the cup of tea sank gratefully into the chair and smiled brightly at the baby being jiggled on the young woman's hip. The baby took a chunky thumb from its mouth and extended its moist hand in Susan's direction.

Susan patted the baby's hand and made cooing noises. She was rewarded with the most beautiful smile and all four women sighed with an audible 'Aw.' The mother hugged the child to her breast and sat herself down again at the table. 'This here is Rosie, my daughter, and her little one, my granddaughter

Lucy.' The last was said with such love and pride that it made Susan feel a tug at her heart.

Susan turned to Stacey with a wide-eyed stare and said, 'But you do not look old enough to—'

Julie, one of the other women cut in. 'Aye, I know. Makes you sick, don't it?' And, digging Jane in the ribs, they both chuckled.

Stacey, obviously used to their banter, smiled. 'I was just seventeen when I had our Rosie. Had to fight tooth and nail to keep her, I can tell you, but … well…' She faltered slightly. 'Our Robbie came good in the end. We got married and, later on, had the others.'

Her lips were held in a tight line as she continued, 'Our Rosie didn't listen to her old mum and was caught in the same way. But I won't let her go through what I did, and we will see her right, will me and Robbie.'

Rosie looked up at her mum. Her look was proud, but you could see the love for her child and her mother radiating out from her. Susan wished that she was able to count on her own family's support in the months ahead, but doubted whether it would be so freely and graciously given. It was all about their standing in society and less about what was actually the right thing to do.

She shuddered suddenly as a chill washed over her. This was not unnoticed by Stacey, and she frowned, unsure what had caused the reaction in her guest, and hoping that it was nothing to do with unmarried mothers. That would just get her back up.

Susan, realising that her involuntary response could be misconstrued, quickly spoke up. 'You did the right thing. I only wish my parents were as supportive and forgiving. It would certainly make my life a lot easier.' She glanced out at the garden to make sure that the children were still playing happily and thus otherwise occupied and would not be eavesdropping on this conversation, as she had the feeling that things were going to get a lot more revealing as the afternoon wound on.

Taking this as her cue to manoeuvre the conversation round to the reason why she had felt so compelled to invite Susan to her home, Stacey settled herself at the table, lit another cigarette and, after inhaling deeply, blew the smoke from the side of her mouth, vaguely in the direction of the open back door, before taking a sip from her cup. She started speaking. 'So, Susan, am I right in thinking that all is not well in the Morton household?'

Watching Susan carefully, she saw the colour start at her throat and slowly flush her cheeks and her eyes become bright with unshed tears. Determined not to embarrass herself, Susan took a deep breath and, looking slightly upwards and not at anyone in particular, she replied in a quiet voice, 'You could say that.' And with the slightest hint of a smile she added, 'I didn't realise that it was quite so obvious, though,' before placing her cup back on the table and wondering where on earth she should start. Instinctively she knew that these women, who she had only just met, had her back and would not use her sorry tale as idle gossip to be casually banded about like the women she knew at the various clubs James had her frequent, much to her chagrin.

Stacey took a sip of her tea and a couple more puffs on her cigarette. She then ground the butt into the ashtray, again blowing the smoke from the side of her mouth so that it did not drift in Susan's direction, and looked directly at her with an open, honest expression on her face. 'I've seen that look more times than I care to remember, in others and also in my own reflection,' she admitted ruefully. 'I always try to help where

I can, to like … you know … pay back them who helped me when I were in trouble.'

Susan watched Stacey intently, feeling safe in the company of these women, like she was cocooned in a warm embrace. She didn't understand this feeling, as she had only just met them, but she trusted her instincts that it was real.

Stacey continued, looking off into the middle distance as if remembering other times from which she drew her wisdom, 'It's the defeated stance – the way you hold yourself: head down, avoiding eye contact, nervous, like a frightened rabbit – as if you are always alert for danger. You won't realise quite how tense you were until it is all over and you can breathe, really breathe freely again. The constant anxiety, headaches, upset stomach, and always feeling on edge… It is all reflected in the cowed way you behave, as if you wish you could disappear and not be noticed ever again. But you also have to hold it together for the children, in front of other people, almost like you are living two lives and the tension will take its toll.'

This was quite a long speech for Stacey, and Susan and the other women nodded solemnly in agreement with her. It seemed like they had all been on the receiving end of some sort of crap at some point or other in their lives, and this seemed to inject Susan with a new-found strength and resolution to do something about her situation.

Susan was about to reply when Robert came charging into the kitchen, swiftly followed by three of the other children. 'Mum,' he said in his most pleading voice, 'can we all walk down to the park together? It's only three streets away and we won't go anywhere near the main road. We'll be safe and we will look after Emma and the other smaller children, I promise. Pleeeease.'

This long-drawn-out word was accompanied with his most endearing innocent smile and his own version of 'Cross my heart and hope to die'.

The other mothers all looked at each other and burst out laughing. Stacey looked towards Susan, 'If you are happy, I don't mind. Tim,' she called to her son, who must have been a similar age to Robert, 'you make sure you look after Lizzie. Hold her hand when you cross the roads whether there is a car coming or not. Robert, you do the same for Emma.'

Susan looked sharply at Robert. 'OK, but no talking to strangers or going off on your own. And you must keep the little ones in sight at all times, OK?'

'Yes,' Robert replied, fist-pumping the air. 'OK, Mum. We will be good, I promise.' And with lots of excited chatter all the children walked through the house to reclaim their shoes at the front door and walk off to the park.

'Be back in an hour,' Stacey called after them.

'OK,' a chorus of voices responded, though how they would gauge the time no one really knew as they didn't own a watch between them and the younger ones couldn't even tell the time. But Stacey seemed to be content that everything was under control, which made Susan feel comfortable, and it really was only about a two-minute walk to the park anyway. In fact, if they moved to sit in the garden, they would probably be able to hear the children playing in the park from where they were.

After the children had left, Stacey made some more tea and suggested that they all sit in the garden, to which Susan readily agreed, as the cigarette smoke was starting to make her eyes water. Rosie laid baby Lucy down in her pram, and she seemed happy enough to kick her legs and play with the colourful plastic shapes hung across the pram and make contented gurgling noises.

Once they were all seated on some garden chairs Stacey spoke again. 'All of us here have had some trauma or other in our lives, and our friendship is what has seen us through. You need to draw on strength from elsewhere sometimes because, believe me, you have little enough reserves of your own.'

Susan nodded in agreement, thinking of how she felt trapped in her relationship with James and powerless to do anything about it, and felt like there was no one she could turn to for support. But, in the space of a couple of days, Sarah had offered her the possible freedom of a holiday where she could potentially orchestrate her long-term escape, and these four lovely women were extending the hand of support and friendship to a total stranger. She felt almost overcome with gratitude and felt the hot, sharp sting of tears at the back of her eyes.

Stacey continued. 'Sometimes you can feel as if you are going mad. You start to question yourself and start to even believe that you must in some way be to blame for what is happening to you, that you must deserve it or be an awful person. You start to lose all your confidence, are isolated from your friends and family and eventually become a fractured shell of the person you were. Does any of this sound familiar?'

Stacey eyed Susan carefully to weigh up her response. If she was wrong in what she suspected about how the great and mighty James Morton behaved at home, she would eat her proverbial hat.

Susan just looked at Stacey in awe. The other woman had basically described her own situation with such clarity and eloquence that she was stunned into complete silence. Stacey smiled a tight smile. There was no joy in being right, no joy at all. Stacey crossed her arms tightly across her chest and just said, 'I thought so. Now what are we going to do about it?'

Tears started to run unchecked down Susan's face. Whether they were from the stunned realisation of her actual predicament, the fact that someone understood and believed what she was facing, or from the loving support radiating from the faces of these other women, she didn't know.

She rummaged in her handbag for a handkerchief, but Stacey handed her some tissues from a box on the counter, just inside the back door, which she took with a muffled thanks. Julie put her arm around Susan's shoulders as she dried her eyes.

Susan let out a deep breath that she had not realised she was holding and straightened her spine.

Stacey nodded her approval. The light was back in Susan's eyes. She would be OK, they would make sure of it.

CHAPTER 27

1936

Louisa decided to skirt past the back door and go and sit on the terrace. She was thirsty and in desperate need of a cup of tea, but she didn't feel up to going into the kitchen yet to make herself a cup and certainly didn't want to ask Maggie to make one for her. If Maggie so much as looked at her the wrong way at the moment she knew that she would fly into a complete rage, which would be out of her control. No, she needed to sit quietly and let her temper subside completely before she burnt all her bridges in one day.

As she sat on the terrace she caught some movement through the open French doors leading into the drawing room and saw one of the cleaning girls that Maggie often drafted in to help out at busy times. She couldn't remember this one's name, but it was Edna or Ethel or something beginning with *E*. She rooted around in her brain but the name just floated out of reach. As it happened, she didn't need to remember it as the girl, seeing the mistress of the house sitting at the table outside, came out and did a sort of half-curtsey and asked her if she needed anything.

Louisa was slightly mollified by the girl's good grace and manners and by her proper addressing of her as the lady of the house, and all this helped to calm Louisa's temper and improve her mood. Smiling briefly at the girl, who she suddenly remembered was called Edith, she thanked her for her concern and asked if she could possibly bring her a pot of tea.

Satisfied that her request would be fulfilled, Louisa sat back in the chair and looked out across the garden, wondering what she should do next. Edward's free time was so limited, and so she was often just left on her own. What little time he did spend at home seemed to be eaten up with the children. Cassy was not quite so demanding, but Tom...

She shuddered. It seemed as though every time some event or occasion or other was arranged that Tom seemed to be behind its scuppering. That boy was a complete nuisance in her eyes, and she needed to try and work a way of getting rid of him so that she could try and carve back some of Edward's attention for herself.

As she was thinking, the object of her irritation came running down the garden and almost screeched to a comedic halt when he caught sight of her sitting on the terrace. Her tea had arrived by then and she was delicately sipping from the fine china cup.

She momentarily halted the movement and then slowly placed the cup back on the table. Tom started walking more slowly up towards the house, realising that there was no way that he could avoid going past Louisa if he wanted to go back inside. After witnessing her behaviour the previous day, he was even more wary of her and was at a loss about what to do or say for the best.

Louisa watched his progress through narrowed eyes. When he was close enough to speak to without raising her voice she said very simply but with enough venom inflected in the words, 'I'm watching you, Tom. Mark my words. Your days of being top dog in this house are numbered.'

Tom looked at her through wide eyes, not fully understanding what the words Louisa had spoken meant, but fully comprehending the threatening tone they were delivered in. As he passed her he glanced quickly out of the corner of his eyes and then scuttled off and into the kitchen.

Louisa sat back in her chair, a smug smile on her face and a warm glow starting to fill her body. She didn't know how she would manage it, especially with Edward so determined to honour his first wife's desire that the children not be sent to boarding school, but she would work something out. Whatever happened, that boy's days of being held in such reverence by his father were numbered.

She sipped her tea and started to think of different ways to be rid of the boy. He reminded her too much of his mother by far, and she was sure that was why Edward doted on the child. It was just impossible to compete with the saintly Sophie. Even after her death she continued to have a hold over her husband and, it seemed, the rest of the family and the staff as well. Louisa would never be able to take her rightful place in the house until that was dealt with. She took another sip of tea and wondered.

Perhaps, she thought with slight distaste, if I were to have a child that might move me up in Edward's estimation. She pondered on that thought for a moment. It wasn't that she disliked children per se. She had used to enjoy the role of nanny and governess. However, the children had seemed much more respectful then, when under her tutelage. But of course, saintly Sophie would have been horrified if they had spoken out of turn, and they had loved their mother unreservedly and would have done nothing to cause her distress or disapproval.

She mulled over her idea. The more she thought about it the better it seemed to her. Edward would obviously be delighted and fawn over her. Once the baby was born the other staff would come around to her, and she could herself get a nanny to help her with the more arduous tasks, such as taking care of the child at night. Yes, this was just the sort of thing she needed to do. Then she would be in a better place to bargain with Edward about sending the boy off to school. She could say that he was too noisy or boisterous and it could harm the baby. She would think of something, of that she was certain.

Feeling very pleased with herself, she placed her cup down on her saucer and left it on the table for Edith or one of the other staff to deal with. Then she went inside the house to decide how best to go about getting Edward to notice her again.

As Maggie walked through the hall carrying a pile of folded linen to put upstairs in the linen cupboard she could hear Louisa singing gently to herself in the drawing room. She frowned, wondering what she was up to now. She didn't trust her, as she always seemed to have some scheme or another up her sleeve.

Sophie had been such an open and honest lady, always with a warm smile and a kind word for everyone she met. In marked contrast, Louisa's behaviour was getting more truculent and disagreeable every day. She was either acting like some sort of Lady Muck, expecting everyone else to run around after her, or trying to ingratiate herself into circles where she would have been openly welcome just from the fact of being married to the doctor, but she seemed to have a knack of alienating herself with her pushy and demanding manner.

Maggie shook her head. *Goodness knows where it is all going to end*, she said to herself, but if tears were not involved she would eat her hat.

Louisa, oblivious to all this, was dreamily thinking of ways that she could renew her husband's interest in her. She would arrange for a nice intimate dinner that very evening for just the two of them. The children could eat earlier, preferably in the kitchen or somewhere out of her hair, anyway. Then she would be all attention and smiles, enquiring after his day, his patients and anything interesting that had happened to him.

She would have to think up something interesting to talk to him about, because spending most of her time inside these four walls didn't lend itself to scintillating topics of conversation. Perhaps she should arrange to go out somewhere, anywhere. She could ask Edward for suggestions, flatter him by asking his opinion. That should work.

And she could start painting again. She had always enjoyed that, and had liked teaching her young students as a governess. Maybe Cassy would even show an interest, she pondered. Thoughts cascaded through her mind like a waterfall. Feeling buoyed up by her plans, she went in search of Maggie to put her dinner idea into operation.

Edward was feeling tired. He had had a busy day with some especially tiresome patients, and was looking forward to going home and putting his feet up in his study with a glass of whisky and one of the latest medical journals he had received, which had an interesting article on some research he was fascinated about.

When he got home he left the car outside. Cedric, who was Maggie's husband, and who looked after the car and the outbuildings, wanted to give it a clean anyway, so it would save him getting it out of the garage.

Edward entered the house through the front door. Louisa, who had heard his car on the drive, came to greet him. She was all smiles and looked like she was dressed to go out. *What have I forgotten?* he said to himself and groaned inwardly. All thoughts of his relaxing evening vanished like mist before his eyes.

'Darling,' Louisa crooned in her overly sweet voice, which was usually accompanied by her wanting something or other.

Edward did not speak but looked at his wife inquiringly as he tried to keep the tension out of his face. 'Louisa,' he said, 'you look nice. Are we going out somewhere? Forgive me if I have forgotten some previously prearranged engagement.'

Louisa smacked his arm playfully and continued. 'No, silly. I just thought it would be good for us to spend some time together, just the two of us. You have been so busy lately and then with poor Tom…' Her voice tailed off for a moment then she rallied. 'Anyway, I have asked Maggie to just do us a simple supper in the dining room so we can have some time to chat. The children have already eaten and are upstairs.'

Edward looked even more confused. 'Chat? What about? Is there something we need to discuss that I am not aware of? I am sorry, my dear, I am very tired. Can it not wait until—'

'No.' Louisa interrupted much more sharply than she had intended, and her eyes narrowed as she saw her perfect plan start to unravel and slip through her fingers.

But then she smiled, and her voice was much calmer when she spoke again. 'Edward, my dear, you have been working very hard, so I thought I would organise this special dinner to show that I have noticed your hard work and so we can get a bit closer, you know.' She lowered her head and fluttered her eyelashes slightly. 'We do seem to have been out of sorts with each other of late, don't you think?'

Edward continued to look a bit bemused, but on seeing the earnest expression on Louisa's face his expression softened and he bent to kiss her lightly on the cheek. 'Thank you, Louisa. It is a very kind thought. Let me just get changed out of my work attire and I will join you directly in the drawing room. Would you be kind enough to pour me a small glass of whisky?'

Louisa beamed at him. This was going exactly to plan. She

had been worried for a moment that Edward was going to be reluctant to play his part in her design, but it seemed to be back on track. 'Of course, my darling,' she said, and smiled shyly at him as he turned and mounted the stairs to get changed.

The smile melted from her lips in an instant and was replaced by her usual determined expression. She would ensure that she got what she wanted from her husband that night. It was her due, anyway, wasn't it? Wasn't that what every wife was supposed to do anyway: produce an heir?

She poured a glass of whisky for Edward and a glass of wine for herself and hurried into the kitchen to ensure that Maggie had fulfilled her part in the plan to perfection. She was just placing Edward's glass on the side table next to his chair in the drawing room when he entered the room. She picked the glass up instead and handed it to him, and then placed her arms around his neck and gave him a long, lingering kiss.

Slightly taken aback by the change that had suddenly come upon his usually – of late – frosty wife, he did not immediately return her warm embrace but stood slightly frozen for a fraction of a second before returning her affections in a similar vein. The hesitation, however, was not lost on Louisa and she worked hard to quell the anger in her breast that had resulted from this slight.

She took a deep breath and moved away from Edward, ensuring that she had a bright, warm smile planted on her face before patting his chair with her hand to bid him to come and sit before asking him about his day.

Maggie called them to dinner shortly after Edward had finished regaling Louisa with tales of several demanding patients, who were suffering from no more than an excessive amount of time on their hands and overactive imaginations.

But they paid him well for his time, and so he could not really complain.

Maggie had been surprised by Louisa's request to have an intimate dinner with Edward, and her suspicions were immediately raised. The sweetness-and-light Louisa was somehow more disconcerting than the usual scowling version. As usual, however, the older woman had said nothing, just nodded her understanding and carried on kneading the dough she had on the kitchen table.

Louisa had laid the table at the end of the dining room furthest from the kitchen door. She had placed a couple of candles in silver candlesticks and put out the best china and silver cutlery. Everything looked beautiful in the flickering candlelight. She poured two glasses of red wine into crystal glasses from the matching decanter on the sideboard and came and joined Edward at the table, where he was busily tucking a napkin into his collar. In contrast, she placed hers on her lap. Maggie had made a simple soup to start. It was some kind of vegetable and tasted lovely. They ate in companionable silence for a while, passing each other condiments and bread. Louisa kept the conversation light.

Edward felt himself relaxing. *This is how it used to be*, he mused thoughtfully. *It is even how it was with Sophie.* A gentle smile crossed his lips at the thought of his beautiful first wife, his first love. He sighed and looked at Louisa, who was eyeing him with interest. 'What are you thinking about, Edward?' she asked in a low, husky voice. After realising that to admit that he had been thinking fondly of Sophie would be a huge faux pas he smiled kindly at Louisa, and said that he was thinking about how enjoyable the evening was and that it was very thoughtful of Louisa to have arranged it all. Mollified by her husband's correct response, Louisa relaxed a little and sipped her wine.

On hearing no more noise of cutlery on crockery, Maggie appeared at the door and promptly came and removed their plates and then bustled back with their main course of a stew, which had been slow-cooking in the oven for most of the day. Cooking it this way meant that it did not matter at what time Edward returned to the house. They both knew that his work often delayed him, and he could not always guarantee to get away when he had promised.

Neither of them having a particularly sweet tooth, they decided to forgo any dessert and instead took a tray of coffee to the drawing room where a fire blazed in the grate. The evenings were really starting to draw in and the large house was often draughty. The long, heavy curtains had been closed against the French windows, which lent the room a cosy and comfortable atmosphere. They both sank into the wingback chairs after Louisa had poured them each a cup of coffee.

Edward sighed and looked at Louisa. 'Well, my dear,' he said gently, 'this has been a most lovely end to a busy and somewhat tedious day. Thank you.' Louisa just nodded and smiled at him. Inwardly she just wanted to hurry through this stage to get to the main event and the reason behind all this effort.

'Shall we take the rest of the coffee up to our room?' she asked, smiling coyly at Edward from lowered eyes. Edward started suddenly. *Now this is a surprise*, he thought, not unpleasantly. Louisa had become something of a cold fish of late and he was always too tired for it to really bother him too much. But he did admit that that would be an even better end to the evening than he could even have imagined, if he understood her intentions correctly.

He looks very pleased, she thought bemusedly. Men were such easy creatures to manipulate, really. She should have thought of this much earlier.

Edward put his cup down on the tray and gestured for Louisa to do the same. Then he picked up the tray and left the room, with Louisa following close behind. She stopped to turn off the light and gave a cunning grin back into the empty room.

CHAPTER 28

1973

Susan felt the relief flood through her body – which was strange, seeing as her position had not changed at all. She was still married to James and, as yet, had no idea of how she was to extricate herself from the relationship. However, just knowing that she had discussed the situation with others, and had not been found to be wanting or crazy, buoyed up her spirits and gave her confidence.

She needed to work out what to do next, where she could go and how she could fund her life without her husband. She looked at the women sitting around the table and took in a deep breath before speaking. 'So, what do I do now? I mean, where do I go? How do I cope for money? I have no bank account of my own. James deals with all the money side of things. He pays all the accounts and leaves me a bit of housekeeping money each week.' Susan started to feel a bit panicky when she realised quite how much she was beholden to her husband.

Stacey looked at her seriously before saying, 'Do you keep any of the money aside?' Susan replied, 'Not really, only the odd pound here and there. James asks for every receipt for anything I have purchased and adds it all up, to ensure that I have not been "squandering" his money,' she said, her voice full of despair. 'I suppose that I could ask my father for help, but I am not sure that he would be willing. The thought of a divorce in the family would be abhorrent to my parents, especially my mother. I don't even know how I will be able to broach the idea of taking the children away. Sarah Peters has kindly offered to write to her sister, as they have a farm, and she has suggested that I take the children there for a holiday.'

Stacey folded her arms and leant back against the door frame and lit another cigarette, as it seemed to help her think. She took a few drags and then blew the smoke out in two perfect rings, which stretched in the air as they floated up towards the sky, gently melting away to nothing. 'OK,' Stacey said, seeming to take charge of the situation. 'How about this for an option? When Sarah hears back from her sister, you arrange to go and stay with her for a couple of weeks. I'm sure that you will be able to come up with a good enough excuse for James. If not, then you can just go when he is at work. Take as much with you as you can carry. I know Sarah's sister. Sarah will have understood your situation too, I am sure, so will be willing to help.'

Susan was looking at Stacey with rapt attention.

Stacey continued. 'They live on a farm, OK, so there is always stuff to be done. You will be able to stay there and help on the farm to earn your keep while you file for divorce. You will need to document, as much as possible, why you are leaving James. You will be able to get free help and advice too. I'll sort that side of things for you. Now, here's the cracker.'

Stacey pushed herself away from the door frame and came and knelt down by Susan and lifted her chin so that Susan was looking directly at her. 'You are entitled to half of everything.' Susan looked shocked and she was shaking her head in disbelief.

She replied, 'You must be mistaken. James would never let me have half of anything. He'd see me dead first.' A shudder ran down her spine and her eyes were wide with shock. Stacey stood back up, arms folded again, her legs slightly apart and a defiant look on her face. 'And that, my dear Susan, is why we need to get you as far away from him as possible before you even give a hint of what you are thinking.'

The children chose that moment to reappear in a noisy jumble of shouts, whoops, balls and hoops. They had obviously had a great time and had revelled in their freedom. They were all smiling and apparently starving and dying of thirst as they fell on the snacks and drinks on the table like ravenous beasts. All the mothers smiled indulgently at their various offspring.

Susan, her mind now completely reeling from the conversation, decided that she should take her leave. She called the children to her from the throng and said her goodbyes to the others.

Stacey walked with them to the door, and the children walked up the path as Susan lingered to say a few words to Stacey. 'Thank you, Stacey. You have given me so much to think about, but more than anything you have given me hope.'

Stacey smiled at her lazily. 'You know where I am. Don't be a stranger, and you can come here at any time, day or night. I'll do what I can to help you.' And with these parting words she closed the door and headed back to the kitchen where the others waited for her.

'There is trouble brewing there – you mark my words, girls. I feel an almost evil hold over that poor woman – a taint, like a nasty taste that surrounds her. It's nothing to do with her personally. She seems to be a really pleasant person, but some evil has its claws embedded deep and it is to do with that husband of hers. But it doesn't even feel as clear-cut as that. It feels strange…'

She stared off into space, almost trancelike, as she pondered over the feelings that were collecting in her stomach area and working their way up to her throat. She shook her head sadly.

'I don't know what we can do to protect her, girls, but we need to be alert.'

Susan was feeling a mixture of emotions: excitement at the thought of finally getting away from James, fear about his reaction and confusion as to how to go about it. She had felt so secure in the group of women, as if they could conquer anything, but now that she was on her own with the children, the fragility of her actual situation hit her full in the face. If she didn't act soon the courage would leave her and she would be stuck in this situation forever.

They arrived back home about 5.30 p.m. Nobody was particularly hungry, as they had all eaten snacks at Stacey's house. Susan thought she would see what was in the house that they could eat later if they got a bit peckish later on. The children ran upstairs to their rooms. They were going to play some game or other that Susan had heard them discussing on the way home. She had been lost in thought so had not really been listening to them, and as they were not bickering or fighting she had just left them to it.

She entered the kitchen and the first thing she noticed was a cream envelope on the table propped up against the teapot. The writing was a bit spidery and was not in a hand that she recognised. Intrigued, she took a butter knife out of the drawer and slit the envelope open with practised ease. She removed the single sheet of paper and read the note:

Dear Susan,

My sister Joyce has replied to my letter, and would be most pleased to have you and the children to stay for as long as you like. There is always lots to do on the farm and she would be most glad of your help if you felt it necessary to repay her in some way, which of course would not be expected of you but your choice entirely.

She would be happy for you to arrive as soon as this weekend. Her address is: Gables End Farm, Shennings Lane, Eartham, West Sussex. They have a telephone, and if you call from the station they will send one of the farm hands to pick you up.

There is no need to telephone in advance. They will expect you from Saturday.

Yours sincerely,
Sarah Peters

Susan stood, one hand resting on the back of a chair with the letter loosely held in her other hand, staring into the middle distance. *Could this be it?* she thought in wonder. *Could it really be this simple?*

She glanced up at the kitchen clock. It was gone 6 p.m. now, and although it would be light for a while yet, she felt that it was too late to go down to the Peters's house to double-check a few things with Sarah. She knew that Jenkins would always keep an eye on the children but, not knowing when James was likely to make an appearance, she did not want to give him any excuse for losing his temper by leaving the children unattended. She laughed mirthlessly to herself. As if he ever cared about the children himself. Just look at his behaviour when Emma had fallen into the river.

A feeling of intense dislike washed over her and galvanised her into action. She needed to make some detailed plans. She had a little money, which she had been saving religiously each week from her meagre housekeeping money, that she intended to use to buy extra treats for the children at Christmas. She needed to pack for herself and the children and to take as much as they could easily carry. And she needed to plan the journey.

She would walk to the station tomorrow after she had been to see Sarah Peters and they could help her work that out.

She was just about to leave the kitchen and head upstairs to start putting her plans into action when she heard the unmistakable sound of a car in the driveway. Her heart started beating very fast and she almost ran to the window to look outside. Sure enough, James's car was parked in the driveway and the man himself was getting out of the car.

Quickly, Susan put the letter and envelope in one of the kitchen drawers under a couple of recipe books – James would never look in there – and walked into the hall to greet her husband, carefully planting the best welcoming smile on her face that she could muster.

James was tired after his drive. He had felt refreshed while he had been away, but had found Clare to be slightly insipid and unstimulating company. Oh, she was OK enough in bed, but to spend any length of time with her had become tiresome in the extreme.

He found himself thinking about Susan, about the time they had spent courting, the gentle teasing and fun they had had before they had moved into this house. He stared up at the large building, craning his neck due to the close proximity of the car to the house. It was a handsome house: Edwardian elegance at its most becoming. It had large stone mullioned windows with black leaded panes forming small rectangles in the glass. The black exposed beams were surrounded by painted pebbledash. It was a lovely house, but somehow it held something of a sinister air.

He felt that familiar anger start to creep around him, and it almost frightened him with its intensity. He did not understand why he felt so different when he was away from the house most of the time – although not always, that was true.

He thought back to the scene he had made at the hospital when Emma had been under observation after her near drowning incident. He didn't understand that either. He didn't often spend much time with the children, but he didn't actually dislike them. He just didn't know what he was supposed to do with them.

His own parents had sent him and his sister to boarding school almost as soon as they could talk, so he had no experience of parenting from them. His peers all seemed to work as hard as he did and spent little time with their families. His parents were still distant and not particularly interested in their grandchildren and Susan's family were similar, especially his mother-in-law. He shuddered slightly at the mere thought of that formidable woman.

However, Susan was different. She was kind and thoughtful, and she never gave him any cause for concern or any trouble. She was a good wife, he supposed, and she always kept the house clean and tidy – which was no mean feat, seeing how large it was.

She was a good cook and also good company, so why did the mere sight of her cause him to fly into a rage these days? He really wanted to be a good husband and father – these few days away had reinforced that belief – so why was he sitting out here in the growing dark in his car, not wanting to enter the house?

He looked up at the house again and saw the soft, warm glow of light illuminating a few windows. The kitchen light was on, so Susan was probably in the kitchen. She would have heard his car pull up, he thought.

He got out of the car and stretched his legs before closing the door and walking towards the front door. As he approached the door the porch light came on and the door opened to reveal his wife standing there with a slightly apprehensive look on her pretty face. This made James feel irritated and sad in turn. He wasn't sure whether the irritation was directed towards him or his wife, and he tried to push these feelings down.

'Susan,' he said with a nod to her as he walked past her into the hall and towards his study, where he placed his briefcase before returning with his overnight bag, which he placed on the floor. 'Er,' he started, 'where do you want this?' Susan looked at him in surprise. James would usually just dump his bag and expect her to deal with it on her own with no thought about how his clothes were laundered and pressed and returned to his wardrobe.

She smiled at him and said, 'Could you bring it into the kitchen? Would you like some supper?'

James smiled at his wife. 'That would be very nice, thank you. I am a bit tired after the drive.' He took off his coat and shook it slightly, then hung it in the cloakroom to the side of the front door. He noticed that the quarry tiles shone and everything was clean and tidy, as always. He picked up his bag and followed Susan through to the kitchen. She pointed to the utility room and he placed his bag on top of the twin-tub washing machine and then came back into the kitchen to see Susan looking into the fridge. The soft warm light highlighted her hair and softened her features.

Susan looked up at James and said, 'You can have soup, cheese on toast, a sandwich... We have some ham, some cheese, or I could make you an omelette. What would you prefer?' She looked at James expectantly, still slightly hesitantly, he thought. But that was no surprise, seeing how he had been behaving of late.

He was hungry but didn't want a big meal, so cheese on toast sounded great. 'Cheese on toast, please,' he said, smiling gently. Susan looked slightly confused, but nodded and busied herself with preparing the meal.

James sat at the table and watched her. He never really spent any time in this room, preferring to sit in the dining room to eat, and had never learnt to cook anything. It was all some sort of mystery to him. His father had been the same and his mother had been happy to deal with all the domestic tasks, as that was how things were done.

He supposed that the world was starting to change more and more now. Women had proved themselves in the war and many women worked full time and raised a family as well. He had plenty of women working in his office, but he had never given a second thought to how they juggled their private lives. Perhaps their husbands helped them. He thought about this for a moment, and it seemed like a very strange concept.

He for one would not have a clue where to start and he didn't think Susan would actually want him to, but the topic had never even been up for discussion. It was understood that as soon as they were married Susan would become his wife and as such would not work. He could not be seen to have a wife who worked. People would question his ability to provide for her and his family as they came along. It would have been out of the question.

He realised suddenly that Susan's feelings about this situation had not only not been ascertained, the thought that she would even have had an independent thought about such things had never even crossed his mind.

He watched her putting the cheese on the bread and placing it under the grill, having first grilled one side of the bread. She looked tired and drawn, he thought, and troubled. *Was that my doing?* he wondered. He suddenly felt full of shame and stood and walked over to his wife and put his arms around her.

Susan was shocked and confused by her husband's show of affection and at first stood stock-still, rigid, with her arms by her side. Then, realising that his embrace was just that, her body softened as she relaxed and she loosely draped her arms around James's back. *What on earth has come over him?* she wondered silently. What had gone on at the conference to return her husband to her as a different man? Why now? Why, when she had more or less engineered her escape, did James choose this moment to start to metamorphose into the husband she wanted him to be?

Her thoughts tumbled about in her brain, each confused image tripping over the next. James held her away from him. She smiled at him but the smile did not meet her eyes. 'I must see to your supper, James, or it will burn,' she said, worried that this may cause him to fly into one of his rages, but he simply let her go and went and sat back down at the table.

A grey mist slipped under the door from the utility room. It weaved its way around the bottom of the cupboards. Its movement resembled that of an eel or some other watery creature, softly flowing into crevices and out again as if in search of its prey. It was a soft grey, not black and threatening as it usually was, and it melted away as soon as it had appeared, unseen by both the occupants of the kitchen.

Susan finished making the cheese on toast for James and placed it on the table in front of him and then started to make a cup of tea while he started eating. She tried to steady her breathing, while also trying to make sense of what was going on.

She really needed to speak to someone, perhaps tomorrow.

Maybe James would go to the office. She could go and speak to Sarah Peters. She was going to see her anyway to talk to her about going to her sister's. What was she going to do about that now? Should she just go with the children anyway? Should she broach the subject with James?

James had finished his supper and pushed the plate away from him. Susan rushed over to take the plate to wash it up, but he placed a hand on her wrist and looked up into her large eyes. She looked just like a frightened rabbit, he thought, and this time it did bring shame and guilt into his heart. 'I'm … I'm sorry, Susan.' His voice faltered, and he couldn't quite meet her eyes.

Susan looked at him in shock. *I must be dreaming*, she thought without humour. What was going on?

'I haven't been the husband to you that I should have been. I don't know why. Sometimes I am filled with such anger, but I don't know why,' he confessed, looking totally stricken now. Susan just stood there silently. She didn't even know where to start to begin to formulate a reply to this sudden confession.

Her silence gave him the space to continue. 'Why don't we go away? We can take the children. They'd like that. We can go to Cornwall or the Lake District. What do you say?'

Susan didn't say anything. She just stood there speechless, wondering what on earth was going on. She had planned her escape – she was really going to do it – but now James was being so … nice. Normal, even. Dare she trust this new James? But this was all she'd really ever wanted, wasn't it?

What on earth was she supposed to do now? Mindful of the fact that she had not yet spoken a word, and seeing the open, expectant look on James's face, she didn't have the heart to turn him down. She replied falteringly. 'Um, well, perhaps, yes. Well, that is to say … a holiday would be most welcome, and the children would certainly love it. Somewhere with a beach where they could build sandcastles, maybe.' She smiled warmly at him and he smiled back.

The mist coiled gently around the bottom of the cupboards. A gentle grey and white, it was like the palest of smoke. There was almost just a hint of movement, and then it was gone.

Chapter 29

1936

Louisa was in her element. She was humming a jaunty tune to herself as she brushed her hair, which fell down her back in golden waves. Edward watched her from the bed, where he was sitting up against the pillow and sipping a cup of tea. He too was happy, if in a slightly bemused way. His first wife had never been one for moods or shows of temper. She had been sweet-natured, gentle and kind, and he missed her sorely, even after the years that had passed.

Louisa was much more of a passionate creature, but this gave over to bouts of moodiness that he found difficult to understand. He tended to deal with them by staying away from her which, he supposed wryly, only incensed her more. However, she could also be loving and fun and full of an infectious energy when she was in good spirits, which she seemed to be right now.

She had been like this for a few weeks now, ever since he'd come home to find her waiting for him with that surprise intimate dinner. He was still not sure what had brought about the change in her, which was much for the better, but he was very glad of it nevertheless. 'What are you doing today, Louisa?' he asked her from the bed.

She stopped brushing her hair and laid the brush down on the dressing table. The brush was very soft, and the handle was inlaid with mother-of-pearl. It had been a wedding gift to her from one of Edward's aunts. 'I was going to walk into the village and then see if the WI needed any help with the village fete.'

Edward nearly choked on the tea he was drinking and

spluttered in a most undignified manner. Louisa rounded on him. 'What, Edward? You're always suggesting that I get more involved in village life, but now you're half-choking to death on your tea when I suggest it.'

Louisa stood indignantly, with her hands on her hips, her chin jutted forward in a familiar way as she rose to take him to task. Edward smiled at her and laughed. 'It's a surprise, that's all,' he countered quickly, not wanting to break her good mood. 'I thought you found that sort of thing stuffy and boring.'

She studied his face carefully to make sure he was not teasing her. Seemingly satisfied, she turned back to the dressing table mirror and started to gently powder her face. 'Well, now I don't. Is that a problem?'

'No, Louisa, it's not a problem at all. Actually, I think you'll enjoy it.' He didn't add that she'd enjoy bossing everyone around. He thought that it was best to keep those thoughts well and truly to himself.

Louisa decided to walk to the village. She had contemplated riding the ancient bicycle that was kept in one of the garages but had decided against it after finding it covered in cobwebs. She would ask one of the gardeners to clean it and oil it for her so that she could make better use of it in the future.

She was feeling very pleased with herself. Her plan was coming along very nicely, and very soon she would have Edward eating out of her hand.

She was just putting on her hat and some thin cotton gloves when Tom came running through the dining room into the hall with a piece of toast in his hand and his mouth full of the bite he had obviously just taken. He shuddered to a halt when he saw Louisa and stood there just gaping at her. Louisa flapped the gloves against one hand and eyed him suspiciously.

'Where are you off to in such a hurry, young Tom?' she asked him.

'Um, nowhere in particular,' he replied, looking down at his shoes, which were slightly scuffed.

She sighed in exasperation. 'Really Tom, what do you do with your shoes? And what on earth are you going to be up to all day today? You really should be engaged in a task to keep you out of trouble. I will speak to Mr Graves and see if there is something you can help with.'

She continued tapping her gloves against her hand while some thought crossed her eyes. Tom remained frozen to the spot, waiting eagerly to be dismissed so he could go and play in the garden, which was where he had been headed before being caught by Louisa. 'I know,' Louisa exclaimed triumphantly, the thought coming to her in a rush. 'You can clean up the old bicycle in the garage for me. Ask Jenkins to help you. It needs washing and oiling and the brakes looking at and whatnot. I'll speak to Jimmy on my way out.' Satisfied now by her great idea, which would kill two birds with one stone, she walked through the drawing room and out into the garden to find Jenkins.

Tom let out a sigh of relief to have been let off so lightly by the task Louisa had decided upon. He liked tinkering with things, and he loved spending time with Jimmy Jenkins, but he wouldn't let Louisa know that. He took another bite of his toast and walked back towards the kitchen. He would wait there until Louisa had gone out and then go and find Jimmy Jenkins.

Maggie was in the kitchen, stirring up some mixture in a huge ceramic bowl. It smelt of cinnamon and Tom was eager to lick the bowl, but knew that he would only be rewarded with a cuff of the ears should he try and get his fingers anywhere near the bowl until Maggie was ready. She eyed him with interest.

'Tom,' she asked, 'what are you doing back in here? And wipe those sticky fingers on that cloth before I'm having to wash jammy fingerprints off all the walls,' she said in a scolding tone.

'Louisa wants me to clean up the old bicycle, so I need to find Jimmy. But I didn't want her to think up any other jobs for me before she left, so I came in here,' he said with a cheeky, impish grin on his face. He wiped his hand on the cloth as instructed and sat down at the table watching Maggie as she continued to mix the bowl vigorously.

'You are a one, young Tom,' Maggie said with an indulgent smile. 'I am sure that Louisa has no idea that the task she has given you is in fact no chore at all but something you will no doubt relish.' She laughed. 'For all her training as a governess she really has no idea about how the minds of small boys work. Now away with you. Go and find Jimmy and bring him in here for a cup of tea and then the bowl will be ready for you. And don't you cast that innocent look in my direction, Tom Winter. I know exactly what goes on in that cheeky little mind of yours.'

With that she put the bowl down on the table, wiped her hands on her apron and went to fill the large kettle with water in preparation for making tea for the three of them.

Tom grinned and pushed himself up from the table and wandered out into the garden, after checking first to see if Louisa was anywhere to be seen. He kept to the side of the garden and ran down to the gate, which led into the orchard. He could smell the faint aroma of smoke and thought that Jimmy would probably be lighting an early bonfire so it could be finished before Maggie wanted to hang out any washing. Nothing put her in such a temper as her clean sheets smelling of smoke and covered in smuts. He grinned, remembering her ire on previous occasions. Usually she was very mild-mannered, but everyone ran for cover if Maggie was in a rare fine temper.

He found Jimmy adding piles of leaves and prunings to the bonfire and stoking it with a large stick. He had his back to Tom so didn't see him approach and he was whistling merrily to himself, his rough shirtsleeves rolled up and his brightly patterned sleeveless jumper showing holes at the bottom, where he had probably caught it on brambles or some other thorned plant. Strands of brown and red wool hung from the hole, and Tom wondered whether Jimmy would be in trouble with his mother for ruining what was obviously her handiwork.

Jimmy must have heard Tom as he got closer, for he turned around and smiled at him. 'I was wondering when you would make an appearance,' he said, grinning down at him. He really liked Tom. He was full of an infectious energy and humour and was always great company. He was so eager to learn and had an inquisitive and intelligent mind.

Tom looked about him as if expecting Louisa to spring out from behind one of the trees, complete with horns and scales and breathing smoke and fire. On catching his furtive looks Jimmy grinned and said, 'Don't worry, Tom. Louisa has gone. She went through the back gate and I believe she is off to help at the WI, so she will be gone for hours. She did mention something about fixing up an old bike and to make sure that you helped me.'

Tom nodded. 'Yes, she told me. I don't mind doing that. It will be fun. But don't let Louisa know, will you?' he added, slightly worriedly. 'If she thinks I enjoyed doing something she tasked me with she will either find me hundreds of other things to do or find something beastly for me to do to make up for it.' Wondering what horrid job she could find for him, he shuddered. 'Oh, and Maggie says to tell you that she is making us both a mug of tea.'

Jimmy grinned. 'Don't worry, Tom. Your secret is safe with me. Now can you just help me finish putting these leaves on the bonfire? We will make sure that it is safe and then go and have our tea and dig out the old bike.'

They walked companionably back down through the garden, where the scent of the blooms added fragrance to the air. The grass was still damp with dew and their earlier footprints were still visible, as were Louisa's. Tom wondered idly whether hers left some sort of sulphurous hue beneath them and smiled to himself. The breeze played with the leaves on the branches and made a gentle musical sound, which the birds sang along to harmoniously.

Everything was peaceful in the garden, and Tom breathed it in deeply. They could hear Maggie humming away to herself as she put two cake tins in the oven. As promised, the bowl with the remnants of the cake mixture stood on the kitchen table complete with two spoons and two steaming mugs of tea. Maggie's tea was on the kitchen counter.

Maggie stood up from where she had been looking into the oven and glanced at the two of them. Her eyes twinkled as she saw both their gazes fixed intently on the cake bowl, like two faithful hounds waiting for permission to eat their dinners. She laughed at the thought. 'Go on, then, you two. Get stuck in.'

They didn't need telling twice, and both of them fell on the bowl like ravenous beasts. When they had finished they both looked at each other and grinned. 'Thanks, Maggie. You're the best,' they said almost in unison. Maggie made a non-committal noise that sounded like a harrumph and shooed them both out of the kitchen.

They put their mugs down on the table and left the kitchen via the utility room, then walked around the front of the house to get to the garage. The double garage doors were painted a shiny black colour and looked quite formidable, Tom thought. The doors were well oiled and opened easily to reveal a cleanly swept floor and all manner of useful things hanging from the rafters, on shelves and in cupboards.

It was cluttered but looked as though everything had its place. There were paint pots, rope, tools, and an old oil patch on the floor. The windows could definitely do with a clean. They were grimy and covered in cobwebs. *Maggie must never come in here*, thought Tom with a shudder.

The bicycle was resting against a bench at the back of the garage. Its handlebars were sort of wedged against an old vice and the screw at the bottom had stuck in the basket on the front, so that Jenkins had to wiggle it gently to free it from the grip of the vice.

Once the bicycle was free he wheeled it to the front of the garage, where there was more light, and took a closer look. The chain was dry and rusty and one of the pedals was hanging off, but the brake cables looked sound. They probably just needed adjusting.

The bike was painted the same black as the garage doors and there was still some of the paint left in one of the cans on the shelf – Jenkins was sure of that – so it would be easy to touch up the paintwork where it had been scratched and rust had set in. There would be some sandpaper in one of the boxes too, so Tom could be tasked with the job of removing the old rusty paint. They spent a pleasant couple of hours sorting out the bike, and when they had finished it looked like new.

Jenkins wheeled it outside to stand in the sun so that the

paint could dry. He thought it wise to make a sign to alert Louisa to the fact that the paint was still wet so that she was not tempted to ride it as soon as she came back. He could just imagine her wrath of displeasure, should any of the wet paint get on her clothes.

Louisa came back around 3 p.m. She had had a good day and felt as though the frostiness she had experienced from the other local women was starting to thaw. As she entered the driveway she saw the bicycle sitting outside the garage. The sun was glinting off the shiny new paint and it was so clean and tidy that it could have passed as new. She knew that Jenkins would have done most of the work, but she thought, slightly wryly, that she would have to also acknowledge Tom's part in this transformation. She studied the bicycle from every angle and was suitably impressed. She entered the house through the front door and placed her basket containing various jars and parcels on the table in the hall while she took off her outdoor clothes.

She brushed down her skirt and fine knitted jumper, picked up the basket and walked towards the kitchen. Tom was coming through the dining room and froze as he saw her coming towards him. Louisa smiled despite herself. 'Well, Tom, I must say that you and Jenkins have created a complete transformation with the old bicycle. Well done.' Tom stood there open-mouthed. He had been expecting the usual jibe or taunt – he knew how to deal with that – but this praise was completely unexpected and threw him completely off his stride. Louisa just walked past him and carried on into the kitchen.

Maggie was wiping down the surfaces as Louisa entered. Louisa placed her basket of goods on the table and smiled at Maggie. 'I have some bits and pieces from the WI ladies. I think there is some jam and also some pickles, some eggs and cheese.

Take a look and see what you would like to do with them. I know that you will make much better use of them all than I ever could, Maggie. Perhaps one day you would be willing to teach me some of your legendary culinary skills.'

Now it was Maggie's turn to look astonished. What was going on? Louisa seemed not to notice and was busily emptying the contents of the basket onto the table. There was a certain glow about her that Maggie noticed as she took in the colour of her skin and the thickness of her fair hair. Louisa looked radiant.

Then the obvious slowly started to dawn on her. Was Louisa perhaps with child? Her glance instinctively lowered to take in Louisa's belly, but there was no sign of any change. But she was young. Often changes were not noticeable for several months in very young women.

Maggie cleared her throat gently, making Louisa look up. Hesitantly Maggie began to speak. 'You are looking very well, Louisa. May I enquire whether you might possibly be in the family way? Your complexion and hair look positively lustrous.'

Louisa beamed with pleasure, even though she would normally have taken offence at being asked such a personal question by someone she had always appeared to hold in mild contempt. 'I believe that I am.' She hugged herself and looked wistfully at Maggie. 'I have not spoken to Edward yet, but I am sure that he will notice very soon, being a doctor and everything. I didn't want him to fuss. I am enjoying helping the WI and being out and about in the village.' She looked slightly concerned that her husband might confine her to the house and even her bedroom as soon as he discovered that she was indeed carrying his child.

Maggie scoffed at her. 'Dr Winter is a sensible man. Of

course he will be concerned with the welfare of you and the child, but he would no more expect you to stay in your room than start climbing the trees in the garden.' She gave out a short bark of laughter at her own joke.

Louisa smiled hesitantly. 'Maggie…' she said quietly. Maggie looked at her intently, willing her to continue. 'What was he like with Sophie when she was with child? What did Sophie do?'

Maggie pulled out a chair and sat down at the table, gesturing for Louisa to do the same. 'Sophie was very spirited, but a kind and gentle soul. She carried on as normal. She didn't suffer from morning sickness or any troubles so just went about her business as usual until she became the size of a house, especially with Cassy.'

She smiled, remembering Sophie's huge bulk with fondness. 'Even then she still tried to carry on pottering about the garden, deadheading the flowers and pruning and the like. We all joked that she would be having her baby out there on the lawn, the way she was carrying on.'

She smiled, but it was tinged with sadness as she remembered the loss of such a wonderful person as Sophie had been. Maggie mentally shook herself and pushed herself up from the table. 'So there is no need for you to be worrying about anything on that score.'

Seemingly satisfied, Louisa nodded her head and left the kitchen to go and find Jenkins to thank him for doing such a good job with the bicycle. She smiled to herself. Maybe this baby would be the making of her.

CHAPTER 30

1973

James had booked the four of them into a little bed and breakfast just outside the pretty town of Keswick. The journey had been long and tiring because of having to make several stops for the children, but they were finally there.

The dark stone of the cottage with its roses around the door and white painted sign stood stark but beautiful against a bright blue sky. The stone mullioned windows with leaded glass reflected the scant white clouds that barely marred the beauty of the glorious day. hung loosely in the sky as if apologising for their very existence.

James parked the car on the street outside and pulled up the handbrake with sharp finality. He smiled at Susan, then turned in his seat to speak to the children. 'Well, we are here at last. Robert, you can help me with the suitcases, and Emma, you can help your mother with the smaller bags.' The children looked at each other and grinned. They had no memory of any previous family holidays so were excited, but also slightly apprehensive. They were thrilled that their father seemed to be much happier, but were anxiously watching for signs that his previous behaviour may make a sudden return.

James got out of the car and addressed his wife. 'Susan, would you be a dear and go and knock on the door and alert the landlady to our arrival, please?' Susan got out of the car and walked up the short path to the front door of the property. She was still slightly wary of her husband's new-found good temper and, like the children, was ever alert to the potential return to his former behaviour. So, although everything seemed lovely on the surface, her level of anxiety was by no means lessened. She sighed to herself. She hoped that in time she would learn to relax and enjoy her husband's company, as she had in the early days of their relationship.

The door was painted a lovely dark blue and had a beautiful stained-glass panel at the top. The door knocker was brightly polished brass in the shape of a fox, whose tail curled up to form the handle. She knocked sharply – two raps – and stood back to await the appearance of the landlady.

When the door was flung open it released a smell of baking mixed with soup and polish. It was a distinctive smell, and for all its assortment of different components was not unpleasant. Mrs Derby was a middle-aged lady, slightly stout and thickened at the waist. Her pepper-and-salt hair had been secured in a tidy bun and she was dressed in smart tweeds with sensible shoes and what looked like woollen tights which, considering the warmth of the day, seemed to Susan to be slightly excessive.

Susan opened her mouth to introduce herself, but Mrs Derby's face broke into a welcoming smile as she said, 'Mrs Morton?' in an enquiring tone.

When Susan nodded and said yes Mrs Derby looked over her shoulder and, taking in the children and James, called out, 'Welcome, welcome. Come on in. I'll show you your room and then I'm sure you could do with a nice cup of tea. You must have had a long journey. Surrey, wasn't it, that you've come from? You must be exhausted. Jim … Jim…'

The last was said at a shout over her shoulder as Susan wondered whether this woman ever stopped to draw breath. She was still talking now. 'Jim's my husband. He'll come and help with the bags. Do you want some squash, children, and maybe a biscuit? Come with me. We will go to the lounge while your parents and my Jim get the bags upstairs.'

The children both looked at their mother for approval and, when it had been given by a nod of the head, they followed the woman down the corridor towards the as yet unseen kitchen. The whole while, Mrs Derby managed to keep up a steady stream of conversation without letting up.

Susan and James looked at each other and started to laugh. It was a rare moment of shared amusement, and Susan savoured it as a warm and relaxed feeling spread over her. They could still hear the distant drone of Mrs Derby's constant chatter when her husband Jim appeared, ready to help them take their bags. Susan wondered if he had to resort to wearing earplugs or if he was so used to his wife that he no longer noticed her or listened to her.

They followed Mr Derby upstairs to a large family room that included a double bed and two single beds, two bedside cupboards, a huge wardrobe, which could quite easily lead to Narnia, and a sink. Mr Derby informed them that the bathroom was along the landing and would be shared with only one other family. The room was bright and cheerful, papered in a stripy yellow print with lemon-coloured bedspreads. There was a small table in the large box bay window and two comfortable-looking green velvet wingback chairs sat proudly in the space, displaying an assortment of plump cushions upholstered in a pretty floral pattern. The whole effect was comfortable and charming, and Susan let out a contented breath.

Mr Derby and James placed the cases on the purpose-built stand inside the door. 'Come down when you're ready. Just follow the sound of the wife,' Mr Derby said matter-of-factly, with no hint of humour apart from the half-hidden twinkle in his eye.

Susan threw herself down in one of the chairs and smiled at James as he closed the door on the retreating back of Mr Derby. She lifted the stiff white net curtain and spied a tidy garden with well-tended rose beds and a view over the rooftops to the hills and mountains beyond. James grimaced. 'Goodness, Susan, I certainly couldn't cope if you talked nineteen to the dozen like that.'

Susan smiled. 'I know. I wonder how she breathes. It was totally fascinating to watch.' Susan felt light with joy. She seemed to have been waiting her whole married life for James to treat her like this. It seemed like his behaviour wasn't showing signs of changing back, either – well, at least at present. She wanted to savour every moment.

Sensing her gaze on him, James reached down and, taking her hand, pulled her into an embrace. He stroked her soft, thick hair and spoke into her neck. 'God, Susan, I've been such a fool. I don't know what possessed me to act the way I have been.'

Susan smiled at him. She didn't understand it either and, although she was still slightly wary that he may revert to his previous bullishness, she wanted to enjoy this new James. 'Shall we go down and find the children?' she asked him gently.

James shuddered slightly. 'I suppose that we must, if only to rescue them from Mrs Derby.'

They walked back down and followed the steady trill of Mrs Derby's constant stream of verbal diarrhoea. They walked down a stone-flagged hallway, which was quite dark, having no windows, but it had plenty of prints adorning the wallpapered walls.

At the end of the passage they stepped into a bright and airy kitchen painted in a bright pale yellow, where a cream Aga was standing proudly against the wall. There was a basket containing a small dog and a ginger kitten curled up together at the base of the Aga and a scrubbed wooden table in the middle, at which sat both the children and Mr Derby. The children were nursing mugs of steaming hot chocolate and there was a half-eaten plate of home-made biscuits in the middle of the table. Bright sunlight streamed through the kitchen window and bounced off the leaves and petals of a pretty floral display on the windowsill.

There was an Edwardian airer hanging from the ceiling, from which hung an assortment of pots, pans, dried herbs and various utensils. A large pot simmered gently on the top of the Aga and released an aroma so delicious that both James and Susan's stomachs rumbled in unison. They both looked at each other, aghast at their bad manners, and hastily at the Derbys, who did not appear to have noticed. The children were stifling giggles behind their hands. Their parents' joint faux pas had not passed them by quite so readily.

'Take a seat, take a seat, loveys. You must be exhausted from the journey. Now what can I get you both, tea? Coffee? A cold drink? I always prefer a nice cup of tea even when it is stifling hot, don't I, Jim? I said, don't I, Jim?' This last was directed at the man who seemed to have been taking absolutely no notice of what his wife was saying.

Mrs Derby waved a hand dismissively in his direction and started on again while simultaneously filling the kettle and setting down some brightly coloured mugs on the kitchen worktop. 'Coffee, please, Mrs Derby,' said Susan, and James too nodded his assent. 'I must say that you have a beautiful home. I adore your Aga,' Susan said wistfully. For all the grandeur of their home in Surrey, this small house was much cosier and more welcoming.

With coffees in hand and biscuits laid before them, the family looked relaxed. Mrs Derby eyed them curiously. They looked as though they had left some trouble behind them, she thought. The lines around both the parents' eyes were deep, and Susan did not seem a hundred per cent relaxed in her husband's company. She was watchful and careful, as though used to dealing with quick changes in mood.

James looked as though he were surprised to be out in the wide world, as if he were seeing things for the first time. There was a certain feeling of freedom about him, but there was also something missing. Mrs Derby wondered idly what that could be. She was well used to reading people. So many came into her life fleetingly. Some returned, but many she never saw again. Her constant chatter put them at ease or on edge. Their reaction to it was interesting to watch, and it was a deliberate ploy used to examine their finer nuances of personality. Her husband thought her slightly mad, but humoured her all the same.

The children sat close together at the table as if the nearness of one to the other offered comfort and strength. They talked in small whispers and cast nervous glances between their parents. Mrs Derby's eyes narrowed. *So it is definitely the father*, she said to herself in conclusion, shifting her ample bosom with her forearms and turning back to the range. She would need to keep her wits about her, that was sure.

They passed a pleasant half an hour or so chattering politely. Mrs Derby offered some suggestions about places they might wish to visit until James stood up and said politely, 'Thank you,

Mrs Derby, for your time and fine hospitality, but I feel that we have taken up enough of your time. Come, children, Susan…'

He placed a hand on his wife's back and guided her and the children out of the kitchen. 'I think we will take a walk down to the lake. Are the gardens still as beautiful as ever?' Mrs Derby replied that they were indeed and that the front door was open until 11 p.m., but after that time they would need to use the key on the little key ring that Mr Derby had given them when he showed them to their room.

With all the pleasantries and thanks completed, the family trooped back down the hallway and out of the front door to the car. James opened the boot to retrieve wellington boots and coats for everyone, and then they started walking down the hill towards the town and onwards to the gardens and lake.

Mrs Derby stood in the front parlour watching them go. She could just make out a swirling white mist accompanying the family. It seemed to be hovering over Mr Morton. Mrs Derby frowned. She would need to confer with her friend Gladys, but if she were not very much mistaken something not very pleasant was afoot, and although it was currently benign it had the potential to become volatile. Of that she was certain. This was further evidenced by the behaviour she had witnessed being exhibited by the rest of the family. Mr James Morton had something dark going on, even though he currently appeared to be having a reprieve.

The family spent a pleasant afternoon walking around the gardens. The children played in the park while James and Susan admired the beautifully artful floral creations. They walked down to the edge of the lake, where a huge gaggle of geese mixed with a few swans fought for the scraps of bread and stale sandwiches happily relinquished by excited children. Susan stood back, having always been slightly afraid of swans, but the children seemed to be enjoying themselves.

James even paid for them all to go out on the water in one of the large boats, and it was wonderful to be transported across the smooth water with the mountains in the distance creating a breathtaking backdrop of greens, reds, golds and purples. 'It must be stunning in the winter, James,' Susan said as she turned to him, her eyes dreamy with joy. 'With the snow on the mountain tops, I mean.'

'Yes, it is,' James replied. 'I spent a lot of time up here when I was younger. I had a cousin who lived just outside Windermere. I wonder where he moved to?' he mused, his hand on his chin in thought. 'I think the family moved to Canada or something.' He shook his head. 'I can't remember now. I did love it so – up here, I mean. The scenery, the walks, the air. It was all so different to Surrey.'

Susan smiled at him and laid her head on his shoulder. He patted her hair and wondered what happened to him to change him so much.

Chapter 31

1 9 3 6

L ouisa decided to tell Edward when he came home from the surgery that evening. She had had a pleasing day and felt happy and relaxed.

As it happened Edward was delayed by the unexpected appearance of a premature baby, and so did not return home until around midnight. He was surprised to see Louisa still awake, reading her book when he entered the bedroom. 'I did not expect you to wait up for me, Louisa. I am sorry. The birth was a difficult one and it was very tricky, but we all prevailed, and mother and baby should survive.'

He sat on the bed to remove his shoes and socks and stopped, then passed a weary hand over his hair. He turned to Louisa, who had placed a hand on his back as a gentle reassurance of her support. 'I understand, Edward. And, had I not had something of great importance to tell you, I would indeed have already been fast asleep.'

Intrigued, Edward paused in his undressing and turned his full attention to his wife. 'Oh, and what, pray, is of such import to keep my beautiful wife from her slumber?' he responded with a smile.

Louisa smiled prettily back at her husband and then, unable to contain her news for one second longer, she excitedly announced her news. 'Edward, my darling, we are to have a child.'

Edward stared for a second and then his face broke into a huge grin, 'Really, my darling…? Well, that is the best news. I should have noticed. I apologise for being so remiss. I presume you are feeling quite well.'

'Very well. In fact Maggie noticed this morning and commented that I was, in fact, blooming.'

Edward reached out and touched her hand. 'You always look beautiful to me, my dear. But yes, I have to agree that there is an additional radiance about you, now that I look more closely.'

Louisa felt her bosom swell with pride at the kind words and relaxed back against the headboard. 'Now, Edward,' she continued, with a stubbornness that Edward had learnt to ignore at his peril, 'I do not want you to stop me from going about my daily tasks and helping the WI, etc. Not when I have only just started and realised that I really enjoy being involved.' She had a haughty set to her jaw that defied him to argue with her.

Edward laughed. 'My dear, when have I ever been able to stop you from doing anything that you wish?'

Seemingly satisfied by his answer, Louisa relaxed her tight jaw and snuggled down under the covers. 'As long as we understand each other,' she said, and turned over to turn out the light on her bedside table.

Edward finished undressing and carefully laid his clothes on the chair under the window. He was pleased about the child, but wondered also about Louisa's determination to carry on as normal. He had expected her to want to be cosseted and fussed over. He shrugged to himself. Either way, he didn't really mind. As long as Louisa was happy the rest of the household seemed to be happy too, himself included.

He got into bed, relishing the cool, clean cotton sheet beneath him, and thought back to the birth he had just attended. So many people were still living in abject poverty, with no access to running water, and doing their very best with so little. He wished he could do more. He knew that at least people in the countryside seemed to have it better than those crowded in the slums of larger cities. But even so, in this day and age, to still have to go to the pump to gather water, to have no bathroom and only an outside toilet…

Edward rolled over to kiss his wife goodnight. She snuggled against him, and he breathed in the sweet scent of her as his thoughts drifted back to the poor woman who he had just delivered of a premature baby in difficult circumstances. The room was as clean as it could be, but it was nothing like how he lived. The floor had been of simple swept stone flags, and five people shared one bedroom. How could that be right?

He sighed and turned over. The poor woman had five children already, and this new addition to the family would need extra care. She was weakened from the birth and the eldest child was only ten, so there was no hope of extra money coming in. Luckily her husband had a job at one of the local farms, but he did not earn very much. He would speak to Louisa and Maggie in the morning and see if they could get some extra help to the family. With these thoughts rolling around his head Edward eventually drifted off to sleep.

He awoke to a new day. Bright sunlight flooded the room and the birds were welcoming in the dawn with great gusto. Louisa was still sleeping soundly next to him, so he gently drew back the covers and got up as quietly as he could so as not to disturb her.

He got dressed and went downstairs to find Maggie in the kitchen. 'You had a late one last night, Doctor,' she said, without looking up from the dough she was kneading at the table. Edward smiled to himself. Maggie seemed to have an uncanny knack of knowing exactly who had entered her domain without actually seeing them.

He chose to keep these reflections to himself and instead said, 'Yes, poor Mrs Jennings. I delivered her sixth baby last night, and it was not the easiest of births.' Maggie looked up suddenly at that. 'Edith Jennings? Why, her babe is not due for another five weeks.'

Maggie rubbed her hands clean on a damp cloth and brushed them down her apron to dry them. She walked to the stove and lifted the kettle to see how much water it held. Seemingly satisfied, she placed it onto the hot plate and started to prepare the pot for tea.

Edward nodded. 'Yes, the baby was slightly premature, but seems to be doing OK. Maggie, I wanted to ask if you, Louisa and perhaps some of the WI members could try and do something to help the family.' Maggie looked at him steadily, waiting for him to elaborate.

Realising that he had indeed gained her full attention, Edward continued. 'The family is very poor. They now have six children, the eldest of who is only ten, and Mr Jennings works as hard as he can but does not earn very much. They are all crammed into a very small space and have so very little. Now Edith will be laid up for a time while trying to care for a premature baby, doing her best to make sure that her other five children get enough to eat and, on top of everything else, ensuring that she has enough milk to feed the infant.' He sighed and ran his hands through his hair.

Maggie put her hands on her hips and looked at him. He was such a kind man, she thought. Always wanting to give more and more. He looked tired himself, she reflected.

She placed a cup of tea down in front of him and said, 'You

leave it to us, Doctor. We always care for our own. You'd be surprised at the support the villagers offer to each other, but I will make sure that they have a hot meal every day for at least the next two weeks. And we can also rustle up some clothes, etc. But,' she added with a word of warning, 'These people also have their pride, Doctor, so we have to be careful how we go about offering our help and support. They won't want to feel like they are a charity case, now.'

Edward stared at her thoughtfully. 'No, I don't suppose they will. I'll leave it to your judgement, Maggie.' And with that he took his tea and headed to his study.

Maggie was tidying away the breakfast things when Louisa came into the kitchen. She was dressed simply in a loose-fitting dress in a pale green check with yellow flowers, and had tied her hair up with a scarf in a matching shade of green. She looked carefree and happy, Maggie thought, as Louisa pulled out a chair and sat down at the kitchen table. Maggie offered her a cup of tea and joined her at the table. Maggie still felt slightly awkward in Louisa's company, but this new version of the mistress of the house was growing on her.

'Dr Winter mentioned helping out Mrs Jennings and her family to me this morning, Louisa,' Maggie began.

Louisa took a sip of her tea and gave her attention to the older woman. 'Go on,' she said.

'I was wondering whether some of the WI women could rustle up some clothes and the like,' Maggie continued. 'I will speak to some of my connections and ensure that there is a hot meal provided for the family every day for a couple of weeks, but they will need other provisions and Edith will be very tired. I am sure that her eldest will be able to help with some of the chores, but they have little money and Edith won't be able to continue doing any ironing for local families like she did before the baby came, to supplement their income, for a few weeks yet.'

Louisa nodded and sipped her tea thoughtfully as Maggie continued. 'They are a very proud family, though, and will not take kindly to charity, so help will need to be offered tactfully.' Louisa felt a stab of irritation just show its head for a second before subsiding almost as quickly as it came. She didn't know if the *tactfully* comment had been aimed at her, but she also supposed that Maggie probably had a point if it had.

At that moment Tom raced into the kitchen like a whirlwind, quickly followed by Cassy. Both children stopped abruptly when they saw Louisa, and their mouths both opened in a mirrored round *Oh*.

Maggie stood up. 'Slow down, both of you, and stop running in my kitchen. You both look like you have the Devil himself after you.'

'Sorry, Maggie,' both children muttered together. 'We came to see if there were any shortbread biscuits left. Tom said that he would eat every last one before I got to the kitchen because I was a slowcoach and couldn't run because it was beneath me, so I thought I would show him…'

Cassy started to trail off as she looked at Louisa. 'Oh, don't mind me,' Louisa said hastily. 'I must be off myself, anyway. I will speak to the other ladies at the WI, Maggie, and see what we can come up with for the Jennings family.' And with that she got up and walked out of the kitchen by the back door and round the front of the house to the garage to retrieve the bicycle.

Maggie chuckled at the two children, who were still standing there wide-eyed with shock at the transformation that appeared to have come over their stepmother. 'Louisa seems to be mellowing, doesn't she?' Maggie said. 'Sometimes things happen in our lives that change our very core. Now, who wants a biscuit?' Pulled out of their dream with the magic word *biscuit*, both children focused their attention on the much more important task of choosing the biggest and best titbit that they could.

Louisa pulled the bicycle out of the garage and pushed it through the gravel and up the slope to the top of the drive, and mounted it once she got to the road. The gravel on the driveway was very thick and made cycling through it very difficult. She didn't want to fall off and hurt the baby.

She had been pleased that Edward had not insisted she give up her WI duties when she was just starting to feel accepted. She was not even starting to show yet, so not even the older ladies could comment on any impropriety on her behalf. She didn't really much care about the work that the WI did – a lot of goodie-goodie nonsense for the most part – but that feeling of belonging and respect made her feel … well, sort of complete, she said to herself with a wry smile. Plus, she actually enjoyed being out and about on the bicycle too. She had forgotten how it felt to have the wind in your hair and the freedom to go where you wanted.

She drew up at the church hall, which served in many different capacities, including various talks and slide shows on different subjects, the Scouts meeting hall and numerous other groups and events as befitted the local community.

Louisa placed the bicycle in the rack positioned for the purpose to the side of the long brick building and went inside. There were a number of women there already, and they looked up as Louisa entered.

'Ah, Louisa,' a stout lady of around sixty with pepper-and-salt hair and a no-nonsense air about her said, as Louisa approached. Her name was Mrs Markham, and she was the current president of the group.

Louisa was startled and looked nervously at the older woman. 'No need to look so terrified, my dear,' Mrs Markham continued with a hearty chuckle. 'We've just been discussing Edith Jennings and her family. As the doctor's wife I am sure that you must have some insight on the subject.'

Now her status in the community was thus recognised, Louisa felt buoyed up with importance and beamed her response. 'Yes, of course. Why, it was one of the things I was going to bring up at today's meeting,' she continued.

The other ladies all looked at her expectantly, and Mrs Markham made some hand gestures which seemed to indicate that Louisa get on with it. 'Edward – that is, Dr Winter – spoke to me this morning, and then I also spoke to Maggie ... that is, our housekeeper—'

'Yes, yes, dear,' said Mrs Markham, with slight irritation. 'Can we get to the point, please?' Louisa could feel the sweat start on her hands and also begin to trickle down her back. She did not want to wipe her palms against her dress, as that would be unbecoming, but under the scrutiny of Mrs Markham she was starting to feel decidedly uncomfortable.

'Yes, sorry... Well, both Edward and Maggie mentioned that Edith and her family would need some extra help, what with the baby coming early and having so many mouths to feed. Maggie also mentioned that we should be careful as the family, though poor, are very proud and would not want to be seen as a charity case.

'Maggie and her friends are seeing that the family has a

cooked meal once a day for a couple of weeks but wondered if we could rally round and come up with some gifts for the baby and mother like clothes and jams, bread, vegetables, etc. Whatever anyone can spare. If we made it like a gift, then it would be more likely to go down better than offering help.' She trailed off, losing steam, but glad that she had managed to remain articulate under such pressure.

Mrs Markham looked thoughtful for a moment or two as everyone waited for her response, and it was with great relief to all, Louisa especially, when her thoughts seemed to gather together to form a smile. 'Great idea, Louisa. Well done. Ladies, let's see what we can do between us all. Louisa, you can deliver our offerings to the family, seeing as you brought the idea to us. One of us can come with you, of course, but I think that this would be a step in the right direction for your furtherance with our cause.'

Louisa was thrilled. Not only had she finally been accepted into the group, but to be given such a responsibility was an honour. 'Of course, Mrs Markham, I would be delighted,' she said, and then excused herself so she could go and wash her hands, which by now were feeling decidedly sticky and unpleasant.

The meeting passed much as usual. There was an interesting talk on flower arranging, and Louisa noted a couple of tips that she intended to try. Towards the end of the meeting, Mrs Markham attended to Any Other Business and waited for a moment to make sure that she had everyone's full attention before she continued. 'Now, you probably all have heard about Edith Jennings's premature delivery of her baby.'

She looked about the room and noticed that several of the members were nodding and some were murmuring gently to their closest neighbour in the hall. 'Well, ladies,' she continued, 'we need to see what we can do to help the family. Young Edith already has a fair clutch of young ones and the eldest is only around nine or ten.'

'Little Amy is ten years old,' came a shout from the back of the hall from one of the Jennings's neighbours.

'Right, so she is ten. So will be able to help a little, but she will be at school during the day and with the others to look after, a newborn who will need extra care and, from what I understand, having had a bit of a troublesome birth, Edith will need some additional help and support. I understand from Louisa here, the good doctor's wife, that the family are very proud and need to be handled empathetically. I would like us to show that we are a caring community, and if you can gather together some "gifts" for the mother and baby Louisa and I will deliver them later this week.' Louisa smiled around the room at the other ladies, thrilled to have been singled out by the president in such a favourable manner. She was almost glowing with pride herself.

The meeting came to a close and the other ladies started to write on a sheet that Mrs Markham's secretary, Elsie Jones, had hastily prepared, to detail what each of the members could donate. Louisa had to think herself. Would she donate something for Edith or for the baby?

Mrs Markham pulled Louisa aside and said, 'Louisa, I was thinking we could take the gifts in a few days' time. It will give everyone a chance to get their bits and pieces together. How about Thursday at, say, eleven o'clock?'

'Yes, Mrs Markham, that would be perfect. Shall I meet you here at the hall? How will we carry everything?'

'Oh, don't you worry about that. I'll get George the baker

to lend me his van for an hour or so. He will be finished with his morning rounds by then, anyway.'

Louisa looked shocked. 'But Mrs Markham, can you drive?' she asked in awe.

'Of course I can drive, child,' Mrs Markham said with astonishment, as if to have any of her abilities questioned was completely unfathomable to her. 'Eleven o'clock, Louisa, on Thursday, and not a minute after,' and with that she strode off across the hall to speak to one of the other ladies.

Louisa stood stock-still for a moment, still shocked by the revelation that Mrs Markham could drive. But, if she had really thought about it, it should not have surprised her. It should not really surprise her either if Mrs Markham announced that she was just popping off to the moon to collect some cheese, so accomplished and formidable was her character.

She smiled to herself and gathered her wits about her before going over to the group of women poring over the list of gifts to be gathered for Edith. She had been thinking and had decided on a particularly lovely crocheted blanket that she had made for her mother before she died and which was currently in a box in the attic. She took her turn and wrote *Louisa Winter: one crocheted blanket, adult size* on the list before saying her goodbyes and retrieving her bicycle from outside the hall to cycle home.

When Louisa got home, she went to look for the blanket straight away. When she found it she took it straight downstairs to the kitchen to ask Maggie for her opinion and also to enquire about the best way to launder it, or whether it just should be placed on the line to air.

Maggie was peeling vegetables at the sink and looked up as Louisa entered the kitchen. 'What have you got there, Louisa?'

she asked, looking at the folded blanket in her arms. 'That looks lovely.'

'It is a blanket that I made for my mother when I was a girl, and I thought that it would be a nice gift for Edith Jennings. What do you think?'

Louisa stretched the blanket out between her hands as she spoke and held it up off the floor so that Maggie could see it in all its glory. 'It is rather lovely. You made it, you say? Does it not have sentimental meaning to you, then?' Maggie was interested and did not say it in a judgemental way, Louisa realised, as she felt that old twinge of irritation rise and drop away just as suddenly.

'Well, it does and it doesn't,' she replied before continuing. 'I spent hours on it, and my mother only had it for a short time before she died, so it is practically new. It seems such a waste not to be used. Oh, I know that Cassy or Tom could have it on their beds, but they have so much and Edith… Well, she doesn't, and it might be something little that could brighten up her world.'

She bit her lower lip, unsure now whether she had made the right decision. Maggie could see the play of emotions on Louisa's face and decided to quickly put her out of her misery. 'Well, I think that it is a wonderful idea. Well done, Louisa. You really seem to be getting in the spirit of things. Do you want me to give it a quick wash for you?'

'Oh, would you?' Louisa replied gratefully. 'I wanted to ask you what was required, but I really have no idea where to start. I don't mind doing it, but don't want to spoil it either.'

'Leave it with me. I'll hand-wash it in the old tin bath. It's too big, really, to do it in the sink. Then it will need to dry flat. I'll get an old sheet and lay that on the lawn and put it on top. It will take a while as it will not be easy to squeeze all the water out of it, but it's set fair for the next couple of days so that should be fine.'

Louisa thanked her and went upstairs to change, as she was now rather dusty from delving about in the attic boxes to find the blanket and wanted to brush the dust off her clothes and wash her face.

Cassy and Tom sat at the bottom of the stairs playing what looked like tiddlywinks. Louisa looked at them suspiciously. 'What are you two doing cooped up in here when it is such a nice day?' she asked them. 'Tom, you especially can't usually be kept indoors for more than five minutes.'

Cassy replied sadly, 'All our friends have gone on a special outing with the Sunday school group and Father didn't remember to sign the letter, so we couldn't go.'

'Really?' Louisa replied stunned. 'Why didn't you ask me to sign the letter?' she asked, realising at once that asking her would probably have been the last thing they would have done. It dawned on her then how much her behaviour had changed since she had realised that she was expecting. Had she always been so unapproachable?

She smiled at the children. 'Well, in the future, if your father is busy, please ask me. Now would you two be willing to donate some of your toys that you no longer play with to a family in the village who are not as fortunate as you both are?'

Cassy and Tom looked at each other and then back at Louisa. They both shrugged and said, 'I suppose,' in unison. They scrambled up and went to their respective rooms to choose something that they could bear to be parted from.

Once they had both found a couple of toys that they really did not mind giving away, the two children convened in Tom's room. Cassy never let Tom into her room. He was far too meddlesome, she said.

Although Tom was much younger than her and really didn't have much to offer in the way of sensible conversation, Cassy really needed to discuss what on earth was going on with their former governess and new stepmother, and Tom was really the only outlet she had in this regard.

They knelt on the cushioned window seat looking out over the garden. They could see Jimmy Jenkins and Cedric Graves looking at one of the larger old trees at the side of the garden, deep in conversation. Cedric was pointing at various parts of the tree and Jimmy was scratching his chin and rubbing his face in equal measure. The sun was casting short shadows across the lawn and the birds were singing in earnest.

'Well, Tom,' Cassy began, 'What do you think is going on with Louisa? I mean – don't get me wrong – it's much better for her to be being nice than being scratchy and horrid all the time. But it feels kind of weird, don't you think?'

Tom looked thoughtful for a moment. 'You don't think that she has been replaced by aliens or something, do you?' Tom was an avid reader and loved his science fiction books and comics.

'No, I don't, silly,' Cassy said, slapping him lightly on the arm, and they both dissolved into a fit of giggles as Tom did an exaggerated monster walk like a small lopsided Frankenstein's monster across the room.

When they had recovered Cassy revisited the question that had prompted their laughter. 'I mean it, though, Tom,' she said, a slight frown appearing on her face as she tried to fathom the sense of what was going on. 'Don't you think it's strange? I mean, one minute she is the epitome of the dreaded stepmother and in the blink of an eye she is all sweetness, light and charity. It just seems unbelievable.'

Tom just looked thoughtful for a minute and then said, 'I don't know, Cassy. Perhaps it has something to do with the baby.'

Cassy looked at him as if he had gone mad. 'Baby? What do you mean, baby? What baby?' Tom shrugged in an uninterested manner adopted by most boys of his age when adults were being discussed as if they were a completely different and unfathomable species best left to their own devices. 'I heard Louisa discussing it with Maggie in the kitchen the other day.'

'Are you sure you heard it right?' Cassy said incredulously. 'I mean, Louisa having a baby? No. Really? Can that be true? Why haven't they told us?' She looked completely indignant now.

'I don't know, Cassy,' Tom replied. 'Perhaps it has nothing to do with us, but if it means that Louisa is actually going to be nice then I'd say it was worth it, wouldn't you?'

He got down from the window seat and walked over to the bed to pick up the train and the soft blue teddy that had been given to him by an aunt who he was not particularly fond of. 'I am going to give these to Louisa. What have you chosen?'

And with that the conversation was over and Cassy was left looking dumbfounded on the window seat.

CHAPTER 32

1973

After the boat had nestled itself gently back against the jetty the Morton family disembarked. Their hair had been blown into an assortment of different shapes and their faces were flushed from the breeze. It was still warm, but the day had taken on a slightly brooding air. The sky had darkened to a dark grey over the mountains and the sun had all but vanished, and the wind was getting up and sending ripples over the surface of the lake. The birds had gone and were swimming en masse across the lake to one of the many small islands that dotted its surface.

'Come on,' James urged his family, looking up at the ominous sky, 'If I'm not sorely mistaken, we are about to suffer a soaking.' Sure enough, big fat drops of rain started to drop heavily from the sky, slowly at first, but they became faster and faster until their rapid break from the freedom of the clouds caused an almost impenetrable sheet of water to cascade down from the leaden sky, drowning everything in its wake.

Within mere moments they were all completely soaked through, yet strangely they were not cold. Rivulets of rain poured from their hair, which was by now plastered to their faces and dripped off their lashes and the ends of their noses and chins.

They all looked at each other in astonishment and just burst out laughing. 'This is the second time this summer we have been caught in the rain, isn't it, children?' Susan remarked as they did their best to shelter under the bandstand in the park, along with an assortment of other people also unlucky enough to have been caught out by the rain.

'Oh?' said James. 'When was that?' Susan looked at him suddenly, realising that this new nice James had only been in evidence for a few short days, and she hesitated for a moment before responding. James noticed this and was momentarily irritated, but mainly with himself for causing a change in the mood.

'I took the children for a picnic the other day.' Susan continued, looking straight at her husband so that he could see that she was being honest and truthful to him. 'We had just finished our picnic and the children were playing when suddenly the heavens opened just like this, and we were drenched. Luckily we were close to the farm cottages and Robert suggested we take shelter with John and Sarah Peters.'

James lifted his chin slightly in a movement which suggested that he understood, but he did not comment any further. Susan, feeling slightly unsure of whether to continue or not but hating the silence, continued. 'They were very kind. Sarah made us a hot drink and gave us all a piece of her famous short-bread and dried out our coats out by the fire. We didn't stay long,' she continued quickly. 'The rain soon stopped, and we came home. I should have listened to Jenkins before we went out,' she said, and half-smiled. 'He said it was going to rain, but the skies were so blue and clear that I thought he must be mistaken. Always trust a gardener, I suppose, when it comes to knowing the weather forecast,' she finished slightly ruefully.

James nodded thoughtfully. 'Was this when I was away?'

'Yes,' Susan replied, wondering where this was leading, started to feel slightly queasy with anxiety, but James just smiled and squeezed her hand, and Susan let out the breath that she had not realised she was holding. The children's shoulders dropped, and Susan realised that they too had been apprehensive about how they father was going to react.

How sad for them, she thought, and hoped, not for the first time, that this new-found kind version of her husband was not just for the holiday. Living permanently in fear of doing or saying the wrong thing was exhausting.

'Shall we find somewhere to have a spot of dinner?' James asked after a moment. The rain was still lashing down and they were soaking wet, but they couldn't stay there forever, and standing still was allowing them to start to feel cold.

'All right,' Susan replied. 'Where do you suggest?' James nodded to a cafe overlooking the lake at the far end of the park. 'There looks as good as anywhere. At least we will be able to get out of the rain and dry off a bit,' he added. 'Are you ready, children? Shall we see who can get there fastest?'

The children looked at their mother suspiciously, as if to ask if this new version of their father was actually for real, but when she nodded and smiled encouragingly Robert and Emma shot off in the direction of the cafe with their parents running behind them slightly more gracefully.

The door to the cafe opened with a welcoming jangle of bells and the lady behind the counter looked up and exclaimed, 'My, my, what a bunch of wet little ducklings you all are. Come and sit by the fire, and we can hang up your coats over here to dry.'

She pointed to the coat stand, which was just inside the door. They all shrugged out of their coats gratefully and hung them on the coat stand that was conveniently situated next to a radiator which, surprisingly for the time of year, was actually on. The coats started to steam gently as the water created puddles on the flagstones beneath.

Once they were seated by the fire and starting to feel slightly more human the lady came over to them with a handful of menus. She distributed these with a kind smile and asked them if she could get them any drinks while they decided on what to eat. Susan replied, 'Thank you. That is very kind. Can we have a pot of tea for two?' She looked towards James for confirmation, to which he nodded his assent. 'And two hot chocolates for the children, please,' she added. The lady wrote this down on her pad and went back to the other side of the counter to start filling the order.

'Well, this is nice, James,' Susan said, looking around at the stone walls, from which hung an assortment of photos of the town and its people over the years, mostly in black-and-white.

The tables and chairs were a higgledy-piggledy collection of mismatched old wooden arrangements with some comfy sofas in secluded nooks with windows that looked out over the lake. There were candleholders on the tables and soft lighting from old-fashioned lamps. The whole ensemble combined to create a comfortable and relaxing atmosphere. There were a few other families and couples dotted about talking softly which added to the ambience.

James agreed. 'We used to come here years ago,' he said. 'It hasn't really changed much. It was just as lovely then.' Susan realised that there was a lot that she did not know about her husband. He never really spoke about his childhood, and she wondered what had happened along the way to change the apparently carefree young boy into the often harassed and angry man. She certainly preferred the man who sat in front of her now.

They decided on their meal and relayed their order to the waitress when she delivered their drinks, and sat back to relax and enjoy their surroundings. 'Well, what do you want to do tomorrow?' James asked them all after they had finished eating.

The children looked astounded once more and glanced again at their mother, as if for confirmation that they had indeed heard the question correctly. They were much more used to being barked at and ordered by their father to do what he wanted immediately than to be offered a choice. That's when they even saw him, of course.

Realising that their father did indeed expect an answer, Robert spoke up. 'What are the options, Dad?' He thought that this was probably a safe bet. He had replied to the question, but was not being so presumptuous as to offer his own suggestions. And anyway he did not actually know what they were, having never been to the Lake District before.

'Well,' his father began, 'we can go for a walk around one of the lakes. There are always farms to visit … and Windermere has a wonderful boat excursion, which can drop us at other towns that we can wander around. There are walks up in the mountains and we can see the wildlife. There are actually red squirrels up here, you know. Ambleside has a quaint little tower on a bridge and… Well, there is lots to do. Why don't you both go and look at those leaflets over there by the door and pick up some that you think may interest you?'

The children looked at each other excitedly and immediately jumped up to run over to the door, where there was a huge display of leaflets covering lots of local attractions and places to visit.

Susan smiled after them fondly and then looked back at James. She placed her hand over his gently and said, 'Thank you for this, James. It really is rather lovely.' She looked so grateful, he thought wistfully. Was it really such a big thing to take his family on holiday?

He thought again about his reasons. He really wanted to get away from that house. It all came down to that house. He felt trapped there. It was oppressive and it seemed to have some kind of hold over him that he didn't understand. *Perhaps we should move*, he thought suddenly. In fact, why not? The house was huge. He had bought it on a whim, as a status symbol, but they didn't need a house of that size. And, if he was really honest, it didn't seem to make any of them happy.

He was just about to suggest this to Susan when the children came running back with a handful of colourful leaflets each. 'Let's order some dessert and look through these,' he suggested, and this time the children didn't look to their mother for confirmation. They whooped their agreement wholeheartedly, without the slightest reservation.

By the time they had finished their dessert and had made some decisions about where they would all like to go over the next few days they had started to dry out a bit. The rain had stopped and the sky was blue and welcoming once more, with only the lightest of wisps of white very high in the atmosphere. The sunlight twinkled on the water, and danced on the raindrops still clinging to some of the petals on the ornamental displays in the park.

A seagull cried as it swooped low over the lake and Susan marvelled at the beauty before her. 'Why, James, it is stunning, isn't it?' She turned and looked at him with such delight on her face that he smiled. 'Yes, it certainly is. Shall we take a walk along the shoreline before heading back to the guest house?' Susan tucked her arm into his and agreed. They set off, the children running before them, not a care between them, and Susan sighed contentedly.

James looked at his wife and hoped that this was how it could be between them now. He needed to broach the subject of selling the house. The more he thought about it the more he believed that the house was at the root of his problems. It was almost like he was two different people. Here, with Susan and the children, he felt like this was how he wanted to be. This felt right.

All the other stuff at home – the house, his work, the pressure – made him behave like an idiot. His wife was beautiful and kind, a wonderful mother, and she really took great care of him and their home. She was always supportive and could be relied upon in any event he happened to find himself, so why had he been tempted away from her and with someone so empty-headed as Clare? He shuddered with revulsion at his behaviour. He suspected that Susan knew, and he wondered why she had never said or done anything about it.

Sensing a chance in her husband's mood, Susan glanced at him. She wasn't nervous, exactly, but was always in tune with his moods – more out of self-preservation than anything else.

A gust of wind seemed to come up from nowhere and blew straight between them, almost like a physical force. It caught them both off guard and forced them apart from each other. A whispered hiss that followed in its wake seemed to voice the word *No*. It was so powerful that they looked at each other as if they had been physically assaulted by a third party.

'What in God's name was that?' Susan exclaimed fearfully. The day was still bright and the children were playing happily, digging in the sandy earth with sticks, drawing patterns and writing messages to each other, before rubbing them out with their feet and starting again. But they both felt chilled to the bone and looked at each other in shocked silence.

'James,' exclaimed Susan, 'please tell me that I didn't just imagine that.'

Susan looked at her husband for confirmation. Her wide-eyed stare, along with her ruffled hair, pronounced her fear. 'I don't know,' James responded, unsure what to say to describe what had just happened. 'It was certainly very strange. Do you want to head back?'

Susan glanced nervously around her and nodded. A strange mist seemed to be coiling its way around the trunk of a tree, but the more she tried to focus on it the fainter it became until she thought that she really must be imagining things.

They called the children to them and started back up the hill to the guest house, with Susan keeping a firm hold on to her husband all the way.

CHAPTER 33

1 9 3 6

It was drizzling slightly as Louisa waited outside the hall for Mrs Markham to arrive to open it up. She had cycled again and, although she was not very wet, she felt slightly damp.

Mrs Markham frowned at her when she arrived. 'You ought to be careful, Louisa. You don't want to get a chill in your condition. Come on, let's have a cup of tea before we go. That will warm you up.' Astonished that everyone seemed to know instinctively that she was expecting, she followed Mrs Markham into the hall, which permanently seemed to smell of polish, wood and feet.

Mrs Markham turned on the lights as she went and bustled into the kitchen. She filled the large kettle at the sink and placed it on top of the stove to heat. Then she turned and fixed Louisa with a steady, appraising gaze. Louisa was yet to say a word, and felt rather nervous under such unmasked scrutiny.

'I must say, Louisa, that you have been one of life's pleasant surprises. I never had you down as a leading member of our little community, but you do seem to have come into your own of late.' Mrs Markham grimaced a smile, which could have been wind, but Louisa didn't want to go there.

'Er, thank you,' she replied cautiously. Mrs Markham nodded – she seemed to approve of Louisa's response – and turned round to start gathering the essential tea-making accoutrements from the many and varied cupboards.

Once she had assembled everything to her satisfaction she turned back to Louisa and continued as if she had been speaking to her all along. 'I suppose that playing the role of doctor's wife and running the home must get a little tedious when you have the exceedingly capable Maggie Graves already ensconced in your house. There can be little for you to do really, I expect. Far better for you to spend your time helping others. It goes down much better in the community, I can tell you. A few people thought that you were too high and mighty to dirty your hands, but you seemed to have proved them wrong in that.' She spooned tea into the pot and waited for the water to announce its readiness with its shrill cry.

Louisa didn't know what to say. Is that really what people had thought of her? She had just wanted to be accepted and thought that holding dinner parties and getting to know Edward's friends' wives was the best way forward, when in reality all she had succeeded in doing was making herself miserable, alienating her family and falling at every hurdle.

She sighed and absent-mindedly started to put away the crockery that the last group of people had left to dry on the draining board. 'I am enjoying it far more than I ever thought possible, Mrs Markham,' she finally responded. 'You are right, of course. Maggie is wonderful and manages everything so much better than I ever could. And yes, I was starting to get bored and resentful, and my aunt had once suggested the WI... Well, it was definitely the best thing I could have done.'

She smiled brightly at Mrs Markham, who was now pouring the water into the teapot. 'Come and sit down, Louisa.' She pulled out a chair herself and sat at the little table, which was painted a pale mint green. 'And do call me Sylvie. "Mrs Markham" sounds like you are speaking to my mother-in-law, and I can do without being reminded of her.'

Louisa gave a little laugh and joined Sylvie at the table.

'Thank you. Sylvie it is.' The tea was poured, and they sat drinking it in companionable silence for a moment before Louisa asked, 'Have we managed to get everything in for the Jennings family that was promised?'

'Oh yes,' continued Sylvie, 'that and far more besides. It is a good job that I have borrowed the van. There is no way we could have carried even half of it between the pair of us. It is all in the van already. We just need to add the bits that you have brought along. Everyone has been so kind and thoughtful. This is such a loving community. When we all get together, great things can be achieved. It was the same during the war.' Sylvie continued. 'We all stuck together then, so there is no reason why we cannot continue to do so, is there?'

Louisa nodded her agreement. 'I agree,' she said. 'I never really understood before. I suppose I was young, but now I totally understand. The feeling of achievement... What for us is a very little thing can make such a huge difference for others.'

She sat, and her eyes became unfocused as she looked into the middle distance. She supposed that things had come quite easily to her, really. Although not born into the upper echelons of fine society her family was a good one: her father was a rector, and her mother was well respected in the community. A position of governess for the Winter children had been a good opportunity and now...

Well, now she was a well-respected member of the community herself, having married the local doctor, so everything was how she wanted it to be. But there was still that niggle, that constant ache that something was missing or not quite complete or right. Was it the child? she wondered silently. Is that what would fill the void?

She came back into the moment and saw Sylvie Markham

eying her curiously. 'Away with the fairies you were, my dear,' she said. Then she stood up, brushed down her skirt and said, 'Come along, then. We have lots to be getting on with. Now where are the bits and bobs you brought with you?' Louisa took the cups to the sink and quickly rinsed them under the tap and followed Sylvie Markham out into the hall, with her voice booming out a running commentary of the itinerary.

Louisa trotted after her. She picked up the parcels from her basket which, luckily, had not got any wetter, as she had had the foresight to park the bicycle under the cover of the little porch entrance to the hall, seeing as it was only the two of them today and it would not be in the way.

Mrs Markham watched Louisa getting the parcels and said in her no-nonsense voice, 'We will collect your bicycle on the way back and I can drop you off on the way to dropping back the van, as it is on the way back. Your house backs onto the lane that runs down to the shops and the station, doesn't it?'

Louisa nodded, surprised that Sylvie Markham knew where she lived. Then, just as suddenly, she realised that of course everyone knew where the doctor lived and laughed at her silliness. 'Yes, that is right. There is a gate in the garden wall. I can push the bicycle down through the gardens. That would be lovely, thank you.'

With a nod and a little shrug Sylvie Markham got into the van, and Louisa settled herself in the passenger seat after moving a couple of egg boxes and a jar of jam. Sylvie turned the engine, shoved it into gear and off they went.

They drove the short distance to the Jennings's house, which was a small cottage in a row down a dirt farm track. It belonged to the farm where Mr Jennings worked and came as part of his wages, which meant that the family had somewhere to live but not much money for anything else like food and clothing for their growing family. The front garden was slightly unkempt and the paint on the doors and windows was peeling, but the windows were clean, and the front step had obviously been recently swept.

Mrs Markham knocked at the door and it was opened by a child of around nine or ten who they both presumed was Amy. Her clothes were old and patched, but she looked clean and tidy enough. 'Is your mother there?' Mrs Markham asked the young girl, who looked at them with a mixture of interest and fear.

'Amy, who is it, love?' came a shout from further inside the house.

'Yeah, she's feeding the babe,' Amy said in a quiet voice, and stepped aside to let the two rather grand ladies in.

The door opened directly into a room that seemed to have several functions. There was a large fireplace to the left over which hung a huge kettle, but most of the room was taken up with a sturdy pine table and there were six chairs around this. There were two wingback chairs situated by the fireplace that were losing their stuffing and which were threadbare along the top of the back of the fabric. They may have once been green but were now faded to almost a brown colour.

There was a dresser against the far wall and various airers scattered about, from which hung an assortment of drying clothes. A battered old clock sat on the mantelpiece, along with a couple of candlesticks, a box of matches and an old vase containing a mishmash of wild flowers. A large ginger cat, which was curled up in one of the chairs by the fire, opened one eye with lazy indifference and glanced at them before losing interest and resuming its slumber.

As they stepped into the room Edith Jennings appeared at the doorway, which must have led to the second room downstairs. She held the baby in the crook of her arm and was hastily fastening up the buttons on her worn cotton blouse. 'Oh my,' she exclaimed and tried to smooth down her hair, which looked sorely in need of a brush. She handed the baby to Amy and said, 'Put her in the crib, will you, love?'

She indicated the little swinging crib which sat to the side of the fireplace. 'How can I help you, ladies?' Edith continued, after watching Amy gently place her tiny new sister in her crib and reassured that all was as it should be. 'It's not often I receive such distinguished visitors. If I had known I would have tidied the place up a bit.' She sounded weary, and looked as pale as the white blanket that Amy had so carefully placed over the sleeping baby.

'Now, Edith, no one would expect you to stand on ceremony when you have just this instant delivered a baby. We come bearing gifts for you and your family. Louisa here is the doctor's good wife, and when we heard that you had been safely delivered of your sixth child, and that she was premature, we decided to bring you some gifts to ease your burden.'

Edith, although obviously weak and exhausted, stood up to her full height of five feet two inches, and with as much force as she could muster said in a very clear voice, 'We don't need no charity, you know. Davy always works hard and does his best for us all.'

Mrs Markham held up a hand to stop the torrent of protest before it could work into a crescendo. 'Now, now, Edith... May I call you Edith?' She didn't wait for an answer before ploughing on. 'We all know what it is like when you have a child, especially when you have other small ones to look after too. It is exhausting. So this is not charity. These are gifts from your neighbours to ease this time and to welcome a new life into our local community.'

Edith still looked unconvinced so Louisa, feeling brave, placed her hand on Sylvie Markham's arm and stepped forward. 'Edith,' she said softly, 'Edward mentioned that you had a time of it. No details, of course – that would not be proper – but he was thinking of you, and when I heard... Well, I wanted to do something, give you a gift. And when I mentioned it to the other ladies at the WI they also all wanted to give you a gift. Giving freely to others is a great joy, so to refuse that gift would cause hurt, don't you see?'

Edith nodded mutely and sank into a chair. Her eldest daughter looked at her with concern etched on her young face. 'Mam,' she said anxiously, 'do you want a cup of tea?' Louisa turned and smiled at the young girl. 'That would be lovely, Amy. Just what the doctor ordered for your mother, don't you think?' Edith just nodded, all fight gone out of her as she wiped her brow wearily with the back of her hand.

Amy filled the large kettle and stoked up the fire. Sylvie went out to the van to start bringing in the items that had been donated for the family and Louisa set out the tea things on the table. Edith had fallen into a light doze by the time the tea was made and the gifts had all been laid out on the table.

Amy patted her lightly on the arm and held out a chipped cup of tea for her, concern still evident on her face. 'I'm OK, love,' Edith said. 'I'm just a bit tired, that's all. The babe had me up most of the night, wanting to be fed.'

She glanced up and noticed that the table was now covered in offerings from a loaf of bread to toys, clothes and a rather beautiful blanket. Tears sprang to her eyes, a mixture of exhaustion and thanks. She tried to speak her gratitude, but the words would not form, so choked with emotion did she find herself.

'Now, now, Edith,' Sylvie Markham said in a blustering tone, 'there's no need for tears. Why don't you have a lie-down while the little one is asleep, and Amy can help us tidy away these things into the correct places?'

As she finished speaking the back door flew open and in came a wave of noise in the form of several young children, a dog and a smiling man with a child of about three on his shoulders and another of about two in his arms. 'What's all this, then?' he enquired in a loud voice, looking from his daughter to his wife and then at the table and the two women standing in his now very full and cramped house.

'These ladies have brought us gifts from our neighbours for the new baby. Isn't that kind of them, Davy?' Edith said quickly, before her husband could jump to the same wrong conclusion that she had. 'Louisa here…' She pointed to Louisa, who smiled at Mr Jennings. 'Well, she's the doctor's wife, and he mentioned the struggle I had to bring Molly into the world. And Louisa mentioned it to Mrs Markham, and the other ladies all wanted to give us something as way of marking her safe arrival.' The two women nodded in agreement.

'Well, then,' said Davy, looking at all the offerings on the table. The children were wide-eyed in awe, never having seen so many nice things. 'I would like to say thank you very much. That is a kind and welcome gesture.'

The tea made, everyone crowded around the table to look at the mountain of gifts. There was something for every member of the family, and lots of treats to eat. The children looked at each other and back to their parents. It was like all their Christmases coming on the same day.

Sylvie opened a tin, which contained some lavender shortbread that she had made herself, and looked at Edith. 'Is it all right for the children to have one of these each? It is lavender shortbread. I am sure they will like it.'

Edith nodded her assent and the children surged forward as one, eagerly jumping up and down to make sure that they were not forgotten. Tears formed in Edith's eyes as she watched her children, made so happy by such a small act of kindness. 'Thank you,' she whispered, and laid her head on her husband's shoulder.

He stroked her hair and looked at the two women who had brought the stack of treasures into their home. 'Yes, thank you, ladies. And would you also please thank everyone who has given so freely today on our behalf? I must be getting back to work now. I'd just popped back for a bite to eat and to take the young ones off Edith's hands for a few minutes so she could have a bit of peace, like. I ate my sandwich while I was out with them to save time... Two birds, an' all that.'

He kissed the top of his wife's head and disengaged himself from her embrace. 'See you later, love,' he said, and with a peck on her cheek he left by the back door.

As her husband left Edith seemed to crumple. The tiredness of the day was falling heavily on her shoulders and, on top of the shock of all the kindness being shown, it was too much.

On noticing her obvious distress Sylvie Markham took charge once more and gently guided her by the arm up the stairs to the largest of the bedrooms, which contained a metal-framed double bed, a small double wardrobe and a chest of drawers. The floors were bare wood with a threadbare rug, and there was a little bedside cupboard on either side of the bed.

There was a cot and also a little Moses basket in the room

too. It looked like the second-youngest child slept in the cot and the basket was for the baby. There was a bowl and a pitcher of water on the chest of drawers. The curtains were thin and would not shut out much light, but because Edith and Davy would probably both be up at first light anyway that hardly seemed to matter.

Although shabby, the room was clean and relatively tidy. There were piles of folded clothes on the bottom of the bed and on the chest of drawers next to the pitcher and bowl.

Edith lay down on the bed and Sylvie covered her over with a thin blanket and said, 'Now you just rest up here for a while. We will take care of everything for a couple of hours. You need to get your strength back or you will be little use to anyone.' With that Sylvie stood up straight and went back down the stairs after having a quick peep in the second bedroom, which held an assortment of beds and very little else.

Once back down in the kitchen she took stock of the brood of children and decided to firstly let them each pick something from the assortment of books and toys that had been donated to the family. This, she thought, would keep them occupied and relatively quiet while they tidied away the other items and decided the best plan of action to give Edith the best help and support that they could.

Louisa held the youngest child on her lap. The baby was still sleeping soundly in its crib. Amy chose a book and a soft toy, both of which had been donated by Louisa's family. She smiled to see the joy that this simple act of giving brought to the young girl. She thought that next time it may be nice to bring Cassy with her so that she could see at first hand how other people lived, and also how it was so easy to make their lives a little bit better.

Amy held out a rag doll to the child in Louisa's lap, which she took shyly, hugging the doll to her chest, and all the while not removing her thumb from her mouth. One of the boys took a wooden train while the other two shared a set of toy soldiers. Amy took a soft woollen blanket and folded it neatly and placed it at the bottom of the crib and also placed a small fluffy brown rabbit in there too. 'Molly can play with that when she wakes up,' she said, by way of explanation.

There were more toys left on the table, so Amy placed them all in a box and put them on top of the dresser. 'Mam and Dad can give these to us for Christmas,' she said.

This girl is wise beyond her years, thought Louisa, and she nodded and said, 'That sounds like a very good idea, Amy.'

There remained an assortment of jars of jam and pickles, which went into the larder, and a large loaf of bread, a pound of butter, two dozen eggs, various vegetables, a string of sausages and a slab of cheese. There was also a cut of meat wrapped up in paper and tied with string. Sylvie unwrapped this and looked about her for the cooking pot, which was at the side of the fire. There was an oven to the side of the fire too. But Sylvie was going to make a stew, as this would last for a few days and feed them all, with little effort required from Edith apart from keeping it warm.

Louisa and Amy helped Sylvie to make the stew, guided by her directions. Louisa's culinary skills didn't amount to much. as she had always had someone to prepare food for her, but she was willing and eager to learn.

Once the stew was made and starting to cook on the hearth Sylvie turned her attention to the other children. They would usually be in school but it was still the school holidays, which was both a blessing and a curse. It meant that Edith didn't have to get the whole of her brood ready and walk them the three miles to school and back, but it also meant that they were all in the house and underfoot. Obviously, Davy had tried to help out in his lunch break, but that was just a tiny part of the day taken care of.

She considered what to do. It wouldn't take Edith too long to get back on her feet, but the more help and rest she got the quicker the process would be. 'Louisa…' she started. Louisa looked up from where she was seated once again – on one of the chairs at the table, bouncing the little girl on her knee. She waited expectantly for Sylvie to continue. 'You were governess to the Winter children when they were small, were you not? I mean, before you married the good doctor.'

Louisa replied slightly uncertainly, not knowing where this conversation was going. 'Yes I was. Why do you ask?'

Sylvie came and sat down at the table. 'Well, I am wondering what we can do to help the family the most. Obviously it is the school holidays and so all the children are at home, and it must be exhausting for Edith to try and look after them all as well as the baby, the house, preparing the meals etc., etc. How would you feel about having the children for a few hours each day for a week or so, just to give Edith the time to get herself together?'

Louisa pondered the idea in her head before replying. She could walk down with Cassy and Tom, collect the children and take them back to the house. If the weather was fine, they could all play in the garden and, if it was wet, they could draw or paint in one of the rooms in the house. It was plenty big enough. 'That sounds like a good idea,' she replied. 'I was going to get Cassy to come with me next time anyway, and Tom has so much energy all the time that the walk here and back will be good for him too.'

Satisfied by her answer, Sylvie got up and went to refill the kettle and put it back on to boil over the fire, having removed the cooking pot and placed it in the oven to the side of the fire where it could now cook slowly for the remainder of the day.

Once the tea was made, she took a cup upstairs to Edith. The baby was now starting to stir so Louisa picked her up out of the crib and changed her nappy so that she was clean and ready for her mother to feed her once she emerged from her well-deserved rest.

She placed the soiled wet nappy in the bucket by the back door and swilled it around with the tongs. Amy said that they got washed once a day in the large metal tub in the garden and were scrubbed on the washing board. They also had an old mangle, which Amy used to get the excess water out before hanging them on the line to dry. If it was wet, then they would be hung around the fire. Amy sounded proud of being able to help her mother in this way.

Louisa had noticed that one of the gifts had been a pile of fresh towelling nappies and muslin squares, as well as baby powder and Milton liquid. It brought a tear to her eye to witness the thoughtfulness of these women in offering strength and support to one another.

Edith appeared back in the kitchen and Louisa handed her daughter over to her for a feed. She settled herself down in the chair by the fire. She still looked tired, but the complete exhaustion that had hung over her previously had now dissipated somewhat. 'Edith has agreed for you to help with the children, Louisa,' Sylvie said in a matter-of-fact way. 'I said that you could come over with young Tom and Cassy tomorrow about 11 a.m. and bring them back after lunch. Does that suit you?'

Louisa nodded her agreement and then they both left, leaving

Amy slicing the bread and buttering it and spreading it with jam for the rest of her siblings. As they opened the door Edith looked up from her nursing baby and in a very small voice said, 'Thank you both so much for all your kindness. It means the world to us, it really does.' Sylvie nodded and Louisa smiled, and they closed the door behind them and walked to the van.

Chapter 34

1973

They more or less marched up the hill. The children, seemingly oblivious to anything untoward having happened, chatted excitedly to each other with their heads bowed together, laughing and giggling to each other.

Susan was relieved. Whatever she had felt down by the lake was not right. There was some malevolence there, and it seemed to be directed towards her and James. It had physically wrenched them apart. James had felt it too, she was certain of that.

She glanced at his face. He was stoically staring straight ahead, but his skin had a pale pallor and there was a firm set to his jaw as if he were clenching his teeth.

The hill back up to the guest house was not overly steep, but the speed that they were walking at made Susan start to puff. She slowed her pace, which meant that she had to disengage herself from her husband.

James stopped and looked back at his wife, who was leaning down with her arms on her legs, trying to catch her breath. He shook himself out of his thoughts and walked over to her. 'Susan, goodness… Sorry. I just… Well, I just wanted to get away from the lake. I was shocked, I suppose. I didn't think about the pace I was setting up the hill. Are you all right?'

His concern threw her momentarily. She was still not used to having this caring version of James. She was expecting him to revert to type at any moment. 'It's OK, James. It frightened me as well.'

As soon as the words were out of her mouth she was worried that she had said too much. To infer that her husband had been frightened was inconceivable. She immediately tried to rectify what she had said, her eyes large and scared. 'I mean... I was frightened. I didn't mean to infer that you had been frightened, James... It was only the wind.'

James put up a placatory hand. 'No, Susan, you are right. I hate to admit it, but I was frightened. Something strange has been happening to me and I don't understand it, and now this...' His words trailed off and he looked back down the hill towards where the lake nestled at the bottom of the valley. The mountains were green and brown in the distance. His expression was taut.

The children, realising that their parents had stopped, paused in their march up the hill and stood watching them, as if waiting for the eruption from their father that would often occur. They huddled together, holding on to each other for comfort.

Susan's gaze was split between the children and her husband. James seemed to realise that everyone was staring at him and pulled himself back to the present. She scrutinised his features for any sign of anger and was relieved when she could see none. Sensing the tension leaving her, the children also relaxed.

James was not consciously aware of what was happening, but he knew that his actions had momentarily caused concern in his family, and it irked him. He pulled himself together and threw on a cloak of jollity and pronounced that the last one to the guest house would be a stinker. Susan smiled and the children hooted with glee as they ran up the path to the guest house. Susan's smile was tinged with concern, though. Something was afoot, and she didn't like it.

They reached the guest house to find the children sat on

the wall feigning sleep, as if they had been waiting ages for their slowcoach parents to catch up. Susan smiled indulgently at them and even James's lips quivered. 'Come on, then,' he said to the pair of them as they walked towards the front door. They opened the door into the porch and took off their boots and placed them neatly on the drying rack and hung their wet coats up to dry. The porch caught the full sun and so hopefully everything would be nice and dry come the morning, as it was lovely and warm in there. They walked down the flagged hallway in stockinged feet and proceeded to climb the stairs to their room.

They had only climbed about three steps when Mrs Derby's voice called out to them. 'Hello, dears. Would you like a nice cup of tea and a slice of cake? You must be cold and wet. Were you caught in one of our showers? It fair old threw itself down from the sky this afternoon, didn't it? I was saying to Mr Derby, "Mr Derby, I said … those poor Mortons are going to be wet through."'

In her usual way she didn't stop for a response and came out of the kitchen, wiping her hands on her apron, and took in their wet hair and stockinged feet. 'I wasn't wrong, was I? No, I thought not. Come away in now, and we will have you thawed out and dry in no time.' Sensing that there was absolutely no point in arguing, as they wouldn't get a word in edgeways anyway, the family meekly trooped back down the stairs and followed the still talking Mrs Derby back into her kitchen.

The little dog jumped out of its basket and started to sniff at their legs as if to discover the secrets of their walk. The children eagerly stroked his small head and patted his little body. Mrs Derby looked over her shoulder and laughed. 'Oh, he will take every bit of attention that you can give him, won't you Hector, duck?'

The kitten, having lost the warmth of his sleeping partner, stretched his way luxuriously out of the basket he had been sharing and yawned widely. He then walked slowly over to the children and threw himself down on his back and started to grab at socks, fingers, and the dog with his sharp claws and teeth. Mrs Derby came over and scooped him up in one hand and admonished him loudly for his naughtiness. The children giggled. Susan and James smiled at them, their previous discomfort momentarily forgotten.

Mrs Derby looked over at them. She could make out a sense of something around them, but it was hazy and fading in and out. She stopped her constant stream of words and stared at them both. James and Susan, realising that they were being studied, looked back at Mrs Derby with interest. 'Has anything happened while you were out on your walk?' she asked them sagely.

'Er, what do you mean, exactly?' Susan replied. James was dumbstruck for the moment.

'Hmm…' Mrs Derby replied, picking up a cup from the draining board and wiping it expertly while never taking her eyes off the couple. The children were oblivious to anything going on as they were too engrossed in playing with the furry animals on the kitchen floor.

'Robert, Emma…' Mrs Derby said. 'Why don't you take Hector into the garden and throw a ball for him? He will love that.' The children were excited and ran to the back door, which opened onto the little garden that they had all seen earlier from their bedroom window. Much laughing and excited barking soon followed.

'Now sit down, both of you. You look as though you have seen a ghost, and there is something strange going on around you. Don't try and tell me any different. I won't have it.' James and Susan looked more concerned now, but did as they were bid and sat down at the large table while Mrs Derby busied herself making tea and buttering some scones. When all was finished, she placed everything on the table and heaved her not inconsiderable bulk down in the end chair.

The light from the kitchen window highlighted the white strands in her pepper-and-salt hair with an otherworldly golden glow and her pink cheeks looked soft and downy. But her gaze was strong and no-nonsense. Her blue eyes were sharp and focused, as if they were determined to get to the truth of the matter. She rather resembled a strict headmistress at that moment, Susan thought, but with a kindness to her which took away most of the fear. Most of it, but not all.

'Something happened while you were out on your walk.' She waved her hand in a dismissive way as James started to talk and he was instantly quiet, which astounded Susan. Her husband was not usually one to meekly comply with another's wishes. 'Well,' Mrs Derby continued, looking from one to the other of her guests, 'who of you is going to start?'

James looked at Susan and cleared his throat with a bit of a cough, raising his fist to his mouth as he did so as if to prevent the words from tumbling from his mouth unbidden. He started to speak but the words came out as a squeak.

Susan leant forwards and put a steadying hand on his arm. She was not sure whether speaking in his stead would assuage his uncomfortableness or anger him with her presumption. She looked troubled, and Mrs Derby, noticing her discomfort, took matters into her own hands and said, 'Mrs Morton, you shall begin. Your husband can then fill in any gaps that you may leave out.' Susan felt James's arm relax under her touch, and she breathed out the breath she had been involuntarily holding before beginning.

'Well,' she said, 'we were walking down by the lake. We had been caught in the rain and were soaked through, so we decided to take shelter in the cafe on the edge of the lake by the ornamental gardens.'

Mrs Derby nodded. 'I know it. Go on.'

'Well, after we had eaten we left, and the children were running along, playing, jumping in puddles, and James and I were walking behind them arm in arm. Then suddenly, out of nowhere, this great gust of wind blew straight at us, forcing us apart, and as it did so I could have sworn that I heard the word *No.*'

Susan looked at James, as if for clarification. He had his head bowed and was looking at his hands, which were resting on the table. 'James,' Susan said, 'did I leave anything out?'

James's head jerked up at the sound of his name, and he stared at his wife bleakly and shook his head. 'We could have been mistaken, I suppose. I mean not about the gust of wind but the sound – the word, I mean.' James faltered in his response. 'It could have been something else. The wind catching in the trees, or…'

His voice trailed off. He was still very troubled by what had happened. It had felt like a huge malevolence blowing through him, bringing to the fore the resentments and the anger that had plagued him at home. He didn't want to return to being that man. This brought him up sharp, as if he had been slapped. 'I don't want to go back to the way I was,' he moaned, sounding desperate.

Susan was shocked by James's outburst and behaviour. He looked hounded and frightened by an anguish deep inside that she had no idea was lurking there. 'What do you mean, James?' she asked him, her hand still on his arm and her head bent towards him. Her hair was falling over her face as she looked up into his, full of concern. 'I don't understand. The way you were... Is this some sort of choice?'

Her face was pale, and she looked at Mrs Derby in confusion. Mrs Derby sort of harrumphed, crossing her arms over her substantial bosom, and frowned. 'I thought that something wasn't right from the moment I saw you arrive. It is like there is a presence around your husband. It is lacking in power and is relatively weak, but it may have gained some strength from the storm, which allowed it to act.'

Susan looked shocked. Her mouth fell open and James just sat with his head in his hands. 'It's the house, Susan,' he said at last. 'I want us to leave the house. It is as if when I am there I act completely differently from the person I am – who I want to be – and it is not fair on you and the children. I am sorry, Susan. I know how much you love the house, but I just can't...' He trailed off miserably.

'James, what? The house?' Susan was shaking her head in confusion. 'I don't love the house, James. It is a nightmare of a monstrosity to look after. I thought it was what you wanted. I would be happy somewhere much more modest. Then perhaps you would not have to work so hard.'

'But the children...' James continued. 'They would miss the garden and their friends.'

Susan laughed. 'James, the children wouldn't care one dot about it. They would quite happily live in a tent if it meant getting some more time from both of us. I am always so busy trying to keep the house clean and tidy, and you are always either at work or stressed and tired.' She stopped there, remembering that they were in the presence of a stranger. She did not want to dredge up the whole sorry saga of their marital disharmony.

James looked up at his wife, a glimmer of hope starting to shine in his eyes. 'Do you really mean that, Susan? I was racking my brains trying to work out how to bring up the subject of selling the house and moving somewhere else.'

Susan smiled. 'Yes, James, I really mean it.'

Relief seemed to flood through him. Then suddenly the room seemed to go very cold, and there was a loud bang as a door slammed upstairs. Susan and James both jumped, and Hector started barking furiously.

Susan and James ran to the door and could see the children both standing together clutching each other while Hector growled and barked at a strange mist that was coiling itself around the tree at the bottom of the garden. 'Get the children inside,' Mrs Derby ordered them as she walked to the door and called to her dog. 'Hector, come here at once.' The children ran into their mother's arms and looked back at the little dog, who now came trotting proudly down the path, having seen off the intruder to his home.

Mrs Derby ushered him inside, where he went and curled up in his basket in front of the stove, eliciting a disgruntled mew from the kitten. 'What was that all about?' Susan asked as the children went up to their room in search of their colouring books.

'I am not entirely sure,' said Mrs Derby, 'but it seems to have its hooks into your husband and that cannot be good. Leave it with me to think on. You will be quite safe in the house. Try and get some sleep. There is nothing more we can do this evening.'

James and Susan made their way up to their room, bone-weary and worried more than they had ever been about anything else in their lives before.

The children were both sitting at the table in the room, colouring happily together, and they barely registered their parents entering the room. After glancing around nervously and realising that everything looked perfectly normal, both James and Susan sighed audibly with relief. This did elicit an interested stare from both the children but, obviously sensing nothing was about to happen to concern them, they returned their full attention to their task at hand.

Susan and James sat on the edge of the bed together, still shell-shocked by the day's strange turn of events. They desperately needed to talk to each other about everything, but did not want to do so in front of the children. It was still relatively early, far too early to turn in for the night, but they didn't really want to venture outside at that moment either. 'Are you two OK there? What are you colouring?' Susan asked them both, hastily trying to both distract herself and reassure the children that nothing was amiss.

'I am colouring in this fairy princess with her beautiful horse,' said Emma, not looking up from the paper and being very careful to not go over the lines. 'Robert is trying to make the tractor look like the one on the farm where John Peters works.'

Robert didn't even look up, so engrossed was he to indeed try and get every remembered detail just right. 'Well, they both look lovely,' Susan said, looking over at James for a second, who was looking past them and out of the window, still obviously very confused and worried.

'Are you both OK here for a minute? Daddy and I were thinking of catching the news on the television in the guest lounge,' she continued. James's head snapped to her as he caught the meaning of her words.

He walked over to the table and ruffled Robert's hair. 'Well, I must say that both those drawings look fabulous. Well done, both of you.' The children looked at each other wide-eyed with shock at having any positive comment from their father. They grinned at each other and continued colouring, each selecting their next pencil colour with thoughtful precision.

'We'll be OK, won't we, Em?' Robert said and Emma nodded.

'OK, then. We won't be long, and we will only be downstairs if you need us.'

Susan grabbed hold of James's arm and the pair of them left the room and walked down the stairs and along the stone-flagged corridor to find the guest lounge, which was thankfully empty. They turned on the ancient television set and turned the volume down low so that it just became background noise, just in case the children did come down to find them and wondered why they were not watching the news.

They each sat down on one of the armchairs, which were placed either side of the stone fireplace looking into the room towards the television. The room was slightly worn around the edges but felt comfortable and lived-in, rather than like a doctor's waiting room.

It was furnished with an odd assortment of chairs and a squashy three-seater sofa, and there was a table at one end. There was a selection of books and games on a tall oak book-case and magazines on both the coffee table in the centre of the room and on the larger table at the end. The curtains were of a brown floral design and the overall decor was of a brown and red theme. The walls were hung with a stripy wallpaper and were adorned with a collection of prints of landscapes and animals. All in all, it worked and felt charmingly welcoming and comfortable, and was not unlike the cafe where they had taken shelter earlier.

They both felt calmer and more relaxed in this space and sensed that Mrs Derby was telling the truth when she said that nothing could harm them in this house. 'Well,' said Susan in hushed tones, 'what did you make of what Mrs Derby had to say?'

James rubbed his hand over his face and through his hair, a gesture that screamed of his uncomfortable inner turmoil. 'I just don't know, Susan. To be honest, I have simply no idea what is going on and it is starting to actually scare me. These feelings are so intense when they come. It sounds really crazy, but I can feel a malevolence that is so strong I can almost taste it.'

He looked at his wife with crazed eyes so full of his mental anguish that Susan felt quite taken aback. This was so unlike the cruel, hard James that she had been determined to escape from. This James was vulnerable and scared and didn't know what to do, which threw her for a moment.

Susan covered James's hand with hers and squeezed it gently. 'You know,' she said gently, 'I have been wondering for a time now whether there was something strange going on in our house. Emma has been acting strangely and you…' She paused, not knowing quite how to put into words the awful way James had been behaving.

She took a deep breath and continued. 'You have been quite, quite horrid at times, James.'

James put his head in his hands and squeezed his eyes tightly shut, as if to try to stem the tears that threatened to spill. He was not successful, and they started to escape through his fingers, leaving salty wet tracks as they were forced by gravity to drop silently onto his knees, where the material of his trousers sucked at them greedily.

CHAPTER 35

1936

Louisa had been humming quietly to herself as she pushed her bicycle down the garden and round into the garage. Young Jimmy Jenkins had been in there at the bench, oiling some of the garden implements, and he started as Louisa pushed open the door from the garden into the garage. 'Oh, Mrs Louisa, you made me jump,' said Jimmy, patting his chest. The oily rag had left a smear on his work jacket.

'Sorry, Jimmy,' Louisa said and smiled at him. 'Could you put this away for me? I will be walking with the children tomorrow so won't need it in the morning, so it can be put right out of your way for now.'

'Right you are, Mrs Louisa,' Jimmy replied, and after wiping the worst of the oil off his hands with the rag and then rubbing them down his trousers he took the bicycle from her.

Tom, who had been lurking in the shadows polishing some toy soldiers, had obviously had his interest piqued at the mention of going somewhere with Louisa the next day, and he stepped forward to enquire of his stepmother, 'Erm, Louisa, where are we going tomorrow?'

Louisa, who had just opened the door to return to the garden, stopped and looked back at Tom. 'Oh, goodness, Tom, how you do manage to sneak about so?' She sounded a bit cross, Tom thought, but that was just usual for Louisa. 'We are going to help with the Jennings children. I thought that Cassy, you and I could walk to their house, pick up the children and bring them back for lunch, and then we could walk them home again.'

'Right,' Tom said and sniffed, not sounding particularly interested one way or the other.

Louisa looked at him but decided that she did not have the energy to engage him in any further conversation, so she just turned and left through the door and stepped back into the warm sunshine that the garden was currently being bathed in. She had decided that she was going to run a bath and have a rest before taking a late lunch on the terrace. She would speak to Cassy later, and hopefully she would show more enthusiasm than Tom just had.

Jimmy Jenkins put away the bicycle and turned back to his previous task of cleaning the garden tools. 'You know, Tom,' he threw back over his shoulder, 'you could have shown a bit more interest in what Mrs Louisa said. You know what she gets like when you and she start on one another.' He had often witnessed the heated spats and exchanges between the two of them and never fully understood what it was that Louisa seemed to have against the young lad. He himself was extremely fond of him and his father quite obviously doted on him.

Tom shrugged. 'I'm not *not* interested,' he said thoughtfully, as if considering his response. 'It's just that... Well, Louisa never seems quite right to me. I don't know exactly what I mean but she is different to me, and not everyone sees that side of her. I don't know. I just don't really like her very much, I suppose.'

'Now, Tom...' Jimmy started to remonstrate with him but stopped himself and said in a very quiet voice for fear of being overheard, 'More people are aware of the conflict between you and Louisa than you would think, you know. But she is your stepmother and you do not really have much choice but to accept it and try your best to get along with her, or stay out of her way.'

He finished with a chuckle and patted Tom's back. 'Come on. Let's see what Maggie has on offer for us in the kitchen, shall we? She will be right pleased, as I have sharpened two of her favourite knives, so we may even get a slice of cake.'

He winked at Tom, and they both walked out of the door and round the back of the house to the kitchen to see what delights Maggie had that they could pilfer.

Louisa was feeling tired. She went up to her bedroom and threw her handbag on the chair. She sat at her dressing table and started to brush her hair, feeling bone-weary. All she wanted to do was sleep.

Her thoughts returned to Edith. *How on earth does she cope?* she wondered. How did she carry on when she was feeling tired but still had a clutch of children and a hungry husband to care for? There was no taking a nap in the afternoon for her. It was just the way the dice of fate were thrown, she supposed. She had been lucky, getting this job as governess then marrying the father of the children in her care. Would she have been able to cope if her fortunes had turned out differently?

She lay on the bed and felt the softness of the pillows cradle her head, and fell asleep almost instantly. She was still there when her husband returned at 4.30 p.m. for a quick snack before evening surgery started.

Edward strode into the room, not realising that his wife was sleeping, and she awoke as he opened the door. 'Oh, Louisa,' he exclaimed in surprise. 'I hadn't realised you were sleeping. Forgive me. Are you not feeling well?'

His look of surprise turned to concern as he reached the bed in one stride and sat down heavily on the edge, taking her hand and automatically taking her pulse, which was reassuringly strong. 'I'm fine, Edward. Just a little tired, that's all. I didn't mean to sleep for so long. What time is it?'

'It's just after half past four,' Edward continued, standing up. 'Would you like some tea?' Louisa shuffled herself into a sitting position. She felt much better for her sleep and she swung her legs over the side of the bed and walked over to her husband, who enveloped her in a warm embrace.

'It's OK. I will go down myself. I missed lunch. I was only going to have a nap for half an hour or so, and I have been asleep for ages,' she continued, checking her reflection in the dressing table mirror and tidying her hair. 'Shall I get you a cup of tea? How long before you need to go back to the surgery?'

Edward checked his watch as if by habit, as he had only just checked the time moments before. He looked thoughtful for a second then said, 'I should have enough time for a cup of tea and a sandwich.'

Louisa nodded and made her way downstairs to the kitchen. Maggie looked up as she entered and smiled. 'I was going to send a search party out for you if you had stayed upstairs any longer,' she said kindly. 'Did you have a nice rest?'

'Yes, thank you, Maggie,' Louisa replied, although she was slightly embarrassed for having been asleep for such a long time. 'Edward would like a cup of tea and a sandwich, and I think I will join him. I am famished. I missed lunch. I was only going to have a nap and then come and have some afternoon tea, but I slept right through.'

Maggie nodded and started gathering together the makings of the sandwiches. 'Can you set the kettle to boil, Louisa? I will make you both a sandwich. How was Edith when you and Sylvie went to see her?'

Louisa did as she was bid and also got the pot and three cups ready, then started to tell Maggie about her visit to Edith

Jennings. 'I was thinking before I fell asleep,' she continued after telling Maggie all the news, 'about how I can just lie down and rest when I am tired. But women like Edith just have to carry on regardless of how exhausted or sick they feel. It must be awful for them, and yet they have had six children. I don't know how she does it.'

She took a sip of her tea and looked at Maggie with wide-eyed astonishment. 'Hmm...' Maggie said. 'Well, in cases like Edith's and those of many other women, they just don't have any choice. At least Edith has a good and kind husband who works hard and tries to do what he can to help. Many others are simply not as lucky, and their conditions are much, much harder. Edith has a cottage, with outside space and fresh air for the children to play in. I come from London, Louisa. The conditions that some families have to live in there would quite turn your stomach.' She stared out of the window as if reminiscing, and, from the shudder that seemed to escape from her involuntarily, they did not appear to be good memories.

Louisa looked at her expression as Maggie continued. 'Three or more families to a house... Families of six cramped into one room where they had to live, cook and sleep, with a shared privy out the back and a yard for communal washing. None of the children had enough food, shoes, clothing or the like and many of the parents didn't either. Life was hard and cheap. Many of the kids, poor little mites, didn't even reach their first birthday, and if the cholera took hold it could wipe out a whole street. And the smell...' She trailed off, a grimace of distaste on her face.

'Well, that's enough about that. So you, my dear young lady, are very lucky, but in a way so is Edith and she knows it too.' Louisa shook her head. 'But it can't be right...' She trailed off again, as at that moment Edward strode into the kitchen and clapped his hands joyfully at the sight of the sandwich Maggie had made for him.

'What can't be right?' Edward asked his wife, then took a large bite of his sandwich and made appreciative noises and nodded his heartfelt thanks towards his housekeeper.

'The state that some families have to live in while others have so much,' Louisa said.

Edward chewed thoughtfully and nodded along as he swallowed and said, 'I agree, Louisa, but the system is a worldwide issue and is not one that can be fixed easily. All we can do, in our positions of fortune, is to give as much help and support to others as we can. It is very commendable, my dear, that you seem to be doing this.'

Louisa bristled slightly at his wording but supposed that Edward did have a point. After all, until very recently, she had been behaving like a spoilt child. Her hands went to her tummy, and she rubbed it absent-mindedly. Edward caught the motion and was quick to ask, 'Is everything all right Louisa? You have not been overdoing things, have you?'

Louisa smiled at him. 'No, Edward, I am fine. I suppose that the fact that I am going to become a mother myself has changed how I see things, that's all.'

Edward looked at his wife carefully. She was very pretty but she seemed to have developed more depth to her character of late, which was far more attractive than a pretty smile and fine manners. 'Well,' he continued, brushing crumbs from his shirt and standing up from the table, 'just remember that in the first three months of pregnancy you will feel tired, as the body is making lots of changes to accommodate the baby. So listen to your body and rest when you need to. Now I need to get back for evening surgery. Thank you for the sandwich, Maggie, and I will see you later, my dear.'

After walking over to his wife he kissed the top of her head and left the kitchen via the back door, then walked around the front of the house and out to his car. He checked the boot as a matter of habit, to make sure that his doctor's bag was safely stowed there, and then jumped in and was off up the drive and out onto the road in a matter of seconds.

Louisa watched him go and then turned back to Maggie. 'I have had everything so easy, and yet I felt like I had nothing. It wasn't until I saw Edith yesterday that it dawned on me. I don't know, Maggie. I have not always been nice, but I have had these uncontrolled rages inside that I cannot stop, and it is as though I want to be mean and hit out.' She looked up despairingly at the older woman, her eyes glistening with unshed tears.

Maggie wiped her hands on a towel and beckoned for Louisa to take a seat at the table. She poured them both some more tea and then looked at her steadily before speaking. 'Do you feel differently now?'

Louisa looked at Maggie as if trying to read her thoughts and then looked away without speaking. She thought about how she had been feeling since she found out that she was going to have a baby and then about how she had been feeling before for most of her adult life. 'Yes,' she said, suddenly excited by the thought. 'Is it the baby, do you think? Can having a baby change you so much, even before it is born?'

Maggie chewed on her lip as she thought about her own mother. She was always moody, up and down, swinging from kindness to downright cruelty at times, apart from when she was expecting. Then she seemed to be much more evenly tempered. She got tired, of course, but the spitefulness dissipated almost completely. 'Perhaps,' she said, and thought that it may be worth mentioning it to the doctor when he came home.

'Have you spoken to Edward about this?' Maggie asked softly.

'No,' Louisa admitted. She groped around in her brain, gesticulating widely, as if trying to come up with a way to describe how she was feeling. 'I had not even realised until now that these feelings were even a ... a thing.' She finally settled on this vague description and started to laugh, relieved that she could sit and chat about something so personal with this wonderful older woman.

'Maggie, I never realised that I could actually feel like I do. It is almost as though I have become free. I want to be nice, instead of constantly feeling hard done by and cold.' She sat at the table, sipping her tea, and the smile on her face lit up the room.

Maggie was pleased for the young woman, but knew, from her own experience, what it was like once the moods fell again. Hopefully the doctor would be able to do something to help even everything out again once the baby was born.

Cassy wandered into the kitchen, looking confused to see Louisa sitting at the table laughing with Maggie. She looked from one to the other with an expression of interest. She sat down at the table and helped herself to a cup of tea. 'What's so amusing, then?' she asked.

'Ah, Cassy,' Louisa said, touching her arm gently, 'I was going to come and find you, but now you are here I will explain to you what I told Tom earlier.'

Cassy looked even more confused now. Louisa was behaving more strangely and out of character by the day. 'Tomorrow we are going to go to the Jennings house and bring the children back here for some lunch and to have a run about in the garden and then walk them home again. This will give Mrs Jennings some well-needed time to rest with the baby without having to look after the rest of her family.'

Cassy shrugged. She liked children. It was fun to play with them. 'I will set up my tea set for the little ones to play with,' she said, smiling. 'It is china and delicate, but if we play with it on the grass then it should be safe enough. I will see what Tom can get out to play with for the boys.'

She finished her tea and jumped up and wandered out into the garden to find her brother, who was probably sitting up in one of the trees in the orchard if she knew him.

Maggie added, 'I will give you a stew and some bread to take back with you so that Edith does not have to make tea for them all too,' and then started to busy herself with making supper.

The next morning dawned fine and clear, which was somewhat of a relief to all concerned, as trying to keep five noisy children entertained indoors would have proven to be a bit of a challenge. Louisa found both Tom and Cassy ready and waiting in the kitchen around 10 a.m., for which she was both relieved and grateful. Edward had wished her well as he left for the surgery hours before.

She had been starting to feel a little jittery at what she had agreed to do, but on entering the kitchen and seeing that she was not to be left alone with this supporting venture, she felt some of the anxiety leave her. 'Come on, then,' she said, as jauntily as she could to her two stepchildren. 'Let's go and get the children and have some fun and games.'

Tom jumped down from the kitchen table, where he had been sitting, and joined Cassy and Louisa as they walked down the garden and through the gate to the lane beyond.

Tom ran ahead while Louisa and Cassy chatted amiably

together. Louisa felt a surge of happiness spread through her and wished that it could always be like that. *Perhaps I should speak to Edward about how I have been feeling*, she said to herself. She had not realised until now that there was really a problem and that she could even feel like she did now. It had just been a normal way of feeling for her.

She liked chatting with Cassy. She was such an open and kind child – very like her mother must have been, she supposed – and she did not even feel any stab of the usual jealousy, which momentarily surprised her.

The sun was warm on their head and backs and as they walked down the lane towards the Jennings cottage. The birds were singing and the air was still and quiet. It was a perfect day.

They could hear that they were approaching the Jennings cottage long before it came into view. It sounded almost as if they were approaching a school playground, such was the noise emanating from the garden at the back of the house.

Edith walked around the side of the house, accompanied by her ragtag brood. She wiped her face with her long apron and unpeeled her second-youngest charge from around her ankles. She looked completely exhausted.

A thin baby's wail started up from inside the cottage, and Amy appeared at the door carrying the squirming infant. Louisa bustled into action. She picked up the small child that Edith had just removed from about her person and handed her to Cassy. She then took the baby from Amy and walked into the cottage, nudging Edith in front of her.

'Amy,' she said in a strong but kind voice, 'please can you get your brothers and sisters ready while I get your mother settled with the baby and a nice cup of tea?'

Amy nodded and urged her siblings out of the room and

started to find shoes. 'Tom, can you please go and help Amy? Cassy, if you could be a dear and fill the kettle, we can make Mrs Jennings a cup of tea and get her settled down with the baby.'

Edith sank into a chair and took the baby, who was still wailing, from Louisa, and started to nurse her. Louisa got the tea things together, and also handed Edith a large mug of water to drink until the tea was ready. Edith thanked her gratefully.

By the time the tea was made, the children were all ready and stood waiting in the small front garden. 'Now, Edith,' Louisa said, 'we will try our best to wear out the little ones, and Maggie has also said that she will make you a stew and some bread for supper, which we will bring back with us. So you are to rest while we are out. We will give the children some lunch, so you need not worry about that either. Is there anything else that you would like me to do before we leave?'

'No, thank you. This is so kind of you,' Edith said wearily.

Louisa nodded. She had noticed that the line was already full of clean washing, so hopefully, with the tea being prepared by Maggie, Edith really would be able to take some time to rest. 'We will have them back around 3 p.m., OK?' And with that Louisa left the cottage and they all set off down the dusty track.

By the time they had reached the garden gate to her home, Louisa was not in the slightest bit surprised that Edith looked as exhausted as she did. The children were so full of energy and, had she not been assisted by Amy, Cassy and Tom, she would have likely flung herself into the nearest ditch to be free of her charges.

The older three children, however, seemed to be having a great time. Their faces were wreathed in smiles, and the excited chattering warmed Louisa's heart. The noise that they made was loud enough to bring Maggie, Cedric and Jimmy out into the garden.

Having reached the safety of the enclosed garden, the older three children had let go of their charges and they were running around, cartwheeling and whooping with excited joy. They saw the blankets laid out with various toys and made a beeline for them.

Maggie walked over to Louisa, her face beaming in delight at the joy on the children's faces. 'Why, it is such a little thing to do, but see how it brings such enjoyment to them.' She wiped away a tear from her eye. 'They will remember this day, Louisa, for the rest of their lives. You mark my words.'

The children were all having a great time. Cassy was teaching the older ones how to spin hoops about their middle and Tom was running around with the boys. It was very noisy, but everyone was playing nicely. Louisa was sitting on the blanket having a pretend tea party with the youngest girl when Maggie called from the house, 'Tom, Cassy, please come and help me with the lunch things.'

They didn't need asking twice, and they sped across the lawn towards the kitchen door. A few minutes later all three of them reappeared, carrying trays of food. Young Jimmy Jenkins carried two huge jugs of Maggie's home-made lemonade and there was also some milk for the youngest girl, but she would probably want to copy her siblings and have the lemonade anyway.

The children's eyes were wide with delight at the sight of so much food. There were sandwiches, little pies, cakes and a large bowl of strawberries and a jug of cream. 'Now come and sit down, everyone,' Louisa said to encourage them.

Maggie had also had the foresight to bring some warm flannels to wipe their hands before they started to tuck into their food – not that they would probably usually bother, Louisa thought with a wry smile.

She helped the little girl, whose name was Mary, to gather some food onto a plate. 'Thank you, Maggie,' she said, and all the children chorused their thanks together too.

Maggie stood with her arms folded smiling down at them all. The sound of a car pulling into the driveway drew interested glances between Maggie and Louisa, and a minute later Edward appeared around the side of the house. 'Edward ... Daddy...' Louisa and Edward's children exclaimed excitedly. 'What are you doing here?' Louisa asked, as he bent down to kiss her forehead.

'Well,' Edward said with a broad grin on his face, 'I heard that there was going to be a party, so I thought I would come and join in. Is everyone having a nice time?' he asked, looking at all the children in turn.

'Yes,' they shouted back, and started giggling.

When the children had once again become engrossed in their food, Edward took a seat on the blanket beside his wife and said, 'It is really nice of you to do this, Louisa. It will mean the world to Edith and the children.'

'I am actually rather enjoying it,' Louisa said, surprising herself by realising that she meant what she said. She *was* enjoying it. 'Tom and Cassy have been great, and they also seem to be having a great time.'

Edward nodded and smiled fondly at his children. 'This house is so large, and we have so much, it is really great to be able to share it and give back to the whole community,' he added. He grabbed a couple of sandwiches and a small pie and ate them quickly, then jumped back up and waved to them all. 'Sorry, everyone, but it was only a flying visit. I have to go and see some patients this afternoon, but it was lovely to see you all and I hope to see you all again very soon.' He winked at Tom and Cassy and then made his way back round to the front of the house and was on his way again.

Louisa hugged herself. She could not remember feeling so happy and content ever before in her entire life. It was true what people said: the simple things do bring the most joy.

The children, having finished their lunch, were once again tearing around and playing various games. She stood up to help Maggie to start clearing away the detritus that the children had left in their wake and felt a sudden sharp jab of pain in her side. She gasped and clutched at her side.

Maggie stopped what she was doing and rushed over to her. 'Louisa, are you all right?' she asked, the concern evident in her voice.

Louisa blew out a long breath. The pain had eased so she managed to straighten up, and was able to mentally scan her body for any other twinges. 'I am OK, I think,' she said, sounding more confused than worried. 'I just felt a sharp jab of pain in my side. I am sure it is nothing. It has gone now.'

Maggie looked at her. Louisa's face was very pale and she looked tired. 'I think you had better go and have a rest. Jimmy and I can take the children back. You need to speak to Edward about this. You have to be careful when you are expecting, you know.'

'I know,' Louisa replied in a small voice. 'You are right. I do feel suddenly very tired. If you are sure it would not be too much for you and Jimmy to walk the children back, I would be very grateful to have a rest.'

'Of course,' Maggie said, flapping her hands at Louisa. She gestured to the plates and bowls on the grass. 'I will just get them to help me in with this lot, and we will be off and leave you in peace and quiet.'

Maggie soon called everyone to order, and a solemn procession made its way into the kitchen, carefully carrying the lunch things to be washed up. Once the tidying up had been done, Maggie, Jimmy, Tom and Cassy took the children home. All of them were carrying a book or a toy that they had been given by Tom and Cassy, and all of them were tired and happy.

Jimmy carried the little girl and she slept soundly against his shoulder. Maggie smiled indulgently as she watched Mary snuggle deeper into Jimmy's neck.

Her thoughts returned to Louisa. She hoped that the pain she had experienced earlier was just a warning to slow down a little and nothing worse. She would check on her as soon as she got back, and also get the doctor to look at her too. You could never be too careful with expectant mothers.

Once the children were safely delivered back home, all full of excited tales for their mother, and the stew put into the oven at the side of the hearth, they made their way back home. Tom was walking with Jimmy, who was pointing out birds and flowers along the way and telling Tom their names.

Cassy fell into step with Maggie. 'That was really good fun, Maggie,' she said. 'I didn't expect to enjoy it quite as much as I did. The children are all really sweet, and were so humble. They didn't expect anything, and their manners were amazing. There was no grabbing for food or squabbling between each other, like at some of the birthday parties I have been to.'

Maggie nodded. 'Manners cost nothing, and for all their humble origins Edith and Davy have taught them very well.'

They reached the garden gate, and all the children trooped through. Tom went off with Jimmy and Cassy followed Maggie into the kitchen. 'Go and ask Louisa if she would like a cup of tea, Cassy,' Maggie said as she took off her hat and laid it on the table. She picked up her apron and tied it on as she continued by saying, 'but if she is asleep just leave her be.'

Cassy nodded and went upstairs in search of Louisa. Cassy knocked gently on her father and Louisa's bedroom door and, when there was no answer, she gently pushed the door open and saw that Louisa was indeed fast asleep. She noticed that she looked pale and was in a very deep sleep, as she had not stirred as she entered the room. She tiptoed out and closed the door very gently behind her and went downstairs to tell Maggie.

Maggie looked up as Cassy entered the kitchen. She had already put the kettle on to boil and was setting out cups on the table. 'Louisa is fast asleep,' Cassy said, as soon as she walked into the kitchen. 'She looks very pale, Maggie. Do you think Father should take a look at her when he gets home?'

Maggie considered this for a moment as she stirred the teapot. 'I think that would probably be a good idea, Cassy. I think that she has probably just been overdoing it, but it is best to be sure in these circumstances.'

She would get Edward to go and look at Louisa the minute he got home. *Something just feels a bit off to me*, Maggie said to herself.

'Now go and tell Jimmy and Tom to come and get a cup of tea and a slice of cake,' she said to Cassy, who obediently went off to do her bidding.

Chapter 36

1973

The relief that flooded through Susan made her feel suddenly exhausted, as though she had been holding herself afloat for a very long time and could now relax.

She let out a long breath and James looked up at her, his eyes red-rimmed from where he had been crying. 'I'm so sorry, Susan. I have been a complete arse.'

Susan smiled at his use of the word. Her husband rarely swore. 'Let's try and put all this behind us and make a fresh start, shall we?' she said to him, and patted his hand. 'I'll see if I can cajole some tea out of Mrs Derby, and we can sit and make some plans. That will help you feel a bit more in control,' she said wisely, as she got up and walked out of the room and knocked gently on the kitchen door.

'Mrs Derby,' she called tentatively, 'may I trouble you for a pot of tea?'

Mrs Derby opened the door and smiled. 'Of course, my dear. Are you in the lounge?'

'Yes,' Susan replied. 'That would be so kind of you. James and I want to have a discussion away from the children.'

'Very wise too,' Mrs Derby said, and started to prepare a tray with tea, biscuits, cups and cutlery.

Susan headed back down the passageway to the lounge and found James looking much more like himself again. He blew his nose loudly into a handkerchief and smiled at his wife as she re-entered the room. 'You know,' he said thoughtfully, 'I have been thinking that the house is so large, and we really don't need something that big. We could sell it and buy something much smaller, and that would give us a nest egg. We could actually move anywhere, you know,' he said, rubbing his chin then sitting back in the chair with his arms behind his head.

'We would need to think about the children's schooling, though, James,' Susan countered. 'They have settled well and have lots of friends, but I suppose they are young enough for it not to matter too much. Whereabouts were you considering?'

'Oh, I don't know.' He gestured with his hands, as if waving away his thoughts. 'I have not really thought about it.'

Susan regarded him then said, 'Well, I would rather not live in a town, James, if it is all the same with you.'

He looked at her for a moment and then nodded his head. 'OK. Agreed. Perhaps I should look to move firms. I could get a partnership somewhere else, maybe. There is a lot to think about, but it feels positive. Do you not agree?' Susan nodded, and then they were interrupted by Mrs Derby bustling in with the tea tray.

'I always find that circumstances will happen upon you if you leave room for them to find you,' Mrs Derby said mysteriously as she laid the tea tray on the table. And with that she left, giving them a parting nod at the door, which she closed gently behind her.

James and Susan looked at each other. 'Well, that was short and sweet for our Mrs Derby,' James exclaimed, and the pair of them started laughing.

Mrs Derby stood in the passageway for a moment nodding her head in silent agreement before continuing down into her kitchen. Things were afoot for this family, there was no mistake

317

about it. Families usually came to stay with her when they were in great need of support and direction, and it was no different this time.

She set about doing the washing-up at the sink, and looked out over the garden as the sun started to set. This was a safe space, but she needed to check that all her protections were still in place. She had a feeling that they were all going to need them before the week was out.

After a surprisingly good night's sleep, the family came down to breakfast feeling refreshed and happy. The children were full of energy, and the family had planned to go for a nice long walk, taking in some of the spectacular waterfalls that the area was famous for.

Mrs Derby had made up a substantial picnic for them and filled a flask with tea for the adults and some bottles with squash for the children. They were going to surprise the children with a trip on the Ravenglass and Eskdale railway. Robert would be ecstatic, and Emma would also enjoy it. From there they could take the four-mile route that took in the Stanley Force waterfall.

James seemed to be as excited as the children as he chivvied them along. 'It takes me back to when I was a boy,' he said, reminiscing with a wide smile on his face. 'I can't believe that I have not come back here for such a long time.'

'It is rather beautiful,' Susan agreed. 'I wouldn't mind living here.'

James stopped tying his laces and looked at her. 'You know, Susan,' he said with a faraway look in his eyes, 'what's to stop us from doing just that?'

He finished tying his laces and jumped up, then grabbed the rucksack that held the picnic hamper and stowed it in the boot of the car. The children followed him eagerly and jumped into the car without any fuss for once.

Susan stared after them, momentarily frozen on the spot from the shock of what James had just said. Could he actually be serious? Would he really consider uprooting them all and moving so far away? It was stunning and he would probably have no trouble relocating to a practice in another town, as he was very well respected in his field.

But move up there? She had only just started to make friends at home. She thought of the warmth and welcoming support of Stacey and the others. Even her family, although she didn't see them all that often, were at least closer and able to help her should she need it. But up there...

What if James suddenly started to act like he had at home? What then? Who would she turn to for help if she knew no one? On the other hand, what if he didn't change back to how he had been and continued to be this lovely kind version of himself? Could she take the risk?

She was still deep in thought when James's call broke her out of her reverie. 'Come on, Susan. Why are you standing there, staring into space? We have a mountain to climb.'

'Yes, come on, Mum,' the children said.

Shaken back to the present, Susan decided that she would have to park those thoughts for now. It was only a throwaway comment, after all, and it would take time to make decisions about what they would be doing, so there was no need to spoil the day worrying about things that would probably never happen.

She picked up her bag and walked towards the car. As she did a gust of icy wind threw itself at her, pushing her into the stone wall bordering the house and causing her to graze her knuckles. She briefly caught the scent of a woman's perfume and the very faint sound of bitter laughter. She cried out in shock as she stumbled.

James was instantly out of the car and at her side. He took her hand and removed a handkerchief from his pocket and gently dabbed at the blood that had started to appear on the broken skin of her knuckles. She had gone very white and he looked at her, concern etched on his face.

'Did you hear that, James?' Susan whispered.

'No,' James replied. 'I didn't hear anything, but I saw you stumble as though you had been pushed. What happened?'

'It was like when we were down at the lake – a blast of icy wind – but this time there was a hint of perfume, and I heard what sounded like cruel laughter.'

'Come and sit in the car,' James said, as he took her elbow and guided her gently to the passenger seat. 'Let's just go for a walk, and hopefully we can get away from whatever strange things seem to be happening here.'

Susan sat in the car and fastened her seat belt. James got back into the car and soon they were off. Mrs Derby stood at the window upstairs in her bedroom looking out at the receding vehicle as it travelled down the road and shook her head. She would certainly have to up her game to ensure that this lovely family was protected from whatever it was that meant to do them harm.

She went into the room next to her bedroom and closed the door silently behind her. The room was lined with shelves containing bottles and jars full of dried herbs and various liquids. There were several bookcases full of old books and a table on which sat an array of bowls and two pestles and mortars. There were charts on the walls, and hanging from an old-fashioned Edwardian airer on the ceiling were bunches of dried herbs and flowers.

Mrs Derby took a couple of well-worn books from the shelves and laid them on the table. She started to gather various ingredients together and began to hum gently to herself as she got to work. Mr Derby paused outside the door, heard the gentle humming emanating from the room, smiled quietly to himself and went downstairs to make himself a cup of tea. *My wife will not be downstairs for a little while*, he said to himself, knowing her as well as he did.

The Morton family had had a lovely day. They had taken the steam train along its narrow gauge track and then gone for a long walk, taking in the beautiful ancient scenery, and marvelled at the power of the immense waterfall. They had sat on rocks in the sun to eat their packed lunch, and the children had run around all day picking up stones and leaves and pointing out birds and even trout in the streams that were so clear you could see right to the bottom. The sun had shone, and the rain had held off all day.

As they all trooped back to the car and started to pull off boots and get ready for the journey back to the guest house, James pulled Susan into his arms and held her tight. He smoothed her hair and drew in the scent of her as he gently kissed the top of her head. There had been no scary recurrence of anything untoward involving gusts of wind or hissed malevolent words. They all felt tired and happy as they settled into the car for the journey.

'Did you have a nice day, kids?' James threw over his shoulder as he negotiated leaving the car park and turned onto the road.

'Yes,' they shouted in unison.

Susan joined into the conversation, a huge smile on her face.

'What did you like best?'

'The train,' Robert answered unsurprisingly.

'The waterfall, I think,' Emma added thoughtfully. 'Are there fairies living by the waterfall?' She asked this with the utmost sincerity, and Susan flashed a look at Robert as he was about to say something that would instantly quash her dreams and make her feel foolish.

'Well,' Susan said quickly before James could say something as equally damning, 'who knows? Apparently only very special people can see the fairies, you know.'

'Have you seen them, Mummy?' Emma asked her mother, her eyes full of wonder.

'I don't think I have, but sometimes I catch a movement just out of the corner of my eye and then I think maybe that could be a fairy.'

Emma giggled slightly. 'Aw, Mum, that is just so sweet.' Seemingly happy now, Emma turned her attention to the I spy book she had been trying to finish rapidly before Robert finished his.

They pulled up outside the guest house and saw Mr Derby sweeping the garden path. There seemed to be leaves covering the garden and they were nearly all green. There was an ornamental cherry tree to the far end of the front garden, and it looked as though it had been the poor loser in a fight with a tornado, so decimated were its branches of its summer plumage.

'What on earth has happened here?' James asked the older man as he walked down the path towards him. Mr Derby just shrugged in his quiet non-committal way and nodded towards the house.

'Just the wind passing through. No harm done.' He carried on sweeping.

'Goodness,' exclaimed Susan, remembering the force of the icy blast that had hit her as she left this morning. Could it have returned and wreaked this havoc and damage on the poor tree?

'Missus is inside. I think she has made some supper for you.'

They thanked him and entered the house. The children ran straight for the kitchen, where they knew that sweet treats and furry friends awaited them.

The adults followed at a more leisurely pace. Mrs Derby looked up as the excited children entered the kitchen. 'Well, now, children,' she exclaimed, her hands on her hips and nodding at them indulgently, 'did you have a nice day?'

'Oh, yes, Mrs Derby,' they shouted, then they both started talking at once. Excited words tumbled from their mouths as they eagerly tried to get the most attention.

'We went on a train, and I collected lots of stones,' said Robert proudly.

'I loved the waterfall and I only fell over once,' added Emma. 'But I didn't cry, did I, Robert?' She looked at her brother crossly, as if expecting him to disagree.

Susan came into the kitchen and laughingly added, 'No, Emma, you didn't cry. You were very brave,' and she patted her daughter on the head.

On seeing Susan and James enter the kitchen Mrs Derby clapped her hands together. 'Now, children,' she said in an authoritarian voice, much like their teachers employed to assure attention, 'go upstairs and change out of your muddy clothes and wash your hands, and then you can have one very small biscuit before dinner.'

Not waiting to be asked twice, and with whoops of excitement, the children raced each other up the stairs to their room. 'Now you two sit down and I'll make you a nice cup of tea. We have things to discuss before the children reappear.' As Mrs Derby turned to put on the kettle and get the teapot ready, she said over her shoulder, 'I expect you saw that we had another little visitor.'

Susan and James exchanged glances and then Susan said, 'If you mean your beautiful tree,' Susan said quietly, 'then, yes, we noticed. What on earth happened? I felt something strong hit me as I was getting into the car this morning.' She sank heavily into the chair. All the colour drained from her face and she looked grey and weary.

'Hmm,' continued Mrs Derby. 'Yes, I was watching that. I have spent most of the day working on a solution for you, and that made the threat angry. And, unfortunately for my poor cherry tree, it bore the brunt of its wrath.' Susan and James both looked very scared now, and Mrs Derby waved a tea towel at them as if to lighten the atmosphere.

'Now, I am not sure what you have attracted to yourself, James, but it is not happy, and it is out for some sort of revenge. It is connected to your home but seems to have followed you here. Although it is connected directly to you it seems hell-bent on taking out the anger on Susan. Have you had times when you have been angry and not particularly pleasant to your wife at home?'

James looked up. His face wore a bleak expression, and he nodded. 'Yes, I have been a complete beast at times. To be totally honest, I am surprised that Susan is still with me.'

Susan reached out and put a hand on his arm. He took her hand and squeezed it gently. 'I didn't understand what was happening, or why I was behaving so badly. I still don't. Are you saying that some "spirit" is affecting me? I mean, that can't happen, can it? I don't even believe in such things. The whole idea is completely preposterous.'

He stood up abruptly as he felt the heat and anger rising in him, which was spurred on by feeling completely powerless to do anything about the situation.

Mrs Derby eyed him with interest and then patted his shoulder. 'Now sit down, Mr Morton, and let me explain a few things to you. It matters not whether you believe in the existence of things you cannot explain. It does not prevent them from existing.'

James spluttered as if to try and refute what Mrs Derby was saying, but she simply held up a hand to still his words. 'Now, Mr Morton, can you see the wind, or for that matter electricity? No? But you cannot dispute their existence. It is similar with other things. Some people live their whole lives and never experience anything out of the ordinary and live in complete ignorance. Others… Well, that is another matter. Now, whatever you believe or don't believe, it doesn't change the fact that you have somehow unwittingly attracted something powerful and malevolent that wishes to do your family harm, and it needs to be stopped.'

At this moment the children came crashing back into the kitchen and all further conversation was halted.

There was no opportunity to take the conversation further until much later in the evening. The family joined the Derbys for dinner, and they all ate in the kitchen. James was very quiet, and Susan kept casting surreptitious glances in his direction, but his eyes remained stoically focused on his plate. The children chatted good-naturedly with each other and the Derbys, and Mrs Derby kept up her steady patter of distracting conversation, for which Susan was eternally grateful.

Once the meal was finished, James offered to help clear away while Susan took the children upstairs to have a bath and get ready for bed. They were starting to tire after their long and busy day, and Susan desperately wanted to avoid their tiredness developing into squabbles. Although she was itching to be privy to the conversation that would undoubtedly unfold between Mrs Derby and her husband, she was also wise enough to realise that being given time alone with the older woman would allow James the freedom to discuss topics that he may feel less inclined to in front of his wife.

Once they were alone in the kitchen, Mrs Derby shut the door gently and stood with her back against it for a moment, studying James. He was undoubtedly a handsome man, tall and straight-backed, but with the inclination towards arrogance and cruelty if not checked. However, there was also a softness to him and an honesty that fought hard against the darker elements of his character. Was he strong enough, though, for the fight that would come? she wondered.

Now, Susan... She was a whole different being. She was tough – a fighter – and she definitely loved this man. Did he know, she wondered, how close he had actually come to losing her? She stroked her chin as she mused. How much should she tell him?

James was feeling very uncomfortable under her scrutiny and started to run a finger around his collar. He looked completely out of place in the kitchen, and it was obvious that he spent very little time in his kitchen at home. 'Well, James,' Mrs Derby said, pushing herself away from the door and walking towards the sink, 'I'll wash and you can dry. Just stack the dried things on the table. We can talk as we wash.'

He looked terrified so she softened her words as she started to talk. 'James,' she began, 'I know that this must be incredibly hard for you. You must be wondering what on earth is going on. In some ways it is interesting that you should have been chosen, as you do not possess the gift like your wife and daughter, but—'

She held up her hand to stay his words as he opened his mouth to interrupt. 'No, James, just hear me out, then you can ask as many questions as you like. The reason you have been "selected", shall we say, over the rest of your family, would be due to your physical strength, I believe. This spirit is very, very angry, but it seems to have a female energy to it. What do you know about your home?'

Now James looked very surprised. 'My home? What do you mean?'

Mrs Derby put the cloth down heavily in the sink, causing small bubbles to fly up and attach themselves to her blouse. She turned to face him. The stern expression on her face informed him that she was very serious indeed and was determined to get to the bottom of the matter. 'Yes, James, your home ... where you live ... the house. What do you know about it? Who lived there before? What happened there?'

James looked at her with a dumbfounded look on his face. He was so confused, and felt as though he was in some sort of strange dream. What could his house have to do with the strange things happening to him? But realisation suddenly dawned on his face. Hadn't he himself spoken to Susan about moving? To bring that thought into being in the first place he must have unconsciously felt that something about the house was not quite right.

Seeing the realisation dawn bright on his features, Mrs Derby nodded, a grim smile on her face. 'So, you have thought of something. Would you like to enlighten me?'

She folded her arms and stood, fixing him with her piercing

eyes. James started to stammer under her intense gaze. 'I…
Well, I mean, erm…'

He faltered, but Mrs Derby did not take her eyes from his
face or say anything so he continued. 'I did mention to Susan
about possibly moving from the house.' He searched his mind
for the correct word to describe how he felt. 'I don't know, but
whenever I am there, I feel angry, I suppose. Yes, I feel angry
and frustrated, and it seems to be directed towards Susan.'

He put his head in his hands for a moment as shame flowed
through him at the memories of how he had behaved to his
kind, sweet wife.

CHAPTER 37

1936

When Edward came home Louisa was still asleep, and Maggie was waiting for him. She walked out of the back door and around the front of the house as she heard his tyres crunch on the gravel drive. He parked the car and reached behind him for his bag.

He looked surprised to see Maggie standing by the door of his car, and concern immediately etched his face with lines. He opened the car and got out quickly, speaking to Maggie as he closed the door. 'What is it, Maggie? Are the children all right? Louisa?'

Maggie patted him on the arm gently to allay his fears. 'Now don't get yourself into a lather, Doctor,' she said soothingly, although he could see that she also did look somewhat concerned too.

Maggie continued. 'Louisa has had a couple of sharp pains and I sent her up for a rest. She has been asleep ever since, and Cassy and I both think she looks a bit pale, so it would do no harm for you to take a look at her. I am sure that she will be fine and that she has simply overdone it a bit, but it's best to be safe than sorry, I always think, don't you?' she added, following behind him as he moved quickly into the house and took off his coat and gloves and handed them absent-mindedly to Maggie.

He went into the small cloakroom by the front door and washed his hands thoroughly. Then, while drying them on the towel, he looked up at Maggie and said, 'I'll go straight up and see her now. She will probably be very thirsty if she has been

asleep for a while, so could you possibly bring us up some tea?'
Maggie nodded and walked back through the hall towards the
kitchen, glad to be able to do something useful. She had a bad
feeling about this and didn't want it to affect the outcome.

Edward bounded up the stairs two at a time and quietly
entered the bedroom that he shared with his young wife. She
was lying on her back, her pale hair fanned out against the
pillow, and her face was indeed devoid of any colour at all. He
took her hand gently in his, and she opened her eyes and looked
at him as if trying to focus on who was with her.

As her husband's face swam into view his name escaped
her parched lips like a whisper. 'Edward,' she said, so quietly,
as if just uttering his name took away the only strength that
remained in her body.

'Well, my dear,' Edward said kindly, brushing her hair away
from her forehead, 'you look like you could sleep for a fort-
night. Do you feel unwell? In pain?' He scanned her features
for any external hint of illness but she just looked pale. Her
head was not particularly hot.

'I had a pain earlier,' Louisa said. 'That is why Maggie sent
me to bed, but it went away and I just feel so very tired.'

'OK,' Edward said. 'Let me take a little look at you. I will
try to disturb you as little as possible, but I do think that you
should have a drink. I have asked Maggie to bring us up a cup
of tea. If you would indulge me, my love, and just drink the
tea, then you may go back to sleep.'

Edward lifted the blankets and checked that there was no
obvious sign of blood on the bedclothes, but everything looked
fine. He took Louisa's pulse and blood pressure and helped her
into a sitting position.

Maggie knocked on the door and came in with a tray of tea

things and some ham sandwiches. Louisa drank a cup of tea and nibbled on one of the sandwiches and then sank back down into the bed and fell asleep almost immediately.

Edward carried the tea tray downstairs and found Maggie and Cassy in the kitchen. 'Well?' asked Maggie, still looking worried. Cassy also looked concerned, Edward noticed, which surprised him a little.

'Well, everything looks fine. It is very early days, so I won't be able to hear the baby's heartbeat or anything yet, but Louisa's pulse and blood pressure seem fine, and she does not have a temperature, so it may just be that she has been overdoing things, like you suggested, Maggie,' he said, wiping a hand across his face as he sat down in one of the kitchen chairs.

'I am a bit surprised, though, as she is very young, but I suppose she was helping with the Jenkins family, and she did walk there and back with the children today,' he said. 'I don't know. We will need to keep a close eye on her. All pregnancies are completely different, so we will just hope that everything turns out OK in the end. Thank you for looking after her, both of you.'

He turned and ruffled Cassy's hair. 'Will you and Jimmy be able to help with the Jennings children tomorrow?' he asked his daughter.

'Yes, Father, of course,' she said immediately, pleased to be able to help out. 'I am sure that Tom will help again too. He really seemed to enjoy himself today.'

Edward smiled. 'Where is Tom, anyway? I've not seen him at all since I came in.'

Maggie snorted with laughter. 'Where do you think, Doctor?' she laughed. 'With Jimmy Jenkins, of course. It's hard to see where Tom ends and Jimmy starts. They are as thick as thieves, those two, but it's not a bad thing. Jimmy is teaching Tom all sorts of useful things. It was both of them who sorted out the old bicycle for Louisa,' she said.

Cassy piped up and said, 'And Jimmy is always teaching Tom the names of birds and flowers. Tom really looks up to him.' Edward smiled. A lot of fathers would not be happy that their sons were spending so much time with the family gardener, but he didn't mind. He was working so much, and Jimmy was just doing the things that he would have done himself had he had a lesser workload. Jimmy was a kind and decent lad. Tom could have much worse role models, so there would be no complaints from him.

'Well, I have some work to do in my study, ladies,' Edward said, with a mock bow to them both, 'if you will excuse me.' He left the kitchen and walked through the dining room and out through the hall into his study, where he sat down at his desk and looked out across the lawn where he could indeed see his son trotting behind Jimmy Jenkins carrying a basket of vegetables that they had no doubt just dug up at Maggie's instruction, and which would most probably form part of the delicious dinner that Maggie would be preparing for them shortly. He averted his eyes from the garden and picked up the papers on his desk and was soon buried in his work.

It was about an hour later that the screaming started.

CHAPTER 38

1973

After the realisation about the house had finally dawned on him, James went upstairs to find Susan tucking the children into bed. They were tired after their busy day. She looked up as he entered the room and saw the haunted look on his face. He looked so tired, she thought – broken, almost.

She smiled at him kindly. He tried to return the gesture, but it felt as if his face muscles were just too weak to comply. Susan turned towards the sleepy children and said, 'Your father and I are just going to get ourselves a cup of tea downstairs. I will leave the door open, so call if you need anything.'

The children were almost asleep already, so merely murmured some sort of response, and Susan gently guided her husband from the room and down the stairs towards the lounge, where she set about making a pot of tea from the accoutrements set on the sideboard for that very purpose. She guided James to a chair, and he sat down as bidden, still not having uttered a word.

Once the tea was made Susan gave him a cup and he held it, looking at the steam rise from the surface of the pale brown liquid as if he had no idea what to do with it.

'Well?' said Susan, gently nudging James out of the deep despair that had seemed to have encompassed his entire being. He looked up as though surprised to see her sitting there, and equally as surprised to see that he had a cup of tea in his hands. His hands were shaking slightly and, afraid that the tea would spill and burn him, Susan reached over and gently took the cup from his hands and placed it on the side table next to his chair. 'What did Mrs Derby have to say that has left you looking as though you have seen a ghost?'

James still looked as though he were in a complete daze, but Susan's words started to pierce the mist that had held him fast in its confusing grip. 'The house,' he said bleakly. 'It's the house. We have to leave. I never really questioned why it was so cheap. I only thought of the prestige of owning such a large house. It was utter folly. What have I done, Susan?' He looked at her now, his face so full of misery that Susan was shocked to the core.

'What do you mean, James?' she said quickly, moving closer to him and crouching down by his side so that she could look up into his face. She placed her hands on his knees and he looked down at her as if seeing her for the first time. He stroked her hair and twirled it around his fingers. Susan brushed his hands away and turned his face so that he was looking at her. 'What do you mean, James?' she repeated more firmly this time. 'What is it about the house?'

James merely groaned and put his head back in his hands. Realising that she was not going to get anywhere with him in this state, Susan sat down next to him and waited patiently, sipping her tea and thinking. She knew that the house had secrets. She had seen and heard things, but that was quite normal for her, and she thought that Emma had also inherited the same ability. She had never been bothered by the house, though. It had always seemed fine to her.

She looked at James. He was a shell of the arrogant and sometimes cruel man who she had planned to run from, but she needed him to be strong now. Perhaps he had just been weak all along, she thought, and that is where his arrogance sprang from – a need to feel important.

Well, she would just have to whip him into shape. They obviously had a big problem that needed to be dealt with and they would have to face it together.

She sat up straight and spoke to her husband in a calm, but firm voice. 'James, we need to sort this out. I can understand that you are worried, confused and potentially even scared, but we have a problem, and I am sure that together we can sort it out. We can speak to Mrs Derby and see what advice she can give us. I am sure that she can help us.'

When he showed no signs of stirring himself out of the gloom Susan stood up and shook him gently by the shoulders. 'James,' she persisted, louder now, 'we have the children to think of. This is not just about you or us. The children need a strong father and a safe home. You need to face up to this and together we can fix it.'

At the mention of the children James raised his tear-stained face. His eyes were red and swollen and full of misery and despair but they were focused now – which was at least an improvement on before, Susan thought.

'OK,' she said. 'That is better. We need to work out a plan of what we are going to do, and try and find out what we are actually dealing with here. Then I think we should try and enjoy the rest of our holiday, as much as we can, and hopefully that will give us more strength to deal with whatever will face us when we return home.'

James seemed to shake himself alert and turned to face his wife. He was starting to look more like himself now, she saw, and relief flooded through her. 'Yes, Susan, you are right, of course,' he said, rubbing at his face with his hands. 'I am sorry. I feel like I have let you all down. Like I always let you down. You do not deserve this, and I will do my best to fix it.'

Susan laid a hand on his arm and looked at him directly. 'No, James, we will fix it together,' she said firmly. 'Now I am going to go and speak to Mrs Derby and find out what we need to do. You can sit here and drink your tea and recover yourself then I think we should go to bed. All this "excitement" is exhausting.' She yawned, handed James back his cup of tea and left the room to go in search of Mrs Derby.

Susan found Mrs Derby sitting at the table in the kitchen. She had an array of small bottles and what looked like four small crudely made dolls on the table in front of her.

She looked up and smiled at Susan and bid her sit down at the table. 'So,' she said in a matter-of-fact voice, 'how is James? Has he any idea of what he is up against here?'

Susan sat down in the chair wearily and shook her head slowly as she brushed her hair off her face and looked at Mrs Derby with eyes filled with despair. 'To be honest with you, Mrs Derby,' she said, looking completely overwhelmed with the whole situation, 'I don't think he actually has any idea at all.'

Mrs Derby rubbed her chin with her hand and looked out of the window at the birds feasting on the bird table. 'I thought as much.' Then she said, 'Perhaps he doesn't need to understand. I know that you have the sight, my dear, and perhaps young Emma does too.'

Susan nodded. 'All my life I have seen and heard things that no one else could, and Emma does too. She has her imaginary friend Tom, but I am wondering now whether he is not quite so imaginary.'

Mrs Derby laughed. 'Yes, well, I think that you are probably right there. She probably doesn't realise what is going on, as she is still very young. But she will, given time. Now back to

336

your husband and what needs to happen next. You say that he is resigned to moving from the house?'

Susan nodded. 'Yes. Funnily enough, he had already spoken about moving before this all started up in earnest. It seems as though he only bought the house out of some sort of ego trip and never really liked it that much. Apparently he managed to get it for a song, so there must have been some reason behind it.'

Mrs Derby looked thoughtful. 'You look into the history of that house, and it won't be too far back that you will find something happened there that is causing all this bother now.' She said *bother* as though it were a nasty smell under her nose.

'I will look at the newspaper archives when I get back,' Susan said, a new determined vigour taking hold of her.

Mrs Derby slapped the table lightly with her hands and looked at Susan. 'Now for the help that I can give you,' she said, and gestured to the items on the table. 'I have made these poppets for you all, and some protection jars.' Susan listened eagerly as Mrs Derby continued. 'Place the poppets under each of your mattresses, and also perhaps put one in James's car or briefcase. On reflection, the car would probably be best. You don't want him pulling the poppet out with his files when he goes to visit a client. That would look very strange indeed.' Susan half-smiled, imagining her husband's reaction if such a scenario unfolded.

Mrs Derby continued speaking. 'The protection spell jars can be placed in the four corners of the house, inside or outside. It doesn't really matter that much, but they must be hidden. You can also splash the infused water in the larger bottle into each of the rooms. I have made a large bottle, as I think that your house has many rooms. Am I correct?'

Susan nodded. 'Yes, it is a very large house.'

'Right,' Mrs Derby said, and nodded. 'You really need to get the house sold and move as soon as possible. It would be even better if you didn't have to stay there while the sale went through, but that probably is not an option.' She looked questioningly at Susan, who shook her head.

'No, I don't think that that would be an option, but I suppose I could go and stay with my parents. But the school holidays will end soon, and they live too far away to get the children to school and back easily each day,' Susan said.

Looking resigned but still concerned, Mrs Derby said, 'Well, we will just have to hope that these protection charms work, then,' as she gathered them all together and placed them in a brightly patterned cloth bag and handed them to Susan. 'Now away to bed with you. Try and just enjoy the rest of your holiday and get your strength back, as I think you are all going to need it.'

Susan collected James from the guest lounge on the way and they both went up to bed together. James was still very subdued, and they didn't speak much. Susan thought that he was probably trying to process all the information that Mrs Derby had imparted to him and thought he was best left to it.

As they got into bed, Susan picked up her book and started to read, while James just lay there looking at the ceiling. Susan put her book on her lap and turned to him and said, 'Mrs Derby thinks that we should just try and enjoy the rest of our holiday and put aside all the other stuff that we need to do until we get home. There is not that much that we can do from here anyway, is there, really?'

James shrugged but then turned to his wife and said, 'You are probably right. I could call an agent and get the ball rolling, I suppose, but it will be much easier to do everything else once we are back. You will need the local Yellow Pages, after all, and there is not much point calling schools, etc. until we know where we will be living. Once we have an offer on the house and we know what we are looking at we can then decide where we want to live.'

Susan looked at him, astounded by his use of *we*. James had never consulted her before and she had just meekly gone along with all his decisions. Noticing her surprise, James grinned and looked slightly sheepishly at his wife. Why had he never seen her intelligence before and done things as a team? She was so much stronger than him.

Perhaps that was his reason. He may have felt threatened by it. Who knows? His head was so full of thoughts all jumbling over each other and fighting for prominence that he didn't have the energy to deal with anything right now. He was so tired. 'Come on,' he said, instead of elaborating on any of the inner turmoil he was currently experiencing, 'Let's try and get some sleep. And then, as you said, we can try and just enjoy the rest of our holiday as a family.'

The rest of the holiday was spent discovering new places and exploring the hills, mountains and lakes in all their glory. They went wild swimming in deserted tarns, watched golden eagles soaring above their mountain eyries and walked until they were on their knees. They ate wonderful home-cooked food, basked in the sun, and got drenched to the skin in the squalls that appeared out of nowhere and left as suddenly as they had arrived, leaving their world glittering with silver droplets.

There was no repeat of the frightening wind or the whispered threats. Susan made sure that they had their protection poppets with them at all times, shoved into a coat or a trouser pocket.

No one seemed to register that this was anything strange. They were just happy to be having a relaxing and fun time.

All too soon it was their last day. They spent this locally in Keswick, taking a boat trip on Derwentwater and then mooching about the town. The children both bought little lambs made from wool with black pipe cleaner legs. They were very sweet.

James was slightly subdued as they headed back to the guest house. The reality of what awaited them on their return to Surrey was weighing heavily on his mind. There would be a lot to organise, but that did not daunt him. It was the uncertainty of what awaited them in the house that weighed heavily on his heart.

Susan glanced at him. She felt it too, but not in the overwhelmingly oppressive way that James had experienced things. She hoped that the protection armour supplied by Mrs Derby would be up to the task. The alternative just didn't bear thinking about.

She knew that she would be able to help James with looking for a new home, new schools and all the domestic things that needed to be dealt with. He would need to potentially look for another job, but in his profession and with his experience and credentials that should not be a problem. She hoped that they would be able to find a willing buyer quickly or they may all have to find alternative accommodation for a while.

Susan tried not to worry about these things and to stay positive on the journey home, but the closer that they got to Surrey the more strained James became. She cast glances at him every few miles and saw that his face was drawn and a permanent frown was creating deep furrows in his forehead.

He had stopped talking about a hundred miles back, and there was just no point in trying to draw him into any conversation when he was this deep in thought. All she could do was stay quiet and hope for the best.

It was late afternoon when they arrived home, and everything was still. James opened the door and carried the suitcases into the kitchen for Susan to deal with the laundry. Susan could not feel anything ominous about the house.

She opened the fridge and smiled. Jenkins had thoughtfully left some milk and cheese, ham, bacon and eggs. And there was a fresh loaf of bread on the table together with a tin of shortbread and a jar of jam, so it may have been Sarah Peters being the thoughtful one instead of Jenkins. Susan felt the warm feeling of gratitude for their kindness spread through her.

The children had gone upstairs to have a bath so Susan sorted through the clothes and put on the first load of washing, then set about making a pot of tea and went in search of James to ask him what he wanted for supper.

CHAPTER 39

1936

Edward threw his papers on the desk and raced from the room. Maggie must have heard the screams too, as she met him in the hall and looked at him with concern and confusion on her face. Edward didn't say a word, but swung himself round the bottom of the stairs and flew up them two steps at a time.

He found Louisa on the floor in the corridor outside their bedroom. Her face was white and contorted in pain and there was a dark red stain on her nightdress, which was spreading, and her ankle was twisted at an alarming angle. He could just see one of Tom's trains jutting out from underneath the nightdress. He dropped to his knees beside her.

Maggie was beside him in an instant. Cassy and Tom's white, frightened faces peered out of Cassy's bedroom door. Maggie quickly went to them and, after saying a few gentle words, she urged them to go into the bedroom and closed the door quietly. She went back to the doctor and helped him to lift Louisa, and together they managed to get her back to the bed. On throwing back the covers they saw that the sheets were already stained with blood.

Maggie busied herself by swiftly changing the sheets. After getting a couple of towels from the linen cupboard she placed them on top of the fresh sheet, underneath where Louisa would be lying. Edward nodded his approval. He spoke gently and soothingly to his wife, who looked stricken and terrified in equal measure.

Another pain ripped through her belly, and she clutched at

herself in much distress. Edward said, 'Maggie, please could you go and get my bag from my study? I will give Louisa something for the pain.' Maggie nodded and left the room swiftly, returning almost immediately with the bag.

By the time she got back Edward had managed to get Louisa back into bed. She was crying now, huge gut-wrenching sobs that came right from the heart of her soul. She felt a despair so intense wash over her, as if she would never be happy again. She leant against her husband and let the pain and the misery engulf her.

Edward held her for a while longer and then went to his bag to obtain some pain relief for his wife. After what Maggie had told him earlier about the sharp pains that Louisa had experienced he was not totally surprised that she was now in the throes of a miscarriage, but still his heart ached for his wife and his unborn child.

He looked at her ankle, which was starting to swell, and strapped it up to make it more comfortable for her. It was then that she turned her gaze on him. It was filled with sorrow but also something deeper, more malevolent and angry, and filled with bitter pain.

'It is Tom's fault,' she spat out with such venom that Edward recoiled. 'I got up to go to the lavatory. I had been sleeping for hours and awoke, and I tripped over one of his toys that he had left on the landing,' she wailed in complete misery.

She looked at her belly. Another wave of pain took her for a moment and then she looked back at Edward and said, 'I fell and then … this.' She gestured to her belly and to the blood. But she couldn't gesture to her grief. 'If I hadn't fallen over and landed so hard this would not have happened,' she said, with a sob of despair.

Edward stroked back her hair. 'Now, Louisa, you know that is not true, don't you?' He looked at her to gauge her sense of reason, but she just stared past him with desolate eyes searching for a way to make it all better again. 'There was already blood in the bed. You saw it for yourself. You were already having pains this afternoon. It would have happened anyway. Sometimes it just does, and there is no reasoning behind it.'

Louisa looked at him with eyes full of contempt. 'Well, of course you would take his side. He is your precious son. Well, I want my own son, my own child. And I would have had one, until this happened.' Pain washed through her body, and she gasped and clutched at her belly once again.

Edward stood up and went back to his bag. 'I will give you something more for the pain, my dear,' he said calmly. 'There is little else to be done now but wait until it is all over.'

While the pain seared through her as her body rejected the darling child that she had so longed for, Louisa's heart grew more and more bitter. With every sharp stab of pain, the malingering anger grew until it was almost a fathomable thing that she could hold in her hand. It had such depth and strength to it that it almost soothed her with its powerful presence.

She felt herself grow calm with steely determination as she lay still on the bed. She would make sure that she got the revenge that was due to her. No one took anything away from her without suffering the consequences.

When Edward popped back in to see her later, he was pleased to see her sleeping peacefully. He was sad, for her and his unborn child – of course he was – but there would be other children and this would just be a distant memory. He would treat her to a new hat or dress and she would soon come round. He was certain of it.

Louisa woke with a start as a cup of tea was placed on her bedside cupboard. Light was starting to filter through the curtains and a light rain was pattering against the window-panes. She opened her eyes and saw Edward looking at her with a sad but kind look in his eyes.

Her thoughts returned to the events of yesterday. The pain had gone. All that was left was a dull ache in her belly, and her heart felt the heaviness of remembering. Edward sat on the edge of the bed and took her hand in his. 'How are you feeling today, my dear?' he asked, looking over her face with concern, taking in the pale skin and tired eyes.

'The pain has gone,' Louisa replied dully.

Edward nodded. 'Yes, that is quite usual. I have run you a bath. I will help you to stand, as you may feel a bit weak.' Louisa allowed herself to be helped up from the bed and escorted to the bathroom. Once he was happy that his wife was not going to faint and hurt herself, Edward left the room to allow Louisa her privacy and, leaving the door slightly ajar, went back to the bedroom to await her return so he could check her over again.

Louisa sank into the warm water, allowing it to wash over her body and remove the stains of the previous day. She was furious with her body for letting her down. And she was distraught due to the loss of her baby and angry because it had been taken away from her. *If this is what happens when you try to do good things*, she thought bitterly, *then that will be the end of my attempts.*

She washed herself in a daze and stepped out of the bath, then grabbed a fresh towel that had been placed on the stand for her use. She wrapped herself in it and made her way gingerly back to the bedroom. She was still bleeding, but at least that awful pain was now gone.

She dressed and got back into bed, and Edward examined her and seemed happy that she would be OK. He left her to rest, promising to come back shortly with a breakfast tray.

Maggie looked up as Edward entered the kitchen. His face was lined with worry and sadness. She nodded towards a chair and as he sat down, she handed him a large mug of steaming tea and studied him as he wearily placed it on the table in front of him. 'So,' Maggie said in her no-nonsense way, 'Louisa has lost the baby.'

It was a statement, not a question, and Edward just nodded grimly as he gingerly tried a sip of tea and then placed it back on the table as he realised it was still scalding hot. 'Yes,' he said and raised his mournful eyes to Maggie's own.

'You do realise that Louisa will not be easy after this. You will need to watch her carefully,' Maggie said. Edward's brows furrowed in confusion. He didn't understand what Maggie was alluding to. Maggie stared at him for a moment longer and then joined him at the table. When she spoke it was in a much gentler voice.

'Surely, Edward, you have noticed Louisa's moods and tantrums and her spitefulness, especially towards young Tom?' Edward just stared bleakly, not wanting to acknowledge Louisa's true nature, which he tried to ignore in his wife.

Maggie continued quietly. 'Her moods had seemed to be vastly improved with her pregnancy, even to the point that she had started to open up to me about how she had been feeling prior to getting pregnant. Surely you must have noticed the change in her.'

Edward nodded slowly. Louisa had been much more pleasant, but then he supposed that he did not incur the full strength of her wrath as it would not be in her best interests to be unpleasant to him. 'Well, she had been much happier, I suppose, and getting involved in community issues. I thought that she was just happy to be having a baby, and had found some friends and things that interested her that could occupy her time. I never thought— Goodness, Maggie, have I really been that blind?'

Maggie patted his hand across the table. 'Sometimes men only see what they need to see and do not fully take in the finer nuances of behaviour unless it directly affects them,' Maggie said in a matter-of-fact manner. 'So, Edward, what are we going to do about Louisa now?' She got up from the table and started to crack eggs into a bowl and beat them into a froth.

'I am not sure what to do, Maggie.' Edward rubbed his face roughly with his hands as though he was trying to wash away all the tension and angst that was to come. 'You know she blamed Tom?' Edward said.

Maggie turned her head to him sharply and stopped mid stir. 'No. What do you mean, she blamed Tom? How could Tom have anything to do with her losing the baby?'

Edward sighed deeply. 'Well, when I found her on the landing, she had tripped over one of Tom's wooden trains, which he had been playing with, and that is how she twisted her ankle. But when I helped her back to bed there was already blood on the sheet, and you said that she had started having pains in the garden.' He paused for breath. 'So ... she had already started to miscarry much earlier in the day.'

Maggie looked forlorn, her face full of concern and worry. 'Edward, this really needs to be taken seriously. You do understand that, don't you? Louisa has never warmed to Tom, but I don't know why. He is such a sweet and kind boy, but he just seems to rub Louisa up the wrong way. It would be best to keep him away from her for the time being, at least until her mental state has improved.'

Edward nodded in agreement. Once Maggie had finished cooking some scrambled eggs and toast and tea for Louisa, Edward carried it all up to her on a tray.

She was lying in bed looking calm, but on second glance Edward noticed a steely glint to her eyes that he had previously not noticed, and started to feel that Maggie may be right. He placed the tray on the side table and helped Louisa to sit up. She thanked him politely, and once she had eaten said that she was tired and wanted to rest.

Edward took the breakfast tray and closed the bedroom door as he left. He placed the tray on the top of one of the dressers in the corridor and went upstairs in search of his son.

He found Tom sitting on his bed playing with a toy train. He was moving it back and forth across the blanket, making quiet chuffing sounds. He did not look up as his father entered the room and sat beside him on the bed, but continued to play with his train as if he were still alone in the room.

Edward watched him for a moment then laid his large hand on top of the much smaller one of his son and spoke his name gently. 'Tom...'

Tom didn't look up at him. He just continued to look at the train in his now still hands. 'Tom,' his father repeated, still gently but slightly louder now – and in a more commanding voice, which demanded a response.

Tom hesitated, but lifted his head and looked at his father for a brief second and then returned his gaze to his hands. His father let out a deep sigh and rubbed a hand through his hair. The child was obviously scared and full of deep emotions. He really needed to get through to him that he was not angry with him and that he had, in fact, done nothing wrong, so he tried again.

'Tom, I need to speak to you. You need to understand something very important, and I need to know that you are listening to me and that you understand what I say. Is that all right?'

Tom nodded silently, but he still did not raise his gaze. Edward was torn between allowing his son to feel comfortable and knowing that he was listening and hearing him. He took another deep breath and then continued, allowing Tom the security of remaining in his current position. 'Tom, Louisa has lost the baby.'

Tom let out a deep sob of anguish before Edward could continue, but he hurried on with his words as quickly as possible so that his son could be put out of the misery that he was obviously going through. 'Louisa has lost the baby,' he said again quickly, 'but it was not your fault. Do you hear me, Tom? It was not your fault. This would have happened whether or not Louisa had tripped over the toy. It was a process that sometimes happens, and it had started much, much earlier in the day.'

Tom looked up quickly, scanning his father's face to ascertain that he was indeed speaking the truth. He scowled in concentration, his eyes taking in every nuance of his father's features, as if he could see beneath his skin and into the very depth of his soul.

He needed to know that this was the truth. That he was not, in fact, some sort of murderer. That by his carelessness his brother or sister had not been killed. The need was so deep and primordial that he almost forgot to breathe.

On seeing the intensity with which his son looked at him, Edward repeated his words again. 'Tom, I am your father. Would I tell you something that was not true?'

Tom considered this for a moment and, as if his brain was assessing every past dealing he and his father had ever engaged in, his thoughts came back with the answer that he could not believe. But believe it he must. His father was telling him the truth. The baby was no more, but it was not his fault.

With relief he threw himself into his father's arms and sobbed and sobbed until his little body shuddered with relief and sadness as the fear and worry that had held him in such a deep grip of despair were washed from his body with the tears. He finally quieted, and his father brushed his hair and murmured words of comfort as he held him tightly against his chest.

Chapter 40

1973

James was sitting in his study, staring out of the window into the garden. The sun was almost setting, and its waning light cast long shadows across the grass. He could hear the birds singing, and it all looked serene and peaceful. And yet he felt a tightness in his chest, a weight that made his very bones feel heavy and cumbersome.

Susan tapped lightly on the door and entered the room to find him in this position. 'James,' she said quietly. He turned and looked at her, his face looking drawn and tired. 'I just wondered if you were hungry. I was going to make us all some supper. Would something light like cheese on toast be enough for you, or would you like something else?'

He looked at his wife. Her face was soft and her eyes were kind and yet they looked at him warily, as if expecting a sharp reaction from him. He sighed and ran his hand across his face and looked back at her with a wan smile on his face and said, 'Cheese on toast would be fine, thank you.' Susan nodded and left the room and walked back to the kitchen to start supper.

James looked back out into the garden for a moment. It would be dark very soon. He stood up and switched on the lamp by his desk and drew the curtains as he felt a sudden chill in the room, a draught as if the door were open.

He turned sharply, but the door was closed. He felt fear grip his heart and he left the room and moved quickly across the hall, through the dining room and into the warmth of the kitchen. It was starting again, he was sure of it. He felt tense and afraid, and silently willed the anger that he could feel coiling in his stomach to dissipate with all the strength he could muster.

He entered the kitchen with such force that Susan jumped and nearly dropped the bottle of milk she was holding. 'James,' she exclaimed, 'you startled me.' She broke off as she saw the whiteness of her husband's pallor and, after putting the bottle down on the table, she went to him quickly and looked into his face, with concern etched deeply on her own. 'What has happened?' she asked him hastily, as she quickly scanned his whole face for answers.

James just looked at her bleakly, 'It's starting again, Susan. I can feel it here.' He placed a hand to his stomach and looked at his wife with his eyes full of fear and dread. Susan searched his face for any of the telltale signs of anger and was relieved when she did not see any.

If she had looked at the ground, rather than at her husband's face, she may have seen the faint misty tendrils pouring in from under the door into the kitchen. They snaked their way slowly along the skirting board, twisting and writhing like a nest of snakes searching out their prey. The mist was so faint and silent that it was almost imperceptible.

Susan led James to the kitchen table and pulled out one of the chairs for him to sit down. He sank wearily into it as the mist evaporated. She handed James a glass of water, which he sipped at gratefully. His rapid breathing slowed and the wild fearful look in his eyes diminished as his body calmed down.

The colour started to return to his face, and he looked calmer and surer of himself. 'God, Susan,' he exclaimed, running his hands through his hair and making it stand up in strange peaks, 'I am so sorry. I do not know what came over me. You must think me a fool.'

Susan stood against the kitchen cupboards and folded her arms about her chest. 'James Morton,' she said in a very strict manner, 'you are no fool. What is happening is very real, and you have every right to feel afraid. In fact, it would be a foolish thing not to be. That would be arrogant and extremely dangerous. We really need to work out what to do for the best and how to handle this...' She searched for the right word. 'This situation,' she finally decided on, still looking intently at her husband.

'Now,' she continued firmly, turning her back on him as she started to prepare their supper, 'we will have our supper, get the children to bed and then try our best to get some sleep. Things will look different in the morning, and you can start to put wheels in motion for us to move. You will feel so much better when you are actually doing something constructive.'

James looked at her and nodded. 'Yes, Susan, you are right. You talk so much sense. Why did I not notice this before?'

She laughed slightly and turned back to him and gestured at him with a spoon in her hand. 'Well, James,' she said, laughing, 'who would have ever thought those words would have come forth from your mouth?' And, still smiling, she turned back to her task as James continued to sip his water.

Out in the dining room Tom stood in the shadows, watching as the mist twisted and coiled around the chairs. He knew that he was powerless to stop the inevitable, which was about to happen.

Emma and Robert were upstairs in Robert's bedroom. Emma had already unpacked her suitcase and put her things away. Robert was sitting on his bed, his suitcase discarded on the floor, when Emma entered his room. She eyed it with derision but did not say anything, as she knew that to do so would incur his annoyance and she wanted to talk to him. Their mother could come out with her own nagging quite well enough, without the need for Emma to add to it.

Robert looked up as Emma entered his room, not complaining for once for her not knocking first on the door. They needed to stick together, as he was sure that there were plans afoot, concocted by their parents, to move. He had heard them talking in the night while they were away. They must have thought he was asleep, or they would never have voiced their plans in his presence.

Emma sat down on the bed and began to swing her legs restlessly. She had seen Tom briefly when she arrived, but he was not in a communicative mood and had left her room shortly after her arrival without an explanation. So she had gone instead to find Robert.

She knew that something was going on but she did not understand what it was, and the feeling unsettled her. She thought that Robert might know more, so she went to find him to ask him.

Robert looked at his little sister's worried face and sighed. 'What do you think is happening, Robert?' she asked him a moment later, in a small voice.

'How do you mean?' he replied, not wanting to worry her needlessly, but also unsure about how much she had overheard herself.

'Well, it feels all wrong and strange,' she said, finding her confidence now that she knew he was listening to her. 'I know that Mother and Father do not seem to be arguing so much – which is a good thing,' she hastily added. 'But…' She drew the word out, her finger on her chin as if considering what to say next, 'something still feels strange and not right, as if they have secret plans that they do not want to talk to us about but that will affect us anyway.'

Robert nodded, somewhat surprised by his sister's comprehension of the situation, even at her young age. 'Well...' He started rubbing at his own chin, a habit so similar to his sister's that it must have been inherited from one or both parents. 'I think that we may be moving.'

Emma gasped in shock. 'Moving? What, from this house? But how, why, where...?' Her little face was flushed in confusion and worry.

'I don't know,' said Robert hurriedly, 'Shush. Be quiet. We don't want them to hear that we know, do we?' Although why he didn't want his parents to know that they knew he couldn't quite explain, apart from the slight frisson of power it gave him to have a tiny secret of his own to hold on to, even one shared with his sister.

'But why?' Emma asked him, now even more confused. She instantly thought of Tom and was worried that she would not see him again, but sensibly kept this to herself. And anyway, she had seen him outside the house, hadn't she? Down by the river, when she had fallen in. That seemed like years ago, but it had really only been a week.

'I don't know,' Robert said, 'but I heard them discussing it while we were on holiday. They must have thought I was asleep.'

Emma thought for a moment before speaking again in a quieter voice, 'What about our friends and our school?'

'I don't know, Em,' Robert replied. The very same thoughts had been flowing through his mind too.

Robert looked down at his sister, whose face was full of worry and concern, and added, 'But whatever happens we will still be together, won't we? I will make sure that you are OK, and Mum and Father too.'

Emma pulled a face when he mentioned their father. It was true that he had been much nicer recently, almost like what she supposed a father should be like, but she was constantly on alert for any slight change in his behaviour that would lead to the sharp slaps that she was much more accustomed to. 'Mm, I suppose...' she said uncertainly, looking up at her brother with her big wide eyes, as if she were inspecting his face for the truth.

'But it won't be the same, will it? What about Jenny and Pippa and Richard?'

'I know,' Robert replied, then added, 'but we will make new friends. Remember when Malcolm and Gemma moved here? They didn't know anyone, did they? And now they have lots of friends.'

Emma considered this for a moment and agreed. 'Yes, that is true,' she said in a much brighter voice. 'I suppose it will be OK. It will be like an adventure.'

Robert patted her on the leg gently, and nodded. 'Yes, that will be just what it will be like. A big adventure.'

Just then they heard their mother's voice calling them down for supper. Robert looked at his sister with a stern expression on his face. 'Remember,' he said in hushed tones, 'no mention of this to either Mother or Father. We do not need them to know that we suspect anything.'

Emma nodded her agreement and drew her fingers across her lips to indicate that they were tightly sealed, and together they went downstairs to the kitchen for supper.

They found their parents in the kitchen together, which was in itself very unusual. Their father was not normally home when they had their supper, and then he usually preferred to eat alone. They did not say anything for fear of upsetting the current mood, which appeared to be, if not happy exactly, certainly non-confrontational. They both took their places at the table and kept their eyes down.

Their father was not aware of anything being wrong, but their mother certainly was. She eyed each of the children in turn and glanced warily at James before speaking in a light voice. 'Well, did you both enjoy your holiday, children?'

They both glanced up at her quickly and exchanged the briefest of looks between them before replying in unison, 'Yes, it was great.'

Susan put her hands on her hips and narrowed her eyes. 'OK,' she said slowly. 'What is up with you two? You are not usually this meek and quiet. Come on, out with it.'

James looked at her in surprise. He certainly had not noticed that anything was amiss at all. As soon as that thought hit him, he was engulfed in a fresh dose of shame as he realised how little he knew his own children. He looked from them to their mother and back again.

Robert looked at his father, trying to gauge his mood. And, sensing that he was not about to get a cuff around the ear, he looked at his mother, and almost without meaning to he mumbled, 'I heard that you were talking about moving.'

Emma gasped and looked at him wide-eyed in shock. 'But Robert,' she said indignantly, 'I thought that we were not supposed to mention that.'

Susan looked a bit shocked herself and glanced at James for support. He placed the newspaper that he had been reading on the table and stood up to speak to them both before saying in a calm voice, 'Well, I suppose that it is better to be open and honest about these things. And since we were not as careful as we had hoped in keeping it from you both… Yes, we are going to be selling the house and moving. We are not yet exactly sure where, but it could really be anywhere. If we find a house we like around here we could stay locally, but both of us are actually up for the challenge of moving completely out of the area and starting afresh somewhere new. What do you think? It will be a great adventure.'

Shocked by hearing both the longest speech given to them by their father as much as by the words it contained, they just sat there open-mouthed for a few moments before Emma mumbled, 'I suppose,' followed a moment later by Robert, who said,

'I guess.'

Susan smiled kindly at them and said in her usual gentle voice, 'Everything will be fine. You can help us decide on the house, can't they, James?'

James looked at her as if the idea was profoundly strange for a moment before smiling himself and saying, 'Yes, I don't see why not. It is time that we did more together as a family, and this would be a great start.'

Excited chatter ensued, with suggestions of what they would like in a new house, from a big bedroom, suggested by Emma, and a garden big enough to play cricket in, suggested by Robert, which was instantly countered by Emma wanting a paddock for a pony and Robert wanting a kennel for a dog.

Susan finished putting the supper in front of everyone. She watched them with a smile on her pretty face. She felt peaceful, and was very hopeful for the future.

Tom stood in the shadows of the dining room by the door to the kitchen. He could hear the laughter and the easy conversation but had a sad look on his face. They would be leaving and he would be alone again.

Then he saw the angry mist coiling about his feet and his sadness turned to fear, as the mist became dark and writhed as if it was full of a hundred snakes. It coiled about the chairs of the dining room and inched its way across the floor, where it disappeared into the wooden panelling of the dining room. This was not a good sign, Tom said to himself. Things were not going to be easy, and danger was certainly close at hand.

Tom watched James Morton walk through the dining room after the family had eaten their supper in the kitchen. This, he thought, was a very surprising development. He could not recall seeing the family eat together, and in particular not in the kitchen.

What has happened to the father? he wondered to himself. He had always seemed to have been short-tempered and morose, but now he seemed almost pleasant. He could tell that the children were still wary of him and that their feelings were guarded, but Susan seemed to trust completely in this change of personality and he did not feel that she was being wise.

He thought to himself for a moment. Yes, he was still only a child, but the things he had seen gave him more experience than most. He knew that Susan sometimes caught glimpses of him, but she never really noticed him properly.

He was concerned about this young family, but felt powerless to do anything to help them. He knew that something was going to happen, and the way that the swirling mist was seething with indignant anger made him realise that whatever it was would happen soon.

James headed for his study. There was so much to do and to think about, and there were many decisions to be made. He could feel the old anger starting to well up in his body and fought desperately to quell it. He felt like he had been on a roller coaster. He was grateful that Susan was willing to stand by him, but, goodness knows, he did not deserve it.

He wanted so badly to be a good man, to be worthy of her kindness, but he could feel the pull of the anger, the melancholy and the despair that made him behave in such an appalling way. They needed to get out of this house, of that he was certain, but where should they go?

He thought about his share in the firm, and this led him on to thinking about Clare. He put his head in his hands. God, what a mess he had made of everything. He wanted to hit out and blame someone for his mistakes, but in reality he knew that it was his fault. His weakness. But if Susan had stopped him… If she had only stood up to him then he would not have carried on being so difficult for so long.

The mist swirled under the door and coiled at his feet. He could feel the anger and resentment starting to rise and stood up abruptly. His head was full of confusion and swirling thoughts, and he knew he had to get out of there. He grabbed his briefcase, which was on the floor by his feet, and marched out of the house. In his haste he did not notice the swirling dark tendrils seeping into the black briefcase as he opened the car door and threw it onto the back seat.

The first Susan knew that anything was the matter was when she heard the front door slam shut. She looked up from the sink to see James striding purposefully to the car, throwing his bag onto the back seat and climbing into the driver's seat. Before she could put down the dishcloth and wipe her hands on her apron, the car shot off up the drive as if the very hounds of hell were after it.

Susan sighed and walked to the table. She sat down at the

end and placed her own head in her hands. It was all starting again. She could feel the house pause as if it were taking a breath, waiting for the next move in its very own game of chess. She felt the familiar sense of weariness fill her to the core and she felt as if she would never have the energy to move again.

The children both heard the front door slam and ran together to look out of their parents' bedroom window, which overlooked the driveway, and saw their father drive away. They looked at each other with sad resignation on their faces.

The hoped-for permanency of the change in their father was slipping away like mist before the sun. 'Come on, Em,' Robert said to his sister. 'Let's go and play a game of ludo until bedtime.' He reached out his hand, which his sister took gratefully, and they walked back across the corridor to his bedroom.

Chapter 41

1936

Louisa stayed in bed for a couple of days, not because she particularly felt ill, but because she really did not want to see anyone. She could not face their concern and pity.

She especially did not want to see Tom, who she blamed for her misfortune entirely. Even though logically she knew that it was not his fault, the bitterness inside her grew like a canker, wiping out all sense and reason. He had blighted her and her unborn child, and he had to pay.

She used this time of self-imposed isolation to plot her revenge. Outwardly she appeared calm, serene, resigned and quietly accepting her loss. Edward was attentive and kind and Maggie brought her endless cups of tea and light meals to tempt her to gain strength after her ordeal.

Nothing was said about the baby, but Louisa knew that Maggie was aware of her mood. She also knew that she must be careful around the older woman. Maggie missed nothing, and Louisa was conscious that she watched her closely. Edward was easily fooled, she thought with bitter irony. Men did not see what was right beneath their own noses most of the time. As long as he thought she was content then that was all that concerned him, and that was a very easy part to play.

On the third day after her miscarriage Louisa decided that she needed to get up. She was getting bored and there was only so much plotting that even she could do. She ran herself a bath and lay back, letting the warm water heat up her thin body. She always felt so cold these days.

Afterwards she dressed and went downstairs in search of breakfast. She found Maggie in the kitchen, putting together a tray for her, and she looked up in surprise as Louisa entered the room. 'Why, Louisa, should you be up already? I was just about to bring this up to you.'

Louisa smiled a thin smile, which did not quite reach her eyes. 'That is very kind of you, Maggie, but I feel like I have been lying around for quite long enough now, don't you? Please could you bring the tray to the drawing room? I think I will sit in there.'

She turned around and walked out of the kitchen, through the dining room and hall to the drawing room. She sat down at the table by the window and looked out into the garden. Maggie followed her with the tray and placed it beside her on the table.

Louisa took a piece of buttered toast from the tray, then bit a delicate piece off and chewed it in distaste. 'I needed some air too,' she said, as if they were carrying on the same conversation from the kitchen. 'I think I will have a little walk around the garden after breakfast and pick some flowers for the house.'

Maggie hesitated for a moment before saying, 'I think that is a good idea, but take care not to tire yourself out.' Louisa nodded but said no more, and continued to eat her toast in silence.

Louisa continued to sit in silence once she had finished her toast and sipped her tea. Everything tasted bland, and even the garden looked colourless and drab. It was as if all the light and colour had been drained from her life. She was dead and was just a shadow of her former self, going through the motions like a ghost. An echo of the person she had been. There was no happiness or joy, not even really any sadness, just a big empty nothingness. She felt like a husk of herself and wondered if she looked different.

She idly wondered whether her reflection would actually stare back at her if she looked in a mirror. She was weak still from the loss of blood, but she knew that it was more than that. It was if, in losing the baby, part of her very essence had been washed away with it.

She stared out at the garden and watched the birds with an utter lack of interest. She was still sitting there when Edward came home after his morning surgery to check on her before he started his rounds of house calls.

She did not even look up when he entered the room. She remained so still that at first he thought her to be asleep, but when he came to her side he saw that her eyes were open. The expression in them chilled him as they looked lifelessly out on the garden.

Edward took her hand in his and spoke her name, but she did not react until he said her name slightly more sharply, and she responded by slowly turning her head and looking up at him with those same dull eyes.

'Louisa,' he asked quietly, 'how are you feeling, my dear? Should you really be downstairs?'

Louisa did not respond for a moment. Then she took back her hand and placed it in her lap and turned her gaze back out of the window before saying, 'I cannot very well stay in my room forever. I feel perfectly well, thank you, just a little tired.' She sighed and turned back to him, trying to force a little light into her face. 'Thank you for asking, Edward.'

He nodded and stood there, looking at his wife. He was at a loss about what to do. She was usually so full of life – feisty, even – that this version of Louisa almost scared him, she was just so cold. Not knowing what else to say, he patted his wife gently on the shoulder and said, 'I will see you later. I have to do my morning rounds now, but perhaps I could pop back and join you for some lunch.' Louisa nodded but did not reply.

Edward left the room and met Maggie in the hall on the way out to the car. He beckoned her over to him and said in hushed tones, 'Can you keep an eye on Louisa for me while I am out? I am not happy with how she seems, not happy at all.' Maggie nodded and agreed and, slightly mollified, Edward made his way out of the house and went on his way to deal with his morning patient list.

Maggie looked into the drawing room on her way back to the kitchen and saw that Louisa was still sitting in the chair by the French windows. She took a deep breath and, after releasing a little sigh, walked over to where Louisa was sitting. 'Would you like some more tea, Louisa? That pot must have gone cold hours ago now.'

Louisa looked up with a faraway look in her eyes, as though she had heard the words but could not quite assimilate them into coherent communication. 'Tea, Louisa?' Maggie said, to prompt her.

Louisa seemed to give herself a little mental shake and focused her eyes on Maggie. 'Tea? Oh, yes, please, Maggie. That would be kind.' Her voice was pleasant enough but flat, unemotional and resigned. Maggie thought that Edward was right to be concerned about his wife. She would try to rejig her morning tasks so she could stay near Louisa, and would see if she could enlist Cassy's help in keeping her stepmother company. She would also make sure that she kept Tom out of her way.

She walked back to the kitchen and found Jimmy Jenkins

rattling the biscuit tin in search of something to eat. She smacked his hands away and said, 'I'll make you a piece of toast in a moment, Jimmy, but I need you to do me a favour today.'

'Oh?' Jimmy replied, looking up with interest and a ready grin on his face. 'Now what might that be?'

Maggie sighed and looked grim as she continued. 'You know that Miss Louisa lost the baby?'

Jimmy's face now became serious, and he took the cap from his head and held it in front of him in both hands. 'Yes, I heard. Poor Miss Louisa. How is she?'

Maggie looked thoughtful for a moment as if trying to choose her words carefully. 'Physically she will be as right as rain in no time. She's still young and, well, these things happen. It is not uncommon to lose your first baby.' Jimmy nodded.

Maggie continued, 'However, it is not her physical state that we are worried about. This seems to have knocked her for six, and she is not taking it well mentally.' Maggie searched for the right words to try to describe how Louisa was behaving. 'She is… She is… Well, she is not quite right. That's all I can really say. What I need you to do, young Jimmy, is to keep Tom away from her. They have never really got on, and Louisa seems convinced that the loss of the baby is in some way Tom's fault.'

Maggie held up her hand to stop Jimmy's protestations. 'I know as well as you do that it is all a lot of preposterous nonsense. But sometimes when a woman suffers such a loss it can cause her to behave in strange ways, and I just do not want young Tom caught in the crossfire, so will you help?'

Jimmy drew himself up to his full height. 'Of course I will help, Maggie. I love young Tom, you know that. Me and him…

Well, we are really close. I will keep him with me all day, you see that I don't.'

Maggie looked at the young man's earnest face and nodded her approval. 'Right you are, then. Now sit down while I make you a cup of tea and some toast. You are making my kitchen untidy with your great bulk.' The broad grin returned to Jimmy's face as he sat down at the table. He knew that he had Maggie's favour when she scolded him like that.

A few minutes later the boy in question entered the kitchen, rubbing sleep from his eyes and looking tired and troubled. It was much later in the morning than he would usually come down. Tom was normally such an early riser, but Maggie supposed that with all the trauma of the past few days he was staying out of the way as much as possible and was most probably not sleeping all that well either, from the look of him.

Maggie and Jimmy exchanged a glance. Then Maggie said, 'Jimmy here has a few things in the garden that he would like your help with, young Tom.' Maggie nodded towards Jimmy as she spoke, and Jimmy smiled at Tom.

'If you don't mind, Tom,' he said, 'you and Miss Cassy will be going back to school soon, so I'd best get all the use out of you that I can.' Jimmy smiled his cheeky, affectionate grin and Tom smiled back.

Tom had wanted to get out of the house to avoid bumping into Louisa, so he was keen to help Jimmy. 'OK,' he said readily. 'What do you want me to help you with?'

Maggie started making some toast for Tom while Jimmy chatted away to him about all the jobs that needed doing, some of which would take Tom out of the house and grounds altogether, as it sounded like several items needed sharpening. This would mean a visit to the ironmongers in the village. Maggie knew they had a grinding machine in there, as she often got one of the men to take some of the kitchen tools to have their blades sharpened.

Jimmy turned to her. 'Will that be OK, Maggie? Taking young Tom into the village, I mean?'

Maggie smiled. 'I am sure it will be fine. I will let Dr Winter know, should he enquire about the whereabouts of his son, but he will be out most of the day, I am sure.'

After breakfast Tom went out to find Jimmy in the garden. He was right at the end by the vegetable patch, pulling out the remnants of a spent crop and digging it over. Louisa watched him trot down the lawn and leave wet footprints in the dewy grass. Her lips tightened and she folded her arms tight against her belly.

She turned away from the window, fury seething through her to the very marrow. It was so unfair, she thought as she hugged herself. The sorrow and pain wracking her body were quickly consumed by anger. How dare he just saunter around the garden without a care in the world, while her little child had not even had a chance at life?

She howled, then forced her fist into her mouth to quell the noise and sobbed silently. She couldn't risk anyone hearing and coming to find her in this state. She needed to be poised and calm. *I can do this*, she thought, as she took deep, sharp breaths to stem the overwhelming tide of feelings that threatened to tip her over into oblivion. *I am strong*, she told herself.

She would get through this one way or another. She had to. She needed to take revenge for the loss of her baby. She had to bide her time and plan every little detail. She sat back down at the table by the French windows and continued to breathe slowly until her heart rate returned to normal.

Tom was completely unaware of Louisa's gaze upon him as he ran down the garden to find Jimmy. He was so relieved to be out of the house and to have something to do that would take his mind off the awful events of the past few days. He was trying his very best to stay out of Louisa's way, but, although the house was not small, it was not so large that one could hide away forever. He would stick close to Jimmy during the day and Cassy and his father in the evenings, and everything would return to normal soon, he was sure of it.

Feeling a bit better, he started to whistle a jaunty little tune as he approached the area of the vegetable patch that Jimmy was working on.

Jimmy looked up at the sound and smiled at him. 'OK, Tom, can you help me pick up all this stuff and put it in the wheelbarrow?' He pointed to the pile of brown leaves and roots. 'We can then have ourselves a bit of a bonfire later this afternoon.' Tom smiled. He loved bonfires.

Louisa paced the room, feeling more and more unsettled. It was becoming difficult to control her emotions and she really needed to get a grip of herself and at least outwardly appear to be calm.

It was Mary's day to come and help Maggie with the cleaning, and Mary knocked gently on the door to the drawing room and pushed it ajar. Louisa scowled at the interruption and Mary made to quickly retreat before Louisa called her back. 'I would like some more tea. This pot has gone cold,' she said, her voice like steel.

Mary scuttled over to the table and picked up the tray, then exited the room in haste. Louisa fanned her face with her hand. It was getting warm, and she didn't really want tea. She would have preferred lemonade to quench her thirst but had not had the presence of mind to think of that when the girl appeared, because she just wanted to be left alone.

She sat in the chair and picked up a book. She tried to read it but could not settle, so she got up again and took a turn around the room. Then she spent a few moments looking at the books in the bookcase and wondered whether she should put a record on to play on the gramophone, but she simply was not in the mood.

Mary returned with the tea tray, along with Cassy, who had become bored reading in her bedroom and had come downstairs in search of something to occupy her. Seeing Louisa in the drawing room, as Mary opened the door, she followed her inside and politely enquired how she was feeling.

Louisa took a deep sigh and replied, 'I am as well as can be expected, my dear, but I am feeling rather restless. Would you care to play a game of cards? I believe it will get rather hot this afternoon, so I may go and have a lie-down later, but for now I need distraction.'

Cassy, who was not very good at cards, agreed reluctantly, but then said, 'I would much rather play ludo or snakes and ladders.'

Louisa thought for a moment. She had enjoyed playing childish games when she had looked after the children, and it would probably be more distracting than playing cards with an unworthy opponent. 'Go and get the board games, then, Cassy. We will play one of them instead.' Cassy smiled and almost ran from the room, a surprised smile on her pretty face.

Louisa sat down in her chair and poured herself another cup of tea. Mary came back with a jug of lemonade and two glasses. Louisa nodded her approval but said nothing to the girl, who looked like a frightened rabbit. She turned and almost bumped into Cassy, who had returned with the box of board games, in her haste to exit the room.

Louisa tutted at her clumsiness, and Mary's face went bright pink to the tip of her ears as she muttered a mumbled apology. Cassy thanked her for bringing the lemonade, and then sat down in the second chair by the table and started to lay out the game.

CHAPTER 42

1973

James parked the car in a lay-by a few miles away from the family home and put his head in his hands. He did not understand what was happening to him. The engine was still running so he turned it off, pulled sharply on the handbrake and stepped out of the car.

The lay-by was close to a well-known beauty spot and the sun was sinking behind the hills, basking everything in its final red glow as it gave up on the day. The hills in the distance started to become darker and shadows crept in from all sides as the sun melted away into oblivion.

There was a little wooden picnic bench set on the grass by a fence, and James walked over to it and sat down. His mind was in turmoil. The anger had risen up within him within hours of being home. While he had been away on holiday with his family he had caught a glimpse of what his life could be. That almost made things worse.

He needed help but did not know where to turn. He just knew that he could not carry on like this. The emotions affecting him were all-consuming, and he was afraid that he would lash out and do something unforgivable. The house... He had to sell that house. It was the only way, but that could take months, and how would he be able to cope with living there all that time?

Perhaps he could send Susan and the children away. They could rent somewhere and look for another house while he stayed here and sold this one. But what about the children's schools?

He pulled at his hair in frustration. There seemed to be no simple answer. Within a few short weeks now the children would be back at school and there would be nothing that he could do. Should he stay somewhere else? What would people think? What would Susan think? He needed to speak to Susan. Oh, why was everything so difficult?

Susan slumped in the chair in the kitchen. She had no idea what to do. She wanted to know where James had gone but also didn't want to know. She was afraid that he may have returned to Clare. But why would he? They had got on so well while they were away that she had started to really hope that there was a way forward for them. At least, she supposed with irony, he had just left the house without resorting to his previous nasty behaviour towards her and the children.

What was it about this house that changed him so much? She knew that there were energies in the house – she had felt them herself – but they did not seem to affect her. Not like they did James, anyway. She felt the cold spots and saw fleeting glimpses in the shadows, she heard the children and saw snatches of their clothes as they ran through the trees, and she heard them calling sometimes. Well, she had heard a particular voice calling for its mother.

But she was used to seeing, feeling and hearing the echoes of time. She guessed that she was just wired that way. Emma too, from the sound of it. James didn't see or hear anything. Of that she was certain. But something in this house seemed to have got its grip on him, and he seemed powerless to resist it.

Susan got up from the table and pushed the chair back underneath. She walked towards the door, glanced around the room, and then turned off the light and made her way upstairs to say goodnight to the children and get herself ready for bed. Maybe a hot bath would help her to settle down and relax a little.

She found both children in Robert's room playing a board game. They seemed to be happy enough, so she left them to it for the moment and went to run her bath. The water ran hot and steamy and Susan poured a cap full of bubble bath under the tap as it ran, letting the foamy scent fill her nostrils and settle her spirit. She went into her bedroom to undress and put on her dressing gown and walked back to the bathroom.

She closed the door and stood in front of the mirror to remove her make-up. The glass was steamed up, so she rubbed at it with the side of her hand then let out a gasp of shock.

The face staring back at her from the mirror with a coldness in its eyes was not hers. Susan turned quickly to look behind her, but she was alone in the bathroom. She looked again in the mirror, and her own startled, pale face stared back at her.

Her heart was pounding in her chest and her breathing came fast and shallowly. She held onto the back of the white wooden chair in the bathroom to steady herself and looked again in the mirror, but it was just her reflection staring back at her. With all the stress, the long journey and James driving off like that with no explanation, had she imagined it?

She sat down on the chair, too afraid to get in the bath until her heart rate returned to normal. She was certain that she had seen another face in the glass – that of a woman with blonde hair who was pretty but cold and calculating, if her glare was anything to go by. She must talk to someone about this house, but who?

Her heart rate having returned to its steady beat, she threw a hand towel over the mirror and stepped into the bath. She let the warmth of the water soothe away her anxious state as best as it could and thought about the house and who might know, and then she almost laughed out loud.

Jimmy Jenkins, their inherited gardener, of course. He had been working here for years. In fact, he was probably nearly as old as the house itself. She would ask him in the morning. For now, all she wanted to do was to try and relax and hopefully get some sleep. She was weary to the bone. *Goodness only knows if James will be back tonight*, she said to herself. But then, she was used to that.

She lay in the bath for a long time, until the water started to become uncomfortably cold. She dried and dressed herself and then went to persuade the children to clean their teeth and get ready for bed themselves. 'Where has Father gone?' Emma asked her as she stroked her head after having read her a bedtime story.

'Oh, I think he had some work to do after being away on holiday,' Susan said, lying, not quite meeting her daughter's eye. Whether or not Emma believed her mother she didn't question her further. Tom sat on the window seat watching them, a frown creasing his brow. The atmosphere in the house was stifling. He wished he could leave, but it did not seem possible.

Susan walked back downstairs after having tucked her daughter in for the night and wishing her to sleep well. She looked in on Robert as she passed his bedroom door, which was at the foot of the stairs, and saw that he was in bed reading one of his old comic annuals.

She wished him a good night too, and wondered whether to go to bed or to go and make herself a cup of tea first. She was very tired, but her body felt restless and her mind was wired, what with James rushing off and then that face.

Her breathing quickened again as she thought about it. She

was sure that she had not imagined it. She needed to talk to Jim. Perhaps he would be able to enlighten her. She hoped that he would not think her fanciful at best or even mad.

She hesitated outside her bedroom. She could hear what sounded like quiet sobbing coming from inside. She turned the handle and the noise stopped. She looked around the room. Nothing was out of place, but it felt cold. 'Oh, for goodness' sake,' she exclaimed out loud. 'I am tired, my husband has disappeared again, and I just can't deal with anything else right now, OK?'

Nothing moved in the room. There was not even a breeze coming from the open window, but the atmosphere lightened softly and the room instantly felt less cold.

Susan nodded and said 'Better,' and thought that she might as well make herself that cup of tea so went downstairs to the kitchen. As she closed the door a candle flickered into life in the jar on the windowsill and a final sob echoed down the years to be released into the room. Then the candle was extinguished with a breath.

Susan felt weary and angry. She just wanted a normal life with her husband and children. She was too tired and overwhelmed to be dealing with the echoes of a bygone age. She was not unfeeling – kindness was part of her true nature – but sometimes she just needed to be left alone to deal with her own feelings and not be swamped with those of others, especially ones that she could do nothing about.

She threw a cup of tea together and walked back upstairs. She was not scared by the strange occurrences in the house – after all, she had lived with such happenings her whole life – but she was unnerved by the intensity of the energy in the house and how it was affecting James.

She wondered whether he had taken any of the protection talismans that Mrs Derby had given them with him when he left so abruptly. She thought probably not. She climbed into bed and sipped her tea. She would try and read for a while until sleep took her.

James was getting cold. The sun had long since departed from this side of the earth, taking with it the last vestiges of warmth, along with any feelings of hope that had once swirled in the murky depths of his thoughts. He simply did not know what to do. He desperately wanted to be with his wife. He realised now that she was the strong one in the relationship. Perhaps that is why he had been such a bully towards her.

He unconsciously recognised that what was lacking in him was in her, and he was in some way jealous of her strength. Or maybe it simply intimidated him. Goodness, but he could do with some of that strength now. But what if he went home and the rage took him again? He would never be able to forgive himself if he hurt her or, heaven forbid, the children. He stood up and paced as he thought, and ran wild hands through his hair until it stood in soft peaks.

He had to go somewhere, though, he realised. He got back into the car and started the engine. His fingers started tapping on the steering wheel as if their drumming could summon up the answers to his plight.

He decided that he would go to a hotel close to the office and from there he would call Susan and explain … explain what? He half-smiled to himself. Explain that the minute he set foot in the house he felt like kicking seven shades out of the nearest object?

Well, he would just have to do his best. He put the car into gear and pulled out onto the road and headed towards the hotel. He just hoped that they had a room for him.

The sound of the phone ringing woke Susan. She sat up with a start. The book that had been resting on her chest where it had fallen after she had succumbed to sleep dropped to the floor, and the bookmark flew across the floor to land under her dressing table.

She cursed silently, grabbed her robe and went downstairs to the hall to answer the phone. She picked it up, silencing the insistent ring, and put the receiver to her ear. 'Susan?' She heard her husband's voice, and a mixture of relief and irritation filled her heart.

'James,' she replied, slightly more sharply than she intended, 'where are you?' Then, softening her tone, she enquired, 'Are you all right? You left in such a hurry.'

At the other end of the phone she heard him sigh. He sounded deflated, she thought, and could imagine him running a distracted hand through his hair. 'I am fine. Look, I am sorry that I left like I did, but almost the minute I was back in the house I felt overcome. I just had to get out, do you understand? I am worried about the strength of the feelings that come over me, and I didn't—' He stopped speaking, unsure how to go on without sounding like a pathetic mess of nerves.

Susan sighed gently. 'I do understand, James, I really do, but what are we going to do? The house might take ages to sell. Do you intend to live elsewhere for all that time? Where even are you?' She had visions of him fleeing back into the arms of his lover and was surprised for a moment how jealous she felt. There had been a time, not that long ago, when she would gladly have driven him over to his mistress's house herself and left him there.

James's response pulled her out from the painful memories, 'I am staying at the Red Lion Hotel. It is close to the office, so I can then start to put the sale into motion tomorrow. I don't know what to do, Susan,' he admitted anxiously, 'but I can't stay in the house at the moment. I can't trust myself.'

Susan thought for a moment. 'I will call Mrs Derby in the morning and see if she can offer us any advice about what to do. Try and get some sleep and call me tomorrow.'

They said their goodbyes and Susan put the phone back in its cradle and walked slowly back upstairs to her room. She felt relief in knowing that her husband was safe and that he was not with his mistress, but the uncertainty about their future worried her. She knew she could do no more tonight, but she would speak to Jim and Mrs Derby in the morning.

CHAPTER 43

1936

The air had a crackling energy to it. Everything was still and the heat was stifling already, and it was not even lunchtime.

Louisa fanned herself with her book. She had played two games of snakes and ladders with Cassy and one of ludo, but she was finding it difficult to concentrate between the inner emotional turmoil building inside her and the stickiness of the day. Cassy had long since grown bored of the game and was currently lying in the garden under the shade of the wych elm, reading a book.

Louisa was tired, but felt too wired to sleep. It almost felt as though her mind and body were being torn in two, between the heady exhaustion that almost floored her and her mind racing with a tumult of bitter feelings. She needed to still herself, but the heat made it too hard to concentrate. Her breathing was shallow and fast. It was like she was losing complete control of herself.

She stood up abruptly, nearly sending the table flying. She needed some fresh air, she realised. That would help to calm her down. She walked to the open French doors, where the curtains hung limply at their sides. It was so still it was as though the earth was holding its breath.

Louisa stepped outside. It was even hotter out there, which did nothing to stem her rising temper. The whole of the raised terrace outside of the back of the house was in full sun. The only shade to be found was among the branches of the wych elm, and Cassy had already taken up that spot. The side of the house that led to the kitchen was in the shade, but it was not a place to sit.

The sweat began to pool between her breasts and trickle down her back. She felt so flustered that she almost started to panic. Then she heard Tom's voice as he chatted animatedly to Jimmy Jenkins. She could not see him fully, for he was almost at the bottom of the garden in the orchard, but the sound of his voice made her eyes narrow and as she looked down she saw that her fists were tightly bunched.

She was so angry. Why should he be outside enjoying his life, having fun, when her own sweet and innocent child had been taken from her?

She paced up and down in the cooler shade of the trees at the side of the house but did not want to be discovered in this state. Not being able to settle her emotions, she headed back into the drawing room and poured herself a glass of lemonade. It had already begun to warm slightly in the heat of the day, and she grimaced at the unpleasant sensation. She glanced at the clock on the mantelpiece. It was just after noon. Hadn't Edward said that he would try and join her for lunch?

She needed to get a strong grip on herself before he arrived, she thought. She glanced at herself in the mirror over the fireplace and grimaced. Her eyes were wild and her cheeks were flushed, but that could have as much to do with the heat as anything else. She would go upstairs, she thought, and splash some cold water on her face and wrists and then have a lie-down until Edward came home.

It was much cooler upstairs in the large house. Someone had opened a few windows, which allowed breezes to drift freely along the corridor and upstairs to the old servants' rooms. Louisa lay on her bed and allowed the cool breeze to drift over her. She was so tired, but her brain would not give in to sleep. The atmosphere was still static, and her clothes stuck to her. She placed the back of her hand on her forehead and tried to still her quaking nerves.

Through the window a bird's song drifted, and this was mixed with the sound of one of the gardeners pushing the mower across the lawn at the front of the house. She could also hear the sound of children playing. She shot up into a sitting position. Why could she hear children playing? Were there children in the garden?

She got out of bed and walked across the long corridor to the lounge, whose large windows looked out onto the garden. She couldn't see any children in the garden, but perhaps it was in the lane beyond the end of the garden. Sometimes sounds could carry further than normal if the wind was blowing the right direction. But today there was no wind. It was so still.

The sky was a deep blue, and there was barely a cloud to be seen. She paced up and down the large room. This had once been the master bedroom when the house was first built, she assumed, back in the days when all the living was done on the ground floor and the house had many servants.

She stopped and peered out of the window again and caught sight of Tom walking back down the lawn pushing a wheelbarrow. *Really*, she said to herself, *Edward needs to do something*. The child was becoming more and more like a ragamuffin urchin every day. He needed to be sent off to boarding school, and the sooner the better. He spent far too much of his time with the servants than was good for him. The son of the doctor needed to be seen to be more respectable.

When Edward returned later he found Louisa upstairs. She was sitting up in bed and had managed to bring her temper under control enough to not be noticeable, though it still seethed in the deepest regions of her heart.

CHAPTER 44

1973

The phone rang out shrilly in the flagged hallway. Mrs Derby wiped her hands on her apron and walked out of the kitchen into the gloom of the darkened hallway and picked up the receiver. She had been expecting the call, and before Susan even had the chance to say, 'Good morning,' Mrs Derby had said,

'Mrs Morton – Susan – is that you?'

Susan smiled silently to herself and let out a deep breath of relief. Her instincts to call this intuitive old woman had been right. 'Yes, Mrs Derby,' she said, and sighed as she leant against the balustrades of the stairs as they met the hall floor. 'It is me. I am sorry to trouble you, but things are not good here and we are out of our depth.'

She proceeded to fill Mrs Derby in with what had happened since their return home. Mrs Derby listened in silence, and when Susan had finished, she took in a deep breath and thought for a moment before responding. The line was so quiet that Susan thought that the connection had been broken. 'Mrs Derby?' she asked, 'are you still there?'

Mrs Derby pulled herself out from her deep thoughts and replied slowly, 'Yes my dear, I am still here. I am just thinking about what the best solution to your predicament would be. This is most serious, and I need to be certain about a few things before I can be sure to offer you the correct advice.'

Susan pulled the telephone cord round from behind the little hall table and hooked it over the banister rail so that she could sit on the stairs. She leant her elbows on her knees and sat patiently waiting for Mrs Derby to finish thinking. She looked around her at the vast hall and at the antique furniture and the huge Persian rug, which dominated the hall floor and hid most of the beautiful parquet floor tiles. And she looked at the stone mullioned windows with their lead-framed windows of tiny rectangular panes and took in the solemnity of the grandfather clock, which ticked away time at the base of the curve of the stairs.

The house was vast, imposing, impressive, but it was not really a home. It was too large and it felt cold and unfriendly, as if it had witnessed too much misery and grief in its life, and those memories clung to its walls like a depressing gloom that the bright sunlight that streamed through the small panes did nothing to diminish or dispel.

Mrs Derby had obviously finished her contemplation, as her strong voice came back on the line. 'I think it would be wise if you all left the house,' she said eventually. 'I get a strong impression that it is not a safe place for you to be, especially for James. The forces are powerful and malevolent, and they want something from James. What this is, I am not sure. The vision is cloudy and painful. I can see a child too, but the child is trying to help.'

Her voice drifted off, as if she was coming out of a trance. When she spoke again her voice was stronger. 'I cannot see it all, but I do feel that you are being warned to leave. Is that a possibility?'

Susan thought back to Sarah Peters's offer of staying with her sister on the farm for a week or so. Maybe they could stay longer and get the children into a school locally, until the house was sold. She would have to discuss it with James, of course, but under the circumstances perhaps she could make her own decisions. 'Yes,' she said to Mrs Derby, 'I think that there could be a way.'

Susan made breakfast for herself and the children and then told them to get ready, as they were going for a walk to see Sarah Peters. The children both cheered, thinking of the possibility of eating some of Mrs Peters's wonderful shortbread. Susan smiled indulgently at them, wishing, with a shake of her head, that her life could be so simple.

They set off around 10 a.m. The sun was shining, and the sky was the deepest of blues. There were just a few high wisps of cloud and a very gentle breeze. The paths were covered in a light dust, and this was blown around in tiny whorls by the breeze. The birds were singing and everything looked bright and glowing, bathed as it was in the light of the sun. The children ran ahead, playing some invented game, and Susan was filled with happiness at the sight of them.

Within twenty minutes they had reached the farm track, and they could see Sarah Peters hanging washing on the line in her garden. Sarah looked up at the sound of the children running down the lane towards her cottage. She put a hand to her eyes to shield them from the glare of the sun and saw Susan much further down the track. She raised a hand to wave and then entered the cottage to put the kettle onto the stove to boil.

She was putting cups, plates and a tin of lavender shortbread on the table when the family reached the cottage. Susan knocked gently on the open door and Sarah called them in. 'Well,' Sarah exclaimed, hands on hips and a ready smile on her round face, 'this is an unexpected but most welcome surprise. Do come in. Sit down. Tea, Susan? Lemonade, children?'

Everyone nodded their preference and Susan sat at the table.

The children, spying a tumble of kittens spilling out of the back door into the yard, exclaimed in delight and looked expectantly at their mother and Mrs Peters. 'Oh, go and play with the little nuisances,' Sarah said as she waved them away with her hand. 'It will stop them getting into mischief in here and tripping me over.'

Susan heaved a big sigh of relief. Now she could speak openly with Sarah without fear of the children overhearing and questioning or worrying about what was going on.

Sarah passed a cup of tea and a plate of shortbread biscuits to her, called the children to come and get theirs and, after they had grabbed their drinks and treats and ran back outside, Sarah closed the door and took her own seat at the table. 'So,' Sarah began, a questioning look crossing her face, 'to what do I owe this pleasure?'

Susan sighed and put down her cup. It rattled slightly in the saucer and some of the liquid spilt over the edge of the cup, leaving brown drips running down the side of the china. 'I was wondering whether the offer to go and stay with your sister would still be open,' Susan said finally. She looked up and Sarah could see the concern and worry etched in the small creases at the side of the younger woman's eyes.

Sarah stirred her tea as she looked at Susan, her eyes scanning the younger woman's face with compassion. 'Is it James?' she asked, taking a sip of her tea as she waited for the answer. The sun shone through the kitchen window, illuminating the swirls of dust in the air and playing with them as they tumbled in their spotlight.

Susan nodded, trying to keep her emotions in check, and she hesitated, not really knowing how to explain the strange situation of her domestic troubles. 'It is … and it isn't. Well, it is James,' she continued hurriedly, 'but it is not really him. Oh, I don't know how to explain this without you thinking me mad, or at least terribly strange.'

Sarah sat patiently waiting for Susan to continue. There was no look of judgement in her eyes, just a quiet acceptance. It spurred Susan on to continue. 'OK, here goes.' She took a very deep breath and the whole story came tumbling out.

'We took a trip away to the Lake District and we stayed with this older couple, a Mr and Mrs Derby, in Keswick. Mrs Derby noticed at once that there was some sort of strange presence around James. And twice, while we were out, we were sort of blasted by this strong wind, which almost knocked us over. And there was a voice...' She trailed off and looked deep into Sarah's eyes, as if willing her to understand.

Sarah just nodded and, patting Susan's arm gently, said, 'Go on.'

'Well,' Susan continued, 'it seems as though this – this thing – has sort of latched itself onto James and it does not seem to like me very much. It explains James's behaviour. He changed, you see, as soon as we moved into the house. He was always a bit distant, but of late he has been becoming ever angrier and almost violent. He scares me, Sarah.'

Susan stopped then. She had been looking down at her hands as she recounted her tale but now she looked up and her eyes were brimming with tears.

Sarah took in a deep breath of her own and looked off into the distance for a moment, deep in thought. 'And you want to leave him, to get away. Is that it?'

Susan gasped but was resolute when she answered, 'No. I do not want to leave him, but we need to stay away from the house. It is where this energy can affect James the most. While we were away it was held at bay. Mrs Derby gave us these protection poppets.'

She reached into her bag and drew out the fabric doll, which was crudely fashioned into the shape of the upper half of a body, filled with herbs and little stones. Sarah took the doll and could feel the strong energy surrounding it. *This Mrs Derby certainly knows her stuff*, she thought approvingly.

Susan said, 'We, the children and I, have kept ours on us at all times, but I think that James left his in the car, so when we got home he found that he had to leave almost straight away as the anger seeped back into him so quickly.

'We need to sell the house and leave the area, but that could take ages, so the children and I need to find somewhere else to stay while it goes on. Or James needs to stay somewhere else. I thought that if we could go and stay with your sister, I could help out on the farm, and it would be cheaper than James staying in a hotel.'

'I see,' Sarah said, filling up both their cups from the teapot.

'So, do you think she would have us for a while longer than a couple of weeks?' Susan asked eagerly, wringing her hands now in anxiety. If this did not work, she did not know what her other options would be.

'Well,' said Sarah, 'I suppose the only option would be to ask her.' She lumbered to her feet and walked to the little book that she kept on the dresser. Although she and her husband did not own a phone in their little cottage, they did keep certain numbers of friends and family, and if they needed to urgently contact one of them. they walked the half a mile down to the telephone box by the track down to the river.

'Ah, here it is.' She thumbed through the tattered pages until she found the entry she was looking for and wrote the number down on a scrap of paper and handed it to Susan. 'Best give her a ring, my dear, and ask her yourself. I don't suppose that it will be a problem. This is, after all, a very busy time of year on the farm, so all help would be appreciated. But what about the young 'uns, their school and that?'

Susan took the piece of paper with such gratitude it was as though Sarah had thrown her an actual lifeline. 'Thank you so much for this, Sarah. I had thought about the schools. We could enroll them in a local school for now. James has spoken about moving away, even potentially up to the Lake District, so the children would be changing schools anyway.'

Susan sighed heavily and placed her cup down on its saucer with unsteady hands so that it rattled before settling in its space. 'Everything is so up in the air. I just don't know what to do for the best, for myself, James, the children…'

Her voice trailed off. The children were still playing outside happily with the kittens, and their cries of excitement were rising and falling in turn with delighted squeals.

'Well, you won't know until you start,' Sarah said, with an authority brought on by a lifetime of helping others. She nodded at the piece of paper on the table with her sister's phone number written on it. 'Phone Joyce when you get home and arrange to go there as soon as possible. The sooner you leave, the sooner you can start to rebuild your life.'

Susan had a sudden thought. 'Do you think that James will be all right? I mean, with us gone, will he actually start the process to sell the house? Or do you think that this thing, whatever it is that seems to have a hold on him, will let him go?' Susan's hand flew to her chest as she considered this thought, and a haunted and panicked look formed in her eyes.

Sarah looked at her with a steadying gaze before she spoke.

'I don't know, Susan, but whatever happens it seems that you cannot be in the house with him, from what you have been telling me. You do know what happened in the house, don't you?'

CHAPTER 45

1936

The sky was so dark, with an eerie yellow light illuminating the bottom of the clouds that spread across the sky like an ominous bruise. The air had a metallic taste to it, and static rippled in waves across the room. It was now mid afternoon.

Louisa looked out of the living room window across the garden to the orchard. There was going to be one hell of a storm. Edward had been and gone. She had tried to settle over lunch, but nothing seemed to still her nerves. She got up and paced the room. She sat down and wrung her hands in her lap. She got up again. She felt like pulling at the roots of her hair to try to release the inner torment that plagued her.

The rage that ran deep inside her was like a writhing black snake threatening to spill over with the storm. Tom was still outside with Jimmy Jenkins, where they were walking side by side. Tom was looking up at Jimmy as he spoke. His eyes were full of focused interest, so keenly was he listening to what Jimmy was telling him. *Are they plotting against me?* she wondered suddenly.

She got up out of her chair and spun around. That was it. They had planned it together, the way for her to be rid of her child. Perhaps Jimmy had told Tom what to do.

Her eyes narrowed as she imagined the two of them together talking about her, then she sat down again in the chair and sighed. She was being ridiculous, she knew that. Some inner part of her mind still clung desperately to reality, while the rest of her mind was spun this way and that in wild thoughts, spurred on with the anguish and emotional longing for her baby.

Tears started to silently slide down her face. She put her hand to her cheeks and was surprised at the wetness that lay on them. *This will not do*, she said to herself. She needed to do something, anything, to rid herself of this paralysing melancholy. She was out of control, she knew that, and it was exhausting, pretending to be normal and happy, and presenting to the outside world the persona that was expected of her.

A bee buzzed lazily around the window frame, bouncing against the glass as if trying to make an exit by throwing itself against the pane with sheer force. Louisa eyed it with contempt. The noise grated on her nerves. She would catch it and put it in Tom's bedroom, where hopefully it would sting the little brat, she thought spitefully.

She picked up a glass tumbler from the silver tray and placed it over the bee. The buzzing noise grew quieter but increased in its intensity, which somehow felt more threatening. She slid a note card under the glass and turned the glass upright, holding the card on top. She held the glass at eye level, inspected the angry bee with relish in her eyes and stepped from the room.

Tom had noticed Louisa in the lounge looking down on him, and he shuddered inwardly. He didn't know why she disliked him so much, so he tried to keep out of her way as much as possible, but it felt as though his very existence irritated her. Cassy seemed to fare much better. Perhaps it was because she was a girl.

Everyone knew that girls didn't like boys, so maybe that was it. Louisa didn't like him because he was a boy, he thought, as he glanced back up at the window from the corner of his eye and stopped walking. What was she doing? He could see her with a glass pressed up against the window. Was she trying to catch something? Would she hurt it?

With no thought for the wrath that he would induce in his stepmother he made for the open French windows and ran through the drawing room, up the stairs and into the living room, but Louisa was no longer there.

Jimmy stood on the lawn and scratched his head. He had been talking to Tom about the best place to see bats and where they roosted when he had taken off across the lawn like a shot. He shook his head and bent down to start deadheading some of the roses. He looked up at the sky. It was so dark that the storm was bound to break soon. The air was positively crackling with electricity and the bottom of the clouds bore an ominous yellow hue.

Tom was confused. Where had Louisa gone? Surely if she was going to get rid of the creature she had caught it would have been simpler to just open the window and let it out. With his eyes narrowed in concentration he walked along the corridor. The door to her bedroom was open but she was not in there.

He walked further along. At the foot of the stairs his sister's bedroom door was also open. The windows had been flung wide to allow a breeze to blow in, but the air was so still that it hung limply with an oppressive heaviness. His confusion continued. Louisa could not have gone downstairs. He would have seen her, wouldn't he?

He started up the stairs to the upper floor towards his bedroom. His feet were light on the stairs as he ran up them, and the thick carpet muffled their sound.

When Tom reached the top of the staircase he glanced towards the other three rooms. The doors were slightly ajar but he heard no noise coming from them. So, curious and slightly cross, he quietly pushed open the door to his bedroom and, in the shaft of light shining at an angle through his window, he saw Louisa standing there.

She turned as he entered. There was a slightly crazed look in her eye, which made Tom stop. He backed towards the door, scared of what she was going to do.

Louisa smiled at him, but there was no amusement in her cold hard stare. 'Well, if it isn't little Saint Tom, the patron saint of all little creatures,' she said mockingly. 'I thought I would bring you a new little pet to look after.' She held up the jar and the frightened insect buzzed frantically, trying to escape its glass prison.

'Let it go, Louisa,' Tom said, his anger at the trapped creature melting his fear away in an instant.

He made to grab for the jar, but Louisa held it up high above her head. 'Uh, uh, uh, little Tom,' she said, waving a finger at him, but having taken one hand off the jar, the piece of card that she was holding on the top slipped slightly, allowing the insect its freedom, which it took immediately. It started buzzing around Louisa's face and she hit out at it, scared of being stung in retaliation for being its captor.

'Leave it alone, Louisa. Why do you always have to be so cruel?' Tom was angry now, which gave him access to all the pent-up frustrations of Louisa's treatment of him that had been buried deep by good manners. They welled up and came to the forepart of his heart in a maelstrom of anguish. He brushed angry tears from his eyes as he made for his bedroom window. 'You little snake,' Louisa said as she moved to grab him, but she missed as he slipped past her, intent only on freeing the poor bee.

He leapt up onto his window seat and wrestled with the

catch on the window. He pushed the window open and the bee, which had been banging itself against the glass, made its escape and flew out into the darkened afternoon.

A rumble of thunder made its way across the sky as a flash replied, ripping through the black clouds like a slash of a sword. Louisa was furious for being spoken to in the way that Tom had responded to her and rushed towards him. He was looking out of the window, having followed the path of the bee until it was out of sight.

Louisa felt herself bump into the boy, and almost in a dream-like state, she shoved him hard. 'If you love insects so much, you little brat, why don't you join them?' Before he even knew what was happening, Tom had lost his balance and was flying through the air, but unlike the light little bee, he had no wings to propel him through the air and could not fly away to his freedom. Instead, his journey only had one outcome, and that was to swiftly connect with the hard paved terrace underneath his window.

There was a sickening thump and a crack as his little body hit the stone flags. Birds flew from the trees, squawking their fright, and Jimmy looked up from the beds to see the little boy, who he had come to think of as a friend, lying lifeless and bloody on the stone. The thunder cracked above, followed immediately by the brightest of flashes, and the rain began to fall in big, heavy drops, like a giant's tears, sizzling as they met the scorched ground.

Jimmy looked up at the window that Tom had fallen from as he ran across the grass, and was sure that he saw Louisa step away into the shadows. He screamed for help and kept on screaming. His cries were full of anguish and fear as he cradled the small boy to his chest, until Maggie and Cedric came running to find out what on earth was happening.

John Peters, who had come to meet Jimmy, as they were due to be going fishing that afternoon, had just entered the garden when he heard the anguished cry of his friend. He ran down the garden at full pelt to see young Tom on the ground. He helped Jimmy to lift his limp body and between them they checked for signs of life, of which they found none.

The rain mixed with the blood on Tom's head and ran in red rivulets down Jimmy's shirt, and dripped onto John Peters's trousers. Maggie, her eyes wide, crouched down beside Tom and felt for a pulse, but she could see from the state of him that he was gone.

Cedric tried to prise the child from Jimmy's arms but he was holding onto him so tightly that they allowed him to carry him into the study, where they laid his broken body on the couch and Maggie fetched a sheet to cover him.

Cassy, startled by the commotion, came to the door and peered in, curious to see what was going on, and then was so shocked and heartbroken when she saw the crumpled body of her little brother being tended to on the couch. Maggie led her out of the room and into the kitchen, where she busied her with making tea for everyone. The doctor was called, as was an ambulance, but it was all to no avail.

Little Tom, the sweetest, most intelligent and thoughtful boy, was dead.

If anyone thought it was strange that Louisa appeared to be absent from all the proceedings, it was not mentioned at the time.

Edward Winter, full of grief and despair, locked himself in his study after Tom's body had been taken away, and did not come out for several hours. Cassy was rocked in Maggie's bosom, and Jimmy was taken down to the pub by Cedric Graves and his friend John Peters.

Everyone was in shock. That is, everyone but Louisa. She was only shocked by her own behaviour and the resulting death of her stepson. But, rather than being remorseful and feeling sad for the loss of her stepson, Louisa's only thoughts were for herself and her concern that she may have been seen by that gardening boy. He would have to go, she thought bitterly. That was the only answer.

The police came, and everyone was questioned, but no one really had much to tell them. Jimmy was not asked that much, and he wrestled with his conscience about whether he should mention that he thought he saw Louisa in the room as Tom fell.

He had half-started to tell John Peters, but something stopped him. He knew that his mistress disliked the boy – it was so obvious to everyone – but to harm him? He became more and more insular, and Cedric started to worry about him. He was looking terrible, haggard almost, and it did not sit well upon the young man.

About three days after the incident Cedric pulled Jimmy aside and sat him down on a seat in the potting shed and closed the door. He made tea on a little stove as Jimmy stared into space, and handed him a mug when he was done. Cedric stood with his back against one of the dusty shelves and, after taking a sip of his tea, which was far too hot, he wiped his mouth with the back of his hand and addressed the younger man. 'Jimmy, is there something on your mind? Apart from the obvious – bearing witness to the tragedy of losing young Tom, that is.'

Jimmy looked up slowly. His eyes were red-rimmed, and deep purple shadows like bruises lay underneath them. He started to speak. 'I thought I saw her, you know, as I was running across the grass to Tom.' He shivered as the full recollection of the memory flooded his senses – the sound of the thump and crack, the electricity of the storm, the weight of the child in his arms and the rain as it poured down upon them both as the gods cried out their anguish at the loss of such a precious soul.

Cedric looked at Jimmy, not speaking, silently urging him to continue. 'I looked up and I am sure that I saw her, Louisa, in the room, just walking away. Why would she be there and why would she not have run down to help us? Where was she during all that happened? She was not outside or in the study, nor did she come down to the kitchen. Where was she?'

The intensity of his feelings and frustration were evident in the tone of his voice, which cracked on the final words as he thought of the loss of his small friend.

Cedric looked ashen. It was certainly no secret that Mrs Winter had no love for the boy, but to be in the room when he fell, and to not be seen afterwards… Well, that was simply not right. *But what should be done about it?* he said to himself. He would speak to his wife. She would be certain to know what the best course of action should be.

Cedric found his wife in the kitchen. He rarely entered the house, having everything he needed in the garage and the outbuildings, and he much preferred to be outside in all weathers. It was all Maggie could do to persuade him to come into their little flat above the old stables at the end of the day, so to see him enter the kitchen took her completely by surprise.

She stopped stirring the pot on the stove, where she was making soup, and looked at her husband quizzically. Her eyes narrowed as she took in his ashen face and troubled brow and her hand flew to her throat. She really could not take any more bad news at the moment. She folded her arms underneath her ample bosom and waited for him to speak.

Cedric let out a long sigh and took a seat at the table. 'Young Jimmy has just told me something that is very troubling, and I am wracking my brains over what to do,' he said wearily, taking off his cap and running a hand over his face and head before replacing it on his head. Maggie watched him, waiting silently for him to continue. He was looking down at his hands on the table and then stared off into the middle distance as if not knowing how to continue.

Eventually he took a deep breath and said, 'I thought that there was something wrong, Jimmy was so troubled. I know that seeing the lad falling to his death in front of him was the most terrible thing to witness and they were so close too, but this was more... I don't know, he just didn't look right, so I sat him down and had a word and what he told me... Well, Maggie, it just isn't right, any way you look at it.'

Maggie watched Cedric as he spoke. He was a kind and gentle man, and they had a bond forged from so many years together. She knew that he would not have come to her unless it was something that he was unable to deal with himself, as he was a more than capable man in anything practical, but in matters like this he was totally out of his depth. 'So you see, Maggie, I don't know what to think. Surely Louisa would not have done anything so bad as to have a hand in Tom's falling, but what are we to think? If she was there, and young Jimmy is certain that that is what he saw, then why did she not scream or come running to help? Like Jimmy said, where was she?'

Maggie looked on thoughtfully as she replayed the afternoon's trauma in her head. They were both right, she thought sadly, not wanting to believe it herself. Louisa had not been there. In among all the terror and sadness, the drama of the incident, she had been forgotten.

But had not Edward or Cassy noticed? Why had Edward not turned to his wife for comfort? The empty bottle of whisky and the smashed crystal glass she found in the study the next morning seemed to answer that question, at least.

'What are you going to do, Cedric?' Maggie asked him as she walked over to him and laid a comforting hand on his shoulder. She could feel his worn flannel shirt soft beneath her fingers.

'I just don't know,' he said, shaking his head wearily and taking off his cap again and resettling it on his head as he contemplated the heavy weight of the shared information that was now bearing down on him. 'We need to tell someone, but should we go straight to the constable, or should we speak to the doctor first? Goodness only knows that he does not need any more bad news at the moment.'

Maggie nodded, 'What about speaking to Louisa herself? Do you think that is an option? I mean, it would only be her word against Jimmy's, and who would stand up better in court, do you think?'

'I know,' Cedric said with an almost defeated note of weariness in his voice. 'But why should she be allowed to get away with it, if she did do something? Goodness knows, we all know that she couldn't stand young Tom. I don't know if the good doctor was totally aware of it. But it was obvious to all of us.'

'Should we just sleep on it and make a decision in the morning?' Maggie suggested sensibly. 'Nothing will have changed by then, and it will give us time to clear our minds and get our thoughts in order. I will finish up here. I don't think that anyone is particularly hungry, so I will leave a soup and some bread rolls, and they can help themselves if they want something. I'll come away to the flat in an hour or so.'

Cedric nodded and stood up. As he did so they heard a slight rustle coming from the dining room. The door had been left slightly ajar. They both turned and looked at each other, and a look of horror and shock crossed their faces as they hurried to see who had been privy to their secret conversation. Maggie was closest to the door and flung it open to see the flash of a blue dress disappearing through the door at the far end of the room.

It was Louisa.

Maggie's heart was pounding in her chest. 'Cedric, go through to the garden and make sure that young Jimmy is OK. Stay with him and don't let him out of your sight.'

Cedric nodded and quickly made his way through the garden. He found Jimmy digging in one of the flowerbeds, but he had been so distracted by his thoughts that it looked as if a rabbit had been burrowing. He looked up in surprise as Cedric came panting across the lawn towards him and looked at him expectantly.

'Louisa knows,' Cedric managed to pant out after grabbing at his knees as he bent over to catch his breath.

'Louisa knows?' Jimmy repeated slowly. 'Louisa knows what?'

Cedric waved a hand at him as if the gesticulation would somehow translate his words into sense. After a few seconds he gained enough breath to continue. 'Maggie and I were talking in the kitchen. I wanted her opinion on what we should do with the information you gave me earlier. The door to the kitchen was slightly ajar and Louisa must have been listening. We saw her leaving the dining room. Maggie wants me to stay with you to make sure you are OK. We just do not know what state Louisa is in mentally, and I think now that we have no choice but to tell Dr Winter.'

Jimmy nodded slowly. 'What should I do?' he said, looking worried, scared and sad in equal measure.

'I think it is best if you just get away from the house. Go and see what that friend of yours John Peters is up to. I'll square it all with Doctor Edward. Not that he is really in any fit state to notice whether his young gardener is here or not,' Cedric said earnestly.

Jimmy nodded, brushed the dirt from his hands and went to collect his bicycle from where he had left it leaning against the potting shed. He looked drawn, as if the whole world rested upon his young shoulders, as he pushed the bicycle down the garden and exited through the gate onto the quiet lane.

Louisa watched him go as she paced backwards and forwards across the lounge. *What am I to do?* she said to herself as her breath came in rapid gasps. They knew. But what did they know?

That blasted gardener had seen her. She should have come down and pretended to be shocked, but in truth she had not wanted to look upon the result of her fit of temper. *Oh, what will become of me now?* she thought as she wrung her hands. Edward would never forgive her for this, and then what was she to do?

She hadn't seen Edward since the ambulance had taken Tom away. She had been shut in her room and he hadn't been up to see her. He had left soon afterwards, and when he returned, he had shut himself in his study. Cassy had gone to stay with her mother's family. So she was left alone in the house with nothing to do but brood.

Why does Edward not think about me? she thought sulkily. If he had thought about her a bit more and sent the child away to school, then this would never have happened. It was all Edward's fault, really. He had brought this upon himself.

She threw herself down in a chair and bit at the side of her thumb until the skin became red and tender.

Edward returned home much later that evening. He really did not know what to do with himself. A locum had come to take care of his patients for the immediate future, as he really was in no fit state to care for them at present.

Maggie had left him a light supper on a tray in the study, covered with a cloth to keep the flies away. He sank into his chair and turned on the desk lamp. The French doors had been left slightly open and they let in a welcome breeze. He had not been allowed to attend the post-mortem due to his relationship to the deceased, but he had been allowed to view the reports.

At least it appeared that Tom had died instantly. He hadn't suffered, so that was one blessing to count. He wondered for the hundredth time how it could have happened. Tom was such a sensible boy. He was always climbing trees and had never fallen. He had the agility of a goat, he reminisced with a sad smile. How on earth could he have fallen from his bedroom window? What had he been doing?

He poured himself a large measure of whisky and took a bite from the hunk of cheese that Maggie had left as part of his supper. He needed to speak to Jimmy again and ask him exactly what he had seen. He would also need to put some bars on the upper windows so that this sort of tragedy never afflicted another family.

I really must speak to Louisa too, he thought, suddenly remembering that he had a wife who was also going through her own trauma, having lost her baby. *God*, he thought as he ran his hands roughly through his hair and massaged his tired face, *does Death stalk me?* His wife, his unborn child and now his son? Who would be next? He sipped at his whisky and allowed the heat to warm and calm him and closed his eyes. He knew there was nothing more he could do tonight.

Louisa lay awake in bed staring at the ceiling, watching the patterns spreading across the room as the gentle breeze toyed with the branches and chased shadows across the room. *Does Edward know?* she wondered to herself. Was that why he did not come to her room and instead stayed downstairs?

What would become of her now? She had no one to talk to, nowhere to go. She was quite alone in the world. Her thoughts tumbled over each other, fighting for supremacy over one another, each one worse and more depressing than the last. She tossed and turned this way and that, tangling herself in the bedclothes until, unable to bear it any longer, she rose from the bed and went to stare out of the window into the night.

Her breathing was shallow and ragged. She put a hand to her throat as if to calm herself but nothing worked. Her skin was starting to chill in the cool night air. The sweat from her anguished tossing in bed was starting to cool upon her skin and causing her to shiver.

Louisa grabbed a robe from the end of the bed and put it on. She opened her bedroom door and stepped out into the darkened corridor. She padded silently down the stairs and saw the yellow light coming from underneath the study door. She paused for a moment, wondering whether to enter the room or to walk on past to the kitchen and get herself a glass of water. She decided to get the water and see if she could summon up the courage to enter the room on the way back.

Edward decided to go to bed. He switched off the light and closed the door behind him and walked up the stairs to the bedroom he shared with his wife. He pushed the door open gently, so as not to wake her and stopped. The bed was a heap of tangled sheets but his wife was not there. He swiftly looked around the room, but she was definitely not there.

Panic flooded to his chest and he staggered backwards. Where was she? After the trauma of the past days he had badly neglected his wife. What if something had happened to her? He spun on his heels and ran back down the stairs and across the hall and flung open the front door. He walked round the house, looking up at the windows as he went, checking the ground carefully, as if he expected to see his wife's lifeless body lying accusingly at his feet.

Louisa returned from the kitchen with a glass of water. As she reached the study door she saw that it was closed and that the golden light that had shown so clearly just a few minutes before had been extinguished. However, there was a steady breeze coming from the front door. She walked towards the door, curious to see what was causing the draught and saw that the front door was wide open. Had Edward gone out? Why would he have left the door open? What was going on?

In her heightened state of anxiety she could not control the maelstrom of thoughts that twisted painfully in her mind, creating visions in front of her eyes like physical forms. He had gone to get the constable.

He knew.

She was going to hang.

There was a loud smashing sound as the glass of water that Louisa had been holding slipped from her hand and smashed into many pieces on the hard wooden floor. Water splashed up her legs and started to form a pool at her feet. But Louisa didn't notice. She had to get away. The voices in her head told her to run, run for her life.

She picked up the skirts of her nightdress and ran through

the door out into the night, her bare feet not noticing the sharp stab of the gravel on the driveway as she ran up the slight incline of the drive out into the road.

Simon Walter, a local vet, was returning home after having attended a difficult foaling up at one of the farms in the hills. He was tired, both physically and mentally, and just wanted to get home to bed. *At least it is summer*, he said ruefully to himself. He was getting too old for lambing in the cold, dark nights. The mare and her foal had both survived, but they had needed his help. The farmer was very grateful, as she was his favourite mare, and the young colt would be a great addition to the farm. But helping him into the world had sapped most of his strength as well as that of the foal's mother.

It was very dark as he drove along the road towards his home at the far end of the village. The bottle of Scotch that the farmer had given him as a thank-you for the safe delivery of the foal started to roll towards the front of the seat, and he momentarily took his eyes from the road to steady it. He did not want it to fall and break. What would his wife say if he and the car stank of whisky? He chuckled to himself as he imagined his wife's face, usually so placid, sporting an uncustomary frown.

Suddenly his attention was snapped back. He must have caught a movement out of the corner of his eye from where he was steadying the bottle on the front seat. His eyes opened wide and a gasp of terror escaped his lips as an apparition reared up in front of his car. He slammed on the brakes, but the rain from the storm the day before had left the road wet and slippery and his tyres struggled to make purchase with the tarmac.

He hit the white-gowned figure full on and came to a stop moments later. He scrambled out of the car and ran towards the crumpled body as it lay motionless on the road.

It was a woman. Her face was fixed in a look of horror that matched his from moments earlier. Her blonde hair streamed out from beneath her head and a trickle of blood poured from her ear and mouth, mingling with her hair and staining it a bright crimson. He knelt beside the body and felt for a pulse, but there was nothing.

He knew that she was dead, and that he had killed her. But he failed to see the smoky tendrils that rose from her body, hovered slightly above her for a moment and then drifted down the driveway towards the house that sheltered in the slight hollow.

He stood up and ran towards the house, following the wisps of smoke, which were hidden from his eyes. He met a man in the driveway, who had just been coming round the side of the house when he had heard the noise of the screeching of brakes and tyres and then the unmistakable crashing sound of an impact.

Edward knew instinctively what had happened, and ran past the stricken man to the road. He stopped short when he saw the crumpled and lifeless body of his wife. He fell to his knees beside her, his head in his hands, and wept. Her lifeless eyes staring up at him, with the expression of shock and horror fixed in them forever, were more than he could bear.

The man rushed back and stood there next to Edward. He placed a hand on his shoulder. All he could do was to keep telling him how sorry he was, that she had appeared in front of him and that he could not stop.

On hearing the commotion, Maggie and Cedric had run out from their apartment above the old stables. They too ran up the driveway, following the sounds of raised voices and muffled sobs. The lights from the van were still glaring but they cast a shadow at the side of the road, so to start with they could not see what the commotion was all about.

As they walked out of the glare of the headlights they looked down and saw the doctor kneeling beside the body of a young woman. The old couple looked at each other in confusion and then back to what their eyes showed them, but their brains found it hard to comprehend. The young woman looked like Louisa, but why was she out on the road in what looked like her nightdress?

Startled back into consciousness, Maggie took charge. 'Cedric,' she said as an order, 'go and call an ambulance and the police. Tell them that there has been a tragic accident, and then put the kettle on to boil. We will need some blankets and something warm to drink.'

Cedric stood looking at his wife in bewilderment for a moment, then nodded and hurried back down the drive to the house. The front door was still wide open, so he went in through the front door instead of heading around the back of the house.

A wisp of grey smoke trailed by his side, swirling about his legs and filling him with a deep sense of unease. He stopped for a moment in confusion. Then he looked again and it was gone, and with it went the dark, empty feeling of hopelessness. He shook himself and put it down to shock. He made the calls and then went to put the large kettle on the stove to boil and grabbed a couple of blankets that had been put on the side in the laundry room for mending, and went back out to see what else he could do.

Maggie was leading the driver of the car down the driveway. He seemed extremely unsteady on his feet, and was still gibbering about someone running out in front of him and not being able to stop. Maggie took one of the blankets from Cedric and wrapped it around the man's shoulders and led him towards the house. 'Go and give that blanket to Edward. He will want something to cover Louisa, and you might want to direct any traffic that comes along. I know that it is a straight road, but we don't want any more accidents tonight.'

Cedric, glad at being given something useful to do, headed back up to the roadside and handed the blanket to Edward, who took it gratefully and gently laid it over his wife's body. He looked down at her. She looked so peaceful that she could have been sleeping. 'How is he?' Edward asked Cedric, referring to the driver.

'Oh…' Cedric replied, surprised that Edward would be asking, but instantly realising that as a doctor he would be concerned. 'Maggie is taking care of him. Do you know what happened?'

Edward shook his head. 'No, but from what he was saying, Louisa seemed to run straight out into the road in front of him. It makes no sense. I mean, I know that she had lost the baby and what with Tom and everything, but I didn't know… I mean, I should have realised…'

Edward put his head in his hands again and started to weep silent tears. The heaving of his shoulders added to the signs of his distress.

Cedric went and stood next to him and put an arm around his shoulders. He didn't want to add to Edward's stress and upset, but maybe an explanation would help. 'Well, Doctor, we might have an answer to your question, but I am not sure that it will make you feel any better.'

Edward looked at the older man with eyes full of despair and confusion. 'What do you mean?'

Cedric cleared his throat and began to tell Edward about Jimmy seeing Louisa in Tom's room as he fell. Edward looked aghast. 'No,' he said vehemently. 'She couldn't have. She wouldn't have.' He was shaking his head as if to erase the thoughts just put there.

Cedric laid a gentle hand on his arm before continuing, 'We all know that Louisa never liked young Tom.' He put up a hand as Edward tried to deny what he was hearing. 'Now hear me out, Doctor,' Cedric continued quietly. 'Louisa never liked Tom. He just seemed to rub her up the wrong way, as some people do, and we know that she had not been right since she lost the baby. I believe that my Maggie spoke to you about it. She was right concerned about what Louisa might do, but we couldn't watch her every moment of the day.'

Edward sank down at the side of the road and sat with his back against the car, his long legs stretched out in front of him as he glanced at the crumpled form of what had been his wife, and then he averted his eyes and stared into the blackness of the night. He felt numb and shocked to the core. He did not know how he would ever recover from this.

The ambulance arrived, as did the police moments later, and from there everything became a bit of a blur. From the marks on the road, it appeared as if the story the young vet had told could be confirmed. He had hardly had time to brake when Louisa appeared in front of him, and there had been absolutely no way that the collision could have been avoided.

The police had arranged for the car to be taken away to the local garage for repair and the vet had been taken home to his wife. The bottle of whisky must have been made of strong stuff, as it had survived the impact of the collision intact. The undertakers had gently taken Louisa away, showing the utmost dignity and respect to her crumpled body.

Edward, Maggie and Cedric sat in the kitchen at the table. The kettle had long since cooled and they each had a large glass of brandy in their hands. Edward looked as white as snow. All colour had drained from his face, and he looked as if a wisp of wind could have felled him.

Maggie glanced at her husband and then back to Edward. She was very worried about him. He had endured so much tragedy in his life. She wondered silently to herself whether this latest episode would be the undoing of him. He would probably be torn between wanting to mourn his wife and hating her just as strongly for robbing him of his beloved son.

CHAPTER 46

1973

Susan's head was reeling. The story that Sarah had imparted to her was awful, but so sad. What a tragic loss of life. *How on earth had the doctor coped with everything?* she said to herself. 'So what happened to the doctor and his daughter?' Susan asked Sarah, who was watching her carefully.

'Oh, I think that he moved to be closer to his family. They lived in London, I believe. The house was rented out to various tenants, but none of them stayed very long. The house has a deeply disturbing energy to it, and some say it is haunted. And others say that young Tom can be heard calling for his mother, poor wee mite.'

'Tom...' Susan said quietly. 'Emma's imaginary friend is called Tom.' She looked up at Sarah in surprise. 'I have often felt a presence in the house and strange things have happened, but Tom would not be causing James to act so weirdly.'

Sarah shook her head, 'No my dear, but Louisa might...'

Susan hurried home with the children. Trying to prise them away from the kittens had been extremely difficult and she welcomed the distraction that they had given them, but now she just needed to get home. She needed to call Joyce, pack some bags for the children, then look at the timetable to find out the times of the trains. Goodness, there was so much to do. She would also need to call James and tell him what she was doing, what had happened in the house and why it might be affecting him.

She was so deep in thought all the way home that she seemed

surprised to find herself at the back gate so soon. She opened it and they all filed through. 'Now, children,' she reminded them once more, 'I need you to go and pack a bag with the things that you would like to take. You will have to carry it on the train, though, and it must also include your clothes, so you can't take too much. I will lay out your clothes for you and put them in the bag and then you can fill the space with what you wish to take. Your father can send the rest of our things on, once we have decided what we are doing.'

Susan opened the kitchen door and they went in. The house felt still and quiet, as though it was waiting for something to happen. Susan walked through the kitchen, placed her bag on the table and walked through the dining room, shooing the children upstairs to get themselves sorted out as she went. She reached the hall and went over to the telephone table, then realised that she had left her bag with the telephone number for Joyce in it in the kitchen. Sighing with exasperation, she called up the stairs after the children, telling them to hurry up and that she would be up to pack their clothes very soon. She remembered that the cases from their holiday were probably still in the laundry room, and she would need to grab them too.

She hastily retraced her steps to the kitchen, but as she entered it she halted immediately. There was a cold chill in the room. Her bag was where she had left it on the table, but it had been tipped up and it looked like there was a smoky mist all around it.

Susan recoiled in horror, and her hands flew to her mouth as if to stifle a scream. She needed her bag, and she could not leave without it. Her purse and her chequebook were in there, and without them they would not be able to get the train.

The smoky mist swirled menacingly, but Susan was determined to leave the place intact with her children. She took a step towards the bag, anger giving her the courage she needed to achieve her task. She grabbed the bag and the mist slipped away.

She was breathing heavily now. She turned to leave but then remembered the cases. She almost ran into the laundry room and there they were, neatly stacked against the wall. She grabbed them and, after turning on her heel, fled the room, closing the door behind her.

The grey mist returned, gathering in density and darkness of colour, and for a moment its twisting tendrils arranged themselves into the shape of a woman before once again slipping away to nothing.

Susan ran through the dining room and slammed that door behind her as well. In the hall she picked up the telephone and dialled Joyce's number. She was still breathing fast, and tried to use the time that the call took to connect to slow her breathing so that she would be able to actually talk once the call connected.

Joyce picked up the phone after a short while. 'Eastham 132,' came her steady voice over the line.

Susan breathed a sigh of relief. 'Hello,' she said a bit haltingly. 'Is that Joyce? This is Susan Morton. Your sister Sarah Peters told me to call you.'

'Susan? Yes, yes. Sarah has spoken about you. You would like to come and stay with us for a while. Is that correct?'

'Yes, please, if that is not too much of an imposition. It would help us enormously.' Susan leant back against the wall and slid down it in relief at being able to start to sort things out and to escape the nightmare that her life had become. They spoke for a little while, making the arrangements, and it was agreed that they would come the next day.

Next she called the train station so she could find out about the train times, and then she called James to tell him what was happening. She could not reach him, though, as he was with a client, so she left a message with his secretary explaining that she needed to speak to him as soon as he was free and that it was quite urgent.

Once that was done, she went upstairs to start to pack. Tom watched her activity from a chair in the hall. He was in deep shadow so she did not see him sitting there, and she was so distracted that she would probably not have noticed him anyway.

He watched on sadly as she made the arrangements on the telephone and then followed her silently as she all but ran up the stairs. He watched too as the grey mist coiled and twisted and thickened in density and darkened in colour. It coiled restlessly against the foot of the grandfather clock and then snaked its way along the finely carved spindles of the staircase. The air felt heavy and oppressive, just as it had all those years ago. Tom was sad that he was losing yet another friend, but understood that they had to go. Louisa was still making him miserable all these years later.

Susan reached her daughter's bedroom at the top of the second flight of stairs. Emma had laid a few things out on the bed to take with her: a couple of soft toys, two books and some colouring pencils and a colouring book.

Susan nodded her approval and started to empty the drawers and place clothes on the bed. Her breathing was rapid and she was starting to feel a little faint. She paused for a moment and looked at her daughter, who was watching her from her place on the window seat. 'Where are we going, Mummy?' Emma asked her mother with wide, innocent eyes.

'We are going to stay with Sarah Peters's sister Joyce. She has a farm close to the seaside in Sussex. Won't that be nice?' She sat down next to her daughter on the window seat. She needed to get her head together, otherwise goodness only knows what she would pack to take with them.

'Is this something to do with what happened to Tom?' Emma asked in such a matter-of-fact way that Susan was shocked for a moment and did not quite know how to answer her.

'What do you know about Tom, Emma?' she asked after a moment's hesitation. She looked intently at her daughter and gave Emma her full attention.

'Oh, not much, really,' Emma replied. 'I know that he died here. He fell from this window.' She pointed behind her at the window, which had bars attached. Susan was shocked but wanted her daughter to continue, so tried to arrange her facial features into one of mild interest.

'Go on,' she said to Emma.

'Well, he didn't fall of his own accord. His stepmother pushed him.'

At that there was a loud bang as the bedroom door slammed shut, and the two of them looked at each other with scared faces.

Susan moved quickly to the door and tried to open it, but the catch seemed to be stuck. Emma rocked backwards and forwards on the window seat, hugging her small fluffy white cat toy to her chest. Susan called down to Robert who, on hearing the noise of the door, had already started to come up the stairs to see what was going on. He pushed hard against the door and managed to force it open.

Susan grabbed handfuls of clothes from the drawers and

wardrobe and shoved them unceremoniously into the case. She put the things that Emma had chosen on top of them and zipped it up. She grabbed the case in one hand and her daughter's hand in the other, and all three of them ran downstairs. Then she shouted to Robert to pack his clothes and to try to be sensible about it while she packed up her own things in her room. She wanted to get out of the house as quickly as possible.

She had just finished putting the last of her things in her bag when she heard the unmistakable sound of James's car crunching on the gravel driveway. She stopped for a second, raised her hand to her throat and took a deep breath. *Thank God*, she said to herself. She grabbed her case and Emma's and called to Robert to hurry up and come downstairs and join them in the hall. Susan all but ran down the stairs with Emma following quickly in her wake, picking up the anxiety coming in waves from her mother. She clung to her mother's side, her face white and her eyes large.

James got out of the car. He had been unnerved by the message his wife had left him and so, without thinking further, he had finished up for the day and driven home to see what was going on. He stopped abruptly on the drive and got out of the car. All seemed still, and as it should be. The birds were singing in the trees and the day was still warm. Just a gentle breeze ruffled the leaves.

He shut the door of the car and walked round the back of the vehicle towards the front door of the house, then opened the door and walked into the lobby. He felt confident that whatever had happened he would be able to help sort it out, and was looking forward to seeing his wife and children. A short time away from the house had cleared the oppressiveness and anger from his body and mind, and his thoughts were so much clearer.

He didn't realise how bad it was until he actually walked back into the house. With each step he took the feelings of resentment and bitterness took him over. He could feel the emotions rising and swirling in him, almost as if a powerful force was taking him over. He shook his head, trying to clear his thoughts and focus, but it was no good.

The swirling mist grew darker. It had been lying in wait for him, swirling above the ceiling in the lobby area, so that the moment he entered it fell upon him like a cloak of despair. The whisperings in his ear grew and he shook his head again, trying to rid himself of the feelings that were starting to consume him.

He entered the hall and saw his wife and daughter standing there, staring at him. Their eyes were wide and full of fear as the anger took him over completely and the hardness behind his eyes flashed as the voice whispered its lies of betrayal to him. 'What,' he said in a hard cold voice, 'is going on?' He glanced from his wife and daughter to the cases in her hand and back again to his wife's face.

Susan blanched. Emma hid behind her mother as Susan took a couple of paces backwards. 'James,' she said in a soothing and calm voice, trying to placate him, 'I tried to call you. I found out what happened in this house. It is not you that is behaving like this. It is her, Louisa. She has been here the whole time and—'

'Enough,' James shouted. He grabbed the cases from his wife's hands and threw them on the floor. 'Where on earth do you think you are going? Do you think you could leave me?' His voice was dripping with venom now. He was so angry that spittle was being forced from his mouth along with the words.

'James, we spoke about this. You agreed. We are going to go and stay with Sarah Peters's sister while you sell the house.'

James's eyes blazed with fury. He continued as though his wife had not even spoken. 'No one leaves this house, do you hear me? No one. Now get back up those stairs and unpack those cases.'

Susan was gripped with fear. Emma was quietly sobbing behind her and Robert – who, on hearing his father's angry voice had not come down the stairs – remained on the landing, watching the scene play out below him, feeling powerless to do anything to protect his mother and sister. He punched the banister and his knuckles became red and sore in his frustration.

As Susan did not instantly move to fulfill her command, James strode towards her and grabbed the suitcase from her hand. Startled, she let go and tripped on the rug, falling painfully on her knees on the hard parquet floor beneath.

She gasped and was momentarily stunned, but she was determined that they were all going to get out of this house with their belongings. With new resolve she pushed herself up with her hands and went after her husband, who had started to climb the stairs, intent on unpacking the suitcases, as if that would prevent them from leaving.

Susan grabbed hold of the banister and swung herself around and up the stairs. 'No, James,' she shouted after him. 'We are leaving. We discussed this. You need to get out of the house too. Look what it is doing to you.' But James did not listen and instead he strode into their bedroom, opened the case and started emptying its contents onto the bed. Susan marched in behind him, anger masking her fear, and grabbed a bag from her wardrobe and started throwing the discarded clothes into that instead.

Fury blazed in James's eyes. He grabbed hold of his wife and all but threw her across the room. She hit her head hard against the edge of the dressing table and her world went black.

Robert, who had been standing outside his parents' bedroom with his hands over his ears to try to block out the sound of the argument, came running into the bedroom on hearing his mother fall. He rained down blows on his father's back. His fear of his father's wrath had been replaced with anger, which was now bubbling over from years of resenting his father's behaviour.

His father, however, seemed to barely notice his actions and brushed him aside as if he were merely an irritating fly. He glanced down at the prone form of his wife on the floor and sniffed in derision. 'She will not leave me. Not now, not ever. How dare she even think about it?' The voices swirled in his head, each one shouting more and more accusations about her actions, until he wanted to do nothing more but still them forever.

James put his hands over his ears, mirroring his son's actions of a few moments ago, and marched out of the room. He didn't even seem to notice that his son was there, and he had forgotten completely about even having a daughter, such were the driving thoughts flooding through his mind.

The dark mist that encircled him was like a poisonous dark liquid. It twisted in and out of his body in its snake-like torment. The voices rose ever stronger in his mind, and a dark and twisted smile formed upon his lips. They would all be together forever in this house, and he knew just how to achieve that.

He strode down the corridor to the stairs and marched down them with intent. Emma was cowering under the stairs behind the grandfather clock and saw him pass as he walked through the hall and into the dining room. Although he resembled her father, he looked nothing like the man who they had been on holiday with only a few short days ago.

She scrambled from where she was crouched and ran upstairs to safety with her mother and brother. As she reached the top of the stairs she heard her brother calling her in a loud whisper. She followed the sound of his voice and found him in her parents' bedroom.

Her mother was lying on her side and there was a small cut on her head. She was moaning gently, and Robert was patting her head with a wet flannel. 'Get Mum's clothes and put them in that bag.' He indicated both the bag and the heap of clothes on the bed with his hand. 'We need to get out of here. Father has completely gone mad this time.'

Emma, white-faced and scared, did as she was bid, as Robert tried to coax his mother out of her stupor. He knew that it would not be long until his father returned. He noticed that Emma had also had the foresight to grab their mother's handbag from where she had dropped it in the hall and nodded his approval at his sister.

Robert managed to raise Susan into a sitting position. She was slowly coming out of her daze, but her head was pounding and she felt slightly disorientated. She tried to clear her head by shaking it, but it just hurt even more. 'Mum, come on, we need to get out of the house,' Robert said to encourage her, and tugged at her arm. 'Father has gone completely crazy, and he will be back any second.'

The thoughts of what had just happened came flooding back to her and fired energy back to her muscles. She pushed herself to her feet and held her head with a groan. Her sight was disturbed with little buzzing lights but she knew that she had to move, and now.

Robert picked up the bag with his mother's clothes and grabbed her arm again. The three of them stole out of the bedroom into the corridor and crept along to the top of the stairs. They could hear their father moving things downstairs. It sounded like furniture. They glanced at each other with questioning looks on their faces. What on earth was he doing now?

The three of them walked slowly down the stairs. There was no other way to get out of the house. They needed to know exactly where James was so they could decide which way to flee. The front door was closest, but there were also doors from the study, the drawing room and the kitchen. It all depended on where James was, and what on earth he was doing.

They made their way down the stairs very slowly. As they reached the turn in the staircase, Susan signalled for them to stop. They could hear a strange crackling noise, and was that smoke they could smell?

Fear rose in Susan's throat. Was there a fire? Surely not? She signalled again to the children to stay where they were and sat down on the stairs so that she could look through the banisters into the hall.

What she saw made her realise once and for all that James had completely been lost to unreason. The noises that they had heard were of him pulling furniture out from the various rooms and piling it against the doors out of the hall. He was then systematically setting fire to each pile with pieces of lit newspaper. Susan scanned the room eagerly, looking for a way out.

There was none.

Susan's mind went into overdrive. They needed to escape, but how? She shooed the children back upstairs and stood in the corridor. 'What is it?' Robert asked her quietly. 'Why are we not going downstairs?'

Not wanting to alarm the children and trying to keep a clear head and think of a way out all at the same time was just too much for her. That, coupled with her thumping head and blurred vision, made her just want to sink against the wall and sleep.

Robert looked at her drooping eyelids and shook her awake. 'Mum,' he hissed insistently, 'What is going on?'

The smell of burning was getting stronger now, and smoke was starting to rise up the stairs towards them. 'Mum…' Robert shook Susan again, and this time she became more alert. She opened her eyes to see her two children looking at her for answers. Emma was whimpering silently, and the fear in her eyes was almost feral.

'Your father has set light to the furniture downstairs. There is no way out of here,' Susan said, defeat echoed in every syllable she voiced.

Robert pulled her up. 'No,' he said and pulled both his mum and sister along the corridor towards the bathroom at the end of the landing. The smoke was getting thicker now, and they were starting to cough.

He threw open the bathroom door and pushed them both inside. They still had hold of their bags, which was some sort of miracle. Susan grabbed a towel, and after soaking it in water she placed it at the bottom of the door to try and stop the smoke coming through. Robert jumped into the bath and started to open the window. In her panic and her dazed state, Susan had completely overlooked the fact that the bathroom window looked out onto a flat roof above the cloakroom downstairs. They may be able to escape after all.

Robert opened the window wide and took a couple of deep breaths of fresh air. He looked down at the flat roof. It was not too far down. If he jumped down first then his mother could hand Emma down to him and she could climb down after.

He turned back to face her to explain what he was thinking and heard the noise of someone running along the corridor. He looked from his mother to the door and back again. The door to the bathroom was not locked. He looked at his mother with panic-stricken eyes and shouted at her, 'Lock the door.'

Susan gazed at him for a fraction of a second. Her befuddled state was making her actions sluggish, but Emma understood immediately and slid the bolt home across the door a fraction of a second before the handle was forced down from outside.

The door vibrated as their father kicked it hard and repeatedly from outside. 'Hurry,' Robert called to his mother and sister. 'We don't have much time.' The smoke was starting to seep slowly under the door as the frame started to splinter. Robert eased himself out of the window and down onto the roof. 'Hand Emma down to me,' he called up to his mother.

Emma was scared but knew that she had to be brave. She allowed herself to be passed down by her arms to Robert's waiting arms. 'Come on, Mum,' Robert shouted back to his mother, the urgency in his voice evident.

The smoke was billowing gently out of the window now and Susan threw the bags through the window, where they bounced off the flat roof and landed on the gravel below. She then all but jumped as the door to the bathroom gave in with a loud crack and was thrown open to reveal James standing there with a maniacal look on his face.

He rushed to the window to see his family climbing down the ivy, which grew in strong vines around the front of the house. James screamed in anger as he saw his family making their escape and bellowed out of the window with a roar that didn't even sound human. He ran back into the smoke as they ran up the driveway towards the road and safety.

James ran along the corridor. The smoke was getting thicker now. He started to cough, and his eyes were stinging. He reached the banister and swung himself round and onto the stairs. The voices in his head were insistent. He must not let his family escape. They should all be together in this house, where they belonged.

As he reached the turn of the stairs he saw that the pile of furniture by the front door was smouldering but not fully alight. He would push it out of the way, he thought, and get out that way. He would then grab his family and bring them back into the house. They would not leave him. They all belonged in this house together, with him, forever.

Tom watched him coming down the stairs. He could clearly see that Louisa was with James. Her anger swirled about him like a black cloud, darker and more intense than any smoke could ever become.

He could see her crazed look mirrored in James's eyes, and he knew that he could not let anything happen to Emma. Emma was his friend. She had kept him company these last few years and she deserved to live the long and full life that had been denied to him.

As James grew level with him, he gently let the toy train that he had been holding in his hand drop onto the tread of the stairs. In his hurry to reach his family, and with the thick, pooling smoke all around him, James did not notice the toy on the stairs and, as his foot connected with it, his ankle twisted beneath him. He lost his footing and fell heavily down the stairs. The back of his head hit with the corner of the bottom step hard, and he was knocked unconscious instantly.

Tom watched as what was left of Louisa left the prone form on the ground and swooped up towards him. Its anger was palpable, but Tom was no longer afraid of Louisa. She could do nothing to hurt him any longer.

Alerted by the smoke, Jimmy had rushed over from his flat after calling the fire brigade. He saw Susan and the children standing at the end of the driveway, still clutching their bags in their hands. He rushed over to them, looking around for James.

When he saw that he was obviously not there he shouted at Susan, 'Where is James? Is he still in there?' Emma grabbed onto her mother's jumper, tears streaming down her face. Robert looked down at the ground.

Susan looked at Jimmy, her face full of angst as she whispered, 'He went crazy, Jimmy. He set light to the furniture. We had to escape out of the bathroom window and climb down the ivy.'

Jimmy set off down the driveway at a run. The bells of the fire engine could be heard as it made its way down the road. Jimmy pushed open the front door, but the heat and the smoke drove him back. Susan and the children stood close to each other, watching the flames start to lick their way round the inside of the window frames. There was a loud crash as the glass shattered and the metal frames buckled and fell inwards. Jimmy ran round the side of the house, trying to find a way in, but every opening he came to was impassable.

The large fire engine lumbered into the driveway and there was a great bustling of activity. Jimmy ran up to them and told them that James was still inside. The fireman he was talking to looked from Jimmy to the building and back again and shook his head.

Susan watched from the safety of the end of the drive. She felt nothing. It was as if her emotions had been severed by the flames that now escaped from all the downstairs windows at the front of the house.

The firemen raced into action, and very soon a steady stream of water was directed at the house. An ambulance arrived and Susan and the children were given blankets and tended to for a few minor scrapes from their climb to safety. The children were anxious not to be separated from their mother, and were allowed to sit in the back of the ambulance while the ambulance man asked their mother a stream of questions.

Emma noticed Tom standing on the grass at the side of the driveway and got down from the ambulance and made her way over to him. Her mother watched her daughter walk across the driveway to the grass and wondered what she was doing. She held the blanket she had been given tightly around her shoulders and sucked the thumb of her free hand. Susan had not seen Emma suck her thumb like that for several years. It had always made her father angry, and he had all but beaten her out of the habit.

The questions from the ambulance man drifted over her as she watched her daughter. She squinted and shook her head for a moment, for surely she could not really see what she was seeing. Emma reached Tom and smiled at him. 'Are you going now, Tom?' she asked him with a sad smile.

Tom nodded. 'I think it is time. I have stayed here long enough, and I think my time has come.' Emma watched as a light appeared from nowhere, and when she looked back at Tom he had faded away.

Susan saw the beam of sunlight hit the drive. The shadow that had looked so much like that of a small boy had vanished. Emma walked back towards the ambulance and stepped up into the back and sat back down next to her mother. 'Tom has gone home now, Mummy,' she said.

And a small smile crossed her lips, for she knew that despite the fire and potentially losing their home, everything would now be OK, and they could rebuild their lives with help from those who cared about them.

9 781838 452254